"Hello, Kasey."

The bottom dropped out of her stomach. She had hoped this day would never come. Tanner Hart. That deep, sexy voice still had the power to jolt her. The way her luck had gone these past few days, she shouldn't have been surprised that he'd shown up at Shirley's funeral.

"It's been a long time," he commented into the growing and somewhat hostile silence. "How's your son?"

Kasey's heart wrenched, though she didn't so much as move. "He's great. He just finished his freshman year at Baylor."

Their eyes met for another millisecond, but that was enough to up the already crackling tension between them.

"How did you know the deceased?" he asked.

"Shirley had taken me on as a partner," she said through tight lips, wanting this conversation to end. Obviously he wasn't aware that she'd witnessed Shirley's murder, and she wasn't prepared to tell him, either. The less he knew about her and her business, the better.

"Look, it was good to see you," she said, anxious to get away. "But I really have to go." Kasey had taken several steps when he spoke, stopping her, her heart taking a nosedive as she swung to face him.

"I have a proposition for you."

MARY LYNN BAXTER

BAXTER

PULSE POINTS

MIRA®

ISBN 1-55166-731-2

PULSE POINTS

MIRA and the Star Colophon are trademarks used under license and registered in Australia, New Zealand, Philippines, United States Patent and Trademark Office and in other countries.

Visit us at www.mirabooks.com

Printed in U.S.A.

PULSE POINTS

One

The parking garage seemed eerier than usual that evening. Kasey Ellis paused and unbuttoned her jacket, hoping to ward off the smothering heat of the July day. Normally she was gone long before the premises was filled with eerie shadows. But the disturbing situation at the office had kept her there, though she had nothing to show for her efforts except a burgeoning headache.

Thinking it was her less-than-rosy mood that was responsible for her paranoia, Kasey shrugged her uneasiness aside and upped her steps to her Toyota Camry. She had inserted her key in the lock when she heard the noise.

Pop. Like a gunshot.

Surely not, Kasey told herself, positive her paranoia was messing with her mind. Nonetheless, she stood motionless and listened while her heart lurched in her chest and her breathing turned labored. Only after she heard the sound again did she spin around.

Even then, she couldn't immediately absorb the scene playing out in front of her.

A man was standing in the shadows with a gun pointed at a woman. Kasey froze and watched in manifested horror as another squeeze of gunfire assaulted her ears. This time the woman sank to the cement like a rag doll whose stuffings had been removed.

Kasey knew she had to do something. Anything, other than stand like she was encased in a huge block of ice. Then she heard another strange sound. Finally she realized it was coming from her. A whimpering erupted from her throat. She felt helpless and vulnerable in the midst of an oncoming bout of hysteria.

She shut her eyes, clinging to the remnant of hope that this was nothing but a contorted, macabre nightmare from which she would soon awaken. But when she opened her eyes, the woman remained crumpled and lifeless.

And the man had disappeared.

Do something, Kasey mouthed silently, making an effort to fight through the fog that dulled her mind, but it was impossible.

She had no idea where she found the courage to move her paralyzed limbs. Later, she credited the force of adrenaline that kicked in, giving her the strength to run to the victim and drop to her knees.

"Oh, my God," she cried when she recognized the ashen-faced woman with the blood-splattered chest.

Her stomach churning and her vision blurring, Kasey lifted her head and took several deep, shuddering breaths, praying again that this was indeed a dream. But when she peered down once more, nothing had changed.

Her business partner, Shirley Parker, remained splayed on the pavement. *Dead.* Kasey lifted her head high again as the stench of fresh, oozing blood filled her nostrils making her dizzy.

Her stomach pitched and heaved, and for a moment, she feared she might faint. Instead she sucked in her breath, and without touching her partner, fumbled for her cell phone, then dialed 911.

"Please, hurry." She didn't even recognize her own voice. It was squeaky and faint. "There's...there's been a murder."

The police station was frigid, though Kasey suspected it was her fractured nerves rather than the temperature that made her teeth clack together. Despite a valiant effort to get her emotions under control, she couldn't seem to do so. She continued to reel from the fact that her world had just splintered into a million jagged pieces.

"Would you care for a cup of hot coffee?"

How else would coffee be? That unasked, but inane, question made Kasey realize that hysteria was once more bubbling close to the surface. Clasping her hands together in her lap and squeezing them seemed to temper that hysteria. But for how long was anyone's guess.

Nothing was able to remove the imprint of Shirley's bullet-riddled, blood-splattered body from her mind.

Kasey shivered again. While waiting for the police to arrive on the scene, she had stayed with Shirley. Her initial reaction, however, had been to jump in her car and drive straight home, lock her doors and crawl into bed. And pretend the nightmare never happened.

She couldn't say what had kept her at the grisly scene. Perhaps she hadn't been able to leave her friend alone even in death. Better yet, remaining had been the right thing to do. The police had been on their way, and she was the only witness to the crime.

Through it all, she had kept waiting for the killer to return and deliver her the same fate, though she didn't think he'd seen her.

But what if he had?

"Here, drink this. Maybe it'll help."

Kasey flinched, then nodded her thanks at the man who handed her the cup. His name was Detective Richard Gallain. Even though a shroud of fog still swirled around her brain, she couldn't help but take note of him. Physically, Gallain reminded her of a bulldog with his slightly bugged eyes, wide full mouth, and heavy jowls. Not a handsome man by any stretch of the imagination, but then he didn't need to be. Putting murderers behind bars didn't require good looks, just a skilled mind.

When he had arrived on the scene, Gallain had asked her if she was all right and what had happened. Somehow she'd managed to make enough sense to tell him what she'd witnessed.

Once the crime lab boys had arrived, Gallain suggested she accompany him to the police department for further questioning.

Now, as she waited for that to happen, Kasey sipped on the dark liquid, but it did nothing to soothe her shattered nerves. The coffee barely hit her stomach before it pitched in rejection. Shaking noticeably, she placed the cup on the desk and folded her hands in her lap.

"Relax, Mrs. Ellis. You're safe here. We're here to help you not hurt you."

Gallain's voice was as strong as his features. And confident. But not abrasive. Impatient was the word. She suspected he was ready to hit her with a barrage of questions, yet he seemed to sense how emotionally fragile she was and was trying to take it easy, something that apparently wasn't easy for him.

"Are you up to talking?" Gallain paused, sweeping a hand though his crew cut. "I don't want to rush you." He let the rest of his sentence trail off but she got the message.

His impatience was no longer veiled, though his voice remained even. Of course, he wanted to rush her. Who was he kidding? She expected him to bark at her any minute, a thought that at one time might have drawn a smile. Not today. Not after she'd just witnessed a murder. And not just a random murder, either but that of her friend and partner.

Kasey took a deep, shuddering breath in hopes of blotting out that painful image, at least for the moment. It didn't work. When she stared into Gallain's sharp green eyes, it was Shirley's white face and lifeless body that she saw.

She blinked when another detective entered the cubicle. A tall man with a kind face, he folded his arms, leaned against the door, then merely nodded at her.

"Mrs. Ellis."

As though being chastised for removing her gaze, Kasey swung her eyes back to Gallain. "I'm sorry. It's just that—" Her words faded into the tomblike silence of the small cubicle, though she was aware that on the other side people were scurrying about and telephones were ringing.

"So you still don't think the killer saw you?"

"Like I told you at the scene, I don't think so, but again I can't be one hundred percent sure." Kasey noticed her voice trembled. She bit down on her lower lip to control it.

"Okay, did you see *him?*" The detective's eyes pinned her with intensity.

"No. I mean I did, but I didn't."

Gallain didn't so much as twitch a muscle at her contradictory response. "You're sure about that?"

"Absolutely. The man who fired the shots was a blur then and still is."

"How 'bout what he was wearing?"

When she didn't answer, Gallain went on, "His clothes. You must've noticed something. His shirt. The color of it, perhaps. Something."

"Not...really." She felt her own frustration building. "Everything happened so fast."

For a second, Gallain stared at her as if he didn't believe a word she'd said. Maybe that was what suddenly roused her out of her traumatized state and forced her upright. She stared back.

He rubbed his chin, then the base of his neck. When he spoke again, his demeanor had softened somewhat. "Look, I don't like this any better than you, but without you, we have nothing."

"Don't you think I want to help?" Kasey rubbed her pounding forehead. "That I'm trying hard to remember? My God, I saw this sicko kill someone." Her tone had risen to a shrill ring.

"Maybe if we gave her some time, Gallain, eased up a bit, she would be of more help."

Both Kasey and the detective cast their eyes in the direction of the other officer who had pushed away from the wall and was ambling toward them.

Before Gallain could take umbrage to another opinion, the man eased down on the edge of the desk and said with a smile, "I'm Detective Hal Spiller."

Fleeting as that smile was, it seemed to enhance the kindness in his face, which in turn bolstered her confidence a notch, something she badly needed.

"Sorry about what happened to your friend, Mrs. Ellis," Spiller added into the loaded silence.

"So am I," Kasey responded in a small voice.

"How far away were you?" Gallain asked, the briskness back in his tone, obviously resenting the intrusion and the rebuke.

"I'm not sure."

"How far is that?" Gallain pressed in spite of the growing frown from Spiller. "I need details."

"A few yards, give or take."

Gallain thrust his hands though his hair again and released a deep sigh.

Kasey's blue eyes flared. "Look, I can only tell you what I saw and didn't see, right?"

"Right," Spiller said, focusing his glare on Gallain.

Gallain shrugged. "Okay, I'll accept that for now. But once you've had time to get over the initial shock, I want to concentrate on the killer himself. I'm betting you saw more than you think."

"I hope you're right, Detective. I want to solve this as much as you do."

"So what about Shirley Parker? I bet you can tell me something about what made the deceased tick."

"I didn't...don't know a lot about her away from the office."

"I understood her to be a friend as well as your partner," he pressed.

Once again Kasey didn't like his tone, but she ignored it. He was just doing his job, she reminded herself, which was trying to find out who killed Shirley. And though she respected that, she didn't respect his method of going about it.

"We were friends, yes, but never running buddies, so to speak. I knew her growing up, even though she was quite a few years older than me. She actually gave me my start in advertising. As a result, I always considered her my mentor. Still, we hadn't seen each other in years until she called me out of the blue and made me an offer I thought I couldn't turn down.''

"What about since you've been back?" Gallain asked, seeming to scrutinize her closer.

"Not then, either.''

"What did you talk about over lunch or dinner? That kind of thing, things women talk about. Perhaps she had a man in her life and discussed him with you.''

"If so, she never said," Kasey replied, "and I never asked.''

He stared at her a moment longer, then released a breath. "So what *did* you talk about?''

"Work mostly.''

"I understand the agency's in deep financial trouble.''

He'd been quick to find that out. She had to admire him. "You understood correctly. We're struggling to stay open.''

"Did Ms. Parker ever tell you why?''

"No, she didn't.''

"What happened when you asked her about it?''

"She told me not to worry about it, that she'd take care of me and the business.''

"And you believed her?''

Kasey jutted her chin. "At first, then I realized I'd been had. Before I could have another chat with her, she was—''

"So what about the books?" he interrupted.

Kasey quickly regained her composure. "From what I've seen of them, there's nothing to indicate where the money went.'' Kasey paused. "Apparently everyone at the agency was kept in the dark.''

Gallain stood. "Seems like the lady had a lot of secrets.''

"What have you found out?" Kasey asked, turning the tables on him.

"Not much. We went over her home with a fine-tooth comb. Nothing there that implicates anyone." He paused. "You still remain our best hope for solving this case, Mrs. Ellis. And I'm not giving up. On you."

Kasey didn't respond. What could she say that hadn't already been said?

Gallain glanced at his partner. "Meanwhile, Spiller here will keep an eye on you and your place for a few days."

"Just in case he did see me," Kasey finished, the tremor having returned to her voice.

"That's right."

Another loaded silence permeated the office. Only Spiller's muffled cough broke it. Kasey rose to her feet and swayed as the room spun. Gallain's fingers circled her upper arm. "Are you okay?"

As quickly as the room had shifted, it settled. "I will be," she lied. After this night, she feared she'd never be all right again.

"Detective Spiller will drive you home, then see to your vehicle. I'll be in touch."

No, please, Kasey's mind screamed in rebellion. She wanted this session to be the end of her involvement. Unfortunately it seemed to be just the beginning.

Two

She was exhausted. However, Kasey knew sleep would elude her, so she didn't bother going to bed. Following a hot bath, which seemed to have wired her more, she made a cup of hot chocolate and sat on the wicker chaise lounge in her bedroom.

It would be nice to sip on the drink, and in between sips close her eyes, maybe even dose a bit. Fear of what she would see imprinted on the back of her lids kept her eyes wide-open. Would that terrifying image of Shirley's blood-stained body ever leave her? Not for a long time, she told herself. If ever.

Kasey gnawed on her lower lip, her gaze veering to the French doors that led onto her tiny third floor balcony. When Shirley had told her about this secluded apartment complex nestled between numerous oaks and pine trees, Kasey hadn't been all that excited.

First, she hadn't wanted to go into another apartment. She had wanted a small house; unfortunately she couldn't afford one. Second, she hadn't wanted to live on the third floor; the thought of trudging up such a long flight of stairs was uninviting.

Now, she was glad to be there. An intruder would have a much more difficult time getting to her. Kasey shivered then reached for the afghan at the end of the lounge even though the July night was so hot and humid, she'd had difficulty in cooling her apartment. Once the coverlet was over her, she shifted her eyes back to the doors. She had to stop dwelling on morbid thoughts and possibilities.

The fact that she wasn't alone, that Detective Spiller was lurking somewhere in the darkness keeping watch on her, should have offered her a measure of reassurance.

"Rest easy, Mrs. Ellis. Nothing will happen to you on my watch," he'd told her when he escorted her to the door.

Somehow she had dredged up a smile. "I'm counting on that."

"If you need anything or if anything out of the ordinary happens, call me on my cell." He pulled a card out of his pocket and handed it to her.

"I'll be fine," she said, not at all certain that was the truth.

He stepped back, then paused. "Don't let Gallain upset you. He's not always that abrasive."

"Are you sure about that?"

"No," he admitted a bit sheepishly.

She managed another smile. "Don't worry. I can handle him. He can't make me see what I didn't see or say what I don't know."

Spiller seemed suddenly uncomfortable as if he'd spoken out of turn. "Protecting you is our primary goal."

Again she was struck by his kindness. As she closed and bolted her door, she wished he'd been in charge of the investigation instead of Gallain. She had never been questioned by the police. Now that she had, it wouldn't go down as one of her most treasured memories.

Maybe that was why Spiller's presence couldn't alleviate her anxiety even though she was home, out from under the prying eyes of his cohort. Her stomach continued to heave as reality struck her like a blow. She had witnessed the brutal taking of another person's life—her friend and partner. Tears burned her eyes, and she blinked several times.

She hoped Shirley hadn't suffered, that she hadn't known what hit her. Kasey pulled the afghan under her chin and once again tried to focus her thoughts elsewhere. It didn't work. Her mind rebelled.

Had the killer seen her?

No. He couldn't have. He had never known she was there.

But what if he had?

That question kept haunting her. What if she was wrong and he was just biding his time until he came after her, thinking she could identify him? That thought almost brought Kasey's heart to a standstill.

Apparently Gallain had thought so or he wouldn't have put her under protective watch. But for now, she was safe in her home. Her gaze touched on things that surrounded her—familiar things such as pictures, plants, books and even her chintz-covered furniture. The fact that the latter needed replacing, and she'd grieved over the fact she hadn't the means to do that, no longer seemed important.

Tomorrow, however, she would have to leave this security and deal with Shirley's untimely death, a death that had a profound and life-altering effect on her.

Kasey reached for the remote control and switched on the television, hoping to catch the late news. No doubt the murder would make headlines on the local stations, as well as in the papers, for days to come. In addition, the gossip mill would be churning.

Although Rushmore had a population of over a hundred thousand, it still had many qualities of a small East Texas town. People made it their business to know their neighbors' business.

Kasey concentrated on the television. News of the bone-chilling murder was indeed being played out in vivid detail. Unable to view the crime scene again, she shifted her gaze and listened, mainly to see if anyone else had come forward as a witness. No such luck.

Kasey wasn't surprised. She had known all along she had been the only person in the garage other than Shirley and the killer. *Who was he?* Who had despised Shirley so much that he wanted her dead? Was her death perhaps business related? Or personal?

A long time ago Shirley might have confided in her and vice versa, but their old friendship had been damaged by recent events. Since her husband Mark's death two years ago, Kasey had been working in an advertising agency in Dallas. While it had been an okay job, it in no way met her financial obligations or fueled her dream of bettering herself, perhaps one day owning her own agency.

So when Shirley had contacted her and offered her a partnership in her agency in Rushmore where Kasey had been born and reared, she had been ecstatic, certain life was about to turn around and take on a new dimension.

"You can't imagine what this call means to me," Kasey had said following Shirley's offer. "Although I'm not anywhere near worthy of this opportunity," she added. "I've only been back in the workplace for two years, and I'm awfully rusty in a lot of areas."

"I don't believe that for a second," Shirley responded. "Besides—"

Kasey cut her off, anxious to square things from the get-go. "More than that, I don't have any money to buy into the business." She paused, trying to figure out how to tell Shirley the truth and keep her pride intact.

She had thought Mark had been a good provider, only to learn upon his death that they were on the brink of financial disaster. For two years she had struggled with her feelings of betrayal and the financial albatross around her neck. To date, she hadn't won either battle.

"We can work something out," Shirley said into the growing silence. "Bottom line, I need help. The agency's grown too much for me to handle alone. I need someone whom I can trust and who will do a good job." She paused with a chuckle. "Kasey Ellis immediately came to mind."

"While those words are so good for my ego, I'm still not sure I'm the right person. After all—"

This time it was Shirley who interrupted. "After all nothing. Remember we go back a long way, and I know what you're capable of doing."

In retrospect, she knew Shirley was right. She had introduced Kasey to the world of advertising, having given her her first job during high school. Kasey had worked summers for her. Although a decade plus separated them in age, they had become friends. While they had lost touch over the intervening years, Kasey had not forgotten Shirley or how much she had taught her about the business.

Shirley had gone on to insist she come to Rushmore, see the agency, then they would talk. Kasey had done just that, impressed far beyond her wildest imagination at Shirley's accomplishments. Maybe the fact that she'd devoted herself to her career, choosing never to marry and have a family, had been the contributing factor to her success in the business world.

"Having seen what I'm all about, are you interested?" Shirley had asked several days later over coffee in the small kitchen in the rear of the agency.

Kasey hadn't answered immediately, studying Shirley from under long thick lashes. The years had been kind to her friend. Though fifty-two, she could pass for forty-two. Her dark, grayless hair was short and stylish. Her complexion was flawless, and her hazel eyes were deep and lovely. The designer suit she wore made the most of her tall buxom figure. Kasey couldn't imagine how she'd managed to remain single.

"So, what's the verdict?"

Shirley's question jarred Kasey back to the moment. "Actually, I'm in awe and slightly overwhelmed."

Not only was the agency housed in a plush high-rise office complex, it had become the largest and most successful firm in the city with a more than adequate staff. The idea that she would ever be a part of something so successful was more than Kasey could take in.

As if Shirley sensed Kasey's inner struggle, she chuckled, then said, "Don't make this more complicated than it is. Just take the opportunity at face value and run with it."

That was exactly what she'd done. That day they had worked out terms of a contract and Kasey had made the move. Now, six months later, she was sowing what she had so hastily reaped. She should have known when something appeared to be too good to be true, it usually was.

Like she'd told Gallain, she had been assured by Shirley that the agency was solvent and thriving.

Shortly after her arrival in Rushmore, the sure thing Shirley had dangled like a carrot hadn't borne out.

Hence, Kasey had felt betrayed once again by someone she trusted. She had been in the process of weighing her options, but now, with Shirley's sudden demise, her options were clear. She had no choice but to close the floundering agency and seek work elsewhere.

Kasey's emotions suddenly surged and that queasy feeling returned to her stomach. What had seemed so wonderful and challenging had turned into a hideous nightmare that showed no signs of ending.

Beside her the phone rang; she flinched. When she checked the caller ID and saw who it was, her bleak situation suddenly brightened. It was her son Brock calling from Waco where he was a freshman at Baylor University.

"Hey, darling, I'm so glad you called," she said to her son, her voice breaking.

"Mom, what's wrong? Are you sick?"

She should've been more careful. Since his dad's death, she had forgotten how Brock had matured far beyond his eighteen years and how intuitive he had become where she was concerned.

"No, but it hasn't been one of my better days." Although she loathed the thought of telling her son what had happened, she had no choice. She didn't want him to hear the gory details of Shirley's death and her innocent involvement from some other source.

"What happened?" he demanded in such a manly, take-charge tone that tears gathered in her eyes.

These last few months, he had been the force that had kept her from sinking into a dark hole of despair.

"Shirley was murdered tonight," she finally said.

"Holy shit!"

She probably should've protested his choice of words, but she didn't, especially when she agreed with his assessment of the situation. "There's more, Brock. I saw it happen."

"Holy shit," he muttered again. "I'm on my way home, Mom."

Suddenly she panicked, the blood in her veins turning to ice. "Don't you dare."

"Why not?"

He sounded shocked and offended and well he should. She couldn't ever remember a time when she'd discouraged him from coming home. Never was she more content and happier than when he was asleep in his bed under her roof. Now, more than ever, nothing would right her upside down world like the sight of her son and the chance to give him a big hug.

Under the present circumstances, however, she couldn't allow herself that luxury.

"I'm afraid, that's why," she admitted without hesitation. "I don't want you involved in any of this."

"Ah, that's not going to happen."

"I know that, son. Still, I think it best you stay away from me for a while." She paused. "I couldn't bear it if something happened to you."

She paused as hot tears scalded her face, having just voiced her worst fear.

Three

"I don't approve."

Tanner Hart gave his attorney, friend and political advisor an off-center smile that bordered on sarcasm. "Thanks for your support."

"What did you expect?" Jack Milstead countered, his round, fair-skinned features etched in a frown that drew attention to his shiny pink cheekbones.

Tanner stretched his lean, taut body as far back in the small chair as it would allow, searching for a more comfortable position. In between working all hours of the night, he'd vented his frustrations on his gym equipment at home; he suspected he'd overdone it.

He and Jack had decided to meet in a coffee shop instead of one of their offices for their weekly get-together. Since he hadn't slept much, he needed some strong stuff to jump-start his day.

This place was one of his favorite haunts, a small, privately owned and operated coffee shop. The smell of flavored coffees and fresh baked breads and pastries always made his mouth water. Thank goodness it wasn't all that frantic this morning. They had found a table in the back, and for the moment, the area belonged to them.

"No way can I give such a foolhardy stunt my blessings,'' Jack added, a pulse leaping in his jaw. ''Not at this stage of the game, anyway.''

''Are you about to lecture me, Jack?''

''If that's what it takes.''

Tanner curbed a sigh. How could he tell his friend to give it a rest, that he knew what he was doing? But crossing Jack was no easy feat, not when he thought he knew best. And most of the time he did, Tanner conceded. Hell, if it hadn't been for Milstead, he wouldn't even be in the race for the Texas Senate.

Jack lived for politics, though he'd never had the desire to run for office himself. ''I work best behind the scenes,'' he'd told Tanner, ''grooming young men like you to run this great state.''

In his late sixties, Milstead was a self-made man who had gotten into the nursing home business at the right time and was now a millionaire several times over.

Tanner had met him and his wife, Sissy, and son, Ralph, before he'd married Norma. They had been old and dear friends of hers. He and Jack had hit it off immediately and in turn had become friends. Tanner guessed he admired and respected him more than anyone else he knew. Holding on to his approval was terribly important to him.

''Cat got your tongue, boy?'' Jack demanded, leaning forward, his eyebrows drawn together in a fierce frown.

Tanner fingered his tie, feeling the humidity as though he were outside. Or perhaps it was his mentor's intense scrutiny that made him uncomfortable. ''Okay, maybe it wasn't the smartest move I've ever made, and probably not great timing, but I felt it was a necessary evil.''

''For a man without any political experience, but

who's entering the final leg of the race, you just don't go firing your ad agency.''

"Why not?" Tanner asked, his deep voice even and cool.

- "Because it could spell political suicide, that's why."

"I disagree," Tanner said with vigor, though his confidence did erode somewhat under Jack's piercing gaze. Still, he defended his actions. "The agency wasn't doing Jack-shit.'' He broke off with another grin. "No pun intended, of course.''

Jack flapped his hand, then ran it though his thick graying hair and on down to his mustache. "Yeah, yeah.''

"Anyhow," Tanner continued, his tone once again abrupt and all business, "it'll work out. Besides, it's a done deal. The Randolph Agency in Dallas is history.''

Jack's scowl didn't lessen. "Well, done deals can be undone. In the political world that's an everyday occurrence.''

"But not in my world." Tanner's tone was rigid. "I make a decision, I stick to it. Just like I've stuck to the issues that I feel passionate about.''

That last pointed remark brought a flush to Jack's already heated features, and he cursed. To date, issues had been the only bone of contention between the two men. Jack had wanted to have a large say in Tanner's platform. And Tanner had indulged him up to a point. But then, he'd had to step in and take charge, realizing that it took fire in one's belly to win big. In order to start that fire and get it roaring, Tanner had to stick to his own convictions.

"All right, I'll keep my mouth shut and hope you

know what you're doing. What does Irene say about it?''

Irene Sullivan was his campaign manager who had hired the agency in the first place.

"I don't know. I haven't told her."

"My guess is she'll shit a brick."

"Probably. Maybe then she'll feel better."

Jack grunted. "Funny. Actually, she's the one you needed to dump. She's too much in-your-face, too ballsy to suit me. I don't know how the two of you keep from butting heads on a daily basis."

"We have our moments," Tanner said, "that's for sure. But overall, she does a good job. She has a mind like a steel trap, and you know how well-traveled she is in the political arena. That adds to her value."

"How 'bout the fact that she's a looker? Are you telling me that doesn't fit into the equation?"

"I'm not screwing her, Jack, if that's what you're getting at."

"I bet it's not from lack of trying on her part."

"How did we get off on this topic of conversation anyway?" Tanner lost his patience. "I can and will handle Irene, keep the bit in her mouth, if need be. So don't worry."

"As long as she does the job," Jack mumbled, "I guess that's all that matters."

Tanner sipped on his coffee. "Like it or not, her strategy, along with yours and lots of others, has turned me into a viable candidate."

"Not a damned easy task, either," Jack muttered with a fleeting grin.

Tanner tightened the harsh planes of his face. "No one knows that better than me. I'll never forget that day you approached me and asked if I was interested in politics. I thought you'd lost your mind.''

"That fateful day wasn't all that long ago, my friend," Jack mused, taking a drink of his coffee.

"It seems like forever. What with trying to jockey my business and my leap into politics, I often wonder what hit me. At times, it's almost driven me over the edge."

"Firing the Randolph Agency was apparently one of those times." As if sensing Tanner was about to fire back, Jack raised his hand in a token of peace. "Sorry, didn't mean to resurrect that dead horse."

"Good, because you're right, it's dead. What you don't know is that I've had to continually kick butt behind the scenes on practically everything they've done—media ads, slogans, posters, letters. You name it. But the real pisser has been the name recognition factor, key to my beating an incumbent. You've drilled that into me from day one. Somehow I never got that point across to that agency."

"In defense of them, you're a perfectionist and a hands-on kind of guy. That makes you hard to work for and with. I don't see that changing with another agency."

Tanner shrugged before a grin tugged his lips downward. "True, but I'd still like for someone else to do the grunt work, especially with this new project I'm working on."

Since he was a longshot for the senate seat in District 2, it wouldn't be wise to let his lucrative developing company suffer. It was his success in the business world that had been the springboard for this venture into politics, an asset that had escaped him until Jack had approached him.

Like he'd told Jack, keeping both his company and his political career afloat hadn't been easy. They had consumed him. He was either working or campaigning 24/7. Not a bad thing, he guessed, especially since his wife's death he had no one to go home to. Work had become a panacea for his loneliness.

"Have you thought about getting someone to mind the company store, so to speak?" Jack said into the short silence. "I don't need to remind you what a formidable candidate Buck Butler is."

"As in ruthless as hell."

"That goes with the territory."

When Tanner didn't respond, Jack went on, "Sometimes I don't think you have the stomach for politics."

Tanner scowled. "Now's a hell of a time to tell me that."

Jack chuckled. "You're honest to a goddamn fault, Hart."

"I'll take that as a compliment."

"Don't, because Butler's sure as hell not. He's conniving and determined. And in the political arena, that can be a winning combination."

Tanner leaned inward and jabbed his friend with brown eyes that had turned black with anger. "So are you trying to tell me something, Jack? That you're sorry you supported me?"

"You know better than that," Jack said, clearly backtracking. "I'm just keeping you on your toes, that's all. Readying you for the grueling months ahead."

"We've been friends long enough for you to know that I can punch below the belt with the best of 'em. And will if I have to."

That was true. You couldn't grow up the way he

had, in and out of the foster care system because his mother's love for the bottle far outweighed her love for him, and not learn a few underhanded tricks. He'd done a lot of things he wasn't proud of, had his share of battle scars, but he'd learned from his mistakes, or so he hoped.

"Maybe you're right," Jack was saying. "Maybe you won't have to stoop to his level and can hold to the high road. With your good looks, easy smile, razor-sharp mind and iron will to succeed, you just might whip Butler up-front and center instead of in the trenches."

"Only time will tell," Tanner responded in a suddenly tired voice.

"So do you have another agency in mind? Maybe a local one this time. The Parker firm would've been a good choice if that Parker woman hadn't gotten killed in that parking garage." Jack paused, his expression turning grim. "I still can't believe that happened. What could that woman have possibly been involved in that cost her her life?"

"I have no idea," Tanner said, "but it's an awful thing. That's one funeral I have to attend."

"You knew her, huh?"

"Yeah," Tanner acknowledged offhandedly, pointedly peering at his watch. "As much as I'd like to stay and shoot the shit, I've got to go. I have meetings lined up the rest of the day."

Jack reached for the bill. "The coffee's on me. You keep me posted."

Tanner stood. "That goes without saying."

The strong smell of coffee still filled his nostrils long after Tanner got back to his office in a plush complex on the west side of town. The affluent side, he reminded himself with a smirk of sorts, thanks in part to Norma Tisdale, his deceased wife.

When he'd married her his senior year in college, many an eyebrow had raised in that small college town. She'd been ten years his senior and from a very prestigious and wealthy family. He, on the other hand, had been a nobody who'd been raised on the wrong side of the tracks.

The two weren't supposed to mix. But they had and very well, too. He knew Norma had died a happy woman despite the pain she had suffered from her heart condition. He had no regrets, having been faithful in his care of her to the day she died. She had rewarded him by leaving him the bulk of her estate. That had been seven years ago.

During those years, he had used the money wisely, and at the age of forty, he was a wealthy man in his own right. And while he seemed to have it all—looks, wealth, power—there was something missing from his life.

Love. He loved no one and no one loved him.

Even so, he didn't feel sorry for himself. He simply buried himself in his work. For now, and maybe forever, that was enough.

You're fucked.

Those words were like a litany inside his skull. He stopped his pacing and placed his middle fingers against his throbbing temples and pressed. Long after he'd removed the fingers, the pounding continued. He needed a fix badly in order to get hold of himself. Pushing the panic button wouldn't do him one ounce of good. It would only serve to bring about his downfall.

He wasn't sorry he'd killed her. The bitch deserved exactly what she'd gotten and then some.

He was just sorry he might've gotten caught. *Might.* That was the key word, the word he'd clung to during the hours since he'd committed the act, since he'd bolted from the parking garage and disappeared into the shadows.

She had seemed to come out of nowhere. If he'd had one more minute, he could've made a clean hit and getaway. Everything had been planned down to the smallest detail, only to have her mess it up. He'd entered the garage long before Shirley had made her appearance and waited. Alone and silent, he had been confident his plan would come off without a hitch.

Dammit, it almost had, too.

Afterward, with his heart beating out of his chest and his teeth knocking together, he'd driven to his sister's house instead of his. He'd unlocked the door and walked in, only to pull up short. Flora had rolled her wheelchair to the table and was drinking a glass of milk.

"Sorry, sis, I thought you'd be in bed," he said for a lack of a better explanation, "or I would've knocked."

"No, you wouldn't have." She angled her head to one side, her greasy, gray curls bobbing with her. "But it doesn't matter, or I wouldn't have given you a key."

"Whatever," he mumbled, feeling his heart settle back in rhythm. He should be kicked for coming here, for perhaps involving her and further endangering himself in the process. He couldn't remember his mother, and his father was dead. His sister was his only living relative, and following the auto accident that left her chained to a wheelchair, he'd done all he could to better her situation. But he could only go so far and no farther. Some things she would not allow him to do, like move her to a larger, nicer place.

The house, so tiny it was stifling, was a battlefield between filth and illness. Dusty old newspapers and magazines littered the threadbare linoleum floor. Roaches feasted on the leftovers in the dishes cluttering the cabinets. The smell of stale piss overpowered the air-fresheners he'd placed in the light sockets.

"What happened?"

Flora's scratchy voice pulled him out of his daze. *Nothing out of the ordinary, sis. I just shot a woman and killed her. No big deal.*

"You look like shit."

Color stung his face at the scorn in her voice. "I had a bad day at work," he muttered.

"I have a feeling it's more than that. Have you been drinking?"

He took a deep shuddering breath. "I wish."

"There's some beer in the fridge. Help yourself."

Beer, hell. He needed something much stronger, but he couldn't tell her that. "Uh, maybe later."

She gave him another odd look. "You sure you're okay?"

"Yeah, I'll be all right. I just stopped by to check on you."

"You're lying," she said in a cracked voice. "But that's okay. I'm used to it."

His temper sparked, but he didn't fire back. No matter how much he did for her, it was never enough. She had become an embittered, shriveled up old woman with an ax to grind.

"I'm going to bed. Lock the door behind you."

"Thanks, sis." His words were coated in sarcasm. "I know I can always count on you."

She gave him another long look, then wheeled herself out of the room. He didn't know how long he stood there, the creak in the wheels sending a chill through him.

It was only after he heard the wailing of a siren in the distance that he moved. He fled Flora's house and drove down every country road he knew. Finally exhaustion forced him to his rented mobile home.

Now, as he continued to pace the floor, he peered at the clock on the secretary in the den. If she'd seen him, he would have been arrested by now. The fact that he hadn't was a good sign. Suddenly he stopped pacing, feeling his muscles uncoil.

He'd done himself right by waiting, by gambling that she hadn't seen his face. He threw his head back and laughed. Quite possibly he'd pulled off the perfect murder. His laughter grew in volume. After all, he had an insurance policy.

He knew her.

Four

Following the release of Shirley's body by the authorities, she was finally being laid to rest. If the number of people attending the funeral was anything to judge by, that was the place to be. It seemed as if half the townfolk had made an appearance at the chapel, perhaps in hopes of viewing Shirley's bullet-ridden body.

If that were the case, then they were disappointed as the casket had been closed. And well it should have been, Kasey thought, standing to one side at the graveside services that had immediately followed the memorial tribute. Though not nearly as congested as the service proper, a goodly number had made the trip to the cemetery.

Shirley apparently had built herself a fine reputation in the community, both as a civic leader and businesswoman. Still, Kasey suspected the majority of attendees were there out of morbid curiosity.

Kasey had known that Shirley's parents were deceased and that she had no siblings. Hence, the only two family members in attendance were two cousins. She had met them earlier and expressed her condolences.

Now, as she forced herself to listen to the final words of the minister, Kasey lowered her gaze, wishing once again that this horrible chapter in her life was behind her.

When she finally looked up, she saw Detective Gallain among the mourners. Her instinct told her he wouldn't leave until he spoke to her. She was right.

"Hello, Mrs. Ellis," he said a short time later.

Though a feeling of dread surrounded her, Kasey maintained her composure. "Good afternoon, Detective."

"Are you feeling better?" he asked, the uncomfortably warm sun catching the frayed corner of his tie, drawing attention to his disheveled appearance.

Kasey nodded as she dwelled on that simple flaw while waiting for him to say what was on his mind. This was his show. She had nothing new to contribute to the investigation.

"I just wanted to let you know I'll be around to your office soon to interview the employees."

"That will be fine, only the agency's closed for the rest of the week." Kasey heard the stiffness in her tone, but couldn't control it. "Out of respect for Shirley."

Gallain narrowed his eyes on her. "Speaking of Ms. Parker, have you thought of anything else that might help catch her killer?"

"I'm sorry, no."

"I'm not giving up on you, Mrs. Ellis. You're still our best hope of solving this brutal crime."

"I know you feel that way. And I wish I could be of more help. I feel terrible because I can't give you the magic words that would nail the creep."

"Just so you don't stop trying."

Did he expect her to dwell on that tragedy? Replay it in her mind in hopes something might click? Apparently so. But she refused to do that, though at night when she closed her eyes, Shirley's body was what she saw. The scene haunted her. If she let it consume her days as well, it would be impossible to maintain her focus and her sanity.

"No small incidents to report?" Gallain pressed.

"Detective Spiller's watching my house."

"Right, but there are other ways to scare the hell out of someone." Gallain's gaze didn't waver. "Like phone calls, for instance."

"Nothing like that has happened." Kasey paused and pushed her shades closer on the bridge of her nose, trying to block out the blinding sunlight. "But I have to say, this all has me really spooked."

"Well it should. Until the killer is apprehended we won't know for sure he didn't see you. It wouldn't be wise for you to drop your guard."

"No one knows that better than me, Detective."

"Later, then."

Kasey could only nod, her throat suddenly too tight to speak as she watched Gallain make his way to the unmarked car and get in. In that moment, he reminded her of the bumbling, fumbling Detective Colombo. Sly as a fox and persistent as the devil. And never failing to get the bad guy.

It was after she paid her final condolences to Shirley's cousins that she saw him. At first she tried to pretend her eyes were playing tricks on her, that the sun's rays had caused her to misfocus. But when he strode toward her, he filled her vision with solid clarity.

Tanner Hart.

The bottom dropped out of her stomach. She had hoped this day would never come. He was the last person she wanted to see. Ever. But the way her luck had gone these past few days and months, she shouldn't have been surprised. Still, it was unfair. Two major blows to the heart in a matter of days were too much.

Kasey longed to turn and run like the coward she was. Only it was too late. Also, her dignity was at stake. The fact she hadn't seen him in almost nineteen years gave her the courage to hold her ground. No longer were they stupid young college students. She certainly wasn't and from the looks of him, neither was he. Far from it.

He looked the success she knew him to be. It hadn't escaped her that he was vying for a Texas senate seat, though she refused to read any of the details of his campaign rhetoric. However, if she'd known he resided in Rushmore proper, and not some other county in the district, she might not have been so quick to take Shirley up on her offer.

Once she'd realized he was in town, she had assured herself they wouldn't run into each other, that their lives were on different tracks, both socially and financially. Apparently she'd been naive or had buried her head in the sand. Or both, because he was in front of her, staring at her out of those dark, probing eyes.

"Hello, Kasey."

That deep, sexy voice hadn't changed. It still had the power to jolt her. Actually, very little about him had changed. He was a mature version of the young man she'd known in college. Maybe his angular features had a few more battle lines, but those were an attraction rather than a detraction. His sun-streaked brown hair remained thick and shiny without any hint of gray, despite the fact that he was forty.

"It's been a long time," he commented into the growing and somewhat hostile silence.

"Yes, it has."

"You're looking well."

"So are you." Kasey didn't know when she'd carried on such a stilted conversation.

"You're living here now, right?"

"Yes." His cologne continued to roll over her in waves. She held her breath for a second, then released it. "How did you know?"

"Does it matter?"

"Not really," she said in a cool tone, not about to give him the satisfaction of knowing that he had disconcerted her.

"I'm sorry about Mark. I know my condolences are long overdue, but—" He let the rest of his sentence go unsaid.

"Thanks," she said in a sharper tone than she intended.

If he picked up on that sharpness, he didn't let on. Instead he continued in that same smooth tone, "How's your son?"

Her heart wrenched, though she didn't so much as move. "He's great."

"And in college."

Kasey didn't know if he'd asked a question or stated a fact. "He just finished his freshman year at Baylor."

"Good for him."

Their eyes met for another millisecond, but that was enough to up the already crackling tension between them. Kasey glanced away from his disturbing gaze, then fidgeted under the boiling sun and the intense humidity. Her body seemed on fire, taking a decent breath impossible. In truth, she suspected the climate had little to do with her discomfort.

"How did you know Shirley?" he asked.

"You mean you don't know?"

Color darkened his face. "No. Regardless of what you think, I haven't been spying on you, Kasey. I just knew you'd moved back. That's all."

She fidgeted silently and didn't respond.

"So did you know the deceased well?"

"Well enough. She had taken me on as a partner," she said through tight lips, wanting this conversation to end. She had already told him far too much.

"My God, I'm so sorry. You must be going through a tough time right now."

"I've had better days."

"Is there anything I can do?"

She quelled her panic and forced her voice to show none of her conflicting emotions. "No, thanks. I'm going to be all right."

"Are you going to remain here and run the agency?"

Obviously he wasn't aware that she'd witnessed her partner's murder. She wasn't prepared to tell him, either. The less he knew about her and her business, the better.

"I'm not sure yet." And she wasn't. Granted, she and Shirley had a binding partnership agreement, and by law the agency should become hers, but that was nothing to brag about. It appeared she had inherited an albatross instead of an asset. However, she saw no reason to share those thoughts with Tanner, either.

All that was important to her was putting distance between the two of them. God forbid that another happenstance meeting should occur. As it was, she was barely keeping her head above water.

"Look, it was good to see you," she said, anxious to get away. "But I really have to go." Kasey had taken several steps when he spoke, stopping her.

"Would you mind if I stopped by the agency?"

Her heart took a nosedive before she swung around.

As if he sensed she was about to give him a negative response, he added, "I have a business proposition I'd like to discuss with you."

Frustration chewed on him.

Richard Gallain cursed under his breath as he sat at his desk, paperwork piled high around him. In fact, his entire office seemed nothing but a mountain of freaking paper. He was working his ass off without any positive results.

The Parker murder had his guts tied in a knot. If he could crack that case, then he just might have a shot at the Chief of Detective position that had recently opened. Passing the written test would be a no brainer, but that wasn't all that factored into the job. He had to be a damned good detective to make the promotion.

Solving this murder was what he needed to boost him upstairs. In order to do that, he needed Kasey Ellis to come through for him. He couldn't help but think she knew something vital to the case, though he didn't think she was holding back on purpose.

She was scared shitless, and he could appreciate that. However, he had reached the conclusion that the killer hadn't seen her, or he would've made a move to silence her. But he wasn't ready to take Spiller off protective watch, not just yet, anyway. Better to be safe than sorry.

The buzzer on his desk sounded. He scrambled to reach the phone underneath all the clutter. The chief's line blinked back at him. He groaned, knowing he was about to be called into the inner sanctum. He was right.

Minutes later Gallain was seated in Chief Harold

Clayton's office, eyeing the chief from his position behind his desk. He was a big, meaty man with features to match, including oversized earlobes. When agitated, he had a habit of fingering one or both of them.

"So what's the latest?" Clayton demanded in his booming voice.

Gallain knew what case he was referring to. For the time being, it seemed the entire department was consumed with the Parker woman's murder. That was why he felt the urgent need to break the case himself. Now.

"I'm working on it," Gallain responded, managing to keep his voice even despite his coiled nerves.

"Apparently not hard enough."

"It was a clean hit."

"Yeah, yeah, so I've been told. But we both know there are no perfect murders."

Gallain felt the color drain from his face. He didn't like the idea that he was being called on the carpet for something that wasn't his fault. And there sure as hell *were* perfect murders. They were carried out every day and the chief knew that. So what kind of crap was he pulling?

"Are you up to the task, Gallain?"

His stomach clenched, but he didn't let on. "Of course."

"Then get results. Someone's on the mayor's ass. He in turn is on mine. Therefore I'm on yours. Get the picture?"

Gallain tightened his lips, then nodded.

"Several new industries are looking at our fair city to relocate. Unsolved murders don't sit well with visiting businessmen. So we need to wrap this up in the win column without further delay."

Gallain stood. "You got it."

"What's the latest with the Ellis woman? Bring me up-to-date on her."

"I'm pressing her as hard as I dare. Either she didn't see anything or she saw something and the trauma has forced it into her subconscious."

"Well, don't let up on her." He paused. "How 'bout Parker herself? Have you found any skeletons in her closet?"

"Not yet, although I haven't talked to her employees yet. Her family didn't know anything. In fact, they couldn't wait to bury her and then haul ass."

"Keep me posted, up close and personal. Like I just said, I don't like getting leaned on."

Me, either, Gallain almost said. If he pissed off the chief, that would nix any hope of a promotion, regardless if he solved the case or not. He couldn't chance that. For the time being, he might have to eat a little shit, but in the end he would prevail.

"You can count on me, Chief."

Clayton flicked his hand. "Then get out of here and get to work."

Five

Tanner stood at the window of his campaign head-quarters and stared down at the morning traffic. Even though it was early, the streets were alive and bustling. Horns were honking and people gathered on various corners waiting for the lights to change. Rushmore was one of the few small cities whose downtown area had maintained its vitality both for business and commerce.

Frowning suddenly, Tanner wiped a gathering of sweat off his forehead. The air-conditioning in the building, or rather the lack of it, left a lot to be desired.

Otherwise, the place was perfect. His campaign manager, Irene Sullivan, had searched long and hard for the right location. The big lofty area had more than ample room for the volunteers to gather, as well as a place to house the loads of campaign materials.

However, his race for the senate wasn't what dominated his mind today. Since he'd seen Kasey, he had been reveling in his good fortune.

Still, he cautioned himself not to get too confident. Or excited. He hadn't pulled his plan off yet. Kasey had to cooperate. Considering her circumstances, he felt she would.

But again, he put the brakes on, reminding himself that she'd rather not have anything to do with him.

Although she had been polite at the cemetery, she'd held herself as aloof as a block of ice.

His confidence eroded at the same time his stomach rebelled against the amount of coffee he'd put into it. Yet he was charged. He was a man on a mission and ready to get with it. Tanner peered at his watch. Irene was due any moment for a strategy session, then he was off to see Kasey.

His stomach roiled, but for a different reason. He should leave well enough alone. To try and resurrect the past even if it was to right an old wrong was never a good idea.

Yep, he should just sidestep that hornet's nest. He had enough going on in his life without taking on added responsibility for someone who detested him. A smirk altered his lips. The truth was, she probably didn't give a damn about him one way or the other.

She hadn't rebuffed him, though, hadn't even told him not to show up at her office. But that final look she had given him said it all. For a split second, he had seen the naked vulnerability behind those eyes.

For the most part, though, she had been cool under fire. He'd have to give her credit for that. But he wondered what she'd thought. Was she remembering that night? Even now, he could still smell her sweet skin, *taste it,* see her moist, swollen lips…

Shit.

Thoughts like that would get him in serious trouble; they would jeopardize any good he attempted to do. But it was going to be hard to keep his distance, pretend they had no past, even if nearly two decades separated them. A lifetime, yet no time at all, now that he'd seen her again.

Time had been most kind to her. She wore her chestnut hair in that just-out-of-bed style men found so appealing. He was no exception. The dusting of freckles across her nose and cheeks was still visible and still a turn-on. She now had tiny wrinkles at the corners of her dark blue eyes, giving her heart-shaped face added dimension and character. Her body now had generous curves—the body of a woman who had had a baby.

While not classically beautiful, she had a quality that was more enduring, more enticing. She had class, an asset he felt still eluded him.

Tanner smothered a sigh, reminding himself that winning the senate seat should command his undivided attention, not a woman from his past who was off-limits to him.

"Did you tie one on last night?"

Both Irene's appearance and raspy voice suddenly grated on his nerves. But when he swung around, he smiled. "Morning to you, too. And no, I didn't tie one on, though I feel like I did."

She raised her eyebrows before quipping, "You look it, too." She walked over to the tiny coffee bar and reached for a cup on the counter.

He watched the swing of her hips in the short, tight skirt that matched her jacket. No doubt, Irene was attractive with auburn hair and brown eyes. But that attraction was in a bold sort of way that was often enhanced by the overzealous use of makeup. She was in her thirties, divorced, and a part-time paralegal. She was smart, ambitious, and like Jack said, ballsy.

Once she had her coffee in hand, she sat down at the glass-topped table and pinned him with her eyes. "Want me to give you a quick massage? Sure would get the kinks out of your shoulders."

Tanner quirked an eyebrow. "I'll pass."

Irene shrugged, but he could tell she didn't like his rebuff. He swallowed another sigh. He knew she wanted more from him than he was prepared to give. So far, he'd managed to keep the line drawn in the sand. Becoming romantically entangled with her would be hazardous to his career and his emotions. Any day, though, he expected Irene to try to cross that imaginary line. He didn't know what he'd do, but for now he wasn't going to worry about it. Other things were far more pressing.

"So what's on your mind?" Irene asked, angling her head. "A change in today's plans, I'm guessing. Otherwise I wouldn't be here."

"I'd forgotten how well you know me."

"Not as well as I'd like."

Tanner shot her a warning glance.

She laughed. "Don't worry, I'm not about to jump your bones."

"I fail to see the humor in that." His tone was short.

"Lighten up, okay?" Her eyes sparked. "Until you come around, I'm happy jumping someone else's bones."

He ignored that last statement, though he fought the urge to throttle her. If she wasn't so good at her job, he might have fired her on the spot. But she was good and without her strategy expertise, he doubted he would cross the finish line a winner.

"So again, what's up?" Irene peered at her watch. "I should be on my way to Dallas even as we speak. In case you've forgotten, I'm due at Randolph's at noon."

"You won't be going."

"I won't?"

"The Randolph Agency is no longer working for me."

Her jaw went slack. "Why not?"

"I fired them."

"You what?" she demanded on a gasp.

"You heard me. I fired them."

"But...but that's crazy, especially when the election's only three months away."

"I've made up my mind."

"Well, minds can be changed," she said in a harsh tone.

That raised his ire, possibly because that was what Jack had pointed out. Dammit, he knew what he was doing. They would just have to trust him. "Don't push your luck, Irene."

The color deserted her face, but her tone remained sharp. "So what do you propose to do?"

"Hire another agency, of course."

"Here?"

"Yes."

She opened her mouth only to snap it shut, clearly at a loss as to how to deal with this latest turn of events.

"I know what you're thinking."

"You have no idea," she responded with unveiled sarcasm.

He ignored that. "I'm hoping to hire the Parker Agency."

She lunged to her feet. "What's the matter with you, Tanner? The owner just got popped, for God's sake."

"I realize that," he said, struggling to hang on to his patience and his temper.

Irene merely looked at him.

"Shirley has a partner."

"Which doesn't mean shit. Clients have been deserting the Parker firm like rats on a sinking ship for a long time now, and you know that. Granted, there seems to be no reasonable explanation, but that shouldn't matter.'' Irene paused as though to get a breath. ''The fact that it's happening should be enough to stay away.''

''The partner's husband was an old friend of mine.''

''So?''

''So, I'm going to hire her.'' Tanner's eyes narrowed on her. ''Do you have a problem with that?''

''You're damn right I do.''

He hadn't consulted her first. Tanner suspected that was what fueled her anger. She wanted to micromanage everything that concerned him. Mainly his life. Not going to happen.

''So where does that leave us?'' he asked.

Irene tapped her foot. ''I'm not sure.''

''Is that a threat?''

''Maybe.'' Irene walked to the door, then turned. ''Screw it. I'll talk to you later when we're both calmer.''

Once she was gone, Tanner plopped down in his chair and put his head in his hands.

The tearoom was hopping. But then it usually was at noon. Hectic or not, Kasey loved eating there because it was also a gift shop with lots of pretties. Today, however, she wasn't in the mood to meander and finger the goods. Instead she was taking advantage of her cousin's company as they sat at a table for two.

''I'm sorry about Shirley,'' Ginger Davenport said, once the waitress had taken their orders.

Ginger was not only her first cousin but a dear friend whose company had moved her here from Houston

several years ago. At thirty-eight she was one year
older than Kasey, and in the process of getting a divorce. Tall and willowy, she had wide-set hazel eyes
and a thin mouth that she made more generous with a
lip pencil.

The fact that Ginger lived in Rushmore had been
another reason why leaving Dallas after so many years
hadn't been so overwhelming to Kasey.

Yet they didn't see each other as often as Kasey
would've liked. Ginger worked for a high-powered in-
vestment firm and traveled often. When they did get
together, however, they made the most of it.

"I'm devastated," Kasey responded, "for more reasons than one."

"I'm sure." Ginger leaned closer and lowered her
voice. "It scares the hell out of me to think that someone you worked with got murdered. I'm guessing you
don't have a clue as to why."

"You're right, I don't." Kasey's voice shook. "I
saw her get shot." She hadn't planned on blurting out
that shocking piece of news. It seemed to have just
rolled off her tongue.

Ginger's eyes widened, and she covered her mouth
as if to stifle a cry. After a moment, she wheezed,
"You were the witness the paper mentioned?"

Kasey nodded, emotion tightening her throat.

"Oh, my God, you poor thing."

"It was awful, Ginger. I've nearly lost my sanity
over it, though I didn't see who pulled the trigger."

"But did he see you? That's what's important."

"I'm convinced he didn't and so are the police.
Otherwise, he would've already made a move
to…silence me. But just to be on the safe side, I've
been placed under protective watch."

"You have?" Ginger's head turned to the right, then left.

Kasey smiled. "He's lurking around here somewhere."

"This is all too mind-boggling," Ginger said, shaking her head. "I know you have to be scared out of your wits. Want to move in with me for a while?"

"No, but thanks. I guess I'm still in shock."

"You've told Brock, right?"

She gave Ginger the gist of that conversation.

"God, what a mess." Ginger's features were pinched. "I wish your mother and brother weren't in Wyoming. On second thought, maybe I don't. You and your mother are like oil and water—you don't mix."

"Since she's been in the nursing home, things have gotten better between us. Still, I wouldn't think of telling either of them since there's nothing they can do."

"What are you going to do about the agency?" Ginger asked, changing the subject.

Kasey sighed. "I'm assuming the partnership's still intact. Even so, I'm not sure I can get it solvent again, especially now, though I might be offered a reprieve of sorts."

Ginger didn't respond right off as the waitress brought their salads. Kasey stared down at hers, and though it looked yummy, she wasn't sure she could eat a bite.

"Eat, cuz," Ginger ordered. "You need nourishment."

"I'll try, but I'm not hungry."

For several minutes, they munched in silence. Then Kasey pushed her plate away. "I can't eat another morsel, or I'll be sick."

"I understand. I feel the same. Imagine that? Me turning down food."

"Sorry I ruined your appetite."

"Under the circumstances, that's not important. Besides, I should skip a lot of meals and drop some of this weight." Ginger paused, then changed the subject. "You mentioned you might be offered a reprieve. I sure hope so. I don't want you going back to Dallas."

"Do you know Tanner Hart?"

"Do *you?*" Ginger's eyes were wide.

Color stung Kasey's cheeks. "Yes. He's from Rushmore and was one of Mark's best friends in college."

"All I know about him," Ginger said, "is that he's running for the Texas Senate against that prick Buck Butler—"

"Why, Ginger," Kasey exclaimed with a chuckle.

"Well, that's what he is. I know because he does business with our firm. And Matt, my soon to be ex, works for his campaign. But that aside for now, what's the deal with Hart?"

Kasey explained about Tanner approaching her at the cemetery.

"You think he might want to hire you?"

"I'm assuming so, since he mentioned business. Still, I find that hard to believe with the election a little over three months away."

"If that is the case, it would certainly be a windfall for you. It would keep the agency open a while longer and keep you here." Ginger's features shadowed. "But for some reason, I get the idea you're not that excited about the prospect."

Actually, Kasey was terrified by the idea that she was even considering such a thing. It was tantamount to playing Russian roulette with the rest of her life.

Tanner Hart would be the last person she would depend on, desperate or not. She should have stressed that she wasn't interested in anything he had to offer.

"Why is that?" Ginger pressed before widening her eyes as she peered beyond Kasey's shoulder. "Oops."

"Oops what?" Kasey demanded.

"Speak of the devil. Tanner Hart just walked in the door."

Six

Kasey couldn't concentrate. Her mind kept wandering.

Following her lunch with Ginger, she had returned to the empty agency. After locking the front door that remained adorned with a wreath in Shirley's memory, she had headed straight to her partner's office and locked the door behind her.

Lately she had become cautious to a fault.

Her plan was to go through Shirley's desk, to see if she could find anything that would give her a clue as to who had taken her life. Too, she wanted to see if she could find any evidence as to why the agency had taken such a downward spiral financially.

At this point, she had no idea what she was looking for. She had taken the general ledger home that the bookkeeper, Nelda Parrish, was responsible for, but it had shown nothing out of the ordinary, which was not surprising.

Kasey's hand faltered. Even now, she found it difficult to invade Shirley's privacy. It felt like she was somehow further violating the dead woman. Temporarily abandoning her task, she looked around. Shirley had made the most of where she spent the majority of her time.

The room was decorated in soft, soothing hues of

green and taupe. Creative artwork adorned the walls, and personal memorabilia was placed just right on various tables and shelves. The ambience bespoke of money and power. But then the other offices were by no means shabby. The company occupied one entire floor of this upscale building thereby proving its former success.

What happened?

That question gnawed at Kasey. Yet she continued to hesitate to open the first drawer. It was then that she heard a noise. With goose bumps feathering her skin, she got up and went to the door. However, she didn't open it. She leaned against it and listened. Several of the employees had keys. After listening a few more minutes and hearing nothing, Kasey felt silly, reminding herself that Detective Spiller lurked outside.

Besides, no one would likely make a appearance today unless it was Tanner. But after the episode in the restaurant, she didn't think that likely.

Following Ginger's bombshell that he'd just entered the restaurant, Kasey had been loath to turn around. Luckily she'd been spared. Tanner and his companion had strode past their table, nodded, then moved on. An immense feeling of relief had left Kasey weak, though she'd fought hard not to let her composure slip in front of Ginger.

"Man oh man," Ginger had whispered, her eyes flashing. "TV doesn't do him justice. He's some eye candy."

Kasey had to laugh, but then she scolded her friend. "Behave yourself."

"Why?" Ginger's tone was innocent. "He's a widower, so he's available."

"You don't know that."

Ginger sighed. "You're right, I don't. I just betcha

he has to beat women off with a stick. I'd have to take a ticket and get in line."

Kasey rolled her eyes.

"Hey, you sure you're not holding out on me, that you don't know more?"

"Yes, I'm sure," Kasey all but snapped, giving Ginger an incredulous look. She had known Tanner had been married and that his wife had died from a heart condition. Mark had told her that. But as to the status of his current sex life, God forbid she had any idea.

"Too bad."

"Hey, are you forgetting you're *not* available?"

"Hopefully I soon will be." Ginger's mouth turned down. "Though I'm beginning to think Matt's not going to ever let me go."

"Yes, he is," Kasey exclaimed in a firm tone. "He has no choice. He can't stop you from getting the divorce. Just hang tough and you'll get rid of him and get what you want to boot."

"I'm counting on that." Ginger's features brightened. "If Tanner hires your agency, who knows what will happen."

Kasey shuddered to think just how true that was.

"It could mean that what you want is finally within reach," Ginger added.

"That's a big if, my friend, so just forget it."

"His offer?" Ginger sounded appalled. "You'd forget that?"

"Yes."

Ginger waved her hand. "Pooh, I don't believe you for a second. If and when he comes with an offer, you won't turn him down. If you do, I'm going to have your head examined."

Now, as Kasey thought back on that part of the conversation, she wished she'd kept her mouth shut, that she hadn't said anything to Ginger. Tanner probably wouldn't even approach her which would let her off the hook. But if he did, she'd have to ask herself why.

He had to know the agency was in trouble, didn't he? Maybe not. He had more important things on his mind than a floundering ad agency. Yet she hadn't mistaken what he'd said. Kasey blew out a breath and tried not to think about him or his intentions. If he called or showed up, she'd deal with him then.

The phone jangled beside her. She answered on the fourth ring. "Parker Agency."

"Kasey, it's Tanner."

He didn't need to identify himself. She recognized his voice the second he'd said her name. "Yes," she said, gripping the phone.

"I'm outside, in my car. Is it all right if I come in?"

"Now?" she asked inanely.

"Yes, unless it's not a good time."

Kasey hesitated, but only for a second. "I'll meet you at the door."

Moments later, she had ushered him into her office, relieved to be back on familiar ground, though her domain was not nearly on a par with Shirley's. In fact, she hadn't bothered to decorate her office, since her situation there had been so tenuous.

"Sit down," she said in as normal a tone as possible.

"Thanks." He lowered his big frame into the chair, all the while looking at her.

It was all she could do not to flush under his scrutiny. "I haven't made any coffee."

He shook his head. "I don't need any more today. I've had more than my share."

She nodded.

"You're not comfortable with this, with *me,* are you?"

Kasey felt the pulse in her throat beat overtime. "I don't know what you mean."

"Sure you do. You wish I hadn't come."

She met his narrowed gaze head on. "If that were the case, I wouldn't have let you in."

"Good, that means we can do business."

"I didn't say that, Tanner."

"Right," he said through tight lips. "I'm getting ahead of myself."

"Before we go any further, the agency's not doing well. I may have to close it."

"All the more reason why you should hear me out." Tanner paused and crossed one powerful leg over the other. "First though, who's the guy hanging around outside the door?"

She knew he was referring to Spiller. Or at least she hoped so, refusing to give credence to the other possibility. "What did he look like?"

Tanner told her.

"He's a detective. I'm under protective watch."

Tanner frowned and eased forward in his chair. That was when she got a whiff of his cologne, that same fragrance he'd had on at the cemetery. She ground her teeth together.

"Why?" he asked, his tone blunt.

She told him.

"Good Godamighty, Kasey, why didn't you tell me?"

She raised her eyebrows. "I didn't think it was any of your business." And still didn't, but she kept that comment to herself. What was the use of further antagonizing him? Besides, it was too late to cry wolf. By letting him in, she had made herself fair game.

"If you're going to work for me, it's my business."

She gasped. "You're awfully sure of yourself."

"Typical politician, right?" Humor quirked his lips. "Isn't that what you're thinking?"

Kasey forced her stiff shoulders to relax and smiled. "That and more."

"Ah, so you haven't forgotten how to do that?"

"What?"

"Smile. The young girl I knew was rarely without a smile on her face."

"I'm no longer a young girl," she snapped.

"That's for sure."

His tone was drawling and his eyes were probing as they swept over her, stopping only after they clashed with hers. She wanted to vent the anger that was charging through her. But something else, something more potent, stopped her—the charisma of the man himself. After all this time, he still had the sexual power to knock her off her feet.

"Did you see the shooter's face?"

His harshly spoken question brought her back to reality. "No. It all happened so fast, it was a blur."

"Then he must've seen you."

Was his tone anxious, or was she reading more into it than was there? "No, I'm positive he didn't, or he would've already come after me."

"I'm glad the police aren't just taking your word for that."

"Me, either, though it's a bit disconcerting to know you're being watched, even if it's by the good guys."

His gaze deepened. "So how are you holding up? Really?"

"Actually, I'm barely holding body and soul together," she admitted, a tremor in her voice.

Tanner's features contorted. "Damn, I hate that this happened."

"I'll be fine, Tanner. It's not your worry."

"You've already said that."

A lengthy silence followed his terse words.

"Look," she finally said, "whatever you had in mind concerning the agency won't work."

"Because you don't want it to?"

"No, because it's not in your best interest."

"Why not let me be the judge of that?"

"All right, how's this? The agency's in such a hole I'm not sure it can make payroll at the end of the week."

Tanner's eyes widened.

"When I came six months ago, everything appeared rosy. Only after I got here did I learn that Shirley hadn't been up-front with me. Financially, the agency's on the skids. I don't know how to be any more blunt."

"Did you demand to know why?"

"Of course, more than once. But she always hedged with the same excuse, telling me the agency had hit a run of bad luck, that it had lost several lucrative clients in a row. I shouldn't have let her get by with that, but I thought since I was so new I would tread lightly and give her the benefit of the doubt. Now I know that was a mistake. She's dead, and the truth died with her."

"The records won't show where the money's gone. You can bet on that."

"Not the ones I've seen, that's for sure." Kasey drummed her nails on the desk. "When you phoned, I was about to go through her desk to see what I could find, if anything."

"Good idea."

"Detective Gallain's due to question the staff and me later this week."

"When you find where the money went, you may very well find her killer."

"Maybe, maybe not," Kasey pointed out. "The two might be in no way related."

"I'm betting they are."

"My point in telling you all this is so you'll get a clear picture of why you should take your business elsewhere."

"On the contrary, my business is exactly where it needs to be. I can keep your business afloat."

"Why are you doing this, Tanner?"

"Will something as simple as I trust you suffice?"

"No."

He chuckled. "It's the truth. I just got burned by a big outfit in Dallas, the Randolph Agency, to be exact."

"How do you know that's not where I worked?"

"Because I checked you out."

That fueled her anger. "You have a lot of nerve."

"There's a lot at stake—my political future."

"Still, I'm not the right person to step in at this late date."

"I disagree."

"I'm flattered, all right. But I've been out of the hands-on part of the business too long. In Dallas I did mundane, grunt work, if you will. That's a far cry from what you need."

"But you're capable."

"Yes," she admitted tersely, "but—"

"If I'm willing to take the chance, then what have you got to lose?"

Kasey opened her mouth to launch another strenuous objection only to then shut it. Tanner's business would indeed keep the agency's door open. Wasn't that what she wanted? Yes. She desperately wanted to remain here, to make a go of this endeavor for her own sake as well as her son's.

If only her savior was anyone but Tanner. She should turn the offer down for that reason.

"Kasey, all you have to do is say yes. It's just that simple."

A bubble of hysteria almost erupted. Simple. God, any association with him was anything but that. However, he didn't know that, she assured herself. Her secret was safe forever.

"Kasey," he pressed.

She took a deep breath. "All right. I'll do my best."

Seven

"So do you have anything in mind right off?" Tanner asked.

"No," she answered with raised eyebrows. "Surely you didn't expect me to."

He shrugged, then grinned, a grin that took her breath. She covered her confusion by saying on a burst of breath, "I don't even know what you're running on, what issues you feel strongly about."

"You mean you haven't been following my campaign?"

A glint in his eye had joined that grin, and she knew he was teasing her. Possibly even flirting. For a moment, she dropped her guard and took the bait, grinning back. She heard him release a gust of air when their gazes held for several beats.

"So are you interested in hearing what I'm about as a politician?"

Kasey spoke around her desert-dry mouth. "Now?"

"Why not?"

"Fine."

"Are you going to ask me if I'm a Democrat or a Republican? Or is that something you happen to know?"

"Actually, I don't."

"I sure haven't made an impression on you, have I?"

"Politics and politicians haven't been high on my priority list."

Tanner's lethal grin appeared again, crinkling the skin at the corners of his intense brown eyes. "Please assure me that's about to change."

"Absolutely."

He wiped his brow in a mocking gesture. "Whew, my faith is restored."

Allowing this light banter to continue between them wasn't wise. As it was, Kasey had already let it go too far. She was no match for him. In her vulnerable state she had to be careful, or she'd be snared again into that web of charm and self-assurance that was so him.

"So what made you decide to run for office?"

"In other words, why would I want to jump in a fishbowl?"

"Exactly. I can't imagine living that kind of life."

Tanner was quiet for a moment. "After the fact, I really think I can make a difference. But I never even thought about running for office until a friend, Jack Milstead, pitched the idea to me." He paused with a shrug. "He was persuasive, and I needed a new challenge. The rest is history, as they say."

"Rich and bored, huh?"

It was obvious she struck a nerve, for he stiffened visibly. "Is that your opinion of me?"

"I don't have an opinion one way or the other."

His lips relaxed and he cocked his head. "If you're trying to piss me off because of another attack of cold feet, it won't work. I'm not letting you off the hook."

Kasey felt heat steal into her face. "So what are you

passionate about? Those passions will determine how I map out the strategy.''

Tanner yanked at the knot on his tie until he worked it loose. ''Ah, much better. Now we can get down to business.''

Kasey reached for a tablet, a pen poised above it. ''I'm ready.''

''Here goes. I want higher pay for teachers—Texas ranks far too low on the pay scale to suit me. I've also devised a more efficient highway system for Texas that will alleviate the traffic problems in and around the major cities. I'm for tightening our borders in order to curb the drug traffic. And last but certainly not least, I intend to put an end to abuse of the elderly, especially in nursing homes. That gets my blood boiling like nothing else.''

''That's quite an impressive list.''

''So you approve?''

''What's not to approve, though it will take Superman to accomplish them.''

He stared at her another long moment. ''Maybe you should keep that thought in mind when you map out my advertising.''

In spite of herself, her lips twitched. ''I might just do that.''

''Have any ideas jumped to mind?'' he asked, grinning.

''Maybe.''

Her hedging wasn't lost on him. ''You're not prepared to share, huh?''

''Not at this point. You'll just have to trust me.''

''I do, or I wouldn't have hired you. I think we're going to make a good team.''

The room suddenly seemed too warm. Or was it the

heat that infused her body under his intent gaze that seemed to peruse her body at leisure? Or was it that she was simply overreacting, reading much more into that look than was there? Regardless, she had to stop thinking about him in any way except that of a client.

Tanner, as a good-looking, available man, was off-limits.

"What about your opponent? I suspect as an incumbent, he's formidable."

"You got it," Tanner countered, his jaws set.

For a few minutes Kasey listened and took notes on Tanner's assessment of Butler, from his successes to his shortfalls.

"When do you think you'll have some layouts ready?" he asked, changing the subject.

"Give me a few days. The staff will have returned, and maybe Detective Gallain will have come and gone."

The mention of the detective's name drew a frown from Tanner. "You won't get rid of him that easy. Count on him being a pain in the ass. But that's not a bad thing until Shirley's murderer is in custody."

Kasey rubbed her temple, then crossed her arms over her chest as if for protection. "I still can't believe Shirley's dead. It's still like a bad dream."

"I'm sure," Tanner responded with grim undertones. "Promise you won't let it get you down."

"I can't. I have Brock and this agency to think about. They both need me."

"And so do I. Don't forget that."

Kasey didn't dare look at him for fear of what she'd see in his eyes. Even so, she was aware of him with every nerve—his big powerful body, how sharp he looked in his sports coat and slacks, the fresh smell of his cologne, the leashed passion in his every move.

"How 'bout I take you to dinner?"

Kasey jerked her head up, then licked her lips. "Uh, no, thanks. I need to get home."

He looked like he wanted to argue, but didn't. "No problem. Maybe another time."

"Maybe," she said in a hesitant voice.

His eyes swept over her once again before he turned and headed to the door. "I'll be in touch," he tossed over his shoulder.

Sweat saturated her body and her breathing was labored.

Kasey felt her heartbeat with every bounce of her running shoes as they slammed against the rubber on the treadmill. Once she and Tanner had concluded their business, she'd been a ball of nerves and her head ached.

Consequently she'd come straight home, changed into her workout clothes and climbed on the machine. She had considered running outside, but the churning clouds had looked so dark and stormy she opted to remain inside.

This grueling exercise session was a good thing. Both her mind and body needed relief. And exercising hard was soul-cleansing.

Even so, Kasey hadn't completely rid herself of the demons raging inside her, most of which centered around Tanner Hart. She wasn't sorry she'd taken him on as a client. She had come to terms with that. But she was nervous from both a professional and emotional standpoint.

She dreaded working in such close quarters with

him. But in order to do the job and please him, she had no choice. However, she mustn't treat him any different than she had countless others in his stead.

Only Tanner was different. He wasn't just any client, and she'd best remember that. She couldn't ever let her guard down around him. Cool and clearheaded were the operative words.

He would be in constant contact. She knew he would want input on every project she worked on. Her discussion with him had proved that.

After he had left, Kasey had sagged against the desk exhausted, feeling as though she'd been caught in a whirlwind. She hadn't remembered him being so full of energy, on such high alert. But then, she hadn't known him all that well despite…

Kasey had tromped down on that thought and gathered her belongings. The office had lost its appeal for more reasons than one. Shirley's absence was a dismal reminder of what had happened. And without Tanner, all the vitality seemed to have deserted the room. She no longer wanted to be there.

Without a backward glance, she had walked out and closed the door behind her.

Now, as she pulled her mind off Tanner and back on her love-hate affair with the treadmill, Kasey blinked against the sweat burning her eyes. Deciding she'd had enough, she steadily lowered the speed button and was soon walking at a slower, but still brisk pace. Sweat continued to cleanse her pores. She reached for the towel draped over the bar and mopped her face and neck.

After a hot bath Kasey lay on the chaise lounge in her bedroom, a cup of chocolate on the table beside her and a legal pad braced on her legs. She had every intention of toying with ideas for Tanner. Whatever she and the staff put together had to be their best efforts. Pleasing him on her best days would be difficult. But challenging. That was the fun part. And the scariest.

Kasey lowered her head and stared. Not only was the yellow page blank but so was her mind. Except for Tanner's face. She blinked, but his image wouldn't disappear nor would details of the fateful night that changed her life.

"You're tipsy, aren't you?"

She giggled and pulled his head down close to hers. "So are you."

"Whoa," he said with a chuckle against her lips, "not so tipsy that I don't know what's happening here. You're about to get me in a heap of trouble with my friend and your fiancé."

"It's his own fault. He deserted me for an old baseball game." She licked her lips and grinned. "And he's the one who asked you to take me, even though I barely knew you."

"Still—"

"You don't find me attractive?" she asked in a petulant, but cajoling tone, running her finger back and forth across his lower lip.

He groaned, then trapped that finger and sucked on it.

"Kiss me," she whispered, grinding her hips into his hardness.

His moist lips adhered to hers in a long, hot kiss.

"Do you know what you're doing to me?" he gasped, pulling back and staring down at her.

"The same thing you're doing to me, making me hot."

Without taking his eyes off her, he yanked open her

blouse and sucked on her nipples until they were wet and torrid.

"I want to touch you," she whispered.

Without taking his glazed eyes off her, he unzipped his jeans, reached for her hand and placed it on him.

She gasped, then with wonderment began to caress the rock hard but soft skin.

"Sweet Kasey," he rasped, jerking down her panties, then leading her to the nearest sofa in the deserted parlor where he spread her legs and entered her.

A moan from deep within her stopped him midway. He stared at her wild-eyed. "Shit, I can't, not when you haven't—"

"Please, don't stop now," she pleaded, lifting her hips.

"But I'll hurt you."

"It'll hurt worse if you don't."

He buried himself in her...

Suddenly Kasey jerked herself upright, her body bathed in a cold sweat while a wave of despair washed through her. Nothing she could ever say or do would excuse her despicable behavior that night so long ago.

She would never forgive herself.

Having grown up in a strict, religious home where guilt was the weapon of choice, Kasey had had little freedom before going away to college. Once on her own, she'd been highly susceptible to the fun and parties of the campus fraternities and sororities.

At one of those functions, she'd met Mark Ellis and soon after they had fallen in love. Or so she'd thought. One evening he had reneged on taking her to a private party. Because she was so upset at not getting to attend, he'd asked a frat buddy to sub for him.

Nothing had prepared Kasey for the charismatic and

charming Tanner Hart. The second they met, sexual tension had leaped between them. After hours of laughing, dancing and drinking, they hadn't been able to keep their hands off each other and ended up making love.

Nine months later and much to her shame, Kasey had given birth to a healthy baby boy.

She had never told Tanner that she'd borne his son.

She had told Mark that she couldn't see him anymore, that she was pregnant with another man's child, a man who would remain nameless. Mark was devastated yet he had assured her that he could forgive her for betraying him, that he loved her and wanted to marry her. He'd gone on to promise her that no one would ever hear the truth from him and that he'd raise Brock as his own.

Kasey, determined not to further humiliate herself or her family, had settled into the role of student, wife and mother, giving up all her dreams of becoming a successful career woman.

Suddenly the phone rang, startling her back to the present. With an unsteady hand and pounding heart, Kasey lifted the receiver.

"Hi, Mom."

"Hi, darling," she whispered around the tears in her throat.

Eight

It had been several days since he'd seen Kasey and she had accepted his offer. Since then, he'd been on a short campaign jaunt that had gone really well considering he'd been in enemy territory, so to speak.

Right now, he and Butler appeared to be running neck and neck according to the loosely taken polls. Jack and Irene, along with the rest of his backers, were jubilant.

"By the time November rolls around," Irene had told him on the way home, "you're going to kick his ass."

He shot her a side glance before concentrating once again on the road. "Don't get too cocky. We're just getting started."

"You had them eating out of your hands."

"Butler's good at that, too, remember."

"He might have a pedigree, but that's all he has. He's just a big bag of hot, stale air."

"I'm sure the same is being said about me."

"Only you'll do what you say you're going to do. He won't. His record proves that." Irene paused, then changed the subject. "You should be excited by the way things are going."

He was, but cautiously excited. He knew that Buck

Butler intended to hold on to his senate seat no matter what the cost.

Though his passion for Texas and the possibility of serving its constituents burned as brightly in him as it did Butler, Tanner had every intention of sticking strictly to the issues. Slinging mud was distasteful to him. He had an idea that wouldn't sit well with Jack or Irene, but he didn't care. If he couldn't win the election on the issues and his reputation as a solid, dependable businessman, then he just wouldn't win.

So far, he hadn't had to worry. Surprisingly Butler had also kept on the high road. Now that Tanner had caught him in the polls, Butler's true personality would likely come out. Underneath that charming, good ole boy facade was a backstabbing bastard.

No one knew that better than Tanner. Years ago, before he'd made it big in his developing company, he'd had a business deal with Butler that had gone sour. Butler had left him holding the bag to the tune of a half million dollars. It had taken him years to pay that off.

Butler wouldn't hesitate to hit below the belt again. He had plenty of ammo—Tanner's past. Butler could have a field day with that if he were able to get Tanner's juvenile records. They were supposed to be sealed, but nowadays, nothing was sacred.

Tanner wasn't proud of his past, but it was obviously something he couldn't change. He was stronger for it. He had learned that life was filled with hard knocks and that if you didn't knock back, you were screwed.

He grew up as an only child without anything—love or amenities. His dad had been killed in Vietnam when Tanner was in elementary school. His mother, weak and whiny, had turned to the bottle for comfort, leaving him to fend for himself.

As a result, he'd been in and out of trouble with the law, often taken away from his mother and put in the foster care system. Then she'd shape up for a while and he'd be back with her. But her good behavior never lasted. She'd get back on the bottle, and he'd be whisked away again.

The year he'd graduated from high school, she died of liver failure. He'd been on his own, had to scrape for himself. Because he was intelligent and had done well academically, he'd received a partial scholarship to college where he had excelled. After graduating at the top of his class, he'd had the good fortune and sense to marry Norma. Under her influence, he'd fine-tuned some of his rough edges. But it had been his combination of book and street smarts that had gotten him where he was today.

Along with his drive, ambition, and love of competition, he had accomplished far more than he'd ever dreamed. And now, he was riding even higher, thriving on his newfound love—politics. If elected, he had a chance to make a real difference in people's lives. That appealed to him.

Still, he wouldn't sell his soul for a seat in the senate.

On the other hand, he would sell his soul for a chance to make amends to Kasey Ellis. Just thinking of her made his heart race. He had seen her twice now, and both times, he'd felt a jolt—a sock deep in the gut that was palatable.

It was just that she was so damn sexy and didn't seem to know it. Her sassy smile, the subtle whisper of passion in the sway of her hips, the way her lipstick looked like she'd been thoroughly kissed, had awakened his carnal instincts.

His reaction was crazy and could go nowhere. However, he couldn't control how he felt. What he could do was keep his feelings under wraps. No one, least of all Kasey, must ever know his true motivation, or she'd slam the door in his face quicker than he could take his next breath.

Contrary to what he'd told her, he had known her plight, known that she'd been in financial trouble since Mark's death, that she was struggling to keep her son in school, and that she'd returned to Rushmore and gone to work for Shirley Parker.

His deep sense of guilt, shame and betrayal had been the driving force behind his underhandedness. He saw a chance to make up finally for some of the pain he'd brought her.

What he hadn't known was that Kasey had witnessed Shirley's death. On learning that, he'd been more determined than ever to help her. Miraculously, she had accepted his offer.

Now, maybe he could start the healing process within himself. Or maybe that wasn't possible. Maybe he would never be able to atone for his sins that night years ago. When he thought about what happened, which was far too often, he got down on himself.

Only a lowlife would take a friend's girl to a party then take her virginity.

Tanner let go of a harsh breath, then rubbed the back of his tense neck, feeling the muscles bunch under his hand. When he raised his head, Paul Darby, the right-hand man in his company, was standing in the doorway.

Paul was big and robust with a wide mouth and cauliflower ears that were more pronounced due to the horn-rimmed glasses that hooked over them. He might be homely, but when it came to overseeing the construction sites, he was a gem. Tanner didn't know what he would do without him, especially now that he'd entered the political arena.

"If this is a bad time, I'll come back." Paul's tone was hesitant.

Tanner motioned him into his office. "Actually, your timing's perfect. My mind should've been on business and it wasn't."

Paul grinned. "Bet you were thinking about the campaign."

Tanner offered no explanation. Instead, he said, "Something's going on, or you wouldn't be here."

"Right, boss, and I sure hate to bother you with—"

Tanner waved his hand, cutting him off. "It's your job to bother me when there's so much at stake."

The project that was underway was one of his biggest ever. Amidst fierce competition, Hart Development Corporation had landed its most lucrative and challenging job to date—building a high-rise office complex and parking garage on the west side of Rushmore.

Construction had started several months back, and for the most part, things had gone smoothly, which had been in his favor since his mind and loyalty were now divided. However, he'd been expecting a setback, knew it was inevitable.

"It's the material," Paul said. "Or the lack of it, rather."

"Have you contacted the manufacturer?"

"Several times."

"What's the excuse?"

"Don't really know." Paul scratched his head. "Can't get a straight answer."

"Damn."

"Like I said, I hated to have to bother you with this, but without material, we're at a standstill, which is something I don't have to tell you."

"I'll see what I can do. But our best bet is to locate another source."

For the next hour, they worked out the particulars of solving this latest debacle, then Paul said his goodbyes and left.

Alone again, Tanner frowned. If he won the senate seat, he'd have to promote someone from the ranks to manage the company, although that didn't sit too well with him. Before he turned politician, he wasn't beneath putting on a hard hat and working alongside his men.

He enjoyed the physical side of construction as much as the mental. Hard labor honed his body as well as his mind. For the time being, however, the senate race demanded he don a tie instead of a hard hat.

His mind having returned to politics, he shifted his gaze to the phone. Should he call Kasey? He was curious if she had anything to show him. Actually, he didn't give a damn whether she did or not.

He just needed an excuse to see her.

Kasey made her way into the boardroom long after the staff had gathered.

Before she had called this meeting, she had assured herself she was up to the task. Her son's timely phone call last evening had elevated her spirits as nothing else could have done. He hadn't wanted anything in particular; he'd just wanted to check on her and chat—all the more reason why the call was special.

However, now that all eyes were focused on her, her courage floundered.

This morning was the employees' first day back since Shirley's murder. Right off, Kasey had picked up on the tone and mood in the office. It wasn't good; everyone seemed to be walking on eggshells.

Now, as she quickly perused her audience, she noted the staff was all present and accounted for, except Monica Lee, the girl Friday who remained at her desk to man the phones.

The department heads, three in all, were sitting together at the table closest to her. Red Tullos, the art director, fit his name to a tee. He was redheaded, red-faced and red-hot tempered. Kasey suspected it was his volatile nature that fueled his creativity and made him one of the best in his field. Temper or not, she liked him.

Left of Red sat Lance Sagemont, the media director. He was a short, small-boned man with a prominent nose that didn't fit his fine features. However, he dressed with an impeccable flare that helped buffer his odd looks.

On the right was Don Hornsby who was in charge of sales and marketing. In his mid-thirties, he was a brash, good-looking young man with a crew cut and well-preserved body. The only flaw that showed was a mole above his upper lip that he fingered constantly. Because of his charm, he was great at what he did.

The remaining staff was made up of a writer, like herself, Dwight Cavanaugh, another artist, Angie Thigpen and the bookkeeper, Nelda Parrish.

"What's going on?" Red finally asked, his booming voice obliterating the silence.

"Yeah, are we out on our ear?" Don chimed in.

Veiled murmurs followed their outbursts.

Feeling her confidence return, Kasey raised her hand. The room hushed. "No one is out of a job here unless they have a problem working with me."

Red spoke again. "How are you going to keep the agency afloat when Shirley couldn't? We all know it's in financial trouble."

His pointed questions were making her job much easier. "We have a new client."

For a moment, the group looked dumbfounded.

"How can one client accomplish that?" Don asked, a suspicious note in his voice.

"Must be one hellava client," Dwight muttered.

"It is," Kasey said, her voice gaining added strength. "We've been hired by the developer and Texas senatorial candidate, Tanner Hart."

"Well, I'll be damned," Lance said, speaking for the first time.

"What he's paying us, plus the other smaller jobs we still have, will enable the agency to keep the doors open until we can prove our worth again."

Angie raised her hand, then said, "That may be a while, what with all the unfavorable publicity."

"And there will be more to come," Kasey said. "Detective Richard Gallain will be here any time to question all of us about Shirley. They are looking for anything that will help them find her killer. I know each of you will do your part to help in the investigation."

Her words met with another silence. Kasey broke it. "Meanwhile, I'll be briefing you on Hart's campaign and asking each of you for your input into the layout. Put your thinking caps on and don't let me down.''

On that note of encouragement, the meeting ended. She was on her way back to her office when Monica stopped her. ''It's for you.''

''What?'' she asked.

''The phone.''

She hadn't even heard it ring. ''Who is it?''

''Tanner Hart.''

She panicked. After that forbidden trip into the past, she didn't want to talk to him or see him. ''Tell him I'm busy, that I'll get back to him soon.'' She needed more time.

Nine

Kasey was both frustrated and excited. She had worked all day yesterday and most of this morning on Tanner's campaign. While her head had been swarming with ideas based on his platform, nothing had gelled, no one theme that would make the man, Tanner Hart, stand out. With the help of the staff, she had come up with numerous sketches and slogans; they were strewn about the workroom on desks and tables. The place resembled a war zone.

But again, nothing out of the ordinary had jumped out at her. At the moment, her frustration was winning over her excitement. Kasey rubbed her temples, trying to clear her dulled mind.

"Want some more coffee?" Don Hornsby asked in a cheery tone, his smile targeting her.

Kasey shook her head. "Absolutely not. But thanks. As it is, I'm already wired to the max."

"You're not alone," Don muttered, turning and pouring himself another big mug of coffee. "Still, I can't stop hitting the high octane stuff. It's keeping me going."

That was when Kasey noticed how tired he looked, how dark the circles were under his eyes. What was his problem? she wondered. The same as hers most likely—lack of sleep. She had been pushing hard since the staff meeting two days ago. They had worked long, intense hours, and the finish line was not yet in sight.

And time was running out.

"Maybe we should get Hart in here to give us his opinion," Red said, shoving a hand through his thick red hair, causing it to stand on end.

"Yeah, why not do that?" Lance chimed in. "I'm sure he could weed through some of this stuff which would give us a better perspective."

Kasey didn't hesitate. "No. When he's brought on-board, I want ideas in place that will wow him."

In fact, she hadn't called Tanner back for fear he would want to know how things were progressing. More to the point, he'd probably want to have input. And while that was certainly his right, now was not the best time.

"You're pushing yourself too hard," Dwight said in his mild-mannered voice.

It was the first time he'd spoken in a while, which wasn't out of the ordinary. He was a strange little man, considered a geek by the others, maybe because he had zero personality and kept to himself. That aside, Kasey had learned that he was talented and valued his ability as a writer. In fact, several of her favorite slogans had been his idea.

"I have to, Dwight," she responded, her eyes touching on each one. "We all do. Remember time is not a luxury we have."

"Hart must've known that when he hired you."

"That he did, Don," Kasey said on a testy tone. "But since I told him our agency was up to the task, we have to deliver."

Don merely shrugged before picking up one of the sketches and perusing it. Though his expertise was sales and marketing, Don also had an eye for design. Shirley had told her that from the get-go, and she had found that to be true. Yet she didn't plan on tying him up too long. He was needed more on the outside to drum up new business.

"So let's get our backsides in the saddle, then," Red said in his loud voice. "The fat lady obviously hasn't sung yet."

Kasey gave the art director a grateful nod, picked up her sketchbook and thumbed through the pages. Not bad, she mused. Some of these ideas were actually damn good, and Tanner would probably be pleased.

She mulled over each, then sighed. Something vital was missing on the pages. Kasey's eyes narrowed, furrowing her brow. Suddenly she knew what it was. Her own brand of creative energy failed to leap off the pages.

Shirley would probably have disagreed, telling her she was too anal, too much a perfectionist, for her own good. Perhaps. But until she pleased herself, she wouldn't please her client.

Especially this particular client.

"If Shirley was here—" Angie Thigpen began, her gaze on Kasey.

Kasey looked up and smiled at her.

Angie flushed. "I'm sorry, Kasey, I didn't mean to imply—"

"It's okay, Angie. I wish Shirley was here, too. We all do. She was the best."

"She was good, all right," Don added, fingering that mole on his lip. "But from what I've seen of your work, you're no slouch."

Kasey flashed him as much of a genuine smile as she could muster. The spoken and unspoken thoughts of Shirley suddenly forced the tragedy back to the fore-front of her mind. As if the others had picked up on that, a sad silence ensued.

Red was the first to break it. "Kasey, how's the investigation coming?" His usual booming voice was now tempered. "Have you heard anything?"

"Nothing. Any day now, I've been expecting Detective Gallain to make an appearance and question us."

"I still can't believe she's gone," Dwight said, his lean features looking troubled.

Red tapped his pencil against a fingernail. "She damned sure deserved better than she got. I'd like to get my hands on the son of a bitch who was responsible."

"You and me both," Don responded, down in the mouth.

"So how are you holding up, Kasey?" Angie asked in a tentative voice. "I can't imagine what you're going through."

Kasey stifled a sigh. "I'm still awfully skittish, that's for sure. And have the tendency to look over my shoulder at odd times. Otherwise—" Her voice faded into nothingness. What else was there to say? What would be the point in telling them she hadn't had a decent night's sleep since the incident? Or how much she beat up on herself because of her inability to identify the killer.

"As long as you're under police protection, you should be all right," Red said.

"I have a feeling that service is about to come to an end," Kasey admitted with a frown, "since I'm obviously no threat to the killer." Just saying that word made her shiver.

Another silence fell over the room.

"Just how bad are things, Kasey?" Lance asked. "Financially, I mean?"

That question dropped into the silence like a small bomb.

Before Kasey could respond, however, he went on, "I know Hart's given us a reprieve, but just how far can that go?"

"Even though I was a partner, I'm pretty much in the dark as to why the agency's floundering. However, I intend to find out."

Another uncomfortable silence descended over the room.

Monica Lee broke it. She stood in the door and said in an uneasy voice, "Kasey, Detective Gallain's here."

An hour later, Kasey faced the detective alone in her office, behind closed doors.

"Did the staff cooperate?" Kasey asked when Gallain was seated in front of her desk.

"Yes, but they didn't know much."

Kasey made a face. "I find that odd. Most of them have been with Shirley from the beginning."

"Seems as if she kept her private life private."

"Surely they were able to tell you something that would help with the investigation," Kasey said.

"Either they're reluctant to confide in me, or they truly don't have a clue."

"Why would they hesitate to tell you what they know?"

"The nature of the crime, Mrs. Ellis. Like you, they're scared and don't want to get involved."

"I may be frightened, Detective," Kasey responded

in a frigid voice, "but I do want to be involved, only I don't have anything else to contribute."

Gallain rubbed his chin. "So you've said." With those succinct words, he stood and opened the door to leave.

Tanner stood on the other side.

Kasey's eyes widened as they met his for a millisecond. But it was enough to cause her heart to skip a beat or two, which added to her irritation.

"Hart," Detective Gallain said in a clipped tone, passing him by.

Kasey watched as Tanner nodded, then responded, "Detective."

Neither said anything until Gallain had left. Then to cover her own nervousness at his unexpected appearance, Kasey asked, "Have you two met?"

"That we have, and you can bet I won't get his vote."

"If that little exchange is anything to judge by, I wouldn't think so."

"Ah, he's pissed because I went over his head concerning an incident with one of his friends. He overstepped his bounds, and I reported him."

When he didn't offer more, she didn't ask, disconcerted that he had just showed up unannounced.

"Why didn't you return my call?" he asked in his low, rusty-sounding voice.

She maintained as much composure as she could. "I haven't had time. I've been busy."

"Is Gallain giving you a hard time?"

"He still thinks I'm the key to solving Shirley's murder, if that's what you mean."

"Don't let him get to you. He can be a royal pain in the ass."

"I can hold my own."

His eyes perused her, and he gave her a lopsided grin. "I'm sure you can."

She turned away, feeling her heart do funny things again.

"Mind if I sit down?"

"Huh, sorry, you'll have to forgive my manners, or rather the lack of them."

He whipped around, his eyes dark and probing. "You're doing it again."

"What?"

"Treating me like a stranger with an ulterior motive in hiring you."

His arrogant assumption infuriated her. "I don't think you want to go there, Tanner. I know I don't."

His face lost its color under the lash of her tongue. "I thought we could be friends."

"Friends?" Her laughter bordered on hysteria. "I don't think so."

"So, do you have anything to show me?"

The sudden change of subject caught her off guard, slowing her response. "I've been working."

"Is that a yes?"

"Actually, it's a no."

He threw up his hands and smiled, but it disappeared just as quickly and his gaze smoldered into her.

She tried to look away but she couldn't.

"Did I ever tell you I was sorry?" he asked in a husky voice.

Ten

Man, he was tired.

He was coming off the road following two days of hard campaigning in rural areas. While invigorating and eye opening, the jaunt had been taxing. He seemed never to stop talking, smiling, or moving. Someone had been in his face at all times.

Instead of heading home and immediately climbing in the shower, he decided to detour by the construction site. Paul assured him things were progressing as well as could be expected on a project of such magnitude, but Tanner wanted to see for himself. The fact that the job had fallen a bit behind schedule, which hadn't gone unnoticed by the company who had leased the complex, bothered him.

Ever though it was after eight o'clock, Paul was still there.

Tanner made his way through the debris and approached him. "It's beginning to look like a building." He raised his eyes and took in the metal frame that seemed to reach to the sky. "You're doing a great job."

"It's your baby, Tanner. I'm just following the plans."

"The ability to carry out a plan is half the battle. Don't sell yourself short."

"The material's due to arrive tomorrow," Paul said, removing his hard hat and mopping his brow with the back of his hand. "Damn, this weather's a killer."

"Don't I know it." Tanner unbuttoned his shirt and loosened his tie. At least he'd had the good sense to leave his sports jacket in the car. "But I've been out in this mess for so long now, I wouldn't know what it's like not to be in a sauna."

"It's tough on the men, that's for sure," Paul said. "But now that the material is on its way, maybe we can kick ass and make up for lost time."

"Ah, so you found another supplier?"

Paul shrugged. "Only time will tell that. But I'm cautiously optimistic that we have."

"Keep me posted. If anything changes, you find me. Meanwhile, I'm going home to hit the sack."

Tanner reached for the cup of coffee on his desk. He'd gotten up early, gone for a run, showered, then made his way to campaign headquarters. But instead of working on an important speech he had on the near agenda, his thoughts were elsewhere. On Kasey. When had they not been on her? The second after he'd left the agency and hit the campaign trail, she had been with him in spirit.

Okay, so he should've kept his mouth shut.

But then that had never been one of his strong suits. He'd never been shy about speaking his mind. Maybe that was why Jack had him figured for a good politician. Tanner smirked as he got up and stretched his arms high above his head.

He should never have referred to that night in any context. And definitely not with an apology. God, the word sorry didn't even begin to cover that sin of the flesh.

When he'd asked Kasey if he'd ever told her he was sorry, she'd been taken aback and furious by his question, and well she should have been. Those gorgeous blue eyes had sparked with anger.

"The past is off-limits." Her voice was brittle as glass.

"I know, but—"

Kasey moved away from him, but the smell of her cologne lingered. He took a deep breath, drawing it into his lungs. If only she weren't such a lovely, mature widow who stirred unwanted longings in him, perhaps he wouldn't be having such a difficult time keeping things on a professional level.

So it was all about sex. Again.

No, it wasn't, he told himself adamantly. She touched him on another level, a deeper level. She was the type of woman he'd always wanted but had never found. And she detested him.

"Tanner, this isn't going to work."

Her words jolted him into action. "Kasey, for God's sake—"

"I knew this was an insane idea," she went on as though he hadn't spoken. "I should've listened to my instincts and told you to take your business elsewhere."

Panic rose inside him but he quelled it. "If it makes you that uncomfortable, I won't bring it up again."

"I don't know."

"I give you my word," he stressed in a gruff voice.

"If I didn't need—"

"The job," he finished for her, "you'd dump my ass, regardless."

A fathom of a smile crossed her lips. "I couldn't have said it better myself."

He grinned outright. "So just count me a blessing."

"Don't push your luck."

He laughed outright, which defused the charged atmosphere. "So when can I see what you've done?"

"I'll let you know." Her tone brooked no argument. "And don't worry, I know I'm under a time crunch."

He had tried to trap her gaze but wasn't successful. "I'm not worried. I know you'll come through for me."

Now, two days later, he still hadn't heard from her. He had reached for his cell to call several times, but hadn't. When she was ready, she'd call him. However, his patience was wearing thin, especially when he wanted to see her again.

Unfortunately the wanting had nothing to do with business.

"Yo."

Tanner looked up and watched as Irene breezed through the door, a sack in hand. The smell of fast food instantly assaulted his senses and his stomach revolted.

"I went by your place first," she said without preamble, making her way to the coffee bar.

Tanner's eyes took in her perfectly done hair and makeup before moving to her designer pantsuit and strapped sandals. No doubt, she was the savvy, career woman on the rise. So opposite from Kasey, though she, too, valued her career.

It was the difference between hard and soft. Irene had hard edges that taunted she wouldn't hesitate to use her looks and brains to get what and where she wanted. Kasey's edges, on the other hand, were soft and refined, embodying the epitome of the old-fashioned ideas that said you waited your turn.

"I hope you're hungry," Irene said, turning back with a plate filled with food.

"I'll pass, thanks."

"Oh, come on, I know you haven't had breakfast."

"You're right I haven't, but I'm not hungry."

"Suit yourself," she replied, a petulant twist to her lips. "So how did your stomps go? I kept waiting for a call but didn't get one."

"Great. I need to revisit those counties soon."

"I agree. I'm assuming Larry came through for you."

She was referring to one of his financial backers and volunteer workers who had accompanied him on the jaunt.

"He did just fine."

"But not as good as me, huh?"

"Stop fishing for a compliment," Tanner said in a harsher tone than he intended. But for some reason, her appearance rubbed him the wrong way, though he had expected her. They were going to reorganize his campaign schedule.

He hid a sigh. Maybe Jack was right. Maybe it was time to rein her in, to put her in her place. And if she walked, so be it. Nah, not a good idea. Changing ad agencies midstream was enough. At this point in his campaign, he didn't need another crisis.

"Are you pissed at me about the other day?" Irene asked.

"What are you talking about?"

She flushed, then said in a sour tone, "Obviously not, or you would know what I was talking about."

He knew, but he saw no reason to give her a green

light to have another of her temperamental fits. She might threaten to leave him, but he knew she wouldn't. When she didn't get her way, she was prone to pull one of her stunts.

"So what's the new agency come up with?"

"I haven't seen anything yet."

Irene's eyes widened in amazement. "Do they know the importance of time here?"

"Yep."

"So what's the holdup? If this person's as good as you say she is, then—"

Tanner raised his hand. "We'll get rolling sometime this week, I'm sure."

Irene didn't respond, as if she sensed she was treading on thin ice. "My but you've been in a grumpy mood lately."

"Sorry, I've got a lot on my mind."

"Of course you do, and I understand that." She walked to where he sat behind his desk, then around behind him. "I have just the cure for what ails you," she added in a cajoling tone.

Before Tanner realized what Irene was about to do, she placed her hands on his shoulders. He stiffened.

"Hey, relax," she coaxed in a low tone next to one ear. "You're too uptight for your own good. This will help work the kinks out."

He stood abruptly and immediately put distance between them. When he looked back at her, her face was white and her lips pinched. His conscience pricked, but not enough to let her continue massaging him.

"I thought you cared about me, Tanner, that we had something going—" she broke off.

He heard the hint of tears in her voice and felt more like a heel than ever. Maybe if Kasey hadn't— To hell with that. Kasey or not, he wouldn't ever get involved with Irene.

"We never had anything going," he said in the kindest tone he could muster. "We're friends and I admire—"

"Friends!" she screeched. "Why, that's an insult."

"I'm sorry you feel that way."

"Sorry. I'm sick of hearing that word," she spat.

"Look—"

"No, you look. You kissed me, Tanner, more than once. And I didn't take those kisses lightly."

Actually, she'd come on to him, flinging her arms around him and pressing her body into his. However, he wasn't going to call that to her attention. Who made the first move was beside the point. Kissing her had been a mistake, a mistake he had no intention of repeating. But how to let her down gently and not add insult to injury was another matter altogether.

"Right now, Irene, I simply don't have the time or the mental resources for a relationship. You're great at what you do, and I depend on you heavily. And would be lost without you. But anything beyond that is off-limits."

Irene gave a nonchalant shrug. "For now, I'll accept that. But I'm not giving up, Tanner. You should know that. I'm convinced we'd make a great couple. We're both power hungry—"

"How 'bout we just drop the subject and get down to work?"

"Fine," she said in a cool tone. "Just remember when you change your mind and need me, I'll be there. And that's a promise."

A shiver went through him. Her words sounded more like a threat than a promise.

* * *

"Hi, Mom. Where are you?"

"Oh, hi, darling," Kasey responded, feeling her evening brighten at the sound of Brock's voice. "I'm at home."

"Cool. I figured you were still at the office. That's why I called on your cell."

"It doesn't matter. I'm glad to hear from you. How's your job going?"

"It's a *job,* Mom."

"That's right, and you should be glad to have it."

He had managed to land a plum job at a construction site in Waco for the summer. He hadn't been able to come to Rushmore to work because of football practice. However, she knew Brock would much rather have goofed off than be tied down to a job, even a short-term one. Unfortunately most of his friends were from wealthy families and didn't have to work.

He did. As it was, she didn't know how she was going to keep him at Baylor for another year despite his partial football scholarship. She had thought about trying to borrow more money from the bank, but fear of rejection had kept her away.

"Mom?"

"I'm still here, son. When are you coming home?"

"Soon as I can. But right now, I'm calling to ask a favor."

"Oh, and what is that?"

"A bunch of the guys are going down to Padre Island this coming weekend."

"And you want to go."

"In the worst way."

"I don't have any objections."

"Good, so you wouldn't mind lending me some money, then?"

"You should have money."

"I'm running kinda short right now."

Her heart faltered. "How much do you need?"

He told her, and she gasped. "Why so much?"

"Ah, Mom, that's not much. We have to have a room for two nights, food, and—"

"Booze. Is that what you were about to say?"

"Come on, Mom, you know I'm not going to do anything stupid."

"You'd better not."

"So are you good for the money?"

Kasey hesitated, her mind scrambling to think if she could scrape together some extra cash.

"When Dad was alive," Brock said on a whiny note, "I—"

"I know," Kasey interrupted. "But you're stuck with me now."

"I didn't mean it that way, Mom."

"You may have the money but don't make a habit of this, Brock."

"I won't, Mom. I promise."

They spoke a few more minutes before he told her he had to go. A short time later she was in bed, staring at the ceiling. Her son was a good kid who didn't ask for much. While he didn't know the extent of her money problems, he knew enough to tread lightly.

But kids would be kids. She just wished she could give him more. Maybe one day she could. Suddenly Tanner's face sprang to mind, and she went cold all over. She mustn't think of the two together.

Ever.

Eleven

He'd had no other choice, though he was pissing peach seeds over the one he'd made. Hell, what else could he have done when he needed a fix and was broke? He'd gotten the money where he could.

His sister, Flora, hadn't known the difference, he assured himself, long after he had snuck into her house and raided her billfold while she was zonked out on a sleeping pill. He figured she'd have some cash as she'd just gotten her check from the government. He'd been right; it was a healthy sum, in fact, which had enabled him to leave her some even though he knew she had money stashed somewhere in that war zone she lived in.

He'd found it once, a long time ago, and helped himself. Flora never said anything to him. Instead she'd simply changed her hiding place. This evening he hadn't had the patience to scrounge around for her stash. He'd been in a bad way; his body had been drenched in sweat, and he felt like his heart was going to explode.

Dammit, he'd had it so good for so long, he'd gotten overconfident, too complacent, that his habit would continue to be fed. Shirley had been such a windfall, such a perfect patsy, that he hadn't bothered to look ahead, make alternate plans in case something went awry.

However, he wasn't to blame. Shirley had been willing and eager to give him anything. Getting what he wanted, when he wanted it, had been so damn easy. And it hadn't been a chore, either. She had been great in bed, eager to please a man several years her junior. Hey, who could complain? Certainly not him. He'd had a rich, hot mama at his disposal, who'd loved to share her body and her wealth.

He didn't know exactly when things began to change, when her attitude began to sour. That shift had been subtle, or else he'd been in such a euphoric state he hadn't picked up on it right off.

That had been his downfall.

"Darling, we need to have a talk," she'd told him one evening following a strenuous lovemaking session.

He'd paused in his efforts to pull on his jeans and stared at her. "What about?"

"I hate to ask, but I have to." Her features were pinched in concern, though her eyes didn't waver off him.

"You can ask me anything," he responded in a forced, nonchalant tone. "You know that."

"I hope so."

He waited while she hedged a bit longer.

"Out with it," he prodded in that same gentle tone.

"I need to know what you're doing with the money I've been giving you."

Every nerve inside him tightened. "Why?"

She seemed taken aback by his abrupt question. Yet she didn't hesitate to answer with another question. "Don't you think I have the right?"

"I didn't think strings were attached."

"They're not." Her voice faltered. "It's just that I can't make it as fast as you're spending it."

"I thought you were using your personal money."

"I was, only it's long gone. Lately, I've had to dip into company funds."

He cursed.

"I know that's not good," she admitted in a rushed tone, "but I wanted to keep you happy."

"And now you don't?"

"Oh, no, that's not it at all." Her eyes were on the wild side. "It's just that I'm in a bit of a bind, having brought in a new partner and all."

"So are you cutting me off?"

"Do you have another woman?" As if embarrassed by her question, she went on to qualify. "It's just that I'm so afraid I'm going to lose you, that what I...we have is too good to be true."

"I'm not going anywhere." He paused for emphasis, his eyes now drilling her. "Unless—" He deliberately left the sentence unfinished, certain she would get his meaning.

Shirley moved toward him and stopped just short of touching him. "If I only knew why you needed the money and where it's going, I would feel better."

"It's going for a good cause, believe me," he said, proud of his ability to lie with a straight face.

"I want to believe that," she said in a pleading voice.

"It's my sister. It's going for her care."

"Your sister? I didn't know you had a sibling."

"That's because we don't talk, we just fuck."

She sucked in her breath. "That sounds so crude."

"Wasn't meant to be, but you know you love it when I talk dirty."

High color tinted her pale cheeks but then she asked, "Why does your sister need money?"

"She's a paraplegic and poor to boot."

An unsteady hand flew to Shirley's chest. "How awful. How come you never told me?"

"I didn't want to worry you with my problems."

"Oh, darling, you can worry me anytime."

He reached for her then and gave her a long, wet kiss, thrusting his tongue down her throat. When he let her go, her breath was coming in rapid spurts. "You're the best thing that ever happened to me."

"Same here," she muttered.

He took her back into his arms, parted her legs and made her come again with his fingers. Afterward, she dropped to her knees, took him in her mouth and returned the favor.

The money never stopped coming. Until she caught him.

He balked against taking a stroll down that treacherous path, but his mind wouldn't cooperate. Every detail was seared on his memory, and he couldn't make it go away.

He'd just gotten out of the shower that evening. Buck naked, he'd strolled into his living room, poured out some powder and inhaled. Immediately he'd felt all the tension ease out of his body and a feeling so exquisite, equivalent to a sexual high, come over him.

He inhaled again.

That was when he heard the key turn. Like a deer caught in headlights, he swung around and stared at Shirley.

"Why, you bastard," she cried, her features twisted. "You lying, conniving bastard." She stepped forward with blazing eyes. "All that song and dance about your sister was a lie."

"No, it wasn't. Isn't."

She went on as though she hadn't heard his response. "You're nothing but a two-bit druggie."

"When did you suddenly become so moralistic?" he sneered. "You had to have known."

"You're crazy," she screeched. "To think you've been snorting my money up your nose, using my money to get high." Her sudden laughter reached a higher decibel. "What a gullible idiot I've been."

He grinned, feeling no pain, the drug working its own particular brand of magic. "You said it, I didn't."

Her hand came out to slap him, only he grabbed it in time, gripping her wrist until she cried out.

"Let me go, you sicko."

He grinned. "Not until you calm down and get a hold of yourself."

She glared at him, but stopped struggling. He let her go.

"So now that you know, what do you intend to do about it?" He knew the answer, of course. But before he could make firm plans, he needed to hear the bad news from her.

"For starters, cut you the hell off."

"I wouldn't advise that."

She laughed an ugly laugh. "What are you going to do about it? You're at my mercy now. No more money. Voilà. No more drugs."

"I have other sources," he bluffed, his high beginning to fade, returning him to the real world with a crash. "There are others who are willing to pay for my stud services."

Shirley's head snapped back like he'd slapped her,

then tears gathered in her eyes. "I thought we had so much more."

He laughed. "God, what a hopeless romantic you are. You're almost old enough to be my mother."

"That's not true," she lashed back, the tears beginning to trickle down her face.

He raked his eyes over her, not bothering to hide his revulsion. "Get the hell out of my sight."

"You won't get away with treating me this way."

"Yes, I will because we both know you can't do without me. You're addicted to what I do to you in bed."

"And so are you. We'll see how you fare in prison."

"Prison."

She laughed again. "Haven't you heard? Coke possession is against the law. I'm going to turn your ass in."

He pushed the panic button, but he didn't let it show. "That wouldn't be smart."

She hadn't bothered to answer. Instead she'd turned and walked out the door. That was when he realized what he had to do. He had to kill her before she made good on her threat.

Now, he brought his mind back to the present and plopped down on his sofa. Chuckling, he indulged in another snort of white powder.

Yeah, the bitch had it coming. If she hadn't threatened to go to the cops, she might still be breathing. As it was, she had met her maker. Or the devil, whichever the case might be.

He chuckled again, closed his eyes and gave in to the feeling that he was flying.

She had a package.

A solid one, too. Kasey couldn't wait to get Tanner's opinion, certain it would be positive. She and her staff had continued their long, grueling hours until the work was done. The television ads were particularly good, she thought, having written them herself. The billboard signs and flyer slogans were strong as well, though she couldn't take credit for those alone. The entire staff had participated, especially Red and the other artists. They had done an incredible job with the artwork.

Still, the underlying theme of the entire campaign bore her mark, which meant she was responsible for its success. Or failure. The thought of failure, however, hadn't entered her mind, having felt her confidence soar once she'd come up with that special ingredient that had been heretofore missing.

Kasey peered at her watch. Although it was after hours, it wasn't too late to call Tanner. It was simply a matter of picking up the phone and dialing the number.

Only it wasn't that easy. While she couldn't wait to show off her handiwork, feel all warm and fuzzy under his accolades, she stalled. Instead her hand hovered above the receiver.

He frightened her.

She was far too aware of him as a man, a man whose seductive power over her had almost ruined her life. Although she'd been very much aware of him that day at the cemetery, she had attributed that awareness to the shock of having been caught off guard at seeing him after so many years.

Now, she knew better. The shock had long worn off and still she felt a thrill every time he came near her. Because she hadn't expected this reaction, she'd been defenseless and still was, especially after he'd broached the subject of that fateful night.

At least, her frigid attitude had stopped an outright discussion of the events. But the fact he'd had the nerve to mention that night had left her feeling vulnerable and upended.

Okay, so her back was against the wall in more ways than one. She'd just have to deal with the uncomfortable circumstances. When faced with other unexpected dilemmas, she'd met the challenge head-on. She'd never been a shrinking violet and wasn't about to become one now.

Another thing in her favor was that she'd become a master at burying her feelings, at holding undesirable people at arm's length. There was no reason why she couldn't resurrect that survival technique and ride out this present storm.

Once the campaign was over, Tanner would disappear from her life. Meanwhile, she'd have to cling to that certainty and think of him as a job and not a man.

Releasing her pent-up breath, Kasey lifted the receiver to dial his number. A knock on the door stalled her hand. Something told her who it was, though she wasn't alone in the office.

"Yes?"

She was hoping this time, when she saw him, she wouldn't feel the impact of his presence. But she did. That jolt zinged her again as Tanner strode across the threshold, looking a tad disheveled and apologetic.

"I bet you'd wish I'd quit just popping up," he said with a hint of a smile.

"Actually, I was about to call you."

"Oh?"

Kasey averted her gaze, but only after she noticed

everything about him—his leashed muscles, his mussed-up hair, the fatigue lines on his face, his dislodged tie. Yet he'd never been more enticing, more sexually potent. And she was never more aware of him.

"It's show and tell time, huh?" he asked.

She looked back at him. But only for a second. However, that was enough to cause a tingle to shoot through her, especially when she saw heat flare in his eyes.

Following a gust of breath, she said, "That's one way of putting it."

"Have you eaten?"

His switch in subjects took her aback. She blinked. "No."

"Neither have I. Want to grab a bite before we get down to business?"

"I'm not hungry."

"You sure?"

"I'm sure."

"Well, I am."

"Maybe after we go through this stuff," she hedged, having no intention of going out to dinner with him.

He grinned. "That'll work."

Twelve

"How much longer are you going to be here?" Don Hornsby asked, sticking his head inside her door.

"Not much longer," Kasey responded, looking up from her work. "I've about had it."

Don's features bore concern as he came deeper into the workroom. "You look worn-out."

"I'm all right."

"Sure as hell could've fooled me," Red exclaimed, striding through the door and giving her a pointed stare.

"I'm going home soon, I promise."

"Just exactly what was it he didn't like?" Don demanded. "You've never told us."

"Ah," Red said, flapping his hand in the air, "he's just your typical asshole politician. What more is there to say?"

Kasey couldn't help but smile, though she knew she shouldn't let Red discuss their client in such an unprofessional manner. At the moment, she didn't have the wherewithal to confront him.

"So are we going back to the drawing board?" Don asked, his concern deepening.

"No," Kasey said, fingering her dark hair. "Actually, he didn't want that many changes, just some tweaking here and there, which I've already done. If those pass muster, then the package is a definite go."

"I wouldn't hold my breath," Red muttered, his face the color of his hair. "I don't trust politicians as far as I can throw them."

Don narrowed his gaze on him. "As long as he's got money and can keep our doors open, who cares?"

"I care," Red shot back, "because Hart can't do that alone. With all the hype still surrounding Shirley's death and that Gallain fellow snooping around and bugging us, no one else is going to touch this agency with a ten-foot pole."

Don turned anxious eyes on Kasey. "I thought Hart would be the shot in the arm we needed to keep the paychecks coming."

"Give it a rest, guys, okay?" Kasey said in a tired voice. "I don't plan to put a Closed sign on the door now or ever." Her voice grew stronger. "Once Shirley's killer is caught and all the publicity dies down, we will rebound. You'll see."

When neither responded, she added, "I'm leaving now. Will one of you lock up?"

A short time later, Kasey let herself into her apartment, wishing she had Brock to greet her. She missed him so much, had never stopped missing him since he went off to college. But she couldn't cling to him forever, though at the moment she wanted to do just that. Then her sound judgment returned, and she was relieved that Brock was away at school.

A shudder went through her. If it hadn't been for his athletic ability, he might have chosen Rushmore Junior College. Before Baylor had come through with a partial scholarship, he had considered that, especially since it had been so much cheaper. In hindsight it would've been disastrous.

She wanted him as far away from Tanner as possible.

Shrugging that thought aside, Kasey made her way into the kitchen, poured herself a glass of iced tea, then went into the living room and sat down. As soon as she found the energy, she would take a shower, then go to bed.

Emotionally she was a wreck.

She had let Tanner get to her. Though it pained her to admit that, it was the truth. He had made her angry and uncertain, a lethal combination where she was concerned.

Their conversation last evening jumped to mind and ruffled her feathers all over again. When she had seen the look on his face after reviewing the layout, her confidence suffered a major blow. Though he'd struggled to mask it, his disappointment had been obvious. But when she'd called his hand, Tanner had vehemently denied it.

"It's good, really good."

"But?" Her voice was wooden.

He shot her a look. "How do you know there's a but?"

"Stop playing games with me, Tanner," she snapped.

He drew back, his eyes widened. "You're really pissed, aren't you?"

"Yes."

"Come on, Kasey, you're making something out of nothing. Overall, the package is strong, but—" He broke off and smiled, a glint in his eye. "Okay, so there is a but." The smile expanded.

She knew he was making an all-out effort to inject some humor into the sudden and potentially volatile situation. What it did was add tension, making her more aware of closeness and his potent charm. Both robbed her of composure and ability to think.

Fearing he would pick up on the chaos clamoring inside her, Kasey moved away.

That gesture was not lost on Tanner. His eyes narrowed and his lips thinned. "Look, if there is a problem, it's with the newspaper ads, but that's my fault and not yours. I just feel we're not quite there yet. The words don't seem to have enough strength or zing to them. Does that make sense?"

"Absolutely. And that's an easy fix. I'll get right on it."

He peered at her out of unreadable eyes. "But again, the total package is a job well done." His voice was low and husky. "I really mean that."

"If you're sure," she said.

"Kasey."

Her head came up and her stark gaze met his. And held.

"I'm sure, believe me."

Their eyes held a moment longer, then Tanner cleared his throat, effectively breaking the spell. But it left her feeling weak and vulnerable.

"I'd better go," he said, in a low, gusty tone. "I'll call you tomorrow."

So far, he hadn't called. And now that the workday was over, Kasey knew she wouldn't hear from him. Suddenly an acute sense of disappointment washed over her, which was ridiculous, of course. Somehow she had to find a way to smother this unwanted attraction that was undermining her good sense.

Otherwise...

Kasey leaped off the couch, furious at what she saw

as a terrible weakness that must be overcome. Draining her glass, she went back into the kitchen to refill it. That was when she heard the noise. She froze. And listened.

Silence.

Moments later she released her breath, only to hear it again. She whipped around and stared through the French doors that led onto her deck. Was someone there? Had someone somehow managed to get past the detective after all?

Her blood turned to ice. Had the killer finally come after her?

Stop it, she told herself. Of course, he hadn't. Her vivid imagination was her own worst enemy. With that assurance, she marched across the room and flung open the door.

A meow greeted her.

She clung to the door handle to keep herself upright, her insides having turned into a quivering mass of jelly. Then she laughed, satisfied her intruder was nothing but a harmless, stray cat. Still, she went back inside and latched the door.

At that moment, the doorbell chimed. A frown marred her brow. Company was not in the offing tonight unless it was Ginger. That thought cheering her considerably, she headed to the door.

Jack's sigh was audible through the phone line. "I said, can we get together?"

Tanner forced himself to pay closer attention to what Jack was saying. "Now?" He peered at his watch.

"Yes, now. It works for me."

"Unfortunately it doesn't for me."

"I thought maybe we might have dinner," Jack

pressed in an exasperated tone. "I have some info on Buck Butler. You need to hear it."

"Sorry, but I have other plans." He didn't, at least not confirmed ones. But he had hopes and didn't want to make another commitment until he knew. Yet he didn't want to appear uninterested when it came to his attention-grabbing opponent who had apparently taken his gloves off and was about to come out fighting.

"Can't cancel them, huh?" Jack asked.

"What about dinner tomorrow night?"

"I can live with that." He paused. "Has Irene told you about Butler taking a jab at you at the Lion's Club luncheon?"

"Yeah, she told me."

"I hope you plan to respond in like fashion."

"We'll talk about that, too."

An expletive forced Tanner to hold the receiver away from his ear.

"That's what I'm afraid of," Jack expounded. "I don't want you to talk. I want you to counterpunch, to knock his dick in the dirt, starting with the new TV ads."

"Later, Jack."

"Dammit, Tanner, don't you hang up on me."

Tanner did just that and with a clear conscience, too. As much as he owed Jack and as much as he admired him, he wouldn't be pushed into steering his campaign in a direction he didn't feel comfortable with, even if the campaign was leaping toward the finish line.

With his lips stretched in a thin line, he peered at his watch again. What he was about to do was a foolhardy stunt, but he was going to do it anyway. He wanted to see her. And that desire was unrelated to business. All the more reason why he should heed his gut instinct and stay there and work on his next speech.

That was tempting, only not nearly as tempting as having dinner with Kasey. Now, all he had to do was convince her. Not an easy task, he told himself, grabbing his sports coat and walking out.

When he stood at the door of her apartment a few minutes later, he noticed he was perspiring more than usual. Funny thing, the humidity wasn't as high as normal. Actually the evening was quite pleasant, the sky clear and star-studded, the breeze balmy. What did that say about him?

That he was insecure when it came to her, which made him feel like an idiot. Still, he wanted to make sure she wasn't still pissed at him. At least that gave him some justification for being here, lame though it was.

After running his palms down the sides of his slacks, he pressed the doorbell.

"It's Tanner," he said in response to her inquiry.

Seconds later, the door opened and he was staring at her in silence. Her cheeks seemed paler than usual, he noted, and her blue eyes darker. Also, her dainty features had a strained look like something had agitated her.

Him probably.

"Mind if I come in?"

She hesitated, then stepped back. Once he was inside, he paused and looked around. The large living area was cool yet its decor had an inviting warmth that was so feminine. So her.

"Nice place."

"Thanks," she murmured.

"Am I intruding?" he asked, noticing she still clung to the doorknob.

"Would it matter if you were?"

Blood rushed into his face. "I'd be lying if I said yes."

"Why did you come?"

"To invite you to dinner."

"I'm not hungry."

"Why did I know you'd say that?"

They looked at each other again, then both shifted their gazes at the same time.

"Are you okay?"

"Am I that transparent?" she asked on a husky note.

Uneasiness shot through him. "Are you still pissed at me?"

"Should I be?"

"Absolutely not."

That old twinkle suddenly reappeared in her eyes. "Actually it's my paranoia. It's working overtime."

"How so?"

She explained about her scare.

"I bet you gave the stray some milk," he said with a lopsided grin.

She grinned back. "I thought about it, but I was afraid he was too wild."

He didn't respond for a moment, trying to recover from the impact that grin had on him. Good thing he had his hands in his pockets and his jacket on or she would be able to see the sudden bulge in his slacks. Hoping to distract her, he rubbed the back of his neck with his hand.

"You shouldn't be here, you know?"

His stomach tightened. "Then let's go out."

"I don't think that's a good idea, either." She paused. "Unless it pertains to business."

"It doesn't," he admitted bluntly.

Her eyes widened.

"Okay, I just wanted to see you away from the office. Is that honest enough?"

It was obvious that she was at war with herself and him. Who would win was anyone's guess.

"I don't want to go out," she said, a slight quiver in her voice.

"So what do you suggest?" He tried hard to hold his eagerness in check, fearing it was premature.

"I'll just make something here."

With that, she turned and headed toward the kitchen. Yet he was powerless to follow. His limbs wouldn't cooperate. First, he was too weak with relief. Second, he was too mesmerized by the way her hips filled out her pants to perfection.

He was playing a very dangerous game, yet he couldn't seem to stop himself. For the moment, he was willing to let the chips fall where they may.

Apparently, so was she.

Thirteen

So she had listened to her heart instead of her head.

When Tanner had admitted his invitation was personal, she had been struck dumb. By the time she'd found her voice, it was too late. He had already crossed the threshold, and she'd been powerless to deny him.

Deny herself.

Now, as she faced him across the small breakfast room table, she looked on in amazement as he finished devouring the chicken salad sandwich, chips and pickles she'd heaped on his plate. In addition, he'd had three glasses of her almond tea.

In between, he had entertained her with humorous happenings on the campaign trail. A time or two he'd even had her laughing outright. Only when she'd feel his intent gaze on her would she be on shaky ground.

By lowering her guard around him, she was treading on the thinnest of ice. Yet she was in no hurry to boot him out.

"Man, that was good."

He pushed back from the table and straightened out his long legs as though trying to get more comfortable. Settle in. God forbid. Still, she couldn't muster the courage to demand that he leave even though the sexual aura surrounding them continued to work on her psyche. She was hard-pressed to keep her gaze off him, and that was a problem.

"It was just plain chicken salad," she finally responded in a weak voice.

"Well, it hit the spot. Actually it tasted better than a filet."

She arched her eyebrows at that. "I doubt that, but I'm glad you enjoyed it."

"You happen to have a to-go box?"

Her eyebrows went a little higher and a smile flirted with her lips. "You're kidding, right?"

He chuckled. "Yeah. I'm so used to eating fast food my body would probably rebel at having two decent meals in a row."

"Fast food is a bad habit to get into."

"Some days I'm lucky to get anything."

"That's not good, either."

"Are you volunteering to feed me, by chance?" His lips twitched.

"Not hardly," she said tersely even though she knew he was teasing her.

"Didn't think so," he drawled.

Kasey rose. "I'll make some coffee and bring it into the living room." She had hopes that he would say he had to go, but he didn't. Instead he got to his feet and began cleaning off the table.

"That's not necessary. I'll do it later."

"Nope. You cooked, I'll clean."

"I didn't cook."

"Well, you know what I mean."

"Tanner."

"Kasey."

They stared at each other—two unmovable objects.

"Oh, all right," she said in a huff, though her insides

were on fire. When he looked at her with that indulgent humor, she found his particular brand of charm even harder to resist.

"That didn't kill you, now, did it?"

"Nearly."

Tanner chuckled. "I didn't know you were so stubborn." Suddenly his features sobered and his voice dropped a pitch. "But then there's a lot I didn't…don't know about you."

Feeling that thin layer of ice threaten to crack under her feet, Kasey ignored the personal reference and busied her mind and hands with preparing the coffee. Meanwhile, Tanner went about his chore of tidying up.

Later, with cups and a tray of cookies, they made their way into the living room. Kasey sat in the big chair. Tanner sat on the sofa adjacent to her. Once again, he seemed to have no qualms about making himself at home and comfortable, having loosened his tie and stretched his legs out in front of him.

They sipped on their coffee while the silence grew around them.

"Anything further on the investigation?" Tanner asked, leaning over and grabbing a cookie.

"Not that I know of. I keep waiting for Gallain to make another appearance, but so far he hasn't."

"I wish Gallain would get off his dead duff and find the killer."

"That makes two of us."

"My gut says you're safe, but I don't think you feel that way, especially when things go bump in the night."

That drew a smile. "As long as it's nothing but a cat, then I'm okay."

"Just be careful." He angled his head and lowered his voice. "Don't take any unnecessary chances."

"I'll try not to."

"Don't work at the office at night by yourself."

"Not even on your project?" she quipped while trying to overlook the possessive note in his tone and how protected it made her feel.

"For sure on that."

A breath exited her lungs. "When I came here six months ago, I had such high hopes of a bright future with the agency, finally accomplishing something on my own for myself. Now, look what a mess my life's in."

"It'll straighten out." Tanner leaned forward. "I have faith in you and your ability."

"I'm not so sure."

"Well, I am. That's why I hired you."

She hoped that was the truth, but she still harbored doubts, only to turn around and reassure herself. He had no way of knowing the truth and never would. Still, she just wished her *heart* wouldn't go bump when he was around.

"Hey, don't get down on yourself," he added in a coaxing tone.

Her eyes flashed. "I'm not. I've never been a quitter and I don't intend to start now."

He didn't respond right away. "You said you wanted to do something for yourself." He paused again. "Does that mean you weren't able to when you were married to Mark?"

Although he knew that line of questioning was off-limits, he'd asked anyway. By rights, she should've told him that was none of his business. But again, if she made a big deal out of not discussing her past, his suspicions might be aroused.

"Yes, but that doesn't mean I wasn't content or happy." Her tone was defensive.

Tanner's eyes raked over her in the tense moment that followed. "That's what I wanted to hear," he said softly. "That was my greatest hope for you."

She hadn't expected him to say that. Feeling her stomach pitch, she bit down on her lower lip. "It's just that Mark wasn't the best at handling money." She couldn't believe she'd said that. But now that she had, she went on, "I didn't know that until after he died," she finished lamely.

"Is money the only reason you went back to work?"

"I had intended to, anyway. But then, it was no longer negotiable."

Tanner rubbed his chin. That was when she noticed how prickly it had become. Despite the fact that his hair was on the light side, his beard wasn't. But then neither was the hair on his strong arms. She swallowed with difficulty.

"You're damn good at what you do. You'll make a great success of this business."

"I wish."

"You don't believe that?"

"It's not that easy. Advertising is so personal. It takes the right combination."

"You hit that combination with me, and I'm hell to please."

"But you weren't pleased, not at first, but you won't admit it."

"That's not true, dammit. But I'm not going to argue the point with you because you'll just get pissed at me again."

Kasey cut him a side glance. "I've already made some changes in the news ads. I hope you'll approve. They're much more hard-hitting without being offensive."

"Do you think I'm on the right track?" Tanner rubbed his chin. "I know you've designed them according to my needs and specs, but you've never really given me your personal opinion. I'd like to have it."

"Oh, no, you don't. My opinion doesn't matter."

"It does to me."

"Even if I'm conservative and you're liberal?"

Tanner's lips twitched. "So does that mean I can't count on your vote?"

For another long moment, sexual tension crackled between them.

"That's none of your business," she responded in a prim, unsteady voice. "Who I vote for, that is."

He chuckled. "Then I'll have to work on that. I'm going to need all the votes I can get."

"I figure you're a shoo-in."

He looked shocked. "Against an incumbent? I don't think so." His eyes darkened. "But I'm curious as to what makes you say that."

"You have looks, money and—" She broke off, realizing how she must sound. Heat scalded her face.

"And?" he prodded with piercing eyes.

Her chin jutted. "Okay, ego."

"I asked for that," he muttered, though his lips twitched again. "At the moment, Butler and I are running neck and neck in the polls. But I don't see that holding for the duration. Maybe this new media blitz will kick butt. Butler's butt, to be specific."

"So much for the high road," she said lightly.

"Ah, so you don't approve, after all?"

"I didn't say that."

"Yes, you did." He sighed. "Look, I'm still not going after Butler personally. Maybe it won't come to that. But again, maybe it will."

"That's why politics leaves such a bad taste in people's mouths."

Tanner reached for the cookie tray and held it out to her. "Speaking of taste."

Without even thinking and without being hungry, she took one. They munched in silence. But she didn't enjoy hers; it tasted like she had a mouthful of grit.

Had she lost her mind? Apparently so. Here she was carrying on a normal, if not flirty, conversation with a man whom she should avoid at all costs.

"How's your mother? I'm assuming she's still alive."

That question took her aback. She hadn't been aware that he knew anything about her family. But then, he had been a good friend of Mark's, and they had kept in touch through the years.

"She's alive, but not well. After she was diagnosed with osteoporosis, she fell and broke her back within two months of Mark's death. As a result, she's in a nursing home in Wyoming where my brother Ben lives."

"Which means you don't get to see her often."

"Not as often as I'd like, that's for sure. I've thought of bringing her back, but—" Her voice trailed off. She had no intention of going into the pros and cons of reuniting with her mother. As it was, she'd let this conversation stray way too far off base.

She stood abruptly. As if he sensed her sudden agitation, he stood as well. Their gazes touched before both turned away.

"My time's up, right?"

She didn't so much as blink. "Right."

"Aren't you going to walk me to the door?" His tone was mocking.

Once there, she held onto the doorknob for support. She didn't intend to look up at him, but the silent pull of his eyes drew her.

Before she realized his intentions, he brushed a finger across the corner of her mouth. "You had a crumb," he said huskily.

Her lips parted on a gasp as he captured her eyes once again and held them. Then groaning, he lowered his head and kissed her. It was a deep gentle kiss, seeming more spiritual than aggressive. But when his tongue touched hers, that changed. The kiss deepened and intensified. Her heart soared and she clutched at him; her fingers dug into his shoulders for support.

But she need not have worried. He apparently had no intention of letting her go, placing a strong arm across her back and molding her against him. She felt every hard plane of his body, leaving no doubt about his arousal.

Then abruptly he pulled away, breathing hard. Without taking his eyes off her, he framed her face in his hands. "Please don't tell me I shouldn't have done that."

She could barely speak around the lump in her throat. "All right, I won't."

"Go to bed," he whispered. "I'll call you tomorrow."

Fourteen

Horace Bigfield was in his mid-fifties with gray hair and a big, strapping body. He had been Shirley's attorney, and now was Kasey's. Today was the first opportunity he'd had to fit her into his busy schedule. Although Kasey felt the partnership agreement was solid, she'd feel much better after this session. After all, she had no idea of the contents of Shirley's will or if it had any bearing on the business. Therein lay her anxiety.

"Good morning, Horace," she said. "Thanks for seeing me."

"Thanks for being so patient." He sat down behind his massive desk with a huff like he'd been running up a long hill. "This has been one more busy week."

Kasey smoothed a wrinkle from her linen pants before she looked up. "I know what you mean."

He scrutinized her closely. "More so than me, I'm sure. What's the latest on Shirley's killer?"

"As far as I know, they haven't arrested anyone."

He tapped his pen against a folder. "That's too bad. Even though Rushmore's a small city, a crime of this magnitude still hits hard. It affects everyone."

"Especially since Shirley was so well-known and liked."

"Well, someone sure as hell didn't like her." Bigfield leaned back in his chair and tapped the pencil against his stained yellow teeth. "I understand you saw the whole thing."

Kasey wasn't surprised by his remark. As predicted, the rumor mill was at work. "That's not true."

"Oh."

She gave him a short version of what happened, hoping then to move on to the business at hand. This was one niggling problem she wanted to lay to rest today, if possible. She didn't like talking about that fateful day in the parking garage. It brought home the horror all over again.

"Damn shame you had to go through something like that."

"I wouldn't wish that on my worst enemy."

The office was quiet for a moment, then Bigfield said, "May I offer you some coffee?"

"No, thanks, I'm fine."

He repositioned his chair and opened the folder in front of him. "I went over the contract again as well as Shirley's will."

"I haven't seen the will."

"It was made before you came on board and before she was murdered."

Kasey fought off a sense of uneasiness. "Meaning?"

"Meaning she left the business to one of her cousins."

Kasey made a face. "Is that a problem?"

"No, but it would have been the smart thing to change her will at the same time we drew up the contract."

"Why didn't she?"

"It wasn't from the lack of trying on my part, believe me. But she kept telling me she wanted to make other changes and needed more time." His features darkened. "Unfortunately she never got that time."

"So where does that leave me?"

"Owner of the agency. Even though Shirley's will disputes that, the contract between you two is legal and binding."

Relief washed through her. "So the agency is mine?" She wanted him to clarify that as an undisputed fact.

"Absolutely. As to her home and personal belongings, this particular cousin has also inherited those. To my knowledge there's no on-hand cash, though at one time there was."

"I would've said she put it into the agency, but since its cash flow is practically nonexistent that's not the case."

"I'll draw up papers with you as the sole proprietor. When the papers are ready, we'll call you."

Kasey stood and held out her hand. "You've certainly made my day brighter."

He smiled. "Glad I could oblige."

Fifteen minutes later, Kasey was behind her own desk, staring into space. Two days had passed since Tanner had kissed her. She'd thought of little else. She had asked herself over and over how he'd managed to knock down that cement wall she'd erected between the two of them. No answer had been forthcoming.

Was she sorry?

No, God help her.

Just thinking about the feelings his lips had awakened made her weak all over. Weak with unfulfilled desire. But then eighteen years ago, she'd felt the same way. Tanner's kisses had affected her like no other man's, including her husband. That was why she'd succumbed to him that night with such blatant disregard for anything or anyone.

But she'd been young and brash then. She couldn't tap into that excuse now. She was older and wiser. That didn't seem to matter, however. His touch had brought unexpected Technicolor into her life where only darkness had been.

What about Brock?

Her stomach lurched. The other night, in the heat of the moment, she had forgotten about her son and what was at stake. In the bold light of day, it hit her like a fist. Yet she still couldn't say she was sorry. While she was pressed against Tanner's aroused body, and his lips were drinking from hers, she'd felt alive.

But that didn't mean she could indulge herself again. *She and Tanner could never be.*

Kasey took a ragged breath and tried once again to concentrate on the layouts in front of her. Realizing she was fighting a lost cause, she decided to do something physical like spend time in her partner's office, clearing out her desk, something she'd been putting off, and something that would expend some energy.

"I'll be in Shirley's office," Kasey told Monica, "if I get any calls."

"Red's gone to lunch, but he was looking for you earlier."

"I'll talk to him later."

Once she was behind closed doors, Kasey didn't waste any time. She sat behind Shirley's desk and began opening drawers, though she felt like an intruder. Shrugging that disturbing thought aside, she continued on. She had brought in several boxes to hold various personal items and began to fill them one by one.

It was in the next-to-last drawer that she found a

notebook. Pausing a moment, she opened it. After perusing the first several pages, she stopped. What she saw listed on those particular pages raised the hairs on the back of her neck.

Hand-written at the top were the words: Date and Amount of Loan. In total, the sum was several hundred thousand dollars. Kasey gasped in astonishment. The last entry was noted only days before her murder.

Who had borrowed that much money? And for what?

Kasey rubbed her head, feeling a headache coming on. Had she just uncovered evidence of blackmail? If so, had Shirley used company funds and managed to cover it up?

More importantly, had she uncovered the reason for her partner's murder? With her heart pounding and her hands unsteady, Kasey leafed through every page.

Even though no name was anywhere to be found in the notebook or anything else pertaining to the money, she knew this information was important.

Gallain should know. Kasey reached for his card, then punched out his number, her mind in an uproar.

What grave error in judgment had she made by trusting her old friend?

"Would you gentlemen please excuse me?" Irene grinned, her eyes touching on Tanner and Jack. "The little girl's room calls."

"Of course," Jack responded, rising to his feet along with Tanner. "I think I'll join you."

Irene cocked her head to one side, her lips spread in a sly grin. "Mmm, wonder how many eyebrows that will raise."

Jack gave her a disgusted look.

"I'll be here when you both get back," Tanner announced in a bored tone, tired of their company. He watched them disappear with relief, though he knew that relief would be short-lived.

When Irene found out that he and Jack were having dinner, she had asked to join them, pointing out a pow-wow was needed. He had agreed and so had Jack.

During the meal itself, the two had managed to hold to a truce. Even so, he wished he was anywhere else but here.

Not just anywhere, Tanner corrected savagely. With Kasey. He'd love a repeat performance of that evening two days ago. But his gut instinct told him that wasn't going to happen. Until he'd made his unexpected move, she'd had a knack for pushing him out, for keeping him at a safe distance.

Considering what had happened between them and the humiliation he was sure to have caused her, he should've kept his libido in check, dammit. But there was something about her that touched him on a level that no other woman had ever reached. And he'd had plenty of women before and after his wife.

Until he'd seen Kasey at the funeral, he hadn't realized how she affected him, of course. In a matter of minutes, the years had disappeared, and they were both young, carefree and uninhibited.

Only they weren't. They were grown-ups with time and circumstances vastly separating them. Still, he'd lucked out and had been granted another chance to make amends. But being the dumb fuck that he was, he'd blown it. Tanner groaned silently. While she had returned the kiss with matching fervor, he knew regrets would follow.

In the wake of those regrets, she might give him his walking papers.

It had been that incredibly infectious smile of hers that had tripped him over the edge that night. Underneath that standoffish facade was a woman made of pure velvet, making her impossible to resist.

No excuse. His mission was to help her, not hurt her further. He had no idea what he was going to say to her. If he got the chance to say anything, he thought with a grimace.

"What's the matter with you?" Jack demanded, pulling out his chair and sitting down. "Did you eat something that didn't agree with you?"

Tanner took the easy way out. "Yeah."

"It's Irene that doesn't agree with me. I wish—"

Tanner cut him off. "Don't start, Jack. Until the election's over, it's imperative that we all get along. If I'm going to win, that is. So bury your hatchet, only not in Irene's skull."

Irene chose that moment to return, effectively stifling Jack's comeback. Their waiter also appeared, refilling their wineglasses. They had dined on the finest of Italian foods accompanied by the finest of red wines.

Tanner watched as Irene raised her glass to her lips and envisioned Kasey sitting there instead. He muttered a silent curse before saying out loud in an abrupt tone, "Let's get down to business, shall we?"

"I have the results of the latest poll," Jack said, then paused, his pink cheeks looking pinker than usual.

"And?" Irene asked, her tone impatient as she cut her gaze to Tanner then back on Jack.

"Butler's regained the lead."

"Damn," Tanner muttered.

Irene chimed in. "All the more reason to start kicking ass, Tanner, on TV, in front of God and everybody, which is something that's not happening.''

Jack gave him a perturbed look. ''I thought you had corrected that.''

''I did. You and Irene need to see final layouts. They hit Butler where he's the weakest. His waffling on a pay raise for the teachers is leading the pack.''

Irene drained her glass, then leaned closer to him, her boozy breath repulsing him. ''That bullshit's all well and good, Tanner. But it won't get votes. We need dirt, darlin'. Mud, if you will.''

''I second that,'' Jack said, his voice brisk.

Tanner looked from one to the other, his jaw clenched. ''Fine. But you'd better make damn sure none of that mud backfires and splatters on me.''

Fifteen

"So what's the latest with you?"

Kasey had barely gotten seated with Ginger at their favorite coffee haunt when the question came.

"Sorry," Ginger added with an apologetic grin. "I should have at least given you time to catch your breath and order."

Kasey smiled back. "No problem."

As if on cue the waitress appeared. When she was gone, Ginger raised her brows. "You're not eating, huh?"

"A latte is all I can handle."

"I see you're still on that roller coaster with your tongue hanging out."

"You got it. We're trying to get Tanner Hart off and running."

"Ah, so how's that going?"

Kasey ignored the twinkle in Ginger's eyes and concentrated on the waitress who arrived with their order. "It's got *me* going, actually."

"Then you're in your element. You seem to thrive on a challenge."

"Believe me, it's that and more." Kasey had no intention of sharing her stupid lapse in judgment with her friend. She wished she could stop dwelling on that kiss herself.

"Anything new with the case?" Ginger asked before putting a bite of scone in her mouth.

Kasey hesitated but only for a moment, then decided she would take Ginger into her confidence on that matter. "Hopefully."

"Oh, really? That's great. It's time that creep was off the streets. Crazy as it may sound, I don't even feel safe." She paused. "I can't even imagine how you must feel."

"It's not easy, especially since they took me off protective watch."

"That's not good, is it?"

Kasey shrugged. "Gallain's convinced he's not coming after me."

"But are you convinced?"

"I'm getting there."

"Good. So back to what's changed about the case."

Kasey explained about the notebook and her subsequent call to Gallain.

"What was his reaction?" Ginger asked. "Was he salivating?"

"Hardly."

"Figures. I've seen that weird-looking guy on TV, and he gives me the creeps."

Kasey didn't answer right off, choosing to take several drinks of her coffee before it got tepid. Ginger did likewise.

"You ought to be ashamed of yourself," Kasey finally said, unable to hold back a grin.

"See, you feel the same way."

"I'll admit Gallain isn't my favorite person, but if he'll nab Shirley's killer then he can stay weird. But since no name was anywhere in that notebook, it may not be the smoking gun I'd hoped."

"I bet it is. When Gallain finds out who she was giving that money to, he might very well find the killer."

"My thoughts exactly, only it won't be easy."

"That's the police's problem, not yours."

"Right. Mine is keeping the agency open after Tanner's contract runs out." Kasey removed the lipstick off her cup with a napkin, then looked back at Ginger. "I have a really talented staff who deserve better."

"So do you. Look what you've sacrificed. Still are. I know you're having a tough time keeping your head above water financially."

"I'm already underwater."

"Why don't you let me loan—"

"No, absolutely not. I haven't gone to the bank yet. But even as I speak, I have Don out calling on companies, trying to drum up business. I know word has gotten out that we're working with Tanner Hart. That has to pull some weight."

"I hope you're right, but with Shirley being murdered, people are leery of getting involved."

"I know," Kasey said, down in the mouth.

"So how's the kid?"

Kasey smiled suddenly, glad of the change in subject. For a while they talked about Brock, then their conversation turned to trivial women's stuff.

Afterward, Kasey asked, "So what about the divorce? How's it progressing?"

"It's not." Ginger's features clouded. "Which sucks big donkey balls."

Kasey laughed. "Okay. Whatever you say."

"Matt's a turd, the floating kind, and always will be."

"Yuk, Ginger," Kasey exclaimed, "that's gross."

"Gross but true."

"I just wish you'd dump on me," Kasey said in a petulant tone. "Every time we're together, it seems my problems monopolize the conversation."

"That's because I'm pretty dull right now. I work and fight with Matt through the lawyers. How exciting can that be?"

"Doesn't matter. I want to be here for you."

"What I want is that piece of eye candy, Tanner Hart, to walk through the door like he did the last time we were here." Ginger's eyes twinkled.

Just the mention of Tanner's name sent her pulses skyrocketing. Then realizing her reaction, Kasey gritted her teeth. "That's not likely to happen. I imagine he's on the campaign junket." She didn't know that, of course, since she hadn't talked with him in a couple of days. Sooner than later she would have to face him again, and she wasn't looking forward to that.

"Aw, that's too bad," Ginger was saying in mock despair.

"You can always stop by the agency, and I'll introduce you."

"That's okay, I'll just stick to my dreams."

Kasey rolled her eyes, then stood. "Let's get out of here. I have work to do."

"When we marry again," Ginger quipped outside the coffee shop, "let's hope it's to some rich old farts so we won't have to do hard time in an office."

Kasey grinned. "I'll pass. I don't want another man."

Ginger gave her a knowing look, then walked off.

Kasey made her way into the art room and pulled up short.

Billboards in vivid colors, with Tanner's name front

and center, lined the walls. Excitement sent Kasey racing forward to get a closer look. Red and Angie had done a fantastic job on the artwork.

Out of the corner of her eye, she noticed the largest table had the latest newspaper ads splayed across it. They were equally good as the signs. Her excitement rose another notch. Vince and Dwight had taken her ideas and worked up a masterpiece. What a great team she had. She couldn't wait to compliment them.

If Tanner didn't like this package, then he couldn't be pleased. Period.

The phone rang several times and no one picked up. Where was Monica? she wondered, reaching for the receiver.

"Parker Agency."

"Kasey, is that you?"

For a second her heart almost stopped beating. "Hello, Tanner." She was barely able to squeeze that greeting through stiff lips.

"Did I catch you at a bad time?"

"No, not at all."

"Can you hear me all right? I'm calling from my cell."

"I hear you fine."

There was a short pause.

"Are you okay?"

She bristled. "Of course. Why wouldn't I be?"

Another pause.

"No reason."

His voice was low and on the husky side. She gripped the receiver tighter.

"I'm out of town, but I'll be back tonight. I'm assuming you have something to show me?"

"Do I ever," she responded with enthusiasm feeling on firmer ground now that they were discussing a safe topic.

"So should I just call you tomorrow?"

"That will be fine." She knew her tone sounded stilted, like she was talking to a complete stranger. But that was the only way she could cope. Just hearing his voice had affected her. She was loath to think about how she would react in his presence. She dared not think about that.

"Kasey, are you still there?"

"Uh, yes."

"Until tomorrow then."

She expected to hear a dead silence indicating he'd ended the call. Only that didn't happen. Although he hadn't said anything more, she knew he remained on the line.

"Kasey—" He broke off, then muttered an expletive. "To hell with it. I'll talk to you later."

For the next few minutes, she walked around in a daze, her heart refusing to settle back into its normal pattern. She couldn't get involved with him. She couldn't.

Why not?

That unexpected question froze her. Where had that come from? She squashed her panic. It was okay to play the devil's advocate. She was simply trying to put things in perspective. Just because she was attracted to him and had kissed him back, didn't mean she'd compromised herself in any way.

She was making much more out of what had happened than was necessary.

"I found you."

Kasey swung around with a start. Monica had stuck her head around the door.

"Where have you been?" Kasey asked.

"In the little girl's room."

"You need me?"

Monica cut her eyes toward the reception area. "There's a man to see you."

"He didn't give you his name."

"No. I figure he's a new client."

Let us pray. "Tell him to come on in."

Moments later a sober-faced man walked in, his hand extended. Kasey judged him to be in his fifties, give or take a year or two. He was tall and good-looking. It was his eyes that gave her pause. They appeared empty.

She shook his hand as he introduced himself. "I'm Burt Parker, Shirley's cousin."

Sixteen

Buck Butler massaged his right jaw, his meaty features steeped in a frown.

"What's wrong, you got a toothache or something?"

Buck stared at Mick Gibson, his number one campaign strategist. A tall, clean-cut young man, Mick was as organized and brilliant as he was loyal. Buck had learned long ago that it was wise to sprinkle young men and women throughout his staff. Of course, the old, wise guards were necessary as well. But it was the young, eager minds that had made his tenure in the Texas Senate work like a well-oiled machine.

A machine that he intended to keep running.

"Did you hear me?" Mick asked in his soft modulated voice.

Buck released such a harsh breath that his full lower lip fluttered. "As a matter of fact, I do. Woke up with my jaw throbbing in the middle of the night."

"You should be at the dentist instead of here with me." Mick's lean features registered his disapproval.

Buck slapped at the air in disgust. "Ah, it'll pass. I took some pain pills a little while ago. They just haven't taken effect yet."

"You'd better hope it passes." Mick didn't sound at all convinced. "If your face swells, you'll be a pretty sight in front of your constituents."

"That's not going to happen." Buck took a swig of coffee. "Let's get down to business, shall we?"

Buck had called Mick into his office early that morning to discuss Tanner Hart. While his plate was full with scheduled speeches and meetings, he couldn't concentrate on any of them thanks to Hart.

Mick opened his notebook and picked up his pen.

"Forget that for now," Buck said in a clipped, cold tone. "What I want to know is how the hell Hart managed to even catch up with me in the polls, much less pass me."

Mick's face drained of color. "We discussed that at length last evening while you were at that fund-raiser."

"And the conclusion?"

"There's no clear-cut answer, I'm afraid." Mick squirmed in his chair as though he were in a hot seat.

"Well, I'm afraid that answer sucks," Buck shot back, sarcasm further altering his gravelly voice.

"There's apparently something about Hart that appeals to the voters, something we hadn't counted on or nailed down."

"Correct me if I'm wrong, but isn't that your job, why I hired you?"

"Uh, right, sir."

That "sir" convinced Buck he'd gotten his message across. Too, Mick's face had now taken on a greenish tint like he was about to upchuck. He had him exactly where he wanted him—his balls on a hot plate.

"I don't intend to lose my seat to that inexperienced, conniving upstart. Do you hear me?"

"That's not about to happen, sir."

"Oh, but it is happening, and that's why I'm pissed." Buck's voice dropped another degree. "With the race heading into the final stretch, there shouldn't even *be* a contest. Hart should be a whipped dog instead of breathing down my neck, for chrissake.''

''We'll take care of that. This surge of popularity is short-lived, believe me.''

''Then you'd best find something I can use on the bastard that will cost him big.''

''As we speak, I have someone on it.'' Mick paused, taking a deep breath. ''But with all due respect, when you found out Hart was challenging you, you told us he wouldn't pose any threat, that you could whip his ass with one hand tied behind you.''

A look of venom darkened Butler's eyes. ''Are you saying this debacle is my fault?''

''Of course not,'' Mick said quickly. ''It's just that since we didn't consider Hart a viable candidate, we didn't do our homework. Now, we're having to make up for lost time.''

Butler lunged out of his chair, his eyes narrowed in a glare. ''He's so goddamn arrogant, so self-assured. In that latest TV ad, he comes across as knowing exactly what the fuck he's talking about. And he doesn't have a clue.''

''Have you seen the one that ran earlier on *Good Morning Texas?*''

Butler felt his entire body stiffen. ''You mean there's a new one?''

''I'm afraid so. He hammers you big time on your voting record, accusing you of missing the majority of the important sessions.''

Butler's top lip curled back. ''Before this is all over, I'll castrate that SOB.''

''You know he's hired a new ad agency. We think that's partially responsible for his change in his tactics.''

"Shut him down." Feeling his insides sting like he was being attacked by millions of fire ants, Butler began pacing the floor, then suddenly stopped midstride and gave Mick a harsh glare. "Stop that bastard any way you can, with whatever artillery it takes."

"You got it."

As though Mick hadn't spoken, Butler stressed, "I want Hart in his place, which is at the bottom of the polls."

"That's not a problem, either. Since he's never been in the limelight like you have, his secrets, so to speak, remain buried. All we have to do is find them and he's history."

"I don't intend to lose this election, Mick." Butler's eyes drilled him. "You'd best make that clear."

"I understand. But again, we—"

Butler cut him off. "I know what you're going to say, but that old dog no longer hunts. I don't want excuses, I want results."

"And you think we don't, sir?"

He heard the defensive note in Mick's voice, and his fury shot up another level. "Listen here, you little twerp, I'm holding you accountable for this fuckup, so I suggest you get off that lofty pedestal before you're kicked off." Butler paused for emphasis. "Is that also clear?"

Mick visibly gulped. "Yes, sir."

"Then get your ass out of here and get to work."

Kasey still couldn't believe she was sitting across the table from Tanner in an out-of-the-way restaurant. Her only excuse was that he'd caught her in another weak moment.

He'd pulled his usual stunt and had shown up unexpectedly at the agency. For her, it had been poor timing. She was still reeling from the shock of dealing with Shirley's cousin who had appeared out of no-where.

While it had taken her best efforts to switch gears in her mind, she had done so. She'd had no choice. Upon learning Tanner was there, the staff had instantly gone on high alert, waiting with anticipation his take on the latest displays.

He'd been more than pleased and had complimented them with sincere words of gratitude. Kasey hadn't re-alized how uptight she'd been until she'd seen the look on his face followed by his words. Relief had made her giddy. And careless.

"We should celebrate," he'd said for her ears alone.

Heat stung her cheeks which she tried to hide by turning her head. "I thought that was what we were doing."

"We are, but I want to take you out to dinner."

She swung back around, her heart beating too fast. "That's not necessary."

"Of course, it is," he argued. "Besides, we need to discuss the next phase of ads, and I'm for doing it over a steak."

If he had made his invitation personal in the least, she would have said no and wouldn't have budged. But he hadn't. He looked and acted as though he'd never touched her the other night, much less kissed her.

Hence, she'd given in and said yes.

Now, as they sipped on wine following a delicious dinner, she perused him from under lashes, looking for evidence that his mood was about to change from im-personal to personal. So far, she had no complaint with his behavior. Still, she couldn't relax for fear that he'd sense that every nerve in her body was aware of him.

As usual, he looked wonderful and smelled even better, though he appeared tired. But who wouldn't be, she thought, trying to operate a business and run a campaign at the same time.

"What are you thinking about?"

His question took her aback, probably because her thoughts were on him. However, she answered him honestly. "You."

He lifted a brow. "I hope it was good."

She heard the teasing note in his voice and tried not to respond. But it was hard. He was too darn good-looking and exciting to remain passive. And if she let herself think about how her lips still tingled from his hungry kiss, she would be lost.

"It was how tired you looked."

He looked startled at her bluntness, then he chuckled. "You don't mince words, do you?"

"Not usually."

"Do I look that bad?" His gaze probed.

Actually you look edible. "No, of course not," she hedged, wishing she'd kept her mouth shut since she hadn't wanted to personalize the conversation.

"Are you sure?"

"Now you're fishing for a compliment." She kept her tone light on purpose.

"Maybe I am," he responded, staring at her over the rim of his wineglass.

She shifted her eyes for fear of what she'd see there. But he wasn't about to let her off the hook. His next words proved that.

"I could say the same for you, that you look fatigued." When she remained silent, he continued.

"Though I'm not sure if I'm to blame or Shirley's murder. I know that's still very much on your mind."

"And I'm still very much looking over my shoulder, too."

"Nothing's going to happen to you." Tanner's tone was firm but rough. "Count on it."

"At the moment, it's neither your job or the murder," she admitted.

"Care to clarify that?"

Kasey expelled a breath, then met his gaze. "I received an unexpected visitor earlier."

He took advantage of her slight hesitation. "I'm guessing it wasn't someone you wanted to see."

"Hardly." She didn't bother to hide her sarcasm.

"What did she want?"

"It was a he. Burt Parker. One of Shirley's cousins. He wasn't at the funeral so I didn't know he existed."

"What did he want?"

"The agency." Her voice quivered.

Tanner's jaw dropped. "No way."

"I'm afraid so."

"So what's his angle?"

"Her will stipulates that he inherits the agency. But it was written before we signed the partnership papers. My attorney told me about it, then said not to worry."

"Then take him at his word."

"It's not that simple."

"Sure it is."

"He's threatening to sue."

"Hogwash."

"He's serious, Tanner." She heard the strident note in her voice and tried to temper it.

"Look, that's what you have an attorney for. Let him earn his money."

"I just don't think Burt Parker's going to simply walk away."

What he didn't know and she couldn't tell him was that it would take money to fight a lawsuit, money she didn't have. But she couldn't lose the agency, either, not to some greedy, money hungry relative who was up to no good and out for his own good.

"When he finds out he's fighting an uphill battle, that you have an ironclad contract—" Tanner paused. "Your contract *is* ironclad, right?"

"According to Horace."

"Then Parker will have to back off. You wait and see. You're worrying needlessly."

"Meanwhile—" Kasey broke off, realizing she'd told him far more than she should have. God, no telling what was really going through his mind. He'd known the agency was already in trouble when he'd come onboard. This latest development had to have him questioning his judgment and her ability.

If he pulled out...

"Kasey."

"What?"

"I'm not going to desert you."

"How did you know?"

His gaze softened. "Your eyes."

Kasey opened her mouth to respond, only her cell phone chose that moment to ring. Without bothering to check caller ID, she answered it.

"Oh, hi, darling. Of course, you didn't disturb me. What's up?"

She listened, then finally told Brock, "Let's talk about this later, okay? Call me tonight."

After shutting off her cell, she tried to fight off a bout of nausea.

"Kasey, what's wrong?"

"That was Brock."

"Is he okay?"

She laughed with no warmth. "He's fine. According to him, he's never been better."

"I don't get it."

"He just told me he's in love and wants to bring her home to meet me."

Tanner grinned. "At his age, I'm betting it's lust."

Kasey's voice was wooden. "That's what I'm afraid of."

Seventeen

Daisy Greer had just been summoned. Normally she wouldn't mind facing Stan Carmichael, chief operating officer of the biggest newspaper in Rushmore. This morning, however, she was trying to meet a deadline, and she simply didn't have time to be bothered.

But when the big boss summoned, you had no choice. Was she in trouble? Again? Probably. With her immediate boss, she stayed in that state. She despised Drew Winthrop, and he returned the favor. But he hadn't tried to fire her. He didn't have the balls. He was afraid of her, and he should be.

If she got the chance to hang him out to dry, she wouldn't hesitate. Better him than her.

Before getting up from her desk, Daisy smoothed her silk skirt over her narrow hips and grabbed her mug of coffee. Moments later, she stood in front of Stan's massive desk. He was a big man with a balding head and well-manicured beard. She wondered why bald-headed men often wore a beard. Surely they didn't think it made up for the lack of hair on their head.

Dismissing that inane thought, Daisy forced a smile. Again, she didn't have time for this. Was she about to be grilled about the mega assignment she'd just completed? She'd been back only two days, and this was the first time she'd seen him.

"Have a seat," Stan said in his low, whiskey-tone voice.

"Thanks, but—"

Stan made an impatient hand gesture. "I know you're working on a deadline, but sit down anyway."

Daisy felt heat rush into her face. "Sorry, I didn't mean—"

He cut her off again. "Yes, you did, but that's all right. It's your aggressive impatience that's made you one of the best news reporters in the state. I wouldn't change a thing about that."

"Why, thank you, sir." Daisy reeled with surprise. For much of her tenure at the paper, she'd had little to do with the head honcho. Instead she dealt with Drew who was too dense to know his ass from a hole in the ground. But Stan was different. He was sharp, with an ear for news. She had the utmost admiration for him.

Still, his compliment had rocked her. As a rule, she wasn't well-liked around the paper. Respected maybe, but liked, no.

"I'm aware of your work, Greer, especially your unconventional approach to news stories."

Since her legs were now a bit unsteady, Daisy welcomed the chance to sit. "Thanks again. I really don't know what to say."

He looked amused. "Since when? You've never had trouble expressing yourself before."

"Okay, I'm flattered and suspicious."

He pitched back his head and laughed. "So you think I have an ulterior motive."

She didn't so much as flinch. "Do you?"

"Absolutely not. You're made for this particular

story. I need a bloodhound and, since you fall under that category, you're the chosen one.''

Daisy had no idea what had brought on these praises from on high. Granted, she had just gotten back from a long assignment on a documentary concerning toxic waste, which was scheduled to run soon. The work had been grueling and challenging, but she had reveled in it, dogging the hell out of the company who was responsible for poisoning people.

Maybe word had gotten back to Stan or maybe he'd seen the piece himself. It didn't matter. She would do whatever it took to work her way up the corporate ladder, even if it was on her back. So far, she'd managed just fine in an upright position, though it hadn't been easy.

Her aggressiveness had cost her a husband, a home and a family. But she had made peace with her choices long ago and was ripe for the pickings, whatever they were.

''I've never seen you at a loss for words this long, Greer.'' Humor remained in Stan's eyes and voice.

''I'm just waiting for you to drop the dangling carrot in my lap.''

''It's a political assignment.''

Daisy moved to the edge of the seat, feeling energized. ''If I have a field of expertise, it's that.''

''That's another reason why you're being tagged.''

Daisy felt her excitement mount. ''So where and what?''

''The Texas Senate. That's the race I want you to target. It has the potential to explode.''

''Suppose you bring me up to speed.''

Stan ran a hand over his sleek scalp. ''Buck Butler's the incumbent. I think you've covered him before.''

"I have. And all his skeletons are out of the closet."

Stan chuckled again. "Maybe there's more."

"If there are, I'll find them."

"That would certainly thicken the gravy, no doubt. While Butler is not to be ignored, it's his opponent I want at the top of your hit list. Tanner Hart."

"I know that name, but I don't know anything about him."

"Neither does anyone else, apparently. When he first announced his candidacy, no one took him seriously, though he's stinking rich and has a great reputation as a businessman."

"As a rule, those assets don't make good political candidates. They usually end up making a fool out of themselves."

"Exactly. But Hart's proved the exception. He's run a smart campaign, hasn't made the mistakes he should have. The latest polls show him right up there with Butler. At one point Hart was even ahead. As a result, the ante has been raised and Butler's coming out fighting."

"A nasty, mud-slinging campaign." Daisy's excitement grew even further. "Just what I like."

"Hart's too smooth, too much a charmer. Underneath, there has to be some dirty laundry. Find it and air it."

Daisy gave him a thumbs-up. "And our circulation will soar."

"Absolutely. The public thrives on other's pain and misery."

Daisy stood. "I'll get on it right away."

Stan shuffled through papers on his desk. He chose one, then extended his hand. "Here, take this. It's a list of political forums and rallies. Pick your poison and go for it."

* * *

He couldn't concentrate. He needed a fix badly, but he knew that was out of the question. So far, he'd managed to do without on the job. To take a snort at his desk or in the john was simply too risky. He couldn't chance getting fired. Even though he didn't get paid all that much, he *got* paid. His salary, with what he'd scraped together by other means, was what kept him supplied.

Today, however, he was having a more difficult time than usual. His insides were crawling and his head bonged, which made concentrating bloody impossible. As a result, it was becoming increasingly difficult to keep body and soul together.

His latest bout with Flora partially contributed to his frantic mood. Last night when he'd raided her house again, she'd been furious. He suspected her mood swing was a result of not taking her medicine, which almost always changed her personality, and not for the good, either.

He'd thought for a moment she was going to call the police, and he'd panicked.

"Don't even think about it," he'd said.

"I'm tired of you using me." Her voice shook with anger.

"I'll pay you back," he lied in a wheedling tone.

"You're a bald-faced liar. You have no intention of paying me back."

"Please, sis, I need some money. Just one more time, and I promise I won't bother you again."

"I wish I could believe that, but you've lied to me too many times."

"Look—"

Her clouded-over eyes narrowed and she bared her

yellow-stained teeth. "Get out of my house and stay out. Otherwise, I won't hesitate to turn you in. Enough is enough."

She turned and rolled out of the room, her squeaking wheelchair grating further on his nerves. For a second, he considered the unthinkable. He almost grabbed her from behind and strangled the life out of her to put her out of her misery. The old hag didn't have a life. In fact, she'd probably appreciate it. She was more miserable than he was.

Hell, he'd already knocked off someone. One more wouldn't make any difference. If he got caught, whether he got the big needle for one or two murders didn't make a difference.

But somehow he hadn't been able to bring himself to commit that evil deed. Killing a lover was a lot different than killing one's own flesh and blood.

Now, as he sat in his office, he fought the urge to claw his skin. Instead he lunged out of his chair and walked to his door and opened it. He saw Kasey in the hallway.

If anything changed, she would be next on his hit list. But so far, she'd remained in line, had given him no reason to kill for the sake of killing. Only time would tell her fate, which was another reason why he couldn't lose this job.

He had to keep a close eye on her. He chortled to himself. He couldn't believe his good fortune. He couldn't have planned things any better if he'd tried. This situation just landed in his lap like a big juicy plum.

He gave a sudden start. She was heading his way. He took a deep, shuddering breath, straightened his tie then squared his shoulders. At best, he looked like hell;

his mirror at home had told him that. Would she notice his disastrous appearance and wonder why? Didn't matter. In the past, his sister had turned into a great alibi when he'd come to work looking like hammered shit. If he had to, he'd reuse the old hag.

He chortled again. They actually felt sorry for him, the caretaker for a poor, helpless sister. Man, his co-workers cut him all the slack he needed. His new boss was no exception. From the get-go, she'd joined the bandwagon. In his eyes, they were a bunch of stupid sons of bitches. But then, hey, he wasn't about to look a gift horse in the mouth. He'd take his good fortune and run with it.

By the time she walked into his office, he actually managed a smile. She returned it, though she appeared distracted.

"Don, I want you in on the meeting this afternoon."

"No problem."

If she noticed his bedraggled appearance, she made no comment. Maybe they were so used to seeing him in this shape, they no longer thought anything about it.

"So that won't interfere with any sales calls you have to make?"

"I'll check my calendar, but I don't think so."

Her mouth turned downward. "I wish you would've responded with an emphatic yes, that you're booked solid with appointments all afternoon."

"With Hart as a client, I'm betting that's going to happen."

"Rather than betting, I'm hoping."

"If he wins the election, word will get around. You know how this town is."

She smiled. "This is one time I'm rooting for the gossipmongers."

''Me, too,'' he responded in as smooth a tone as he could muster.

She peered at her watch. ''The meeting will start around two. Don't be late.''

Don't be late, he mimicked silently to her back as she walked away, his features twisted bitterly.

Just who the hell did Kasey Ellis think she was ordering him around? She owed him a favor and didn't even know it. He laughed silently. Without him, she wouldn't now be the head knocker in this agency.

Shirley Parker would still have that honor. But he'd taken care of her, and if the need arose, he'd take care of Kasey, too.

Meantime, he'd continue to watch and make sure she stuck to her story that she couldn't identify him. If that ever changed, then he'd just have to silence her.

He laughed again. Wouldn't Kasey shit a brick if she knew the killer worked for her and was watching every move she made? For a moment he was tempted to tell her for the sheer pleasure of seeing the look on her face.

Then he'd be the stupid one. Nah, he'd just bide his time. Hell, he might even hit her up for partner himself but not before he put the make on her.

His adrenaline kicked in. Hey, Shirley had fallen for him, why not this Kasey Ellis? If he could manage to play his cards just right, stranger things have happened.

Eighteen

He was good.

Kasey saw that right off, though politics was something that had never really interested her. She had always perceived politicians as dishonest and boring.

Tanner was neither. Dangerous. That better described him, at least in her own mind. For her that danger had to do with his incredible sex appeal. She tried to ignore her heightened excitement as she watched and listened to his smooth words and tone.

She couldn't ignore his commanding presence on the podium like he was born to be there. The sun bore down on his head, highlighting the golden threads in his hair. His tanned skin also benefited from the sun, taking on a healthy glow. Yet underneath all that in-your-face attraction was a decent man, Kasey sensed, who meant what he was telling the crowd. And that crowd seemed to hang on to his every word.

Even though he was in a shirt and tie, he didn't look rumpled, despite the insufferable humidity. That, combined with the heat, made it difficult to breathe.

Or maybe it was Tanner, the way he affected her, that caused her shortness of breath.

When he had asked her to join him at this rally, she had balked. But he refused to take no for an answer, explaining her presence would help her get a better handle on his agenda in order to plan the next series of ads.

Because that made sense, Kasey had agreed.

She had also wanted to get out of the office. Since Shirley's death, it seemed she had lived within the confines of those walls. However, her motives hadn't been that simple. She'd wanted to be with Tanner, though that admission was terrifying to her peace of mind.

Also, thoughts of Brock had plagued her, kept interfering with her work. While she wanted her son to be a normal teenager, she didn't want him getting seriously involved with a girl. Not at this juncture in his life. While he was in college, she wanted him to have lots of girls.

But no one could tell her anything at that age. Maybe that was why she was so frightened for Brock. She didn't want him following in her footsteps. That thought chilled her to the bone.

"You're Kasey Ellis, aren't you?"

Kasey jumped at the sound of the unexpected voice. She turned and stared into the pink face of a man who smiled at her around a cigar.

"Didn't mean to startle you." He shot out a hand. "I'm Jack Milstead."

"Pleased to meet you, Mr. Milstead. Tanner's told me about you."

He eased down on the bleacher next to her. "You're doing a great job for Tanner," he said without mincing words. "And I have to tell you, I wasn't for him switching firms at this late date, either."

"I'm glad you're pleased," Kasey acknowledged, feeling a renewed sense of pride.

"Well, just keep up the good work, you hear?"

"I'll do my best."

He wiped his brow. "Damn, but it's hot."

"Don't I know it." Kasey had covered herself with sunscreen, but still the sun felt like it was baking her skin.

Milstead's gaze shifted to Tanner. "Even though he's sweating, he still looks cool."

"Cool under fire."

Milstead lifted his eyebrows. "Good analogy. Ought to use that on a slogan."

"Use what?"

Kasey turned and stared at a young woman who had climbed the steps and paused beside them. Kasey had never seen her before, but that obviously wasn't the case with Jack. He stood abruptly, though his features remained impassive, and made the introductions.

"Ah, we finally meet," Irene said, not bothering to extend her hand.

Kasey's instincts told her Tanner's campaign strategist didn't like her. The expression on her face and in her eyes told her as much. Kasey suspected she knew the reason—jealousy. Too bad she couldn't reassure Irene that she had nothing to fear from her, that Tanner was a client and nothing more.

Liar.

Ignoring that zing to her conscience, Kasey forced herself to be pleasant. "It looks as though you've steered Tanner's campaign in the right direction."

"Tanner's had a lot to say about that," Jack put in.

"Not about to give me one ounce of credit, are you, Jack?"

Despite her smile, Kasey picked up on the contempt in Irene's tone. Her gaze bounced between the two. Was Tanner aware of the trouble in his camp? Most likely. She figured very little got past him.

However, some people delighted in making trouble; she suspected Irene was one of those people. She couldn't help but wonder why Tanner kept her around.

Shrugging that somewhat disturbing thought aside, Kasey focused her attention back on Tanner who was answering questions right and left. The crowd remained enthralled, eating out of his hand.

The phrase "a born politician" rose to mind.

"If I have my way," Jack said, sitting back down, "he's going to be governor of this great state. After that, who knows."

"I'm not sure Tanner's that ambitious." Irene sat on the other side of Kasey, then looked at her. "What do you think?"

Kasey could read the curiosity in her eyes. There was something else as well, though she couldn't quite identify it. "I have no idea one way or the other," she said.

"Sure about that?"

Kasey bristled inwardly. She didn't like Irene's tone or her loaded question. This woman thought way too much of herself and her position. She would love to give her the attitude adjustment she needed, but it wasn't worth the effort. Furthermore, it wasn't any of her business. If Tanner was willing to keep this troublemaker around, that was his business. And his problem.

"Come on, Irene, give the lady a break." Once again Jack didn't bother to mask his contempt.

Irene flashed Jack a go-to-hell-look before turning her gaze on Tanner who had just stepped off the podium to a loud and boisterous applause. He was making his way toward them.

Thank God, Kasey thought, more than ready to distance herself from his cronies as well as the all-consuming heat.

"I thought Butler would've made his appearance by now," Irene said. "He's due to speak next."

"Apparently you've forgotten he's chronically late," Jack pointed out while smiling at Tanner who had been stopped by an avid supporter.

Kasey stood and headed toward him. Jack and Irene followed suit.

"I see you've all met," Tanner said, his eyes sweeping over them.

Kasey thought she picked up on a thread of anxiety in his tone, but she wasn't sure. What she was sure of was that his gaze lingered on her a tad longer than the others.

"Yeah, we did," Jack said, smiling at Kasey then slapping Tanner on the back. "Great job. You had 'em eating out of your hand."

Irene gave him a bright smile. "Jack's right, you were smashing."

"I was hardly that," Tanner said with impatience before focusing his attention on Kasey. "I'd like to hear your opinion."

That low, silky sounding voice seemed to caress her. Kasey swallowed hard, feeling like she'd just been placed on the proverbial hotseat. "From what little I know about campaigning, you did great."

"But did he win your vote?" Irene pressed. "That's the key."

Before she could respond, Tanner said in a light tone, "Hey, give her a break, okay?"

Irene didn't argue, but from the way her face tightened, Kasey knew she was pissed at Tanner for his offhanded dismissal of her question. And of her.

"Come on, I'll buy us dinner," Jack said into the growing tension.

Tanner shook his head. "Thanks, but no thanks. I'm sure Kasey has to get back."

"That's right, I do."

Jack nodded. "Another time, perhaps."

"You can take me to dinner," Irene said with a smile that did little to temper her catty tone.

"I'll pass," Jack muttered.

"Hey, knock it off." Tanner then turned his back on them and circled Kasey's elbow. "We're out of here."

At his unexpected touch a shiver darted through her. But Kasey didn't let on and hoped he didn't catch on. Soon she would be back at her apartment, out of the line of fire.

It was a while, however, before they managed to make it anywhere near his vehicle. Numerous supporters stopped him. Kasey stood by and admired his handling of each person who wanted to shake his hand and say a personal word. Tanner seemed to have a knack for making them all feel special.

He was indeed a born politician. Someone had to do it, she guessed. She was just glad it wasn't her or anyone close to her. That kind of life held no fascination or interest for her. The thought of anyone snooping into the nooks and crannies of her life made her shudder.

"At least I didn't have to confront my opponent," Tanner said, breaking into her thoughts as he opened the passenger door to his vehicle.

"Wait up, Mr. Hart, please."

At the sound of the excited voice, both swung around. A tall, slender woman with dark hair worn in a bob, was hurrying toward them. When she stopped in front of Tanner, Kasey noticed she didn't have even a smidgen of makeup on. Still, she was attractive in a wholesome sort of way. But there was a hard glint in her eye that made Kasey instantly leery.

"I'm Daisy Greer from the *Chronicle*. I've been trying to get to you all afternoon."

"What can I do for you, Ms. Greer?"

Though Tanner's tone was pleasant, Kasey heard the hesitation in it. This reporter hadn't fooled him, either. Not surprising, since he already had a ballsy woman on his staff.

"I'd like to ask you some questions."

"Now is not a good time."

"Is that a no?" A hard glint darkened her eyes.

Tanner smiled. "Actually it's an invitation to stop by my office."

"What makes you think you can beat Buck Butler?"

"Later, Ms. Greer."

"What are you hiding, Mr. Hart?"

Tanner didn't flinch, but Kasey saw his eyes narrow and sensed he was pissed by her question and her persistence.

"Don't make me regret my offer, Ms. Greer."

She smiled, then replied smoothly. "Just be ready to answer some hard questions."

"I'm looking forward to it."

It was only after they pulled up in a restaurant parking lot that Kasey realized Tanner's intentions. "I wanted to go home."

"After we eat, you will."

"Tanner—"

"Don't argue, okay?"

Given his testy tone, Kasey decided to cut him some slack and herself. "I am hungry."

"Me, too, and I could use a drink."

Moments later, they were seated at a cozy table for two in a garden room surrounded by lush flowers and greenery. Among such a cool tranquil setting, Kasey felt her wilted body and spirits suddenly revive.

"What a great place," she said, once the waitress had arrived and taken their orders.

"And the food's good, too."

Her eyes widened. "I'm really impressed."

He chuckled.

The waitress brought their drinks, then disappeared. Tanner held up his glass; she answered with hers. "Here's to a smooth finish and a win."

"I'll drink to that."

They were silent for a moment, then he asked, "So what did you really think?"

"About what?" she asked in an innocent tone, though she knew exactly what he meant.

"Aw, so you're going to make me beg for a compliment."

Kasey rolled her eyes. "You did great, but then I don't have to tell you that."

"No, you don't, but it's nice to hear."

"Lack of confidence is not one of your weaknesses."

A twinkle appeared in his eyes. "Maybe I'm faking it."

"Sure you are."

Tanner laughed outright, then he sobered. "So what's your take on the reporter?"

"I'd rather be interviewed by a rattlesnake."

He laughed again. "My thoughts exactly."

"Sounds like she's out for blood."

"Along with trying to uncover my dirty laundry," he responded in a cold tone.

"Will she find any?"

His gaze was unflinching. "It's not so much what she might find, but what she'll misrepresent to the media, that worries me."

"Guilty until proven innocent, which is scary."

Tanner stared into space. "And the innocent part no one ever hears. A politician's worst nightmare."

Their food arrived then, and they ate in a comfortable silence. Despite his volatile personality, he was easy to be with. It was after they were served coffee that Tanner restarted the conversation.

"Think I should tell her I can't see her?"

"Hey, I'm the wrong person to ask."

"No, you're not. Your instincts are sound, which makes your opinion valuable to me."

"In that case, I don't think you have a choice. You've already opened Pandora's box, so to speak."

"I know, but I'll end up just antagonizing her. You watch and see."

"Especially if she thinks you're trying to hide something."

"Everyone has something to hide." Tanner's eyes bored into hers. "Right?"

For a second her heart almost stopped beating. *Does he know? Of course, he doesn't. It's just your paranoia working overtime.* "Maybe," she said.

"I'll admit I have a checkered past." He paused and wiped his brow with a white handkerchief. "What with going in and out of foster care, I did a lot of things I'm not proud of. And though my juvey records are supposed to be sealed, that doesn't mean they can't be gotten to."

"What if that happens?"

He shrugged. "I'll have to deal with it."

Kasey sipped on her coffee, her mind troubled. He was right. He didn't have to say anything one way or the other in order to hang himself. A hint of misconduct was all it would take to smear him and subsequently defeat him.

"So?" he asked.

"So what?"

"Have you decided if I'm worthy of your vote yet?" He was half smiling.

While she was glad he had lightened the mood, this teasing side of him was much more threatening to her peace of mind.

"I want you, Kasey."

Her eyes widened and her nerves tightened.

"I can't deny it any longer," he added in a husky tone, his eyes delving into hers. "But then, you already know that."

Her lips parted on a gasp, totally unprepared for his seductive bluntness.

"Having said that," he went on, "I don't plan on doing anything about it." He paused, his gaze melting into hers. "Unless you want me to, that is."

"Tanner, I—"

"Before you say anything, there's more."

"I think you've said enough," she told him in a shaky voice, her heart splintering in a million different directions.

"Probably, but I have to get this off my chest. When I saw you at the funeral, it was like the years had disappeared and we were back at that party. I felt those same forbidden, exciting emotions, that same craving—"

Her hand went to her chest. "Tanner, please don't."

His eyes looked tormented. "I wish that night had never happened, for your sake. But for mine, I have no regrets."

"It won't work, Tanner." She could barely speak around the tightness in her throat. "And I don't have to tell you why. We're no longer young and irresponsible. We made a mistake. Let's not make another one."

Tanner's smoldering gaze held hers. "Like I said, it's your call." He didn't say anything else for a long moment. "It would help if you could look me in the eye and tell me you don't feel the same way, that you don't have a tug-of-war going on inside of you right now."

Though she met his gaze, the words wouldn't come. Her denial froze in her throat.

"Then for God's sake, why can't—"

Suddenly Kasey stood. "Please, I can't do this anymore. I want to go home. Besides, you promised." Her gaze speared him.

"You're right," he admitted with pained reluctance. "And I'll keep that promise, too, no matter how much I may not want to."

Nineteen

Dread knotted Gallain's stomach.

Any moment now he expected to be called on the carpet once again. The chief wasn't known for his patience or his forgiveness. He was about ready to explode, and Gallain knew he would be on the receiving end of Clayton's wrath.

The case simply wasn't coming together. More to the point, nothing was bloody happening. Dead ends. Nothing but dead ends. He'd covered every base possible, talked to everyone even remotely connected to Shirley Parker, and he'd come up empty.

Gallain lunged out of his chair and walked to the window in his cubbyhole. Through the limp, broken blinds, he watched the office personnel, cops and other detectives scurrying about. He lived to be here, lived for his job. The thought of losing it made him sick to his stomach.

He took several deep breaths which calmed his erratic heartbeat. Even if he didn't solve the Parker murder, he wouldn't get the boot. But he might as well. Clayton would make things so tough on him, he'd be miserable.

His wife wouldn't help, either. Just this morning she was complaining about how broke they were and when was he going to get a raise. A raise was out of the question if he didn't nail Parker's killer.

Dammit, he had to find that perp. He didn't give a hang about the promotion for the money, despite his wife's constant nagging. He wanted the promotion for his own self-satisfaction. Gallain muttered a curse.

If only the Ellis woman could be of more help. Or even someone at Parker's agency. When it came to Parker personally, her employees acted dumber than a box of rocks. How could you work for someone and not know something about them?

Easy. Hell, no one at the station knew he was married to a bitchy shopoholic and had spawned two kids who weren't worth a shit. Apparently Shirley Parker didn't encourage fraternizing in the workplace, either.

That left Kasey Ellis. She still remained his only ace in the hole. The more he was around her, the more his gut told him she'd seen more than she was telling. He would just have to keep up the pressure, keep urging her to think about that evening, until something clicked in her mind.

When she'd called him about the notebook she'd found listing the staggering amount of money Parker had either given away or loaned someone, he'd gotten excited. However, that excitement had been short-lived. While he felt the money might have something to do with her death, he hadn't been able to prove it.

It seemed as though Shirley Parker hadn't had a life outside the ad agency. But his instincts told him otherwise, which meant that if he kept digging, he might get lucky and uncover something.

In the meantime, he'd continue to gently pressure Kasey Ellis.

The light on the phone finally caught his attention.

He groaned. The chief. He was being summoned for another ass chewing.

Gallain swore as he walked out.

"When are you coming to get me?"

"I can't right now, Mom."

"Why not?"

Kasey tried to keep her mother's strident pleadings in perspective. But it was hard. Lottie Hobbs had always taken the guilt route to bring her only daughter to heel, keep her on the straight and narrow. Even though Lottie's mind wasn't as sharp as it used to be, she hadn't lost that particular skill.

"This place is awful," she whined.

Kasey squeezed the receiver. "Now, Mom, you know that's not true."

"Yes, it is," Lottie lashed back. "And I hate you for making me stay here."

"It was your son's idea." The instant she said those words Kasey wanted to retract them, but it was too late.

"That's because you didn't want me."

Kasey stilled herself against Lottie's attacks and sniffles. "That's not true. I did want you. And I still do."

"Then come get me. I want to go home."

Tears trickled down Kasey's face. "If I came after you, Mom, I couldn't take you home."

"Of course, you could."

At one time Lottie had known their house had been sold, but like so many other unpleasant things, she'd chosen to block that out. Or else she couldn't honestly remember.

"I'm planning to come see you soon," Kasey said, changing the subject.

"I don't believe you."

Lottie's tone was both forlorn and belligerent. Both broke Kasey's heart.

"I hope to bring Brock with me."

"Brock. Oh, that sweet child. How is he?"

"He's fine, Mom. But he's no longer a child. He's in college."

"Oh, dear me. That doesn't seem possible."

"I know. I find it hard to believe myself."

A short pause.

"Come get me, Kasey. Now. Or the Lord's going to punish you. You just mark my word on that."

Kasey blinked back a new onslaught of tears. She couldn't do this anymore. Lottie would never give up. Once she had something on her mind, she would harp on it for days. In order to shut her up, you either gave in or gave up.

"Mom, I have to go. I love you and I'll call you again soon. I promise."

Once the dial tone sounded in her ear, Kasey replaced the receiver and let the tears flow. Despite the fact that her mother had often made her life miserable by trying to control her, she hated the idea that Lottie was in a nursing facility so far away from her. Between the facility and her brother, she knew Lottie was well looked after. But that wasn't the point. Lottie should be with her. Daughters were expected to take care of their mothers.

Maybe that was why the old guilt had come back to haunt her. Before the latest disastrous turn of events, she had considered bringing Lottie back to Texas, had even discussed that possibility with her brother.

But once again, circumstances beyond her control had thrown a wrench in that plan. Until Shirley's murder was solved and the agency settled, she couldn't give her mother the time and attention she would require. For now, she was better off where she was.

Kasey had just repaired her makeup when the phone rang. Since she was due at the lawyer's office shortly, she considered ignoring it. But when she saw it was Brock, she picked up.

"Hey, darling."

"Hi, Mom."

"Did you have fun at Padre?"

"Man, did we."

"Uh, did your new friend go?"

"Of course."

Dread filled her. "I thought maybe you two might have split by now."

"No way," he said in a heated tone. "We're in love."

"So you told me."

"When can I bring her home?" he pressed. "She wants to meet you."

"Oh, Brock, I don't know." Kasey felt terrible for continuing to stall him. But she wasn't ready to share this young girl with her son or encourage that relationship. "Things are still up in the air around here."

"That's why I need to come home."

"Then come, but alone."

"Aw, Mom, come on. You're not being fair."

"Look, we'll talk about this later, okay? I have an appointment with my attorney even as we speak."

"I'm about to get mad at you, Mom."

"I know and I'm sorry. I love you."

By the time she hung up the second time, her head was pounding. Would her life ever straighten out? Suddenly she longed for someone strong to lean on, someone to pour her heart out to.

Tanner.

Kasey sucked in her breath and held it, feeling blindsided by her subconscious. How could she betray herself like this. How could she long for the arms of the man she most feared? It didn't make sense. Since they'd had that intimate dinner conversation two days ago, she hadn't been able to get him off her mind or his passionate declaration.

I want you, Kasey.

And she wanted him. The memory of how good sex had been between them flamed eternal. That heightened the madness. Hysteria bubbled inside Kasey. The problem was, Tanner saw nothing wrong with them making love, having an affair. He saw their meeting again as fate. A second chance.

While she might want him with every fiber of her being, she wouldn't let him wear her down, make her do something she would regret for the rest of her life. She was no longer strong enough to suffer the consequences of such an action.

Fighting off a bout of nausea stemming from her pounding head, Kasey relegated thoughts of Tanner to the dark corner of her heart, then dashed into the bathroom and swallowed a headache capsule.

Fifteen minutes later she was sipping on coffee in Horace Bigfield's office, staring at him over the rim of her cup.

"I might as well get straight to the point."

"It's not good news, is it?"

"No. Burt Parker has filed suit."

Kasey's stomach bottomed out. "I'm not surprised, though I was hoping otherwise."

"Me, too."

"If he found someone to represent him, then he must have a case."

"Not necessarily. Some idiot attorney has sugar-plums dancing in his head because of Shirley's murder. Thinks he's going to get some press time out of it."

"Can he win?" Kasey asked, feeling completely bombarded by circumstances beyond her control.

"I don't think he has a snowball's chance in hell, but—"

"We still have to fight him, and that takes money."

Bigfield rubbed the back of his thick neck, narrowing his eyes on her. "And that's a problem?"

"A big one," she admitted. "But don't worry, you'll get paid."

"I'm not worried. Don't you, either."

"What happens now?" Kasey asked, getting to her feet, unable to sit still another second.

Bigfield also rose, his bold features hardening. "We fight to win, anyway we can. But again, you don't worry."

Worry. Her worry?

The moment Kasey got behind the wheel of her car, she put her head down and sobbed.

"If it's trouble, I don't want to hear about it." Although Tanner smiled, he meant every word he'd said.

Paul stopped, pivoted, then headed back toward the door.

"Where the hell do you think you're going?" Tanner demanded, scowling.

The foreman swung around, his features serious. "I was taking you at your word."

Tanner's scowl deepened. "Take a load off and say what's on your mind."

"We've got more problems," Paul said, hat in hand.

Tanner muttered an expletive. "Just what I don't need."

"Me, either." Paul plopped down in the nearest chair. "The fight—"

"Fight?"

"Yeah," Paul responded red-faced. "It started with two guys exchanging words, then shoves."

"Where were you?"

"In the hut reviewing plans."

"Go on."

"The next thing I knew, they were exchanging blows. By the time I got there, the whole crew was involved."

"So why didn't you and the foreman break it up?"

Paul's flush deepened. "One of the guys pulled a gun."

Tanner gave him an incredulous stare, then said in a cold tone, "You'd better tell me no one got shot."

"They didn't, even though the idiot fired the gun. Of course, someone called 911, and you know the rest of the story."

"Dammit, Paul, it'll be in all the papers."

"Maybe not, but I wanted to warn you, anyway."

"Get back to the job, and don't let anything like this happen again or I'll fire your ass."

"Yes, sir."

Once he was alone, Tanner gritted his teeth and eyed the bar. He longed for a drink, but he wasn't about to take one. The mood he was in he wouldn't stop until he was dog drunk. While the episode at the job site was certainly disturbing, that wasn't what had his nerves on edge.

He wanted Kasey, and she wasn't cooperating. That was gnawing at his insides. Get over it, he told himself. Find someone else to share your bed. Hell, Irene was ready and willing. That thought turned his stomach. That was the problem. He didn't want another woman. Hadn't wanted anyone else since Kasey had come back into his life.

Tough shit, Hart.

She wasn't about to let him share her bed, and he might as well face that fact. Disgusted with himself and with his thoughts, he plowed a hand through his hair, then headed to the bathroom to change into his running attire. Maybe a three-mile run would relieve his mind as well as the ache in his groin. Damn, he hoped so.

Twenty

Hopefully she didn't look as bedraggled as she felt. Kasey peered closer in the mirror in the office bathroom and frowned. Actually she looked worse. Her skin and hair looked dull, and there seemed to be more tiny lines around her eyes. She wasn't surprised. These last few weeks had played havoc with her mind and her body. That crying jag in which she'd just indulged hadn't helped, either.

Once she left the lawyer's office, she'd had every intention of going straight to the grocery store. However, one glance in the mirror on the visor changed all that. She'd headed here to the agency, for damage control.

The complex was quiet for a Friday afternoon. Several employees had taken the afternoon off with her blessing. They had all been working such long hard hours to get the Hart campaign off to a stellar start that she didn't begrudge them the time off. First thing Monday morning they would all have to hit the drawing boards again, especially as the new billboard signs were not quite up to par.

A sigh filtered through Kasey's lips as she walked out of the bathroom. She wished she'd told Brock to come home even if the girlfriend had to come with him. She missed her son, and it seemed like ages since she'd seen him. So why didn't she just drive to Waco instead? Her day brightened considerably. If he could fit her into his plans, that would be a workable solution.

Even though Shirley's killer continued to pose no threat to her, she still hadn't let her guard down. The thought of the person who had shot her partner in such a cold-blooded way running loose on the streets kept her fear factor high. She wondered if Gallain and company would ever find him. Of course they would, she told herself. With all the sophisticated tools at their disposal, it would happen. It was simply a matter of time.

Meanwhile, Kasey worked hard on keeping her paranoia at bay and trying to function as normal as possible.

"Mrs. Ellis."

Kasey jumped visibly before swinging around. "You scared me half to death."

"Sorry," Detective Gallain responded. "Your receptionist told me you were in here."

"You should've knocked." Kasey stared at him while rubbing her cold arms that felt like chunks of lead.

"I did, only you apparently didn't hear me."

Kasey stiffened, unwilling to take responsibility for his ill manners. Would she ever learn to tolerate this man? She had her doubts. His bulldog looks and frigid demeanor frightened her. Or closer to the truth was that he made her feel ill at ease as though she were under suspicion.

"What can I do for you, Detective?" Kasey asked, forcing an even tone.

"Give me a description of the man who shot your partner."

She took umbrage to that and said as much. "Are you being flippant?"

"Hardly."

He didn't like her, either. Too bad. He should just leave her alone, and they would both win. She didn't think that was going to happen. He continued to assume she was holding out on him. To date, she'd been unable to convince him otherwise.

"I'm still counting on you, Mrs. Ellis." His expression was keen.

"If anything changes, you'll be the first to know."

"So you said," he responded, cracking his knuckles.

"Look, Detective, how many times are we going to have this conversation?"

"As long as it takes to jog your memory."

Kasey gritted her teeth. "For the last time, I don't have a memory to jog."

"I think you do," he said bluntly.

Her response was equally as blunt. "If you don't solve this case, what happens?"

"A killer goes free."

"Nothing else is at stake for you?" If she hadn't been seething inside, she probably wouldn't have counter-attacked. Could someone be arrested for smart-mouthing a cop?

"I have a job to do, Mrs. Ellis," he said, "pure and simple."

Kasey jutted her chin. "You've made that quite clear."

"Then we understand each other."

Fury snuffed out a comeback.

"One way or the other, I intend to get this creep off the streets," he added.

With that, he pivoted and walked out of her office

as quietly as he'd entered. Kasey sagged against her desk, feeling more washed out than ever. What a horrible little man. She was beginning to fear him and his tenacity almost as much as she once feared the killer.

"What did he want?"

Kasey gave a start as Red stepped into her office. Don followed on his heels.

"The same as always," Kasey replied in a forlorn voice.

"He thinks you know more than you're telling, right?" Don said, leaning against the door frame.

Kasey nodded. "That's about the size of it."

"What a self-absorbed little prick," Red exclaimed in a huff.

Don tongued the mole above his lip, then spoke. "I wish he'd get lost and stay lost."

"Look, guys," Kasey said, shifting her gaze off Don, repulsed by the way his tongue kept going to his mole. "I'm leaving for the day. We'll start fresh the first of the week."

"You watch out, you hear?" Red said to her back.

Kasey swung around. "What does that mean?"

"Knock it off, Red," Don said, giving his cohort a harsh look. "You're deliberately spooking her."

Red looked apologetic. "Didn't mean to."

"It's all right, Red," Kasey said. "We're all on edge, especially me."

She still felt that way a short time later as she made her way up and down the aisles of the grocery store. Although she'd been there a while, her cart was practically empty. Nothing looked good to her except the fruit. But she couldn't live on fruit alone. Since she'd left Dallas, she'd lost several pounds. She didn't want to lose any more.

But it was no fun cooking for herself. Maybe she should ask Tanner... As quickly as that thought was born, she killed it. Even so, her heart didn't settle. It continued to beat much too fast. If she made dinner for anyone, it would be Ginger.

Realizing she'd passed up an item she wanted, Kasey parked the cart to one side and turned, smashing into a hard, smelly body.

Kasey recoiled, then froze. Her already out-of-control heart lunged into her throat as she lifted her head and stared. A scroungy-looking man with longish dirty hair was so close to her she could see the flecks in his cold green eyes that pierced hers.

Oh, my God, it's the killer.

Terror traumatized her.

The man's empty eyes took another quick tour of her body, then he turned and strode off.

Shaking, Kasey bent over, fighting off an acute attack of nausea. When she no longer felt like gagging, she straightened.

"Ma'am, are you all right?"

A plump, matronly woman stood beside her, her face etched in concern. "I will be," Kasey said in a weak voice. "I'm just a little sick to my stomach."

"If there's anything I can do, I'll be glad to."

Kasey gave the woman a wobbly smile. "Thanks. You're too kind. But I'll be okay."

"If you're sure," she said with seeming reluctance before moving on.

Somehow Kasey managed to find the wherewithal to pay for the items in her cart and drive home. It was only after she was locked behind closed doors did she breathe. Even then, it was labored.

Had he been Shirley's killer? The way he'd looked

at her... Kasey broke off with a shiver. Of course, it wasn't. Her imagination was her own worst enemy.

While trying to reprogram her mind, Kasey made her way into the bathroom and stepped into the shower, getting the water as hot as she dared. After slipping into a pair of lounging pajamas, she headed to the kitchen only to end up with a glass of iced tea and nothing to eat. The thought of food was revolting.

She eased onto the sofa at the same time the doorbell pealed. Frowning, she uncrossed her legs and made her way to the door. After peeping through the hole, her stomach did another cartwheel. Although the image was somewhat distorted, it was obvious who was there.

With trembling fingers, she unbolted the door and opened it.

Tanner angled his head, his eyes roving over her. "I'm sorry," he said in a husky tone.

She licked her lips. "For what?"

"Poor timing."

"Is this a business call?"

"No," he said, his voice deeper and huskier.

Kasey's mouth went dry. "Do you want to come in?" She realized how stupid that question sounded, but it was too late to retract it.

"If that's all right."

She moved aside and let him pass, thinking inanely that he wasn't at his best, either, like the heat had gotten to him, zapped him of his energy. She guessed he'd been out campaigning. Despite his disheveled appearance, he looked good. Too good. He smelled good, too, a combination of sweat and cologne, a powerful aphrodisiac in her weakened condition.

Once she found the courage to join him in the middle

of her living room, an awkward silence hovered over them. Neither seemed eager to look at the other.

Finally Tanner cleared his throat. "Are you okay?"

"What makes you think otherwise?"

"Your eyes. I saw...see fear in them."

Her lips parted, her mind in a whirl. She wished she hadn't scrubbed off her makeup or had dressed in something less revealing, readily conscious of her nakedness underneath her pajamas.

"Kasey."

The pull of Tanner's rough, sexy voice drew her eyes back to his. For a moment their gazes locked. Kasey's heart hammered against her chest. The way he was staring at her was insane. More insane was that she had let him in.

"I—" Kasey's voice broke on a sob, which further mortified her. To break down again was unthinkable for fear of the consequences. Yet she ached to say to hell with restraint and fling herself into his strong arms for the comfort she so badly sought.

Only it wasn't just comfort she craved.

As if he read her mind, raw lust suddenly glinted in his eyes, then he groaned and reached for her. Wordlessly she went into his arms and draped her arms around his neck, clinging to him. For the longest time, he seemed content to just hold her.

Kasey couldn't say exactly when the body temperature changed. Maybe it was after she released a deep sigh that made her aware of how her nipples had hardened and were pressing into his chest. She felt herself stiffen.

"Oh, no, you don't," Tanner whispered against her neck.

His hot breath and lips against her skin buckled her knees. She clung that much tighter.

"This is so good, so right," he muttered before sinking his lips onto hers.

Tongues met, then sparked while his hands slid down her body, cupping her buttocks. Her next breath stopped in her throat when she felt his rock-hard penis against her pelvic bone.

"Where?" A savage edge roughened his voice.

Pulling away, she grabbed his hand and led him into the bedroom, refusing to think about what she was doing. The moments were hers. She wasn't about to lose them.

Clothes were quickly dispensed with and soon they lay on top of the duvet, skin against skin, lips against lips.

"You're more beautiful than I remembered."

She felt herself drowning in his deep eyes. "So are you."

"Especially your breasts."

She gulped.

"They're perfect."

She ran her hands down his leg.

He gasped. "Oh, please don't stop."

She circled him with her hand, her thumb concentrating on the moist tip.

Moaning, he dipped his head and latched on to a nipple and sucked.

"Oh, Tanner," she whispered achingly.

Following another groan, his lips targeted the other breast while a hand parted her legs just wide enough for him to cup her there. He eased two fingers inside her.

She bolted on a cry, then began frantically to massage him until she felt the moisture increase.

"Please," he begged, "I want to come inside you. Now."

"Yes, yes."

With glazed eyes holding hers for several beats, he thrust inside her, uniting them in moments shared, mindless bliss.

Twenty-One

She lay with her back to him, her body in a fetal position.

He was so still and quiet he had to be asleep. She tried to control her erratic breathing but it was difficult. She wanted to awaken him and tell him he should go, but the words stuck in her throat.

She didn't want him to go. What they had shared had been incredible, had carried her to dizzying heights. She craved more of the same, more of his seeking hands and thrusting body. The scariest part was that this feeling was more than just sex. When she was in his arms and he was inside her, she no longer felt alone and afraid. At least not of strangers and things that go bump in the night.

But Tanner was no stranger. *He was the father of her child.*

Suddenly Kasey wondered what would happen if she woke him up and blurted out the truth. Confessed everything. What would his reaction be? Though her mind screamed rejection of that forbidden thought, it wouldn't go away.

All the more reason to keep her distance, to treat him with professional respect and nothing more. But after tonight, that was going to be hard, if not impossible. Even now, she dreaded for him to leave her.

However, she knew he had to go and she had to let him.

An affair was out of the question. To indulge herself again would be asking for trouble. Though she knew her secret was safe to the grave, it was not wise to play with fire. And that was exactly what Tanner was.

Still...

"Hey, you."

His husky spoken words brought her onto her side to face him. To her dismay, she felt tears well up in her eyes. It was the way he was looking at her, with his heart in his eyes, that triggered that emotion.

Tanner reached out and removed a stand of hair off her cheek. "It's okay. No one's going to hurt you."

Only you.

"Something frightened you today, didn't it?" he asked. "I sensed that the second you came to the door."

"Yes," she admitted with simple honesty.

"Tell me what happened."

She did.

A string of harsh profanities followed. Then he held her close in comfort for several minutes before putting distance between them. "Trust me, everything's going to be all right."

"No, it's not," she gulped.

"As long as I'm breathing, no one's going to hurt you." Cold determination underlined each word.

Kasey licked her lips. "I'm sure I just overreacted."

"I'm sure you did, too, but that's to be expected."

"That's no excuse."

He kissed her again. "Don't be so hard on yourself. You've been through hell and it's not over yet."

She didn't say anything for the longest time. Then

finally she asked on a tremor, "When is it going to end?"

"You're not just talking about the murder are you?"

"No."

His eyes darkened and he grimaced. "Does that mean you're sorry?"

She knew he was referring to their lovemaking. "No, but I should be."

"Why?"

"You know why."

A sigh filtered through him. "Because of Mark."

"Partly, I guess," she responded in a strained whisper.

"You shouldn't feel guilty."

"I know, but guilt's my middle name."

"Look at me."

The pull of Tanner's voice drew her eyes back to his. "Last night was perfect."

"It was, wasn't it?"

"I loved being inside you again."

Her breath caught. "I felt the same way."

"Then why are you fighting us? Fighting me?"

"You know why."

"No, I don't." His voice was anguished now.

"I wish things were that easy for me." *Careful, Kasey. You're treading on thin ice.*

"The difference between us is that I don't want to forget anything about that night. Everything that happened, the way I touched you, the way you touched me is forever seared on my brain."

"Tanner, please, I don't want to talk about that night."

"Then we won't." He leaned over and grazed her

trembling lips with his. "Just don't shut me out, okay? I couldn't stand that."

"We're working together," she whispered inanely.

"You know what I mean."

"This is not right."

"It's *so* right."

"I should never have let you in."

"But you did."

"I know," she said again in a weak voice.

The pad of his thumb caressed her lower lip. Hot desire made her weaker. "Don't."

His eyes probed. "Don't what?"

"You know."

"Make you hot?" His words were an impassioned whisper as his finger continued to massage her bottom lip.

She could only nod.

"And make you want me again?" His voice had dropped another decibel.

"Yes," she said though tight lips. "Are you satisfied?"

"Far from it." He reached for her, pulled her against him and aligned her body with his.

She heard his shallow, labored breathing and felt him press hot and hard into her belly.

"Now I'm satisfied," he whispered in a guttural tone. "Or nearly, that is."

He kissed her again, a deep, searing kiss that left her dizzy and breathless and clinging to him.

"I won't really be satisfied until I'm making you come," he told her, his breath warm and caressing.

Just once more, she promised herself. What could it hurt? When the time came, she could walk away. She had what it took to do that. She also had what it took to banish her guilt into the dark corners of her heart and grab the moment.

"Kasey?"

"What are you waiting for?" she asked, thick-tongued.

He groaned, parted her legs and thrust inside her. Kasey closed her eyes and gave into the sensations rocking her.

"Dammit."

Tanner looked up from the paper then crumpled it in his big hand before tossing it aside. The gun incident at the construction site had made the front page of the paper. Although he knew that was possible after the police became involved, he had hoped something else would take precedent over the incident.

He should've known better.

Anything he and Butler did out of the ordinary seemed newsworthy. Jack had warned him that privacy as he'd once known it would cease to exist. He hadn't thought that would bother him, that his skin was thick enough and his confidence high enough to handle that downside of politics.

He wasn't so sure now. Especially when everything seemed to get blown way of out proportion.

The article made his company look bad. Made his employees look bad. Made *him* look bad. The accusatory tone of the piece had Daisy Greer's stamp on it. He'd bet everything she'd been on the scene.

Why the hell did she have her stinger out for him? Why couldn't Butler have been the unlucky bastard on the other end of her poison pen? Suddenly disgusted that he was wasting his thoughts and energy on an ambitious broad who would apparently do whatever it took to get ahead in her profession, Tanner deleted her from his mind.

He focused his attention back to the half-written speech in front of him. But the words on the page seemed to all run together. He tossed down his pen, stretched back in his chair, then glanced at his watch.

His luncheon appointment with Jack was nearing. In light of the article, he wasn't looking forward to that meeting. Jack would be livid. He wondered if Kasey had seen it and what she was thinking.

He fought the urge to pick up the phone and ask her. Not a good idea, he told himself, especially after last night and this morning.

He'd hated leaving her. It had taken every ounce of willpower he possessed not to awaken her one last time and make love to her. He had squirmed, feeling like his balls were about to explode. Yet he'd contented himself on watching her sleep, concentrating on the rise and fall of her full breasts, remembering the feel and taste of them in his mouth and hands.

The dusting of freckles across her face had made him smile. But it was her lips that he concentrated on. They were perfectly shaped and so kissable. They had done unbelievable things to his body, made him feel sensations he'd never felt before, not even the first time they made love.

Now that he'd found her again, he couldn't bear to give her up.

But when dawn had broken, Kasey had awakened and stared at him stark-eyed. "You're still here."

He tried to smile, but his efforts failed. "That's not good, huh?"

"No."

Tensing his jaw, he shoved the covers back and

stood, conscious of his nakedness. But he didn't care. Maybe he wanted to tempt her one more time, make her realize what she was giving up.

He turned back to her and her face was flushed, though her gaze didn't waver. Their eyes held for what seemed like an interminable length of time.

"Please, I want you to go."

"Don't worry. I'm going."

Out of the corner of his eye, Tanner saw her watching him while he got dressed. When he reached the door, he swung back around, his gaze sliding over her. "Later," he muttered.

Now, as Tanner pulled his thoughts back to harsh reality, he stared into space and fought off a sense of hopelessness.

"I caught you."

Tanner gave a start. Irene. The last person he wanted to see. "Come on in."

"Have you seen today's paper?" she asked, striding deeper into the room.

"Yep."

She shook the paper at him. "I don't have to tell you this is not good."

"That doesn't even warrant a response," he replied on a sour note.

Though color surfaced in her cheeks, Irene's eyes continued to flash. "Sarcasm doesn't become you."

"Then don't invite it."

"My, but you're in a pissy mood this morning."

He gave her a pointed stare.

"After this article, I guess you have a right to be."

The article had nothing to do with his piss factor being high, but he didn't bother to tell her that.

"By the way, where were you last night?"

That blunt question infuriated him further. "Since when are you keeping tabs on me?"

"Since you hired me to run your campaign and since you kissed me."

"Dammit, Irene, will you stop harping on that kiss. It was a mistake for both of us and you know it."

Her lips thinned. "For you maybe."

"I have to go meet Jack."

"So you're not going to tell me where you were, huh?"

"No, I'm not."

"Are you seeing someone?"

Her perception shocked him, but he didn't let on. He just didn't say anything.

"One of these days, Tanner, you're going to get what's coming to you, and I hope I'm around to see it."

"What did you want, Irene?" he asked, trying to keep the ice out of his tone. As it was, their relationship was tenuous. He smothered a sigh. For someone who'd always had a way with women, he was suddenly batting zero.

"Never mind," she lashed back.

"Tell me."

"Why?" Her mouth curled. "Your mind is obviously not on business anyway."

He bowed his shoulders and his eyes glinted. "You're pushing your luck."

"Oh, all right," she exclaimed in a waspish tone. "That Greer woman came to see me."

Before he could make a comeback, she turned and stormed out of the office, slamming the door hard behind her.

"Great," he muttered. "Just bloody great."

Twenty-Two

She should thank Tanner.

The thought of doing that, however, made her palms clammy. Still, she owed him. The new client she had just signed was a friend of his. Bob Jefferies had told her how pleased Tanner was with her work on his behalf. Of course, Kasey hadn't taken full credit. Her staff had worked alongside her and still were. Until the election was over, satisfying Tanner was an ongoing project.

Though Jefferies wasn't in politics like Tanner, he appeared desperate for help. He'd taken over an established but floundering business and was determined to turn it around by advertising in a big way the changes he'd incorporated.

The new, lucrative contract was both a boost for her self-esteem as well as the agency's. If their client list continued to improve, she could make a dent in some of the debts. At least she was able to meet payroll. For the time being, that was a big plus.

Kasey eyed the phone. *Call him.* It had been three days since they had made love. Even though she hadn't seen or talked to him since, she had thought of little else. She had replayed in her mind every intimate detail of their time together.

This morning in her office those thoughts were still

with her. She had made love to him. Again. As an adult. But she had known what she was doing. She'd had a choice and she'd made it. And she had given back as good as she'd gotten, she reminded herself, feeling her body suffuse with heat.

So what now? She had to see him, and she couldn't pretend they hadn't made love. She just hoped she had enough willpower not to let her guard down again, not to fall susceptible to his lethal brand of charm.

He was not for her. She had to keep telling herself that. Tanner was a problem she didn't need. Already she felt overwhelmed by the load she was carrying. Dealing with her own financial woes and struggling to make the agency solvent in the face of a threatened lawsuit should have been more than enough to keep her mind occupied.

If not, there was Shirley's unsolved murder which left a killer running the streets scot-free. Despite her brave facade, the episode in the grocery had proven how vulnerable she was.

And Brock. She couldn't forget about her son. She was determined to see to his physical and emotional needs. He was the love of her life and her top priority.

Thinking about her son and what was at stake brought Kasey sharply back to reality and back on target.

Her cell phone rang. Glad of the interruption, Kasey reached in her purse, sure her caller would be Brock. Without bothering to check caller ID, she answered it.

"Morning."

Her breath faltered. "Good morning to you."

"Two things," Tanner said.

"All right." Kasey sat down, fighting off the weakness invading her system.

"Any more scares from strangers stalking you?"

"No, but then I haven't been back to the store."

He chuckled, which served to lighten the building tension. "Good." Then his voice sobered. "I don't think it's a good idea for you to be alone."

"Thanks for your concern," she responded in a light tone, "but I'm okay. My imagination is my own worst enemy, I'm sure."

"I hope you're right. But I still worry."

"Don't," she said, clearing her voice.

There was a long silence.

"By the way, thanks," she finally managed to say.

"For what?"

She figured he was being deliberately obtuse, but she indulged him nonetheless. "Recommending the agency to your friend."

"Ah, so Bob made it by."

"And hired us."

"He won't be sorry."

That compliment pleased her. "We'll do our best."

"So where are you?"

"At the office."

"On Saturday?"

"Where are you?" she asked pointedly.

"At the campaign office."

This time she laughed. "So—"

"So all work and no play makes us dull."

"Dull works for me," Kasey responded a trifle breathlessly while trying to heed the warning bells going off in her head.

"I don't believe that for a second."

"You said there were two things." She purposely changed the subject.

"Right. I have to go to a carnival. I want you to go with me."

Kasey was glad she was already sitting down. "No can do. I have to work."

"Come on, surely you can take a little time off."

"I'm in the middle of designing your billboards."

"We'll work on them together. Later."

Kasey stalled. "Why are you going to a carnival?"

"Actually, it's a fair. I'm one of the featured speakers at a rally there."

"I see."

"So is that a yes?"

"You drive a hard bargain."

"I'll pick you up shortly."

"Tanner, I didn't say I'd go." Kasey didn't bother to curb her frustration.

"Sure you did."

With that he hung up, leaving her staring at the phone.

Despite the pressing heat, it was a gorgeous day. It had rained last evening which seemed to have cleansed the earth. Everything looked fresh and smelled clean. The sun, in all its glory, had obliterated the clouds. Trying not to frown against the strong rays through her shades, Kasey fanned herself and looked around.

The fairgrounds were teeming with people scurrying about. Children were having a ball, especially on the rides. A whiff of tantalizing popcorn drifted past Kasey's nose. She inhaled, then focused her attention back on the podium where Tanner was finishing his short speech.

He'd told her that his scheduled appearance was supposed to be short and to the point and promised she wouldn't be bored. She had almost laughed. Bored was something she wasn't with Tanner. He was much too dynamic and controversial for that.

And much too attractive.

Just looking at him was a treat. He was dressed in a short-sleeved sport shirt and casual slacks. His bronzed skin glistened with sweat under the boiling sun adding to that attractiveness. The wind had played havoc with his hair, which also worked in his favor.

Like the first rally Kasey had attended, the boisterous crowd gathered in front of him was eating out of his hand. But then she was guilty of the same thing, much to her shame and chagrin. Still, she wasn't sorry she'd given in and come with him. Surprisingly, the tension had been bearable even in the close confines of the car.

For the most part, they had kept the conversation on an impersonal level. They had talked at length about the potentially damaging news article about the incident at the building site and how it might affect his campaign.

"Surely you don't hold yourself responsible," she said early on in the discussion.

"You're damn right I do."

"That's crazy. Even if you had been there, the same thing would've happened."

"You're wrong. They know better than to pull that kind of shit with me."

"But you can't be in two places at one time."

"And that's my problem. I need to be on the job site and I need to be on the campaign trail." He shrugged. "So what do you do?"

"That's where choices come in."

He took his eyes off the road and gave her a look

that upped her heart rate. "Like the one you made this morning."

She swallowed, then nodded.

"I'm glad." His tone was low and husky. "I've missed you these past few days."

"I've missed you, too," she said, folding her hands tightly in her lap. "But that doesn't mean I'm going to do anything about it."

He blew out a harsh breath, focusing once more on the road ahead. "I'm not going to stop trying to change your mind."

"You're wasting your time."

"No commitments, huh?" She heard the bitter edge in his voice.

"That's right. That's the way I like it." Her tone sounded almost flippant, but that was the only way she could cope, especially since she was trapped in the vehicle with him and could think only of touching him.

"You drive a hard bargain, Kasey Ellis."

"So I'm told."

Tanner laughed, which once again snapped the tension crackling between them. "So are you game to ride any rides?"

"You've got to be kidding."

"Which means no."

"I'm a 'fraidy cat. I'll admit it."

"I don't believe that for a minute."

"Okay, it turns my tummy upside down."

"That I believe."

She shuddered. "I wouldn't even ride those creaky things with Brock."

Mentioning her son made her realize how off track the conversation had veered. She had stiffened visibly, a gesture he'd apparently picked up on because he hadn't said anything else the rest of the way.

Now, as she watched him step off the podium and make his way toward her, she tried not to react. But she couldn't help herself. Passion raged inside her. The thought of making love to him was uppermost in her mind, and no matter how hard she tried to delete that image, she couldn't.

Would she ever regain peace of mind as she once knew it?

"A penny."

At the sound of his rich voice, she whirled around, thinking she probably looked like a deer caught in headlights.

If he thought so, he didn't react. Instead he asked, "Are you sweltering?"

"Pretty much."

Tanner's eyes perused her. "You don't look like it."

She turned away, not trusting herself to meet his gaze for fear it would mirror her own. "I sweat quietly," she told him inanely.

He pitched his head back and laughed. "I'll have to remember that."

"The truth is I'm dressed for the occasion, which is dumb luck since I didn't know I would be going to a carnival."

Thinking she would be working in the empty office all day, she had put on a pair of capri pants, matching knit top and sandals. The one thing she hadn't done was apply sunblock to her sensitive skin. She crossed her fingers she wouldn't burn.

"I hope you weren't too bored."

"With all these weird people to watch, no way."

"So you weren't listening to my speech."

"Sort of."

His lips twitched. "Well at least you're honest."

"You asked."

They had walked several yards when a man's booming voice called out, "Hey, Hart, wait up."

Tanner froze visibly then muttered a curse. They swung around and faced a short, stout man with beady eyes. "Hello, Butler."

Now she knew why Tanner's reaction had been so negative. Still, it was Tanner who first extended his hand.

"Who's your friend?"

"Kasey Ellis meet Buck Butler," Tanner said in a polite but cool tone.

She didn't blame Tanner for his reaction. In her estimation, when it came to sizing up character he was on target. She didn't like the man, either, especially after he held her hand a tad longer than necessary, a move that didn't escape Tanner, not if his grimace was anything to judge by.

"Heard your speech," Butler said.

"I saw you in the crowd."

Butler wiped his brow. "Not bad."

"I'm glad you approved."

Kasey noticed Tanner made no effort to hide his sarcasm which wasn't lost on Butler.

His large features tightened. "Too bad about the article in the morning paper."

Tanner didn't bother to reply, which Kasey thought was rather wise on his part. Butler smelled blood and was out for more.

"No comment, huh?" Butler had a smirk on his lips.

"No comment."

"Maybe you'll comment on this," Butler hammered. "I was wondering if you're up to debating me."

Tanner snorted. "Now why would I want to do that? You're the one who's sputtering at the finish line."

Butler's features twisted. "You'll pay for that remark, Hart, at the polls."

"Good luck, Butler."

Kasey felt Tanner's hand surround her elbow, urging her past his opponent. Once they were out of earshot, she turned toward him. "Nice fellow."

"If I had a choice between picking shit with chickens and being around Butler, I'd choose the chickens."

Twenty-Three

"You're really not going to debate him?"

"Not on your life."

Kasey didn't say anything.

"I take it you don't approve?"

They had returned to her office and his latest ads were strewn about the worktable. For a while now they had been discussing the pluses and the minuses, though Tanner found it hard to concentrate on anything other than Kasey who was much too close for comfort.

"I didn't say that," she replied, crossing to the fridge on the other side of the room. "Would you care for something to drink? I'm sorry I didn't offer sooner."

"Only if it's beer."

She cocked her head. "No beer, not here at the office."

"I knew better." He smiled with a shrug. "Thought I'd ask, anyway."

"How 'bout a Coke?"

He made a face. "Do I have to?"

"Not if it's that painful. But it won't rust your pipes or anything as serious as that."

His smile widened. "You sure about that?"

Becoming flushed at his teasing, she turned her back, exposing her delectable derriere.

It was all he could do not to grab her from behind, whirl her around and kiss her. She looked too damn sassy and adorable for him to keep his hands to himself, though he sensed she had no clue how she affected him. The fact that she didn't realize just how sexy she was made for a real turn-on.

What she had on didn't help any. Her outfit was designed to tease a man, especially the pink top that molded her tiny waist and hugged her breasts so that her nipples were visible even through her bra.

All afternoon those nipples tantalized him, made his mouth water to put his lips on them and suck them, something he'd taken delight in doing during their marathon night of lovemaking.

So far he'd managed to keep his lascivious thoughts and libido in check. His instincts told him that while she might not be sorry they had made love, she wasn't ready for a repeat performance. Hell, she'd said as much. Since he'd been given the unexpected gift of her company the entire afternoon, he wasn't about to blow it now.

He would just bide his time and slowly chip away at her armor. He didn't know how he felt about her— hadn't looked that deeply inside himself—but what he did know was that he wanted to be with her, didn't like it when she was out of his sight.

"You don't like the billboard ideas, do you?"

Realizing she had taken his silence as criticism, he jerked his head up. "What makes you think that?"

"Because you're so quiet."

"I was giving them the once-over," he said in a lame tone, uncomfortable that his mind was on her rather than on business.

She gave him a disbelieving look, then held out a can to him. "Here's your drink."

He took it and guzzled some of it down. Then he looked at her with his features contorted. "God, this stuff is worse than I remembered."

"It's much better for you than beer," she said primly, though her eyes were twinkling.

"You love punishing me, don't you?"

Their eyes met for a long second. Sexual tension leaped between them, heating his blood. As if sensing their teasing was getting out of hand, she looked down and concentrated on the layouts.

"What you and your staff have done with the bill-boards is really good."

He watched her visibly sag with relief before she raised her head. "Thanks. We've been working hard."

"It shows. Now we have to get them up."

"That's taken care of. The company's coming Monday. Your face and platform will be splattered all over your district."

"Can't get too much of a good thing," he said in a glib tone, hoping to relieve some of the tension inside him. Man, but he was uptight. No, he was damn horny and couldn't do anything about it.

"After meeting your opponent today, I'm convinced you'll unseat him."

Tanner raised his eyebrows. "While that's music to my ears, he's not going to lay down and die."

"You're right about that. When he looked at you, his eyes were shooting daggers."

"I'm sure I returned the favor. When he held on to your hand longer than necessary, he came close to landing on his ass."

Kasey's lips parted, and her eyes widened in surprise. "That wouldn't have been smart," she said huskily.

"I know, but sometimes I don't do smart."

"He's a jerk. I sensed that right off."

"A jerk who could kick my butt in the polls, especially after that article hit the paper."

"I've always heard that bad publicity is better than no publicity at all."

"That's a dicey call. All it takes is one fluky thing and your constituents can turn on you. For some unknown reason, that Greer woman is determined to go for my jugular and feed the fire."

Kasey's features grew pensive. "Maybe she and Butler are in bed together."

He narrowed his eyes on her. "Literally or figuratively?"

"Maybe both." Kasey lifted her slender shoulders. "It happens, right?"

"Every day. But don't worry. What he does has no bearing on me. I'm not about to give in or give up. I'm in this for the long haul and determined to win."

"Then I hope you do," she said, shuffling through some papers.

He watched her dainty hands for a long moment, then turned the subject off him. "What about your situation?"

Kasey's hands stilled. "Which one are you referring to?"

"The cousin who wants the agency?"

A shadow fell across her face. "As far as I know, he still plans to take me to court."

"If I can help—"

She cut him off. "Thanks, but no thanks."

Her abrupt brush-off rankled. Maybe it was because

he wanted to be more to her than a great one-night stand. If her strained features were anything to go by, he wasn't.

"You're much too hardheaded for your own good."

Kasey stiffened. "How would you know?"

"You're right, I don't." His reply was short.

A heavy silence fell over the room during which he finished his Coke, more for something to occupy his hands than anything else. Again, it was all he could do not to grab her and kiss her until she melted against him.

Get a grip, Hart. She was right to keep him at arm's length. The last thing he needed was a serious affair. The timing was poor and the priority not there. She apparently had enough sense to figure that out. But then, he was thinking with his dick and not his head.

"If there are no changes in the billboards, then—" Kasey's voice trailed off, adding to the awkwardness of the moment.

"Hey, Mom. How's it going?"

With her heart lodged in her throat, Kasey swung around, her mouth open. *"Brock?"*

"Oh, honey," she cried, dashing forward and giving her son a big hug. When she pulled away, she realized she had tears in her eyes. "It's so good to see you."

"It's good to see you, too."

She knew she must sound like she'd been winded, but that was exactly how she felt. Hopefully Brock hadn't seen or overheard anything he wasn't supposed to.

It was after she released him that she noticed his gaze fixed on Tanner, his eyes lighted with curiosity.

Her heart instantly sprang back into her throat, making further speech impossible.

"Hello, Brock." Tanner crossed the room with his hand extended. "I'm Tanner Hart."

"Mr. Hart," Brock said. "Nice to meet you."

"Same here."

Kasey's gaze darted from one to the other, terror keeping her silent. *Brock and Tanner in the same room. Impossible. That was something she had hoped would never happen.*

But it had and she had to contend with it. Still, her first and last thought was to take her son and flee the premises. What if Tanner recognized subtle similarities in their features? While none were particularly striking, Kasey was aware of them.

He was tall and robust like Tanner and had the same light brown hair with flecks of blond. But then so had Mark. Another plus were Brock's blue eyes, a replica of hers. Bottom line—Brock looked like himself—a great-looking, confident young man with a bright future in front of him, a future she'd protect at all cost.

"I'm an old friend of your mom and dad's," Tanner explained.

It was Tanner's matter-of-fact statement that forced Kasey to gather her scattered wits about her and function as normally as possible under the circumstances. "And a client," she stressed. "In fact, we were working on his project."

"Cool," Brock said, walking over to the table to look at the billboard concepts.

"I guess I'm still in a state of shock that you're here," Kasey put in, determined to derail any personal contact between Brock and Tanner. If only Tanner would leave. Since he didn't seem in any hurry to do that, she'd have to work around him.

"Got anything to drink?" Brock asked.

"I'll get you a Coke," Tanner said, turning his back and heading for the small fridge.

Brock nodded toward Tanner with raised eyebrows, a question in his eyes.

Kasey ignored his blatant gesture, though her heart did another somersault. "You're looking good," she told Brock, clearing her throat. "Handsome as ever."

"Aw, Mom." Brock's big foot pawed the carpet.

Kasey realized she'd embarrassed him. However, she'd meant what she'd said. Pride swelled in her as her eyes remained on him. Although it had only been several weeks since she'd seen him, it seemed like much longer. Maybe it was because so much had happened during that time.

However, being with her son never failed to put things in proper perspective. In the long run, nothing mattered except Brock's well-being.

"So how long are you planning to stay?" she asked into the descending silence.

"I'm not sure," Brock said in a hedging tone. "Depends."

"Okay. Look, why don't we head for the house? I'm sure you're starving."

"Man, am I ever."

"Why don't I take you two out to dinner instead?" Tanner smiled. "I know a great steak place."

Brock's eyes cut to Kasey. "Sounds great to me. How 'bout it, Mom? Wanna go?"

No, Kasey wanted to shout. Damn Tanner. She fought the urge to attack him like a banshee. How dare he encroach on her time with her son? He had to know she resented his sustained presence. Short of being rude and making a scene, she had little choice but to bite her tongue and endure.

Yet she heard herself ask, "Are you sure you wouldn't rather I fix something at home?"

"Nah," Brock said, "that's too much trouble and I'm too hungry."

"Then let's go," Tanner responded. "I'll bring you back to get your cars."

"That okay, Mom?"

"Fine," she said, though she felt like she had lockjaw.

Thirty minutes later they were seated in a restaurant that Kasey could never have afforded, their orders taken and drinks in front of them. Resentment continued to swell inside her at Tanner's high-handed interference. But again, she kept that thought quiet, reminding herself how important it was not to raise a red flag.

"So has spring training started?" Tanner asked.

Brock's eyes lit up. "You're a football fan, huh?"

"You bet. Actually I'm a big Baylor Bear fan."

Kasey felt his eyes on her. "Did you know that, Mom?"

"No, I didn't." She tried to keep her growing agitation from showing, but she wasn't sure she'd pulled it off. Tanner's gaze on her was piercingly direct.

"We should be pretty tough this season," Brock said, "if everything comes together."

"Are you a starter?" Tanner asked.

"If I stay healthy, I will be."

Kasey's hand went to her chest. "Don't say that. The thought of some big oaf hurting you makes me crazy."

"You wouldn't know it if they did." Brock grinned. "When I'm on the field you keep your eyes closed."

"Who told you that?"

"Never mind. But it's the truth, isn't it?"

"So what if it is," Kasey admitted, a churlish note in her voice.

Both guys laughed.

"Hey, Mom, how come you haven't asked me why I'm home?"

Kasey was taken aback. "I didn't know you needed a reason. You never have before."

"True," he said a trifle down-in-the-mouth. "But I usually call."

"Is something wrong?" Kasey asked, feeling an added tightness in her chest.

"Not wrong exactly." Brock slid his gaze off her. "I got laid off today."

Kasey gave a start. "Oh, no."

"I knew you'd go ape shit which is why I didn't tell you over the phone."

"What happened?" she asked, ignoring his colorful description.

He shrugged. "Not enough work. And since I was the last hand to be hired, I got the ax."

"You'll just have to find something else. That's all there is to it."

"That's not easy, Mom. You know I have practice every day. That severely cuts down my choices."

"I know that, son," Kasey countered with forced patience. "But the deal was, if you stayed in Waco, you had to work."

God, she hated having this discussion in front of Tanner. At the moment, she wanted to pinch her son's head off for bringing it up over dinner. She dared not contemplate on what was going through Tanner's mind. Not that she cared, she told herself.

"Well, I can't come home."

Kasey picked up on the strident note in Brock's voice, deepening her anger and her despair. "Look, let's not talk about this any more now. I'm sure Mr. Hart's not interested, so—"

"That's where you're wrong," Tanner said. "In fact, I was about to offer a solution."

"Oh?" Terror squeezed the breath from her.

"How would you like to work for me, Brock?"

Twenty-Four

"**I** wish you'd stop pacing. You're making me dizzy."

Buck Butler glared at his wife, fighting the urge to tell her she stayed dizzy. But he refrained. Now was not the time to take on Clare, not when her dear old dad was contributing heavily to his reelection campaign.

He had put up with her wild spending sprees, her endless charity functions and her dedication to the bottle. All for money. Even though he was from a prestigious family with ties long past the Civil War, they didn't have money. When his parents died, they were broke. He had soon learned that pedigree without big dollars to back it up wasn't worth much, except that it had gotten him Clare Riley.

But his allegiance to a woman he despised behind closed doors was wearing thin. He didn't know how much longer he could bear to remain married to her.

While he had no claim to fame in the looks department, she was even worse. She was much too thin, causing deep wrinkles in her face and extra flesh to sag from her neck. Even though dear old dad had offered to pay for a face-lift, she wouldn't hear of it. Pain was not her thing. On the other hand, if Dad had offered him the opportunity, he would have jumped on it.

Cosmetic surgery for him. Wouldn't that knock a few dicks in the dirt and give Clare's snotty friends something really juicy to talk about? Looks aside, it was the daily grind of living with an airhead that was making his life miserable. When the kids left home, he had promised himself he'd move out and file for divorce.

But then he'd entered politics and the rest was history.

At the moment, Buck longed to be with Joy, his latest fling who was young and energetic and made him feel like he could jump over the moon. However, he hadn't seen her in several months. With the senate race full steam ahead, he'd been afraid he'd get caught literally with his zipper down, so he'd kept away.

God, he could just imagine the brouhaha an affair would cause. Clare and her old man would hang him out to dry even if Harry had reaped mega benefits from his son-in-law's stint as a Texas senator of standing.

Buck aimed to keep that status no matter how many cold showers he had to take or how many martinis he had to down to keep himself on track. He loved his job, loved the power it brought him. Once he served another term in the senate, he planned to move onward and upward. He had his eyes set on Washington, D.C.

If Tanner Hart thought he was going to derail his plans, then he was dead wrong.

"For crying out loud, sit down," Clare said in a strained, petulant tone. "What has you in such a dither, anyway?"

"If I'm bothering you that much, why don't you leave?"

Her coffee cup shook as she set it down. "That's a rude thing to say."

"So it's rude. Get over it."

Her pale features tightened. "You're becoming unbearable to live with, Buck."

"Get over that, too."

She stood tall and straight, seeming to gather her dignity about her. "I'm going to pretend we didn't have this conversation because I know you're upset."

He laughed a bitter laugh.

"You're behind in the polls. That's bound to have you upset."

The fact she knew that shocked him. Probably one of her rich-bitch friends told her, gleefully rubbing it in. Or better still, it was Daddy who had broken the news. A new poll had come out yesterday. It showed Hart slightly ahead of him. Screw polls. He hated them and tried to ignore them, but no one would let him. Now his wife was getting on the bandwagon. *Screw her.*

"It hasn't upset me," he bit back, stopping his pacing and looking at his watch. "Because it's only temporary."

"When are you due back in Austin?"

"Tomorrow," he said in a clipped tone.

There was a long moment of silence during which he felt her eyes burn into him. He turned away.

"I'm not going to give you a divorce."

The hair froze on the back of his neck. Yet he managed to whip around and stare at her. "Where the hell did that come from?"

"I know about your little flings, Buck."

Again speech failed him.

"You think I'm an idiot, that I don't know what goes on with you, but I do."

His first thought was to deny the accusation, but

from the look on her face, he thought better of it. She'd caught him with his hand in the cookie jar, and it was going to take some finagling to get it out.

"How did you find out?"

"I have my ways."

"Dammit, Clare, don't try to best me at this game," he retaliated in a harsh, aggressive tone. "You won't win."

He was posturing, but he had to try and save face any way he could. Raising his voice had always been an effective tool to intimidate her. Why not now?

"I hired a private detective."

Again, he was too flabbergasted to speak.

"And it wasn't Daddy's idea, either." Clare lifted her shoulders and smiled an empty smile. "I was just curious who you spent your time in bed with since it's not me. And hasn't been for years."

He felt anger contort his face. "And whose fault is that?"

"Not mine."

The ease with which she challenged him added to the bitter gall that rose up the back of his throat. "I don't have to stay here and listen to this garbage."

"Yes, you do. If you want to win the election, that is."

"Don't you dare threaten me." He walked closer and got in her face. "Daddy isn't my only asset, so you just back off."

"Or what?"

His features twisted. "You'll be sorry."

Clare backed up. "I don't think so. Holding on to your senate seat is all that matters to you. You're not about to do anything that will jeopardize that."

"I wouldn't be too sure," Buck said harshly.

"Who knows, we might not have to worry about it. Tanner Hart might just beat you." Her voice was rich with dark humor. "Now, wouldn't that be something?"

She was getting her rocks off by baiting him. He coiled his hand, prepared to reach out and slap her, only she stepped farther out of harm's way. However, her taunting didn't stop.

"I'd be real careful where I dipped my wick. Daddy wouldn't be nearly as understanding or forgiving as me."

"You bitch."

"I won't give you a divorce. For all the misery you've put me through, you don't deserve one. My only aim in life is to punish you with my continued presence in *your* life."

Realizing that he was close to losing the hold on his temper, Buck clenched his fists to his sides. "Once this race is over, I'm leaving you."

"We'll see," she said in a light, arrogant tone.

His fury climbed to new heights, but again he held it in check.

Clare smiled. "I'm going to my room now. Have a nice day, darling. I'll see you this evening."

With that, she turned and walked out of the room, leaving him choking on his own spittle.

"Excuse me, sir."

He addressed the housekeeper without turning around. "What is it, Sophia?"

"You have a visitor, sir, in the parlor."

"Thanks," he muttered.

Sensing he was once again alone, Buck sucked in a deep breath, then let it out. He did that maneuver until he no longer wanted to put his fists through the wall. Still, he checked his image in the huge mirror hanging above the buffet. None of his seething emotions were visible. Outwardly he appeared cool as ice.

Plastering a smile on his lips, Buck made his way to meet his guest, his hand outstretched. "Hello, Daisy. It's so good to see you."

"Same here, Senator." Her eyes roamed around the room. "Nice pad."

"Thanks." He gestured toward a comfortable high-backed chair. "Please, have a seat. Would you care for coffee and pastries? Or just coffee?"

"No thanks to both."

"Then we'll get down to business."

"That's what I'm here for. To whip up on Tanner Hart."

Buck smiled, feeling his self-confidence return in force. "Lady, I like your style."

"Mom, talk to me."

"I've already had my say."

"Come on, you're not being fair," Brock whined.

She had found her son in the kitchen munching on a bowl of cereal long before he should've been up and long before she'd even had her first cup of coffee. Now, she was sitting at the table with him, working on her second cup and having a conversation she didn't want to have.

"Why can't you just find another outdoors job in Waco?" She knew she was being unrealistic, that what she'd asked was close to impossible. But desperation was making her take desperate measures.

Working for Tanner was simply not an option. However, she apparently hadn't gotten that across to Brock.

"Mom, it was dumb luck that got me the job I just lost," Brock declared, that whine still in his tone.

"I thought you wanted to be outside."

"I did, but I really had no choice since that was the only part-time job available. But now that I have a chance to work in my field, how can I turn that down?" He shoved his empty bowl out of the way. "And why should I?"

Because I'm terrified you'll find out the truth.

Of course, she couldn't voice that numbing fear. Ever. But she had to come up with a valid reason soon or she was going to lose this argument and lose face at the same time.

"I just don't think it'll work."

"Well, I do." His tone was as blunt as hers was lame.

"He's here and you're in Waco."

"Mom, you're not thinking. He's asked me to improve and maintain his Web site. That can be done anywhere. And since Computer Science is my major, he's offering me the perfect opportunity to do what I love and to make money as well." He paused and took a breath. "And isn't money what we…I need most to stay at Baylor?"

"Yes."

"Then I'm going to do it."

"Even if I don't approve?" she asked with a heavy heart.

"This time, yes."

She held her silence as she got up and crossed to the sink. Although she stared out into the morning, already bathed in harsh sunlight, Kasey didn't so much as blink against the glare. Her mind was in a turmoil. Damn Tanner for interfering further in her life, for dropping that bombshell in the middle of dinner.

The second after Tanner had made his offer, fear had closed Kasey's throat so tight she couldn't speak.

"Gee, Mom, did you hear that?"

"I heard," she murmured, barely keeping her fury in check.

"What did you have in mind, Mr. Hart?" Brock asked, excitement spilling from his voice.

"I need someone who's good on computers. Do you qualify?"

"You bet," Brock responded eagerly. "Computer Science is my major."

"Then you're the man I need."

Kasey cut in, "Don't I have a say in this?"

Both men stared at her as though she'd just hailed from Mars, which heightened her fear and irritation.

"Of course, Mom. But what is there to say but yes? I need a job and Mr. Hart just offered me one."

She'd had no suitable comeback for such logic. So in order not to make a complete fool out of herself, she hadn't said anything more. But that didn't stop her resentment from festering.

Tanner should've kept his mouth shut. More to the point, he shouldn't have invited them to dinner which would have negated this conversation altogether.

But since that hadn't happened, she had to try and salvage what she could out of last evening's disaster.

"Mom, I don't understand what's wrong. You're working with Mr. Hart. Why are you suddenly acting like he's got something contagious?"

Kasey shook her head to clear it. "That's ridiculous."

"No, it isn't. I'm going to be making more money than on the construction site, plus gain the experience. How can that not be a deal?"

"All right, Brock. If that's what you want, I'll accept it."

He scratched his head. "I just wish I knew why you're so mad at me."

"I'm not mad at you. What do you say we don't talk about this anymore?"

"Okay, let's talk about Nancy." Brock frowned. "Or is that another sore subject?"

Kasey forced a smile. "Of course not. I want to hear all about her."

"I'm in love, Mom. What do you think about that?"

I think it's awful and my heart is breaking in another place.

Kasey forced a smile. "I think it's time I met this young lady."

Twenty-Five

Tanner sensed Kasey was angry. Correct that. He *knew* she was angry. Somehow he had to try to patch things between them. But how? He'd thought about just showing up at the agency or the apartment like he'd often done. The agency he could justify, but her apartment was a harder call.

He let go of a deep sigh as he lay in bed and stared at the ceiling. Despite the early hour, he should be up and dressed. His agenda for the day was full and running over. In fact, he didn't know how he was going to be in ten places at once.

Irene kept him booked too closely. He felt like he was running nonstop on a treadmill. However, he intended to take time out of his busy schedule and work with Brock. Though he had others to whom he could delegate that chore, he wanted to do it himself. Irene could just have a hissy fit. He didn't care.

Kasey, however, was a different matter. It bothered him that she was miffed. But he thought he'd come up with the perfect solution to a suddenly bad situation. And while he was sincere when he'd told Brock he needed someone to manage his Web site, he would've never thought about the kid until the loss of his job.

And Brock had been so excited, which had made him feel like he'd done something worthwhile. Too, he was actually looking forward to working with him. What a great kid. What a great job Kasey and Mark had done with him.

If only he'd...

Tanner swore, then got up and sat on the side of the bed only to have the room spin. Bending over he rubbed his head, hating himself for tying one on as he'd done last evening. But he was lonely and frustrated. For him that was a deadly combination.

It had been two days since he'd had dinner with Kasey and Brock. When they had parted, he had told Brock he'd be in touch.

So far, he hadn't found the courage.

Tanner's lips twisted into a sneer. Since when was he afraid of anything? Not since he'd been shuffled in and out of foster care and beaten when he hadn't towed the line. He'd learned at an early age that fear was something you never showed for it gave others power over you.

He'd lived by that creed until now.

How had things suddenly gotten so complicated, so out of control? He'd had his life all mapped out. He was so close to obtaining respect and status on his own merit. Not because of who he had been married to or the amount of money he had, either. Dedication and hard work had made him who he was today.

His company was booming. And now he had a chance to become a part of the Texas senate where he could really make a difference. From there was anyone's guess. The sky appeared to be the limit.

He had no attachments, no one he need be overly concerned about other than himself. Simple, right?

Yeah. Then Kasey came back into his life. That was when he began to fall apart emotionally.

"Damn," Tanner muttered, rubbing the back of his tight neck.

How much longer was he going to sit there and wallow in self-pity? Maybe all day. Had he fallen in love with her? Was that why his guts were tied in knots?

If that were the case, then he was screwed. While Kasey might have enjoyed making love to him, he could guarantee that was as far as she'd let herself go. She was a textbook case. Guilt kept her attached to the past, and unless she got past that, then a future between them was hopeless.

Yet he ached for her. Not just for sex, either. All right, he admitted, he did crave her that way. Right now he was hard as a brick bat just thinking about her and how responsive she'd been to him, how she'd used her lips and hands to...

"Ah, to hell with this." Tanner bounded off the bed and traipsed naked to the shower. Even the blast of cold water failed to temper the heat roiling inside him. The only thing that would appease that was having Kasey join him.

The erotic thought of soaping her, then backing her against the shower wall and taking her there, sent his blood pressure soaring and hardened his dick even more.

Giving in to the weakness invading his limbs, he leaned against the stall himself, closed his eyes and let the water pound him.

"I'm so glad to see you, Ginger. You're like a ray of sunshine."

They parted after giving each other a brief hug.

"I'm glad to see you, too, kid." Ginger's eyes sobered. "Though I have to say, you're no ray of sunshine."

Kasey laughed and it felt good.

"I didn't mean that the way it sounded, of course," Ginger clarified in a mollified tone.

"Yes, you did, and that's all right because it's the truth."

Kasey had managed to lure Ginger away from her job long enough for them to meet for a quick cup of coffee at their favorite haunt. After the previous night's cleansing rain, the humidity was low enough that they could sit comfortably in the courtyard.

"I'm so glad you called," Ginger said, after blowing on her large cup of mocha supreme covered in whipped cream. "I was about to pick up the phone and buzz you."

"Something must've been on your mind because you never call me anymore."

"I know, and I'm sorry. Jerk face is driving me nuts."

"Matt's not willing to budge, huh?"

"Nope. He doesn't want a divorce and is doing everything in his power to stop it."

"Well, just tell me when the contested hearing date is and I'll be there."

"Good. I'm going to need all the support I can get." Ginger paused. "But what I really wanted to tell you is that Matt's spouting off about the election. He's claiming that Butler's assured of a win. Does he know something on Hart that's so damaging, it could be a knockout punch?"

"I have no idea," Kasey said, "though I hope not. I've worked too hard on Tanner's advertising for him to get beat by that pompous you-know-what."

"So you've met the asshole?"

"That I have."

"Now you know why Matt fits in their camp so well." Ginger's tone was bitter.

"Tanner's trying to stick to the issues."

"Well, he can forget that. Rest assured Butler's peeing up one leg and down another because of the change in the polls. He's in for a fight he hadn't counted on. He's not about to stand still for that."

"So get ready for a real mudbath, huh?"

Ginger made a face. "More like a bloodbath, I'd say."

"Thanks for the warning. I'll tell Tanner."

There was a short silence while they sipped on their coffee and munched on their croissants.

"So what's going on with you?" Ginger asked. "You look like you're run ragged."

"I am, though Brock came home and lifted my spirits."

"You sure about that?"

"Well, he lost his job, and he declares he's in love."

"Ouch."

"The job problem is solved, or so I think."

Kasey told her about Tanner's offer, though she was careful to keep her voice devoid of any emotion. But that was hard. When she thought about the two of them working together, even from afar, she nearly lost her mind.

"Kudos to one and persimmons to the other."

Kasey laughed, then sobered. "What can I do about Brock and Nancy? I can't bear the thought of them—"

"Getting it on?"

Kasey gulped. "Yes."

"Well face it, honey. That's probably happening even as we speak."

Kasey felt the color drain from her face. "But he's just a child. He's my baby."

"Not anymore. He's nineteen and horny."

"Oh, God, Ginger, I can't stand it."

"Sure you can. He's a good kid, a responsible kid, which means he's probably taking precautions."

"Maybe I should find that out."

"If he were my kid, I know I would."

"I knew I needed to talk to you. I already feel better."

"So what's new with the agency? Is that Parker guy still after it?"

"As far as I know."

"Well fuck," Ginger exclaimed.

Kasey laughed.

"And Shirley's murder?" Ginger asked.

"Nothing new, or at least not that I know of. I haven't even seen or heard from Detective Gallain in several days."

"I wish they'd hurry up and catch that son of a bitch."

"I can't bear to think about it, so I don't."

"I'm glad you have Hart and his campaign to keep your mind occupied. He's a blessing in disguise."

Suddenly Kasey longed to confide in her friend about her personal involvement with Tanner, how she'd lost her head and let him make love to her. But she couldn't because she couldn't justify to Ginger why that wasn't smart, why she could never have a serious relationship with Tanner.

"What's eating you?"

Kasey felt color sting her cheeks. "Nothing."

"And you're a liar," Ginger whispered, leaning forward. Then her eyes widened. "Have you and Hart taken a liking to each other? After all, you're in each other's pockets. And he's helping out your kid. Now that I think about it, stands to reason there's some heavy duty hanky-panky going on."

Kasey's jaw went slack. Ginger was much more intuitive than she'd ever guessed.

"Great day in the morning." Ginger practically whooped. "Why, you're actually getting a little."

"I'm going to kill you," Kasey spat, trying desperately to cover up her stupidity.

"Oh, give it a rest, honey. Like I've told you before, you're single and over twenty-one."

"Do you mind if we talk about something else?"

"You could do worse, you know? Tanner Hart's going somewhere. There's no reason why you can't hitch onto that wagon and go right along with him."

Kasey ignored her and peered at her watch instead. "Don't you have to go?"

Ginger stood with a warm chuckle. "All right, I'll let you off the hook for the sake of our friendship. But for God's sake, lighten up."

Lighten up.

If Ginger only knew how much she *had* lightened up, she wouldn't have said that, Kasey told herself, fighting back the rising hysteria as she made her way into the agency.

It was paramount she calm down. Her job with Tanner wasn't finished yet. Until it was, she had to conduct herself with detached professionalism. Once the election was over, she wouldn't have to deal with him again. As far as Brock was concerned... Kasey stopped her mind from going down that path. She couldn't cope with anything else right now.

The agency was a beehive of activity. For that she was glad. She had plenty of work to keep her busy, especially in light of the new client. Too, Don Hornsby's aggressive sales methods had brought in more business.

The object of her thoughts was coming out of the workroom just as she was heading towards her office. "Morning, Don. I was just thinking about you."

He paused midstride and stared at her. Yet he wasn't seeing her, Kasey thought, then felt like an idiot. Of course, he was seeing her. His gaze was steady on her. Still, there was something wrong, though she couldn't quite nail it down in her mind. He looked different. Sort of spaced out.

She voiced her thoughts. "Are you okay?"

"Uh, I'm fine," he said, clearing his throat. "It's my sister. She's going through a tough time."

"Do you need some time off?"

"No, but thanks." He fidgeted from one foot to the other.

"By the way, I want to thank you for getting out and pounding the pavement and bringing us those new clients. With your eye for design as well as your marketing ability, you've become a real asset to the firm."

"Thanks. I appreciate you telling me that."

Since he seemed in a hurry to end the conversation, Kasey told him she'd see him later and walked into her office only to pull up short.

Irene Sullivan rose from Kasey's visitor chair. "I hope you don't mind the intrusion. But I thought it was past time you and I had a little talk."

Twenty-Six

"Hey, Mom, you still mad at me?"

"I was never mad at you, son, only—" Kasey's voice faltered as she eased into her desk chair at the office. She hadn't been at work too long when Brock called. He was back in Waco, and she missed him terribly. Would that ever change?

"You acted mad," Brock went on. "Real mad. And you never told me why."

"Maybe it's because I don't know," Kasey admitted with pained reluctance.

"Well, anyhow, what I'm doing is really neat."

"Ah, so you've already started."

"Yeah. Tanner—"

"Tanner?" Kasey didn't bother to hide her shock and dismay. "Don't you mean Mr. Hart?"

"He's the one who told me to call him Tanner," Brock said, a defensive note in his voice.

Kasey wanted to scream. "You were saying?"

"That we've talked a lot on the phone and I've been online since." Brock paused. "I just hope I'm doing what he wants."

"I'm sure you are," Kasey said through tight lips.

"I guess we'll soon see. I'm about to do a test run, so keep your fingers crossed." He paused again. "Even though you don't approve."

"You sure know how to make me feel guilty."

"Aw, Mom, give me a break."

"I'm trying really hard."

"You know, Tanner likes you even if you don't like him."

Kasey felt her heart turn a somersault. "Have you two been discussing me?"

"Not really. He just told me what a great job you've done for him."

"That's good," she responded hastily, then changed the subject. "It was so good to see you. I don't want you to wait that long to come back home."

"I won't, especially since I'm working for Tanner now."

Although that wasn't what she'd had in mind, Kasey didn't say anything. The key to surviving this latest crisis was to keep her mouth shut, smile and endure. The project would probably end when the football season started. That and Brock's studies would keep him too busy to work for Tanner. Or so she prayed.

"Mom, you still there?"

"Of course."

"Look, I gotta go and get to work. I'll talk to you soon."

"You be careful and I love you."

"Love you, too."

Once the receiver was back in place, Kasey rubbed her head, refusing to acknowledge that a headache was nibbling around the edges. Before it got out of hand, she reached in her desk and removed an over-the-counter medication. Once she'd swallowed a couple of the pills, she focused her attention on the designs in front of her. For once, she wasn't working on Tanner's campaign. Instead she was jotting down ideas for one of the agency's new clients.

After concentrating undisturbed for a while, Kasey got up, stretched her back muscles, then walked to the window. Another clear, sun-filled day greeted her. But she knew the beauty was deceiving. Outside, the heat and humidity were suffocating.

A sigh filtered through her lips as she turned and made her way back to the project. Refocusing was hard, though, once her concentration had been broken. She felt fractured, at loose ends.

Tanner was responsible for that. Every time her mind became idle, thoughts of him filled it, especially when she thought of him in context with Irene, his campaign manager.

Even now, several days after the fact, Kasey still wasn't sure what had precipitated that visit. She wondered if Tanner knew about it. Next time she saw him she planned to ask.

She had invited Irene to sit down, of course, out of courtesy more than anything else. And curiosity, too, mainly because she'd sensed the woman didn't like her when they'd met at the rally.

"I guess you're wondering why I'm here," Irene had said without preamble.

"I'm assuming it's about Tanner's ads."

"You're right."

Although Irene was quick on the response, Kasey wasn't convinced she spoke the truth. She suspected Irene had an ulterior motive, though she couldn't be sure.

She was dressed to the nines, Kasey noticed with a tad of envy, which added to her attractiveness. Designer suit and shoes adorned her slender but curvy frame. But as before, she had on too much makeup, making her appear older and harsher than necessary.

"Would you care for something to drink?" Kasey asked in a cool, polite tone.

"No, thanks. Actually I can only stay a minute. I just stopped by to tell you what a great job you and your agency are doing for Tanner."

Kasey was taken aback as her smoothly spoken compliment didn't jive with the hard glint in Irene's eyes. "I'm glad you approve."

Irene smiled. "If I didn't, he wouldn't be working with you."

Meow.

"The two of you seem to work well together," Irene went on in the same smooth tone.

Since Kasey didn't know where this conversation was going, she refrained from saying anything she deemed incriminating. "That's because he's easy to work with."

"But that's about to change."

Kasey's only response was to raise her eyebrows.

"Since he's going to be on the road so much, I'll be your direct contact." Irene angled her head. "Do you have a problem with that?"

"Not at all," Kasey replied in an equally smooth tone.

Irene stared at her through veiled eyes, then stood with a smile. "I knew you'd see it my way. I told Tanner as much."

Immediately after delivering that final loaded punch, Irene left. For the longest time afterward, Kasey had nursed her fury in silence. Now, having rehashed that conversation in her mind, she felt that fury surge again.

Irene Sullivan had come to her office for only one

purpose—to stake her claim. Tanner belonged to her, and she had wanted Kasey to know that.

Was he sleeping with Irene? That question gnawed at her. The thought of Tanner making love to that woman with the same intensity and fervor as he'd done with her turned her stomach and made her green with jealousy.

The ringing phone jerked her back to the moment at hand. Mindlessly she answered it.

"Can you get away?"

No matter how often she heard Tanner's low, sexy voice, it never failed to affect her. This time goose bumps broke out on her skin and her mouth went dry.

"Not if I want to earn a living," she responded a trifle breathlessly, forgetting for the moment how angry she was at him.

"Would it helped if I begged?"

"No," she said, around her rapidly beating heart.

"If that's what it takes, I will."

"Tanner—"

"I have another rally this evening. I want you to come with me."

"What about Irene?"

"What about her?"

"Why doesn't she go with you?"

"Because I don't want her to."

Kasey sucked in her breath, then let it go, her mind in chaos. She wanted to go. She ached to see him, though she knew that was a bad idea.

"I want you." He paused. "Only you."

Those intimately spoken words sent a shaft of longing through Kasey. She eased back down in her chair. "All right," she said weakly.

"I'm on my way."

What had she done? The answer came quickly to mind. She had dug the hole deeper and pulled the dirt in on top of herself.

She saw Daisy Greer thread her way through the crowd with a sinking heart. Kasey's gaze darted back to Tanner who was in the process of answering questions now that he'd finished his speech.

She sensed he was definitely aware of the unwanted guest by the instant tightening of his features. Maybe Greer would surprise them both and be on her best behavior. *Yeah, right.*

However, Daisy didn't jump right in with a question. It wasn't until Tanner was thanking everyone for their attendance that she called out, "How about abortion, Mr. Hart? How do you feel about that?"

Tanner stiffened as a refrigerated silence fell over the crowd. Then a man hollered out, "I'd rather know how you feel about gays adopting children."

"Thank you again, ladies and gentlemen, for your attention, but my time is up." With that Tanner bounded off the podium and made his way toward her.

Kasey had stepped to the outskirts of the crowd and was waiting.

"Let's get the hell out of Dodge," he said against her ear before latching onto her elbow and thrusting her forward.

"Mr. Hart."

They could have pretended not to hear Daisy Greer, but since the reporter was on their heels, that would've been a definite slap in the face. Still, Kasey sensed Tanner considered doing just that by the way his features tightened along with the grip on her elbow. His fingers were hard and warm. She shivered inwardly.

"Shit," he muttered under his breath.

Tanner turned around first. Kasey followed reluctantly, wondering how a person could put himself through this kind of anguish. But then people who decided to step into the political arena had to know the score. She frowned. The thought of opening herself up for all the world to see was appalling. Nor could she live with anyone who did that.

Her breath caught in her throat. Where had that crazy thought come from?

"Mr. Hart, any particular reason why you refused to answer my question?"

Kasey watched Tanner give Greer his lethal smile. "Like I said, my time was up."

"How long can it take to say I'm pro choice or I'm pro life?"

That lethal smile didn't waver, but Kasey guessed he was seething underneath.

"Longer than I have to get the facts straight," Tanner responded. "But my offer still stands for a personal interview."

"I don't have time to waste, Mr. Hart."

The insult struck its mark. Tanner's anger was almost palpable. Yet Kasey had to admire his cool under fire.

"That's your call, of course."

"That woman's nothing but a package of poison," Tanner commented a short time later once they were settled in a booth in the rear of a coffee shop.

"I agree." Kasey drummed her nails on the table. "Do you think she'll ever leave you alone?"

"No, but I don't think she'll show up at my office."

"Why not?"

"When she drops a grenade, she's the type who likes an audience." His features were grim. "And she knows I know that two can play her game."

"But what if she does take you up on your offer?"

"I can handle her."

"Better you than me." Kasey shuddered. "She gives me the willies. She's out for blood and makes no bones about it."

"My blood, to be exact, compliments of Butler, I'm sure."

The waitress brought their glasses of iced coffee, which shut down their conversation. Once she was gone, the silence lingered. Kasey watched as Tanner tilted his head back and took several consecutive gulps. Her gaze fixed on the long, bronzed column of his throat as he swallowed. When he put the glass down, their eyes met and held.

Feeling that sexual tension crackle between them, she looked away, taking the image of his big, sweat-drenched body with her. It was when he was all rumpled and hot that he was the most attractive to her. Heaven help her, but she would love to feel that damp skin...

"Kasey."

"Yes," she said quickly, trying to control the heat she knew flooded her face.

"Thanks for coming today." His dark eyes were probing. "I know you didn't really want to."

"It's okay," she said. "I love getting out of the office."

"And sweltering in ninety-five degree heat." He half-smiled. "What a great way to spend an afternoon."

"So what *is* your stand on abortion?" she asked,

deliberately switching the subject, for her own self-protection.

"I have a feeling it isn't the same as yours."

"I guess we won't know until you tell me."

"What if I don't want to talk politics?"

"Even if I want to know?"

"Okay, I'm pro choice."

"I was afraid you'd say that."

"I take it you don't agree."

"You're right, I don't."

"See, now you're angry."

"No, I'm not."

"I knew that would happen. That subject does it every time."

"You're right, we shouldn't discuss politics."

"So can we agree to disagree?"

She tilted her head. "I bet I could change your mind."

He chuckled. "If anyone could, it'd be you."

"Maybe I'll take my best shot someday."

"I'd like that, actually. Means you'll still be around."

She felt color invade her cheeks. "I didn't mean that."

"I know, but I did."

"Tanner—"

He reached out and grabbed her hand, turned it over and caressed her palm. Heat, pooling at the apex of her thighs, made her shift positions. "Don't," she said in an unsteady voice.

"Don't tell you how much I want to make love to you right now?"

"Yes."

"Too late. I've already told you."

"I—"

The rest of her reply was interrupted by his ringing cell phone. Muttering an expletive, he reached for it. Moments later, Kasey watched the color drain from his face, leaving it pasty white.

"What is it?" she asked around her sudden fear.

"A floor just collapsed in one of my buildings."

"Was anyone hurt?"

"Yes." His tone was harsh. "One of the workers."

"Oh, no, Tanner."

He stood. "Come on, we're going to the emergency room."

Twenty-Seven

"How does a glass of iced almond tea sound to you?"

Tanner cut his eyes toward her, too shocked to speak. They had just left the hospital and pulled up in the drive of her apartment. He had planned on seeing her to the door, then heading home, though he'd dreaded walking into his empty condo. Most likely he'd console himself by hitting the liquor cabinet. Almond tea sounded much more healthy and safer.

"Like manna from heaven," he said. "Why?"

"I have some in the fridge."

"Are you inviting me in?"

She released a breath and met his gaze head-on. "Yes."

"Are you sure?"

She didn't hesitate. "I'm sure."

"You trust me?" His tone was low and gravelly.

She rose to the challenge. "Should I?"

"No."

"Then—"

"Yes, you can trust me."

Tension spread like wildfire between them as their eyes met and held.

Not about to give her time to change her mind, Tanner got out of the car. Once they were inside her cozy apartment, he headed for the sofa. God, he was beat, both mentally and physically. If he didn't get some rest soon, he felt as though he might collapse which would be a first for him. His aides had often compared him to the Energizer bunny—he could go on and on.

Tonight, however, had just about done him in.

"You look exhausted," Kasey said, a slight quiver in her voice.

She was nervous about having asked him in, second-guessing herself, he'd bet. While he'd like nothing better than to drown his troubles in her delectable body, he'd hold himself in check. Somehow.

"I am," he finally answered, peering up at her as she stood in the middle of the living room watching him. He wasn't the only one in need of a hot shower and sleep. She was also exhausted. Yet the weary droop of her shoulders and those circles under her eyes, or the vulnerability in them, didn't detract from her beauty. Something deep inside him stirred, making him suddenly want to hold her and just comfort her.

"I'll be right back," she said in her soft voice.

The second she disappeared, Tanner rested his head against the sofa and closed his eyes. Before he could get his swirling thoughts under control, however, she was back with a tray in hand. A pitcher of iced tea, glasses and sandwiches were neatly arranged on a tray that she placed on the coffee table in front of him.

He roused and sat up. "Hey, you're quick."

"How so?"

"You whipped up these sandwiches in nothing flat."

She smiled which suddenly erased some of her fatigue. "I can't take credit. They're from the deli."

"Beggars can't be choosers."

"In that case, help yourself."

She poured their tea and took her glass. He noticed she bypassed the sandwiches. "Not hungry, huh?"

"No. Not in the least."

"They're good," he said, having taken a bite.

"I'm glad."

He peered at her, then all but threw down the sandwich. "Actually it tastes like a wad of sawdust. No offense."

A smile flirted with her lips. "None taken."

He sighed, then drained half the glass of tea. "Now, that's really good."

"It's my specialty."

He watched as she took a sip, then lowered her glass. She flushed under his steady gaze. He turned and repositioned his weight on the sofa, feeling his features turn grim.

As though she read his mind, she said, "We have to believe he's going to make it."

"He has to make it," Tanner stressed through tight lips. "He can't die."

"I know you feel personally responsible, but it was an accident."

He didn't say anything for a moment. His mind was veering in too many directions. "I'm not so sure about that."

Kasey's eyes widened. "But how could it not be?"

"Paul, my assistant, whom you met, pulled me aside and told me he had suspicions."

Her lips parted. "What kind of suspicions? I mean—" Her voice faded into nothingness.

"Faulty material would be my guess."

"Oh, Tanner, I hope not."

He lunged off the couch and flexed his muscles while his gaze locked with hers once again. "If that's the case, can't you just see the field day the media's going to have with this, especially that Greer woman. Why, she'll be all over me like fleas on a hound. Only I don't give a shit as long as Carl makes it.''

A frown marred Kasey's features. ''I'm going to hold on to the fact that it was just an accident.''

He smirked. ''Maybe your positive attitude will rub off on me.''

''Maybe so.''

They were quiet for a while during which he paced the floor.

''You were really good with his family.''

''I care about my employees, Kasey.''

''It shows. I wish the media could see that side of you.''

''Thanks,'' he muttered, pleased that he'd *pleased* her. ''But that's not what they're looking for.''

''You're right. They're looking to smear you.''

''And that's too damn bad.'' Tanner's tone was bleak. ''We should both want only what's good for Texas.''

''Would you care for some more tea?''

He paused midstride. ''Am I making you nervous?'' ''Yes.''

He chuckled, which helped to relieve the tension inside him as well as in the room. ''Okay, I'll take you up on that.''

She refilled his glass. When he took it from her, he made damn sure he didn't graze a finger. His emotions were waiting for an excuse to explode. Touching her would be the catalyst that set them off. He didn't dare chance that. Just being with her was the next best thing to touching her. He should learn to be grateful for the small things.

With that in mind, he once again downed half the tea in one go. When his eyes lowered, they landed on the small opening in her blouse which allowed him access to the creamy slope of a breast. His breath froze in his throat, then he forced himself to swallow. Still, his eyes wouldn't budge. He watched as her breasts moved up and down with each breath she took.

As if she could read his mind, her mouth parted. Maybe he was imagining things, but he could've sworn he heard a small whimper escape. Heat flared inside him. "Kasey," he said in a cracked voice.

She rose and grabbed the pitcher. "I'll go get a refill."

A refill wasn't needed, but he didn't point that out. It was best she left the room before he did something he'd regret. If he touched her again, he wanted it to be her idea not his.

When she returned, he had managed to regain control of himself and his libido. Dammit, he should be thinking about Carl Neufield lying in a hospital room unconscious from that lick on his head. Instead he was thinking about how much he wanted to seduce Kasey.

"I feel bad," he said into the silence.

"Why?"

"For keeping you up."

"Don't. I probably couldn't sleep anyway. I'm too keyed." She raised her hand and rubbed the back of her neck. When she did, his eyes landed once again on that opening in her blouse.

A bead of sweat popped out on his upper lip. Coughing, Tanner forced his gaze off her and said, "I bet I'm headlines in the paper again tomorrow."

"You don't know that."

"I'm counting on it," he muttered harshly. "Butler

will be cheering from the sidelines.'' His tone was bitter. ''Count on that, too.''

''How could someone politicize something like that?''

''Easy. They get off on it.''

''That's awful.''

''If it's something other than an accident, and I should know by morning, she'll crucify me.''

''Stop thinking like that. You're just borrowing trouble.'' Kasey got up and made her way to him, stopping just short of touching him.

He plowed a hand through his hair before meeting her eyes again. The heat between them flared again. He sucked in his breath and held it.

Long moments ticked by.

''Maybe you should go,'' Kasey finally whispered, licking her dry, lower lip.

He yanked her against him and held her so tightly that she felt his rock-hard muscles push into her slender frame. Then leaning back, he took her lips in a long, slow-building kiss that left her breathless and weak.

''Please don't make me,'' he pleaded against her ear, his hot breath sending shivers though her.

''No.''

''No what?''

''No, I won't make you go,'' she responded, gladly giving in to the hot and hungry desire that raged inside her.

''You won't be sorry.''

''Yes I will, but I don't care.''

''I want you so much.''

His lips adhered to hers, and he ran his hands under her blouse, wandering across her back where he unclasped her bra. He went from one breast to the other, kneading them.

Only after he pulled her close against him again did he mutter, "The hell with these clothes."

Holding back their frantic need for each other, they pulled away just long enough to undress. Never removing his gaze from her, Tanner reached for her and sank his lips back onto hers.

His hands made their way down her back and over her buttocks. He traced his fingers down that forbidden path between her cheeks. A gasp of excitement and wonderment split Kasey's lips in consecutive gasps.

"Like that, huh?" he muttered from deep within his throat.

Too weak to speak, she nodded. His finger found the hot entrance between her legs. Without erring, he thrust a finger into her moistness. She squeezed her thighs together, holding it there as he began to thrust it in and out.

"Oh, Tanner, I'm—"

"Go ahead, darling, let it go."

Following his throaty command, she pitched her head back, closed her eyes, and cried out, giving into the exquisite sensation that pelted her body.

Once she had climaxed, he urged her into the bedroom and onto the bed. He braced his hands on either side of her, nudged her legs apart with a knee, and thrust into her. While staring down at her, he moved in and out ever so slowly.

"Stop torturing me," she pleaded.

"That I can do."

Locking her arms around his waist so as to better anchor him inside her, their bodies joined in a frenzied ride until both cried out in spent satisfaction.

* * *

Tanner had a love-hate relationship with erotic dreams. He loved them because they made him feel great. He hated them because he had to wake up.

He didn't know when he realized the exquisite feelings pounding his body weren't from a dream. Perhaps it was when he remembered he'd made love to Kasey again and that she was still with him.

Bending over him, actually.

"Kasey," he heard himself grind out.

"Mmm?"

"What are—" His sentence ended on a deep-seated groan.

"You don't like it?"

"I love it," he said, barely able to talk.

Her tongue lashed him again.

"Oh, yes, yes."

Her mouth surrounded the tip.

"Kasey, Kasey."

"Do you love this, too?" She sucked.

His buttocks bolted.

"Good, huh?"

"Best ever."

"I can do even better."

"That's...not necessary."

"Are you sure?"

"Kasey—" He latched on to her hair and dug his fingers into her scalp.

"Yes?"

"You're...going to make me come."

She sucked harder.

Twenty-Eight

Kasey had awakened a few minutes earlier feeling somewhat disoriented. But when she saw Tanner sitting on the side of her bed, his sinewy back to her, things fell into place. She jerked her eyes off him and stared at the ceiling, her heart beating overtime.

"What time is it?"

Kasey rolled over and looked at the clock on the bedside table. "A little after three."

"I'm glad you slept," he said in a low, raspy voice.

"You didn't?" she asked.

"I kept seeing Carl Neufield's battered body and the frantic look on his wife's face."

"It wasn't your fault," she pointed out in a gentle tone.

"God, I'd like to think that, but since I'm not sure, I—" His words played out on a harsh note.

She ached to comfort him, but she didn't know how. Like Shirley's murder, Carl's accident was another of those awful situations that only time would take care of.

"I should go," he said in that same raspy tone.

"I know."

"Look at me. Please."

Reluctantly she did as he asked. Her eyes were all over him, devouring him.

"I could be persuaded otherwise."

Her breath came hard and fast. How could he want any more sex? They had made love almost continually throughout the night. "You're insatiable," she said in a husky voice.

"Only when it comes to you." He reached out and covered a breast.

"Would you like some breakfast?" she asked, quickly moving out of his reach.

His eyebrows shot up. "Are you cooking?"

"Of course."

"You're on. But I'll help."

"That's not necessary."

"Sure it is."

Not daring to consider the consequences of her offer, she got up and reached for a robe that was draped across a nearby chair. When she swung around, he was standing.

Naked.

For a moment, she was robbed of speech. The light from the lamp that they'd left on throughout the night fell just right on him. His six-pack abs and burgeoning manhood reheated her blood. Only by sheer force of will was she able to transfer her gaze back to his face. That wasn't much better. With mussed up hair and a growth of whiskers, he looked rough and dangerous.

And sexy as hell.

"Don't tell me you're embarrassed." He chuckled.

"Of course not," she exclaimed, her breath catching.

His chuckle broke into full laughter. "Yes, you are. After last night, I find that mighty hard to believe."

"I'll be in the kitchen," she muttered in a terse tone.

His laughter followed her. Damn him, she thought, clinging to the cabinet for a minute, groping to get her bearings. He offered to go; she should've let him. Her son's image suddenly rose to mind, and she sagged against the counter.

Why couldn't she be strong when it came to Tanner and sexual fascination with him?

"Need any help?"

Without turning around, she said, "No, I'm about to make the coffee."

"At least let me do that." He crossed the kitchen and before she could offer further protests, he reached for the filters.

Shortly, the coffee, bacon, eggs and biscuits were done, and they were at the table eating in silence. At least Tanner was. Every bite she took seemed to curdle in her stomach. Not so with him. He had wolfed down the entire contents of his plate which she'd heaped high.

His eating habits reminded her so much of Brock. Her stomach completely revolted at that thought, which forced her to push her plate away.

"Do you ever eat?"

"When I'm hungry."

"I'm ravenous."

"No kidding."

He paused, his cup midway to his lips, a twinkle in his eye. "You shouldn't be such a good cook."

"I've had a lot of practice," she said lightly, wishing again she'd kept her mouth shut. The idea that she had made hot love most of the night then fixed breakfast for her lover was ridiculous.

"I could get used to this." He reached for her hand. "How 'bout you?"

Startled, her eyes widened as goose bumps feathered her skin.

"You're jumpy as a cat on a barbed-wire fence."

Kasey withdrew her hand, but the damage was done. That touch had set off every pulse point in her body.

"I'm not jumpy."

"You didn't answer my question."

"I know."

His eyes pierced hers. "Which tells me the answer is no."

"I don't want any commitments, Tanner."

"I'm not asking for any. I just want us to be together."

She shifted her gaze. "For me, that's commitment."

"What are you afraid of, Kasey?"

She got up abruptly and walked to the sink, then realized she was empty-handed. When she was around him, all rational thought seemed to leave her.

"I won't hurt you," he said to her back. "And I sure won't hurt your son."

Her body went rigid. "Leave Brock out of this."

"I know you're pissed because I asked him to help me."

She turned around and crossed her arms over her breasts. "Could we not talk about this right now?"

His lips flat-lined. "I don't want to stop seeing you."

"We see each other almost every day."

"You're being deliberately obtuse," he said in an irritated tone.

She kept her silence.

"All right, Kasey, I won't push. But I'm giving you fair warning, I want you in my life and I'm not going to go down without a fight."

"We're too different, Tanner. Our lives are on different tracks. But that aside I—" She broke off.

"Look, right now, there's too much turmoil in my life for you to add to it. Why can't we just work together?"

His hot gaze raked over her. "I think you know the answer to that. All I have to do is touch you—"

"Stop it," she lashed out. "And please, just go."

When the door to her apartment slammed a few minutes later, she flinched.

"I'm assuming you've seen the papers, son?"

I'm not your son, Tanner wanted to say, but he refrained. It wasn't Jack Milstead's fault that he was out of sorts. It was his own fault for getting involved with a woman who meant more to him than a casual lay. She was fast becoming his obsession.

"Actually I haven't."

After he'd left Kasey's, Tanner had returned home, taken a shower, then crashed. He'd awakened late and had headed straight to the hospital to check on his injured employee.

The second he'd stepped out of his vehicle, Daisy Greer and the others had pounced on him.

"Are you cutting corners on the job, Mr. Hart?" she had demanded.

"Absolutely not."

"Can you prove that?"

"Yes," he'd lashed back.

"If Carl Neufield dies, will you assume responsibility?"

He'd never ever considered striking a woman until that moment. Instead he'd told her. "I have no further comment."

Now, he forced himself back to the conversation at hand. "You're joking," Woody Lamar said with disbelief, switching his soggy cigar to the other side of his mouth.

Woody was one of Tanner's chief financial backers who chose to remain on the sidelines. Because of the latest debacle, however, Jack had urged him to get involved. Tanner didn't have a problem with that. Even if he did, he couldn't afford to bite the hand that fed him.

"Nothing about this is a joke, Woody."

"Well," Jack said in an ill-humored tone, "the goddamned media's having a field day with the accident. You and your company are headlines."

Tanner ignored the sick feeling invading his stomach. "I've already been on the receiving end of Greer's sharp tongue and poison pen. I'm thinking I held my own, but we'll see."

He paused, settling his gaze on Jack. "By the way, thanks for asking about Carl." His tone was sardonic.

Woody removed the cigar, then ran a hand over his bald head. "Who the hell is Carl?"

"The worker who fell through the floor, almost killing himself."

"I guess I didn't get his name," Woody mumbled under his breath.

"You know I'm concerned about him," Jack said, ignoring Woody's comment. "But I'm also concerned that this latest screwup is going to cost you the election."

Tanner almost said screw the *election*. But he didn't mean that. He wanted to win the senate seat as much as ever, only not at the expense of a man's life.

"If the guy doesn't die, then maybe there's hope," Woody said. "What are his chances for a full recovery?"

Tanner leaned back in his chair. "Good, according to the doctor. But he's awfully banged up and still in intensive care."

Jack swore.

"So was it an accident?" Woody asked.

"I'm waiting for Paul to get back to me on that," Tanner replied. "He and the police are working together to try and determine the cause."

"If it's faulty material, then—" Jack broke off with a savage shake of his head, making his pink cheeks jiggle.

"I'm not ruling that out," Tanner said, blowing out his breath. "We ordered from a new supplier." He grimaced.

"Just as long as your crew didn't cut corners."

Tanner's eyes narrowed to slits. "I can guarantee that didn't happen."

"How?" Jack demanded. "You're rarely on the job site."

"I trust Paul." Tanner's tone was cold and brooked no argument. "And he's there. Practically 24/7."

"I just wish for once some of Butler's luck would rub off on you, Tanner," Woody chimed in. "Why can't you land in a tub of shit and come out smelling like a rose same as Butler?"

Despite his less than flattering comment, Tanner was relieved to see a smile on Woody's face. Still, he knew Woody was serious. Right now, things couldn't look grimmer.

"By the time that female reporter gets through with him," Jack said, "he'll drown in that tub of shit."

"Dammit, Jack, stop talking about me like I'm not in the room."

Jack glared at Tanner.

Tanner's fury rose. "Are you saying I should throw in the fucking towel?"

"You know better than that," Jack said.

Tanner's eyes continued to drill him. "This is the second time I've gotten that feeling, and I don't like it. From now on, I'd advise you to keep those kinds of comments to yourself."

He was furious and he wanted them to know it. What had happened on the job hadn't been his fault or his foreman's. If the supplier had shipped faulty material, then it would pay. He'd see to that.

"Hey, guys, calm down," Woody injected. "We're all on the same side here."

Tanner held his silence, not about to apologize.

"I have to agree with the guys, Tanner. It seems you're determined to give Butler this election on a silver platter."

All eyes faced the door.

"Hello, Irene," Jack said in an unamused voice.

Tanner turned stoic as Irene strode through the door. *And let the second round of fireworks begin.*

Twenty-Nine

She hadn't seen or talked to Tanner in several days.

Kasey tried not to let that bother her, but it did. She missed him, though she was loath to admit that even to herself. At certain moments during the night and day, she did acknowledge that. Her heart would almost break at the impossibility of their situation.

She wanted Tanner and he wanted her. They also needed each other during these trying times. Brock's situation, Shirley's unsolved murder, and the pending lawsuit with the agency gnawed at her continuously.

Tanner fared no better. He was under siege as well from the media. To date no definitive decision had been reached as to what caused the ill-fated accident. Hence, the investigation was ongoing. And so was Tanner's campaign even though it was a bumpy ride. The polls bore testimony to that. His popularity was up one day and down the next.

In spite of their emotional attachment, she could never have him. So why did she continue to punish herself? Perhaps it was because she had never experienced this heady, breathless feeling, *this rush,* she felt with him.

If that wasn't love, then it was the next best thing. That frightened her even more. How could she have let him invade her soul?

She had always considered herself a strong person, one who played by the rules and who learned from her mistakes. Or so she'd thought. Her involvement with Tanner had proved otherwise. But in defense of herself, he had snuck in the back door of her life, caught her when she was the most vulnerable.

Still, she couldn't blame him. If she were to give in to her heart's desire, she and her son would both suffer. She had spent a lifetime guarding her secret, and she would continue to do so.

"My, but you're deep in thought."

Kasey shook her head to clear it, then turned and smiled at Red who had just ambled into the workroom. "Not as deep as I should be." She'd been there since dawn but to her chagrin didn't have much to show for it.

"From the looks of things, I'd say you've been kicking butt."

Kasey sighed. "In my case, looks can be deceiving."

"Oh, I doubt that," Red countered before easing his rear onto a high work stool.

"Doubt what?" Don Hornsby asked, making his appearance into the room.

Red gestured with a hand. "Never mind."

Don shrugged, then also took a seat.

"What happened to you?" Red asked, peering closer at Don. "Did you tie one on last night?"

"That's none of your damn business," Don snapped, glaring at Red.

"Enough, okay," Kasey said. Though she couldn't help but notice that Red had grounds for his comment. Don looked different. Acted different. He had gone from one stool to another yet hadn't taken a seat on either. Agitated was the word. And his eyes, there was something about them that just didn't appear right.

"Am I late?"

"No, you're not." Kasey smiled at the media specialist, Lance Sagemont, as he strolled in. "In fact, you're right on time."

Lance was silent, though his gaze seemed to peruse his surroundings, finally resting on Don. "What happened to you?"

"Will y'all get off my back?" Don demanded fiercely.

"I think that's a good idea." Kasey stood. "Besides we have a lot to cover in a short period of time."

Don peered at his watch. "I have a meeting in an hour."

Kasey assumed his meeting was with a prospective client, which might not be so good, considering Don obviously wasn't having one of his better days. But all in all, she could find no fault with him or his work. In fact, he'd been bringing in clients right and left, albeit small ones.

"How are we on the Hart ads?"

"That's the main reason for the meeting."

"We sure have our work cut out for us," Red pointed out, "what with him getting hammered in the press."

Kasey reached for a pen. "Exactly."

Lance rubbed his chin before crossing to the worktable strewn with papers and posters. "If you ask me, Butler's ads border on slander. He's all but accused Hart of trying to murder that poor guy who took a tumble."

"The way I see it, we have no choice but to give

Butler a dose of his own medicine,'' Don put in, shoving a hand through his wiry hair.

"Although I haven't spoken to Tanner in several days, I know he would agree,'' Kasey said. "So let's get down to work and do some major damage control.''

They called in the other staff members and soon ideas and sketches were drawn and verbal ideas discussed. Kasey felt a thrill shoot through her, realizing once again how much she liked what she did, how much she wanted to make a success of this business. If only she could do that and have Tanner...

Kasey gave her head a savage shake. Now was not the time to woolgather. As it was, the day was shaping up to be a long and exhausting one.

"Okay, people,'' she said, "listen up. I have an idea.''

Daisy Greer glanced at her watch.

Damn, she was running much later than she had intended. She should've been out of the office long before now, especially if she wanted to get that last important interview of the day.

But she couldn't snub her boss, and he was the one who was responsible for detaining her. He called her into his office and wanted to know her modus operandi. Once she'd gone over her continuing strategy, he'd dismissed her but not before saying, "You're doing great. Keep up the good work.''

Those encouraging words had been music to Daisy's ears in light of the flack she'd caught from others who were rallying behind Tanner Hart. Last evening, she'd even received a threatening phone call, telling her she'd be sorry if she didn't stop persecuting him.

"Go fuck yourself," she'd told the caller before slamming down the receiver.

Now, as she readied herself to go into another battle, she grabbed her notepad and purse only to pull up short when the phone rang. She considered ignoring it, but didn't. A wise choice, she soon learned. It was Buck Butler.

"Why hello, Buck."

"I just wanted to let you know what a fine job you're doing, young lady."

Her self-confidence swelled to new heights. Two pats on the back in one day. Unheard of. Her future glowed brighter by the second.

"I'm glad you're pleased," she said on a giddy note.

"Pleased. That doesn't even begin to describe my feelings."

"Well, I certainly didn't plan on having this good fortune fall into my lap. You have to know that."

"The fact that you took full advantage of the situation makes you the crackerjack reporter you are."

"I think Hart's finished."

Butler chuckled. "Well on his way, that's for sure."

"But just in case we encounter a stumbling block, I'm keeping the pressure on. I'm working several other angles."

Butler's chuckle deepened. "You won't be sorry you jumped on my bandwagon."

"Is that a promise?" Daisy asked boldly, then waited with bated breath.

"You bet."

Thank God, the day was about over.

Kasey finished straightening the worktable, then leaned back and over, stretching her sore, aching muscles. Everything felt cramped, even her bones. Despite her exhaustion, it had been a productive day. Tanner's new television and radio ads and billboard signs had been designed, ready for his approval or disapproval, whichever the case might be.

Her plan now was to go home and take a long, hot soaking bath, then go to bed.

Without Tanner.

That out-of-the-blue thought robbed her of breath. Kasey's hand flew to her chest; she felt her heart beating out of sync. Closing her eyes, she breathed deeply, trying to right her suddenly skewed mind.

It didn't work. Thoughts of Tanner continued to pound her. Why hadn't he called? She had pissed him off, that was why. Still, she expected to hear from him concerning the advertising. He wanted that senate seat a lot more than he wanted her.

"You're nuts," Kasey muttered to the empty room, all the while gathering her personal gear in preparation to leave. She headed out to her car and was in the process of unlocking the door when she heard another vehicle pull up beside her. She swung around. She was suddenly filled with a sense of impending doom.

Daisy Greer was already out of her car and heading toward her.

Kasey swallowed her groan of despair and plastered a smile on her lips. "Hello, Ms. Greer."

"I'm glad I caught you," Daisy said without preamble.

"And to what do I owe this visit?" Kasey tried to keep her voice neutral, but she failed. Sarcasm nibbled around the edges of her question. And fear. This woman was a walking lethal weapon whom she had hoped to avoid at all costs. She was gunning for Tanner and wasn't shy about making that known.

"I thought it was time we had a chat," Daisy said.

Kasey's fear elevated. "About my partner's murder?"

"We can start with that, if you'd like."

"I have nothing to add to my original police report."

"That's too bad, since the killer's still walking the streets. That doesn't bode well for any of us."

Kasey gritted her teeth to keep from lashing back at the obnoxious woman, telling her to get lost.

"If and when you do remember something, I'd like an exclusive story. Would you agree to that?"

Kasey had to hand it to her. The woman had gall. And to be a reporter in these times, it took that and more. Balls and moxie. Daisy Greer had more than her share of both.

"I don't think Detective Gallain would be too thrilled," Kasey said at last.

"We'll see," Daisy said, then pulled out her legal pad. "Is there somewhere we can go and sit down?"

"I really don't see that we have anything to say to each other."

"We can talk about Tanner Hart."

"What about him?"

"He's your client, right?"

"Yes."

"And your lover as well?"

The silence was ominous while Kasey stared at her in horrified disbelief. "Excuse me?"

"Since you know him so well, do you think he's capable of putting profits before human life?"

Fury flared inside Kasey and she spat, "Get out of my face and out of my way."

Thirty

Paul Darby couldn't keep his fingers off his several days' growth of beard. He continually pawed at his face which got on Tanner's nerves. But then everything got on his nerves these days. He was on a short fuse.

"What's with the hair?" he asked shortly after Paul had arrived at his corporate office.

Paul frowned in obvious confusion. "Hair?"

"Yeah, that's growing on your face."

The color red invaded his features. "I just thought I'd see what it was like."

"And?"

"It itches like bloody hell." Paul grinned sheepishly.

"With this weather as hot as it is, I don't see how you stand it."

"Is that what this meeting's all about?"

"Not hardly," Tanner muttered.

"Didn't think so."

Tanner moved from behind his desk, then perched on the edge of it. "Want some coffee?"

"Nah, I have a thermos full in the truck."

Tanner knew he'd stalled long enough, but he loathed telling Paul the latest kick in the teeth. But he had no choice.

"What's wrong, boss? I know it's not Carl because

I just came from the hospital, and though he hasn't regained consciousness he's still hanging in there.''

"I know.''

Silence prevailed for a long moment.

"But again that's not why I'm here, right?'' Paul pressed.

"Right,'' Tanner admitted on a sigh.

Paul merely looked at him as though he had all the patience in the world. Tanner admired and envied that laid-back attitude even in the midst of crisis. He was just the opposite. His insides were as twisted as barbed wire. And not just because of the accident on the job site, either.

His obsession with Kasey was taking precedence over everything. He had to get control of his runaway emotions or lose himself in the process. He'd had a lot of women, including a generous, loving wife, but he had never given himself emotionally to her or any of the others.

Only Kasey.

"Tanner, what's going on? You're spooking me big time. I've never seen you like this.''

Tanner pulled his mind off Kasey and onto the problem at hand. "We're being investigated.''

"Investigated. As in how?''

"A criminal probe into our building practices.''

"You mean—'' A string of curses finished Paul's sentence.

"I mean we're getting hung out to dry.''

"But on what grounds, for chrissakes? It has to be more than Carl's fall. It was an awful accident, but that's all it was and nothing more.''

"We both know that, Paul. Unfortunately, others don't.''

Paul's green eyes flashed. "Buck Butler for starters."

"Well, he's sure taking advantage of the accident, no doubt about that. He's determined it's going to get more than its fair share of media time."

"Dammit, can't we stop the investigation before it gets started?"

"If I try to interfere, then it'll look like I…my company has something to hide."

"But you have the right to defend yourself."

"Oh, make no mistake, I'm going to do that." Tanner paused while his eyes drilled his assistant. "Are you absolutely sure the materials from that new supplier met standards?"

"Dammit, Tanner—"

"Hey, don't take this personal, Paul, because it isn't." Tanner's tone was hard.

"How can you expect me not to take it personally when I'm the foreman?"

"Because it's not about you. It's about me. Who I am."

"Politics," he muttered.

"I know you're doing your job," Tanner stressed, ignoring the muttered comment. "I have complete confidence in that. But this is going to get sticky at best and nasty at worst. So I have to know if there's anything going on I need to know about. I don't want anything to bite me on the ass when I'm least expecting it."

Paul looked him in the eye. "I swear on my kid's head that I saw no fault with the material and that no corners were cut for any purpose."

"Then we have nothing to worry about."

"But just the hint that there's wrongdoing on your part is going to hurt you in the polls."

"Already has."

"Though not for long," Paul said, his voice strong with confidence. "When the team gets through with their snooping, they'll be eating dirt."

"They plan to backtrack, look into our other jobs." Tanner's tone was grim. "That's not going to be quick or easy."

"So what are you going to do?"

"Offer my cooperation and not stand in their way."

Paul stared at him from under hooded brows. "I don't know why anyone would want to be in politics. You're like a goddamn sitting duck just waiting for someone to take a shot at you. I just don't have the stomach for that kind of abuse."

Tanner stared into space. "I'm beginning to wonder if I do."

"Any special instructions?" Paul asked, toying with his hard hat.

"Nope." His jaw clenched. "Just continue to do your job."

The second he was alone, Tanner expelled his breath and stared at the phone. He'd received a zillion calls in light of this latest situation and needed to return them. But he didn't want to. He only wanted to call Kasey. And not about business, either.

For the first time since he'd entered the political arena, he felt the urge to chuck that responsibility, regain his anonymity, go after Kasey, and whisk her away.

In your dreams, Hart, he told himself, fighting off the feeling of darkness settling over him. He shuddered to the ringing of the phone.

* * *

Kasey put the paper down, her brows drawn in fierce concentration.

No wonder she hadn't heard from Tanner. The media had latched on to the tragedy at the construction site like a bulldog on a bone, showing no signs of letting up. He was up to his eyeballs in trouble.

She wished there was something she could do to help ease his pain. Then realizing the slippery slope her thoughts were heading down, she jerked herself upright.

Tanner Hart's problems were none of her business. If she allowed herself to think otherwise, then she would open herself up to further misery. As it was, she felt like she'd been strapped to a torture rack and was being pulled apart.

He had become her secret passion.

He could never know that, however. No one could. She refused to admit she had fallen in love with him. But if she examined deep within her heart, she feared that truth would come to light.

If only...

The buzzer sounded on her phone. Hoping the caller was Tanner, she reached for it. "Yes, Monica?"

"Your attorney's on line one."

Crushing her disappointment, Kasey picked up. "Hello, Horace."

"Just wanted to let you know a court date has been set for the hearing," he said without mincing words.

Her stomach revolted. "I want him to just go away."

"He will soon," Horace said in a promising tone. "He doesn't have a leg to stand on. However, if he wants to be made a fool of, then we'll let him."

"I hope you're right. The thought of losing the agency—"

"Don't think like that. It's not going to happen."

"If you say so."

"I say so."

He gave her the date, then rang off.

What next? Kasey asked herself, sinking her head into her hands, fighting off her growing despair.

When she finally lifted her head, her gaze unwittingly drifted to the worktable filled with Tanner's latest ads, still waiting for his okay. If he didn't call her today, then she would have to call him. Now that his name was being dragged through the mud it made it that much more imperative to get those new aggressive TV ads working for him.

"Hey, Mom."

Stunned speechless by the sight of her son in her office doorway, Kasey could only sit and stare at him with her mouth gaping open.

"Yep, it's me in the flesh," Brock continued, his whole face bathed in a grin.

"Surprising me is becoming a habit." Having said that, she got up and gave him a fierce hug.

That was when she looked beyond his shoulder and saw that he wasn't alone. Frowning, she pulled back and stared up at him. Brock turned and motioned the young girl to his side, circling her waist with his arm.

Kasey didn't have to ask who she was. She knew, and her heart plummeted to her toes.

"Mom, this is Nancy Dittmer, my fiancée."

The humming of the refrigerator was the only sound in the kitchen.

Finally Brock said, "I've pissed you off again, haven't I, Mom?"

"I wish you'd stop using that phrase," Kasey responded in a testy tone.

Brock pressed his lips in a thin line and just looked at her.

Kasey turned away, smothering a scream of frustration. Ever since he'd shown up at the office late in the day, she had been rabid to talk to her son in private. As luck would have it, she had stumbled into the kitchen around midnight, only to receive yet another surprise.

Brock was sitting at the table, munching on a peanut butter and jelly sandwich and drinking a glass of milk. She had poured herself a glass and joined him at the table.

Now, as she faced him under terribly strained conditions, she didn't know where to start. She had so much on her mind and in her heart, she felt like she was choking.

Her baby, engaged?

Impossible.

She had misunderstood him.

Much to her heartfelt regret, she hadn't.

Moments after he'd introduced Nancy, she had learned that Brock had needed to talk to Tanner in person about the Web site and decided that he'd bring Nancy with him. Kill two birds with one stone, he'd added.

A simple explanation that packed a powerful wallop.

"Thanks for being nice to Nancy even though you don't like her," Brock finally said.

"You're missing the point," Kasey stressed. "It's not a matter of liking her. It's a matter of the engagement."

"I know I can't afford a ring."

"For God's sake, Brock, I'm not talking about a ring. I'm talking about you actually thinking you want to marry this girl."

"I know I want to marry her. We're in love."

Kasey couldn't help herself. She rolled her eyes. "You don't even know the first thing about love."

"That's not fair, Mom," he countered in a belligerent tone.

"Fair or not, it's the truth. What about getting your education then playing pro football? That's always been your dream."

"It still is. Nancy thinks me playing ball for a living is just great."

Kasey groaned inwardly all the while wanting to grab her son and shake some sense into him.

"Look, Mom, we're not getting married for a long time, so stop wigging out. I just wanted to tie her up so no one else would. You can see for yourself how beautiful she is."

It was true. Nancy was indeed an eye-catcher with her dark wispy hair, dainty features and peaches 'n' cream complexion. However, Kasey suspected she was short on brains, though she hadn't had any time alone with Nancy to verify that. Once they left the office, she had taken them out to eat then back to the apartment where Brock hadn't left Nancy's side. They had watched movies until bedtime.

"She likes you, Mom. She thinks you're cool."

Unimpressed, Kasey took a breath, then asked, "Are you two…intimate?" God, she hated this, but like Ginger had told her, she had to know. She couldn't keep her head buried in the sand, only to regret it later.

Silence.

"Mom, I can't believe you asked that."

"Don't 'Mom' me. If you are, I hope you're using protection."

"I am."

Her baby making love.

No.

She hadn't heard that.

She didn't believe it.

Tomorrow she would wake up and find this all another terrible dream.

Kasey struggled for a decent breath to continue, trying to mask her fear and her disappointment.

"Come on, Mom, everybody does it."

She felt her face grow hot. "That doesn't make it right."

"You want my friends to think I'm gay?"

"Stop it, Brock," she cried out. "I don't care what your friends think. I only care what's best for you."

A shutter seemed to fall across his features. "Don't ask me to give her up, Mom, because I won't."

"So that's the way it is, huh?" she asked, fighting back tears.

"Yeah, that's the way it is."

"Just promise me you won't do anything stupid."

"Like get her pregnant?"

"That for sure, or run off and get married."

"I promise I won't do, either."

She reached across the table and grabbed one of his big hands and squeezed it. "I love you, you big oaf." Tears trickled down her face. "You're all I have."

"Aw, Mom, give it a rest. It's gonna be okay."

Her smile caught on a sob.

"Aw, Mom," he said again, "you're making me feel real bad."

"Sorry, son. It's just that I had such big dreams for you."

Brock's face blanked out. "Do you mind if we change the subject?"

"It's fine with me," Kasey responded in an uneven voice.

"I finally got Mr. Hart on his cell."

Kasey forced herself not to react, though another scream wanted to break through her throat. "Oh?"

"He wants us all to have breakfast in the morning." Brock cocked his head to one side. "I told him that was okay. Hope you don't mind."

Thirty-One

Sweat oozed from every pore in his body. He felt like he'd been sitting in a sauna for hours. But that was nothing compared to what he was going to feel like when he got to hell. And burned forever.

Don Hornsby bit down hard on his lower lip. Even after tasting blood, he didn't let go. Frightened and desperate, he shook all over like he had the rigors.

Yet he couldn't stop himself. It was the desperation that drove him, making him attempt this disastrous deed. He'd run out of options. He had no other way to get the money to feed his habit. He'd stolen from his sister until she had nothing left except her government check, and she'd beat him to it. She had already cashed her check and spent it.

Breaking into a stranger's house and stealing something worth pawning was the only way out of this earthly hellhole. Without the drugs, Don simply couldn't function. Snorting up and getting that incredible high was what he lived for, what he got out of bed for each morning.

If he couldn't have his fixes, he didn't want to live.

He hovered in the darkness barely able to breathe. The smothering heat and humidity gave him the feeling of being covered in a wet blanket. Otherwise, the weather was in his favor. No stars lit the sky. No moon, either. Only clouds and they played to his advantage.

Splayed against the fence, Don tried not to move a muscle. He wanted to listen for human sounds. Unfortunately his body wouldn't cooperate. His need for a snort of cocaine made his limbs twitch and his stomach pitch.

"Holy shit," he muttered before bending over and dumping the contents of his stomach.

After lifting his head and swiping the back of his mouth with a hand, he slumped against the fence. God, he felt awful. He could swear millions of ants were crawling over his insides. He massaged his arms. He wanted to scream. He wanted to run.

He did neither. He forced himself to remain where he was and stared at the back door of the house while trying to clear his head. If he was going to pull this off and not get his ass arrested, he had to clear his mind and force himself to concentrate on nothing but getting in and out of that house without being detected.

Could he do it? Did he have the guts to do it?

Damn straight he did.

Piece of cake.

His intended victim was his sister's elderly neighbor who lived alone. And had more money than she had sense. According to his sister, Agnes Cargill supposedly kept wads of cash stashed in the house.

If Flora was wrong, he swore he'd wring her scrawny neck.

Don took several deep, sucking breaths and made his way onto the rickety back porch. Fearing he'd step on a rotten board that would squeak like a pig in distress or snap under his weight and wake the old lady, he walked very gingerly until he reached the door.

There he relaxed, suddenly remembering old Agnes was almost deaf. Another factor in his favor since he planned to pilfer through her house until he found some of that cold cash.

Picking the lock turned out to be a no-brainer. Once inside, the musty stench that assaulted his nostrils reminded him of Flora's pigsty. Pushing that aside, he tiptoed deeper into the shadows. First thing he located was the old lady's bedroom. She was apparently sound asleep with the covers pulled over her head.

He eased the door shut, then flicked on his low-beamed flashlight. Once in the living room, he looked around. An old secretary-like desk caught his eye right off. A perfect place to stash some cash, he told himself, feeling his adrenaline kick in.

Placing the flashlight on the desk flap, he rummaged through the nooks and crannies. Moments later, he struck pay dirt. His hand came in contact with a wad of bills.

"Praise Jesus," he muttered under his breath after licking the sweat off his lips with his tongue.

That was when he heard a noise. Fear froze him, rooted his feet to the sticky linoleum. Then, with his heart pounding out of his chest, he grabbed the light and slunk into the shadows.

"Is someone there?"

That was when he saw the old woman, standing in the doorway, her robe askew and her white hair standing on end. But that wasn't what held his attention and further immobilized him, causing spittle to gather at the corners of his mouth. She was wielding a sawed-off shotgun.

"Hey, Don, got a minute?"

Don pulled up short on the way to his office and whipped around. "What's up, Red?"

"I'm about to get some coffee. You want some?"

"Sure, why not?"

They made their way into the small kitchen where the smell of fresh coffee filled the air. The thought of partaking made Don's stomach roil again, but he didn't say anything. Instead he reached for a cup and filled it, then sat across the table from the artist.

"What's up?" Don asked.

"I'm glad to see you looking better."

That comment triggered an alarm inside Don, but he didn't let it show. He sat as stoic as possible. "Thanks."

"For a while I thought you were about to tip over the edge, and I was worried."

"Really?"

"Yeah, really. You'll have to admit that lately your behavior has been pretty squirrelly."

"Just some personal problems I had to get straightened out," Don replied in what he hoped was a nonchalant manner. But his insides were wound tightly.

"I know your sister—"

"Have I screwed up somewhere and don't know it?" Don interrupted. "Is that what this conversation's all about?"

Red's face mirrored his name. Then he muttered, "You know better than that. You've been working your ass off like the rest of us and it shows. I just thought maybe you might need someone to vent to."

"Since I don't, I suggest we both get back to work." Don kept his tone light, though it was hard when his insides were a tangled mess of nerves. He was definitely having difficulty walking that fine line.

He couldn't continue to come to work looking like hell one day and a crown prince the next. Today was crown prince day, since he'd managed to buy enough coke to get high. In fact, he felt goddamn superhuman, like he could walk on water.

"My wife and I are having a little get-together at our house this weekend, a pool party to be exact. I've asked Kasey and most of the staff. Are you interested?"

"Thanks. I'll let you know."

Once he was back in his cubbyhole of an office, Don sat down and opened up a file. But he couldn't concentrate or remain seated. He was too full of energy. But he knew this euphoric feeling wouldn't last beyond his money, and that panicked him.

He wasn't about to repeat last evening's desperate move. Hell, he was lucky to be upright and breathing. That crazy old bitch could've blown his freaking head off. He lunged out of his chair, sweat pooling in his armpits.

You would think after he'd had the guts to shoot Shirley at point-blank range, an old lady wouldn't have held him hostage.

But *she* had the gun.

The only thing that had saved his ass was that she turned out to be almost as blind as she was deaf. When her crackling voice had demanded to know who was there, he'd almost messed in his pants.

Thank goodness, he'd had enough discipline to remain splayed against the wall without so much as breathing. She had stood there for a few minutes longer, peering into the darkness. Then she'd lowered the gun, and mumbling to herself, turned and went back into the bedroom.

Trembling, he had snuck out of the house.

Now, in the light of day, he couldn't believe he'd actually pulled off that stunt. He wouldn't have to stoop to that level if he was getting paid more money at the agency, he thought bitterly.

Suddenly a switch went off in his head, his thoughts turning to Kasey. He'd ask her for a raise. The agency's financial situation had vastly improved, thanks to his getting out and pounding the concrete. Kasey owed him big time. Besides, she seemed to like him. Even better, he liked her.

Another thought struck him. Maybe after he'd snorted another high, he'd ask her out. He hadn't had any since the last time he'd screwed Shirley.

Wouldn't that be a hoot if he ended up inside his new boss's pretty panties. Hell, no telling where that would lead.

Don's chuckle burgeoned into full-blown laughter.

"You have a great kid, Kasey."

She hesitated. "I think so, but then I'm prejudiced."

"He's exactly what I needed on this project."

"So you two worked through the problems with the Web site."

"That we did. It's up and running great guns."

"Good."

Kasey felt Tanner's piercing gaze on her, but she chose to ignore it. If she had her druthers, any discussion about Brock would be off-limits. Under the circumstances, however, that was impossible. She still couldn't believe how fate had played such a trick on her by bringing Brock and Tanner together.

Since she didn't want to raise questions she wasn't about to answer, then she'd had to keep her mouth shut and endure. Thank goodness, Brock and Nancy had returned to Waco. Until another problem arose, her son was out of harm's reach. At least where Tanner was concerned.

"You're worried about him, aren't you?"

"Yes," she admitted before she thought.

Once they had finished breakfast, which had gone much smoother than she'd ever imagined it would, and Tanner and Brock had talked business, the kids had piled in the car and headed back to Waco.

She and Tanner had come to the office where he was in the process of assessing the agency's latest work on his behalf.

"I agree he's much too young to tie himself down to one girl."

"I tried to talk some sense into him, but my advice fell on deaf ears."

"I'm not surprised. When I was his age, I was as headstrong as they came."

Like father, like son.

"Even if I'd had a mother who gave a damn," Tanner continued, "I wouldn't have listened. That's just part of growing up."

"But what if he does something stupid and marries her?"

"He won't."

"How can you be so sure?"

"Because he respects you."

"But he loves her," Kasey responded from the depths of despair. "Or so he says."

"He's in lust." Tanner paused, then added in a low, thick voice. "Just like we were."

Her stomach bottomed out and her lips parted.

"Sorry," he muttered, clearing his throat. "That was out of line."

Recovering her composure, she turned her back on him.

"Kasey, I know how you feel about that night, but until we talk about it," he stressed, a strident note in his tone, "it's going to continue to keep us apart."

She swung back around. "There's no *us,* Tanner."

"It doesn't have to be that way."

"Yes, it does."

"Why?"

"Because it just does."

"That's no reason."

He closed the distance between them, his eyes burning down into hers. "I'm crazy about you and I think you feel the same way."

"No, I don't," she denied fiercely.

He grabbed her and kissed her hard. When he let her go, they were both breathless.

"Your lips say otherwise," he said huskily.

Thirty-Two

If only he'd stop fingering that mole.

More to the point, if only she hadn't accepted Don's invitation to lunch, she wouldn't be sitting across the table from him. Kasey shifted her gaze while taking unusually long sips of her iced tea.

Apparently, when he'd issued the invitation, he had caught her in a weak moment. And she felt sorry for him, too, though she couldn't say why. Maybe it was the situation with his sister that often made him come to the office looking like he'd been run over by a truck.

Whatever the reason, she was here and she had to make the most of it. The deli he'd chosen was bursting at the seams inside so they had opted for a table in the outer courtyard in order not to have to wait.

Now, Kasey was sorry. No amount of lush plants and flowers could detract from the smothering heat.

"This wasn't such a great idea, was it?" Don asked.

She faced him and put her glass down. "I'll survive," she said lightly. "You're the one with the coat and tie on."

He shrugged. "I'm okay."

They had ordered and were waiting for their salads. It was all she could do not to squirm under his sudden penetrating gaze. She liked Don, though she didn't know him all that well and didn't care to. As long as he did his job that was all that mattered.

"How 'bout some more tea?" he asked eagerly, reaching for the pitcher.

She held out her glass. "Thanks."

"I appreciate you doing this."

"No problem," she responded, beginning to feel really weird in addition to experiencing bad vibes.

The waitress chose that moment to bring their food. They ate in silence for a while, then Kasey pushed her plate aside. Food was the furthest thing from her mind. Ending this ordeal was all she could think of, though nothing out of the ordinary had happened. He'd been the epitome of good behavior.

"Was your food not good?"

"It was delicious."

"You sure? Feel free to order something else."

"It's okay, Don. I'm fine."

He flushed as if he realized he was pushing a tad hard. "I guess you're wondering what's going on."

She gave him a lame smile. "That did cross my mind."

"Hey, apparently they'll let anyone eat here."

Kasey spun around, grinning widely, then stood and hugged Ginger. "I'm so glad to see you."

"Me, too." Ginger's glance landed on Don before coming back to her, a question mark in her eyes.

Kasey quickly made the introductions. Though Don smiled and held out his hand, he didn't appear overjoyed at the interruption. But she was delighted.

"Are you alone?" Kasey asked.

"Not for long."

"Too bad. I was hoping you'd join us. Don and I are just having a boring business lunch."

"Thanks. Maybe another time." Ginger paused. "I'll call you later."

"I'll talk to you then."

Once she had left both Kasey and Don sat back down. For a moment an awkward silence followed.

Don was the first to break it. "I like you, Kasey, and I think you like me."

"That's true," she said with cautious reluctance. "I have no complaints with your work."

"That's what I'd hoped to hear."

When he didn't embellish on that statement, she became more confused. What was going on? What did he want? If he had something to say, she wished he'd just spit it out so they could get back to the agency. She didn't have any more time to waste.

"Don, we really should get back to the office."

"Not yet. Please."

She lifted her eyebrows and stared at him pointedly.

"I do have reasons for asking you for lunch."

Ah, so he did want something. Kasey's curiosity deepened.

"First off, I'd like to take you out to dinner some evening."

Kasey's mouth gaped. She couldn't help it. "As in a date?"

"Why not? You have to know I'm attracted to you."

Kasey shut her mouth, too flabbergasted to speak. "Look, Don—"

"Please, don't say no without hearing me out."

"I really don't think—"

Again he interrupted. "I've seen you look at me, too."

This time Kasey had no trouble speaking. The words just blurted out of her mouth. "Only as an employee,

Don. Nothing else." She hoped she had let him down gently, but she didn't know if she'd accomplished that or not. Who could say? He was turning out to be such a strange duck.

"That could change."

"No, it can't. It won't."

Something flared in his eyes, something she couldn't quite read before it disappeared. Whatever it was increased her discomfort and made her furious that she had put herself in this position. What had she been thinking?

"I'm not giving up."

"I won't have your personal feelings interfering with your work, Don." Again she tried to be as gentle as possible for as long as possible.

"Don't worry. I would never do that. My work is too important. It's all I have."

"At least we're on the same page there," she told him with relief.

"That's why I'd like you to consider taking me on as a partner."

For the second time in a matter of minutes, Kasey's jaw went slack.

"Get the hell out of my way," Tanner barked to the reporters, fury tightening his throat.

"Come on, Mr. Hart, talk to us," one short, wimpy-talking guy pleaded. "Give us a break."

"I'll give you a break, all right," Tanner lashed back. "I'll break your arm if you don't get that thing out of my face."

"You do and I'll sue you," the reporter retorted.

"And I'll back him up," still another said.

"Let him go, Jacob," Daisy Greer chimed in.

"Since he won't talk, we'll have to assume he has something to hide." She paused. "Especially after this second incident."

Tanner didn't bother to make a comeback. Instead, he skirted around the reporters and headed to where Paul stood waiting for him. Out of the corner of his eye, he noticed the media didn't attempt to follow. Had they tried, it wouldn't have done them any good. They weren't allowed in the construction zone.

"Was anyone hurt?"

"No, not this time."

"Thank God."

Paul made a hand gesture. "Actually it's a bloody miracle, considering the damage."

Tanner let his gaze peruse the site, then he motioned to Paul. "Let's go into the shack. I don't want to see or talk to anyone else."

Once inside the metal building, Tanner removed his coat and tie, then rammed his hands through his hair.

"What the hell happened?"

Paul grimaced. "Same as before. A portion of the structure just caved in without warning."

"Shit," Tanner muttered harshly.

He'd been wrapping up a speech to a ladies' luncheon when he'd gotten the call that a wall had caved in. Not bothering to ask any details, he'd left immediately and headed here. Unfortunately the press had beat him.

"I'm sorry about those goddamn vultures."

Tanner knew he was referring to the press. "Did they take a stab at you?"

"They tried."

"I'm assuming you didn't say a word."

"I know when to keep my mouth shut."

Paul's tone told him he'd taken umbrage at his

words. Tanner couldn't help that. He was making no apologies to anyone. What he wanted was answers and damn quick, too. This latest incident had raised the ante to an explosive level both jobwise and careerwise.

"Sorry, but I had to hear you say it."

"I understand," Paul said, letting go of a deep sigh. "It's just a matter of time until this place is crawling with investigators."

"Have you had a chance to inspect the area?"

"Yep." Paul thumped his hard hat. "And again, the material looks sound as concrete."

"Then what the hell is going on?"

"Work, man. Work. This kind of shit happens all the time, but since you're—" Paul broke off, red-faced.

"In the limelight," Tanner said bleakly, "it puts the company under a microscope."

"Exactly." Paul's tone was dark.

"Well, that's just the way it is, and we'll have to live with it. I want to win that senate seat because I think I'm the best man for the job."

"I didn't mean—"

"I know you didn't. But I know this is a lot tougher on you than me since the day to day, hand to hand grind is your responsibility."

Paul's features turned fierce. "That's what you pay me big bucks for, and I'm not about to let you or myself down."

"That goes without saying. But even though there isn't a rat in the woodpile, the media will put one there. Already has, for that matter, meaning we have to cover the company's ass."

"And you have something in mind, right?"

"Yeah. We need to do our own investigating." Tanner rubbed his neck. "And I know just the person to handle that. He owes me a favor."

"Let's get on it, then."

"I'll let you know the details as soon as they're worked out. Meanwhile, I'm headed to my office." Tanner grabbed his coat and walked to the door. "Keep me posted."

"Ms. Sullivan's in your office," his secretary told him the second he walked into company headquarters.

Tanner groaned silently. Irene was the last person he wanted to see right now, though he realized there were forest fires that had to be put out, and she was the one to start the damage control.

On the way here, he'd talked to Jack on his cell, trying to soothe his ruffled feathers.

"Have you spoken to the press?" Irene asked without preamble.

"No, I refused."

"Good. Suppose you tell me what this latest fuckup is all about."

He told her as much as he knew, which at this point, wasn't much.

"Dammit, Tanner, what else is going to happen?"

"It's going to be all right."

"The hell it is," she rebutted, her eyes flashing. "Two megahits in a row will be tough to overcome."

"This brouhaha won't cause me to lose the election," he said coldly.

"I wish I could be so sure."

"It's your job to see that it doesn't."

She laughed without humor, then threw in her own brand of sarcasm. "I'm not superwoman."

"Okay, then, I'll handle it."

A panicked look came over her face. "Not an option."

"Then—" He purposely didn't finish the sentence, but he didn't have to. She got the message.

"You'll be bombarded at the barbecue rally this evening."

"I'm aware of that," he responded in a tired voice.

"I'll call Jack and the others for a conference call. We'll map out a plan."

"Fine." His eyes drilled Irene. "Before you do, I need a moment alone."

Her chin bowed. "I should be able to hear anything you have to say."

"I don't think so." His tone was frigid now. "This is personal."

"Whatever." Irene flounced to the door and jerked it open.

Once she was gone, he felt ashamed. He shouldn't have taken his frustrations out on her. So she stepped on his nerves with her forceful ways. He should just ignore that as he had in the past and not let it bother him. Lately he couldn't seem to do that. He couldn't seem to let anything go. He made a big deal out of everything.

That was because his insides stayed tied in knots. Kasey was the reason. He wanted her so much he literally ached. She was all he could think about. He had tried to fool himself into thinking he had his emotions under control, that he could keep his distance if that was what she wanted.

He knew better.

Without wasting any more time, Tanner picked up the phone. Moments later, he said in a low, tense tone, "Kasey, it's me. I need to see you."

Thirty-Three

"Did anyone ever tell you that you were a good sport?"

Kasey thought for a moment, then cut her eyes up at Tanner who was staring at her from across the picnic table. "Not that I recall."

Tanner smiled. "I find that hard to believe. But in any event, I'm telling you now."

"Well, I have to admit the smell of barbecue mixed with the stifling heat isn't the way I would choose to spend an evening."

"Aw, and miss all this?" Tanner teased, sweeping his hand across the park filled with adults, children, and pets, some sitting at tables wolfing down food while others milled around.

Her heart did a somersault under that glint in his eye. He looked so sexy dressed casually in a pair of jeans, T-shirt and boots. When he'd called and asked her to attend this political function with him, she had barely hesitated. She had ignored her conscience and told him yes.

Perhaps it had been the dejected note she'd heard in his voice that swayed her. Or rather the sound of desperation, like he was on a tight leash that was about to break. She refused to attach a reason to her action, though she hadn't wanted to be alone with her own

thoughts, especially after that unsettling lunch with
Don Hornsby. The gall of that man still had her reeling.

"A penny."

His husky tone forced her to look at him again.
"They're not even worth that."

"Why don't you let me be the judge of that?"

"Okay." She told him about Don and his bizarre
behavior.

Tanner frowned. "Have you ever given him any reason to think you were interested in him?"

"Of course not," she snapped. "He's a nice man
and a good worker, but that's as far as it goes."

"He should run for office, then," Tanner countered
sarcastically. "With his inflated opinion of himself,
he'd be a winner."

"That inflated opinion seemed just to come out of
nowhere. Until now, he's always been just one of the
staff who spoke up only when he had something to
say." Kasey shook her head in wonderment. "I don't
get his sudden aggressive behavior."

"Does he know about the cousin who's after the
agency?"

"They all do."

"He didn't mention that?"

"No. I'm telling you, this just came out of the blue."

"You straightened him out, right?"

"In a heartbeat, but I'm not sure he heard me." She
looked toward the podium, then back at Tanner. "Anyway, I'm not going to worry about Don."

"Has the court date been set?" Tanner asked.

"Yes, but still I'm hoping the suit will simply go
away."

"My attorney can make that happen. You want him
to take a crack at it?"

Kasey gave a start. "Thanks, but that's not necessary."

"I know it's not necessary," Tanner replied in a slightly irritated tone, "I'd just like to help make your life easier."

"I didn't mean to sound ungrateful," she said, feeling herself flounder in unfamiliar territory. Since Mark's death, she was used to solving her own problems. Even if she wanted his help, she couldn't accept it. She'd already reached the danger point in letting Tanner invade her life as much as she had.

"You're just stubborn is the way I see it." Tanner's tone was a bit gruff.

Kasey didn't answer, suddenly distracted by a youngster chasing his dog nearby. Tanner's reserved table was under a huge oak whose full foliage offered some respite from the late evening sun and its sting. He hadn't been off the podium long after surrendering it to another candidate.

"Are you ready to eat?" he asked.

"Not yet. It's still too hot."

"I second that," he said, taking his hand and swiping it across his brow. "Like I said, you're a real trooper letting me talk you into this."

"I came willingly," she said in a slightly breathless tone.

His gaze held hers. "I'm glad."

Don't, she wanted to say because it couldn't last. She was indulging herself once again. But soon it would have to end. When her work for him ended, then they would end. She just prayed her heart wouldn't be broken into such small pieces that she couldn't mend it. If so, it was her own fault. From the get-go, she'd known what was at stake and she'd ignored it.

"The new ads are great," he said, severing their eye contact and the silence. "Did I tell you that?"

"You did."

His gaze slid over her. "But we may have to change them yet again."

"How so?"

He told her about the second accident that morning on the construction site.

"How awful," she responded in dismay. "I'm surprised no reporter grilled you about that."

"They tried even though they don't know the whole story. But they will, after they read the morning paper. The shit will hit the fan again."

"But if it was another accident—"

"It doesn't matter. The fact that it's happening to me and my company is fodder for Butler. Trust me, he and that ballsy reporter, whom I'm convinced are in cahoots, are making the most out of my problems."

"Still, you seem to be holding your own in the polls."

"That's not good enough," Tanner pointed out grimly. "Before Carl got hurt, I was starting to gain real momentum."

"So what's your next move?"

"Punch below the belt, same as Butler."

She paused. "I can do that. All I need is the green light."

"We'll see," Tanner told her in a noncommittal tone, flicking a bug off his arm.

For a second, Kasey was fixated by the flexed strength of that tanned, muscled arm and long fingers. She swallowed and turned away, thinking about how those fingers alone had made her climax over and over.

Feeling her face suffuse with color, she pretended to

bend down and scratch her ankle. When she raised her head, Tanner was staring at her through dark, heated eyes. "You look lovely."

"Sure," she said, followed by a nervous laugh. "With my body all clammy from sweat."

That intensity in his eyes jumped to another level. "I know how to remedy that." His voice was low and hoarse.

Change the subject, she told herself. Don't take the bait. "How?" she eked out.

"Lick every drop off your body."

She sucked in her breath and held it while her heart went crazy. Had she no shame? How could she let him talk to her like that? Because that was what she wanted too. She'd love to feel his tongue on her flesh...

"Dammit, Kasey," he muttered savagely, his eyes never wavering.

She shook herself with a savage gesture. "I think I'm ready for something to eat."

She heard him expel a harsh breath before he got up.

"I'll be right back," he said seconds later.

She watched him as he strode in the direction of the tables loaded with different types of barbecued meats and side dishes. But his progress was slow as he was stopped every few steps by an outstretched hand and a friendly greeting.

Ah, the life of a politician, she thought. The more she knew the less it appealed to her. But Tanner was a natural. He was strong and confident with an inflated ego. She supposed that was what it took to stomach others' constant interference and roll with the punches delivered below the belt.

Her son possessed some of those same traits. Again, like father like son.

Despite the heat, Kasey felt chilled. She had to stop letting those kinds of missiles attack her without warning.

"I hope you're hungry."

She gave a start and peered up at him, glad her eyes were protected by her sunglasses. She was terrified to think he might read forbidden thoughts. "Jeez, look at the food."

Tanner chuckled. "You could use some meat."

"No pun intended, right?"

"Right."

"No way will I make a dent in all this." Her eyes shifted to the huge paper plate in front of her, crammed with brisket, links, potato salad, cole slaw and beans. His was equally laden.

"Give it a try, anyway," he encouraged around a mouthful of food.

They both listened to the speaker while they ate, though from time to time, Kasey felt his gaze rest on her. She strove to keep hers averted for her own protection. Sexual tension was too close to the surface. One look, one touch could set off an explosion.

"It's actually delicious," she finally admitted, smiling at him.

"I just hope mine doesn't sour in my stomach once Butler makes his appearance."

Her fork stuck in midair. "Do you want to leave before that happens?"

"Not on your life."

"It's your call."

"And rob him of the pleasure of taking a pot shot at me in person? No way."

She laughed outright. As she lowered her head, their eyes locked.

"I don't want to stop seeing you. Ever."

Her heart wrenched.

"Well, well, if it isn't Kasey Ellis with the esteemed Tanner Hart."

At first neither Kasey or Tanner responded to the intrusive voice. They continued to stare at each other as though they were alone and not surrounded by throngs of people.

"And sitting here mooning over each other. Who would've ever thunk it."

The familiar voice brought Kasey's head around. Tanner followed suit and was the first to speak. "I don't believe I've had the pleasure." His voice shook with suppressed anger.

"Matt Davenport," Kasey said, her own fury rising at the sight of Ginger's vile husband. "He works for Butler and—"

Tanner stood, chopping off her sentence. "What can I do for you, Mr. Davenport?"

Though Tanner's tone was now smooth and clear, Kasey knew he was trying to come to grips with his anger. His eyes were hard and a muscle ticked in his jaw.

"You can tell Kasey here to leave my wife alone."

"Get lost, Matt," Kasey said before Tanner could respond.

Ignoring Matt, Tanner turned to her. "Who is this guy?"

"My cousin Ginger's abusive husband."

"Hey, bitch, watch your mouth."

Before Kasey could react to that threat, Tanner's hand flew out and grasped Matt's shirt, jerking him within inches of his face. "I suggest you apologize to the lady."

"Let me go, you bastard," Matt spat.

"Not until you do what I said."

"It's all right, Tanner," Kasey said in an uneasy tone, realizing they had created a scene.

"The hell it is." Tanner tightened his hold on Matt whose face was crimson as though he was being strangled. "Apologize."

"All right," Matt screeched. "I'm sorry, Kasey."

Tanner let him go so quickly and unexpectedly that he landed on his butt in the dirt. With hatred burning in his eyes, he scrambled to his feet. "You'll be sorry for this. Just wait until Butler exposes you for what you are. You're one of those greedy bastards who risks others' lives in order to line your own pockets."

Kasey watched in horror as Tanner got back in his face and said, "Go right ahead and try it. But know that I'll return the favor by letting the public know that Butler's not the family man he pretends to be, that he works his mistress over on a daily basis."

Matt's features froze but not before his mouth fell slack.

"Now get the hell out of my sight before I knock the fire out of you."

As if Matt had no doubt Tanner would do just that, he turned and slithered off.

"Come on, let's get out of here."

After they were in the car, Kasey turned to him. "How did you know about Butler and his mistress?"

"I didn't. I don't."

Kasey's eyes widened. "You mean—"

"Yep. I just made it up. Two can play this game, you know."

Kasey groped for a suitable comeback. When nothing came to mind, she merely stared at him while he started the car and drove off.

Thirty-Four

"Hey, Kasey."

She looked up and gave him a smile, though it was less than enthusiastic.

Ah, no matter, Don thought. Any way you cut it, a smile was a smile. Maybe she'd been thinking over his proposal, actually giving it serious consideration.

"Look, I'm more than busy," she told him. "Can't this wait?"

"Not really."

She seemed taken aback by his bluntness, which he tempered by a wide grin. "I have the promise of a new client. A real coup, in fact."

A light flared in her eyes. "Hey, that's great."

Don plopped down on the edge of her desk like he had the right. "Want to hear about it?"

"Of course, but now's really not a good time. Tanner's ads are due out today."

"By the way, I noticed where he's back up in the polls."

"I saw that, too, which is good."

"We can take part of the credit."

"Some, you're right."

He snorted. "Some. That's way too modest. It's your kick-butt-in-a-nice-way strategy that put him on the high road to victory. He ought to be kissing your feet."

"Even if that were the case, it's not just me. It's all of us."

"I'll admit that."

Kasey angled her head. "Let's get together later and talk."

He paused for what he thought was just the right amount of time, then leaned forward. "I hope you're giving some thought to what we discussed over lunch."

He watched the high color drain from her face.

"Actually I haven't," she said.

Keep your cool, Hornsby. Don't let her rile you. Remember you catch more flies with honey than with vinegar. He shrugged. "Hey, no problem. I'm a patient guy. I can wait until you get accustomed to the idea."

Her eyes widened, then she said in a testy tone, "I'm afraid you'll be waiting a long time."

Don smiled. "We'll see. Meanwhile, I'll continue to bust my ass and bring in more business. That's how I'll prove my invaluable worth to you."

"Don—"

He cut her off with a grin and a wave. "See you later."

When he reached his office he closed the door, ducked down behind his desk, pulled out his drug paraphernalia and took a quick snort. Instantly he felt the kick. If he had to, he could walk on fucking water.

He chuckled out loud. Man, was he good, or what? By damn, he was going to get away with murder. Imagine that. And no one was the wiser, certainly not that inept Detective Gallain. Why, he couldn't find his ass with both hands much less pin Shirley's murder on him.

Yeah, things were definitely going his way. He'd make himself indispensable to Kasey, and she'd come around to his way of thinking. It was just a matter of time. As long as he could get his hands on the magic white powder, by whatever means, then nothing could stop him.

He headed to the workroom, laughing out loud.

"What's with you, Hornsby?" Red asked, passing him in the hall. "Get laid, by chance?"

"Maybe," Don quipped. "You jealous, by chance?"

"If I didn't know better, I'd say you were on something."

"Yeah, right," he muttered with another laugh as he kept on going. But when he reached the workroom and realized it was empty, he slumped against the wall like a deflated tire. He'd best be more careful.

She hoped it wouldn't come to firing Don. Kasey rubbed her forehead, then laid her pen down. He had turned into a major headache, one that had caught her unawares. What on earth had gotten into him? She still couldn't believe his audacity.

Partner?

Never.

Go out with him?

Double never.

So how did she convince him of that without creating a big scene? Perhaps she couldn't. If he didn't come to his senses, perhaps he would indeed get his walking papers.

Kasey shook her head, dismissing Don from her mind. He wasn't worth worrying about. He'd get over his delusions of grandeur. If not… She let that thought trail off in her head.

She had much more important items on her agenda.

She'd talked with Brock last evening, and he and Nancy remained joined at the hip, much to her chagrin. She'd tried again to talk some sense into him, but her words hadn't dented his resolve. In order not to alienate him completely, she'd finally backed off and moved to football and computers.

Her son was having the time of his life. And while she was still opposed to his working for Tanner, it didn't seem to be a problem, at least so far. Long distance definitely had its advantages. If Brock had been here, she wouldn't have stood for it.

Oh, yes, you would, she reminded herself. She wouldn't have had a choice.

Thrusting that unpleasant thought aside as well, Kasey got up and stretched her back. She'd been sitting behind her desk for hours working on their new client's ads for the opening of a new store. So far, she was quite pleased with what she'd come up with. She hoped he would be, too.

If the new deal flew, it would mean another windfall for the agency. That combined with what Brock was earning from Tanner would keep the wolf away from her door a bit longer.

The phone jangled beside her.

"Hey, Ginger," she responded enthusiastically, easing back into her chair.

"Matt has finally agreed to a settlement. You're the first to know."

"Well, praise the Lord. What changed his mind?"

Ginger giggled. "I'm inclined to believe Tanner actually knocked some sense into him."

"Think so?"

"Stranger things have happened. As far as I know, Matt's never been bested by anyone. I'm just sorry I wasn't there to witness Tanner making him a new buttonhole.''

''It was something to see, all right.''

''Matt's talking about suing Tanner. That's the way that jerk thinks.''

''Surely he's not that stupid.''

''Trust me, he is,'' Ginger said.

''He's no match for Tanner.''

She had never seen that volatile side of Tanner. And while his actions had given her an incredible sexual rush, she would hate to be on the receiving end of his temper.

''By the way, how is our hero?''

Kasey let the ''our'' slide by. ''Fine, I'm guessing. I haven't seen him since the barbecue. He's been hot on the campaign trail.''

''It shows, too. Despite his run of bad luck on the construction front, he's rebounded and is busting Butler's balls in the polls again.''

Ginger's unladylike terminology drew a spontaneous laugh. ''It appears that way.''

''You sound down. Are you?''

Kasey didn't bother to contain her sigh. ''Just a lot on my mind, that's all.''

''The unsolved murder, for one.''

''I'm not looking over my shoulder quite as much,'' Kasey said, ''but the fear's a constant niggling in the back of my mind.''

''Damn, but I wish that idiot detective would nail the bastard.''

''He's waiting on me to do that,'' Kasey declared in a despondent tone.

''That's why he's an idiot.''

Kasey chuckled again, already feeling much better

just talking to Ginger. "When are we going to get together and celebrate your good news?"

"Not until the divorce is a done deal. Knowing Matt, he's liable to change his mind at any given moment."

"Hopefully that won't happen."

"If not, I'm putting you on notice. We're going to hit some clubs and find us a man."

Kasey laughed. "Heaven forbid."

"Don't give me that. You need to get laid as bad or worse than me."

Kasey felt heat invade her face and was glad Ginger couldn't see her. "I'm making no promises," she said after clearing her throat.

"Next time you see Tanner, give him a big hug for me."

"I'll let you have that honor," Kasey responded lightly.

"I'll look forward to it. Meanwhile, keep me posted on what's going on."

"I will."

Kasey hung up only to have the phone jangle under her hand. Irritated at another interruption, she snapped, "Hello."

"Did I pick a bad time?"

"Yes, no," she said breathlessly.

Tanner chuckled. "I'm glad the no came last."

"Are you home?"

"Yep, for a while anyway."

Silence.

"That's your cue to say I'm glad." His voice had dropped even lower.

"Okay, I'm glad."

"And that you've missed me," he pressed.

Another silence, during which her heart refused to

settle. He was flirting with her, and she was letting him. But when he turned on the charm which he was doing, she was doomed.

"Okay, I'll say it. I've missed you." His voice had dropped another octave.

She swallowed. "You didn't call."

"Not because I didn't want to, believe me. You were on my mind constantly."

Kasey crossed her legs and squeezed them. "I thought about you, too."

"That wasn't so bad, was it?"

"What?" She was being deliberately obtuse.

"Admitting that."

"Yes."

He laughed warmly. "I want to see you." He paused. "Actually I want to be inside you so badly I can't stand it."

She gasped and clutched the phone tighter.

"Does the truth shock you?"

"You shouldn't talk to me like that." Her voice lacked conviction.

"I have an obligation at a nursing home this evening. Come with me, please."

You can end this madness right now. Save yourself further heartache and pain. It's a matter of a simple no.

"All right."

Tanner slowed his gait to match Kasey's as they made their way down another corridor of the nursing facility. They had attended a performance in the activity room put on by several of the residents. It had been a riot, especially since she hadn't known what to expect.

When they'd first arrived, she'd been shocked that Tanner hadn't chose an upscale facility instead of a bona fide nursing home. Here, most of the residents were unable to care for themselves.

"You're really into this, aren't you?" Kasey cut her eyes up to him.

"I told you the elderly are one of my passions."

"It's not for show." Kasey's sentence didn't end with a question mark.

Still, Tanner raised his eyebrows. "And you thought it was, just to get votes?"

"No...yes...maybe."

His jaw tightened, then he said in a fierce tone, "If I'm elected, I'll make a difference. You'll see."

"I hope you do. Nursing home abuse is on the rise and that makes me furious, especially since my mother's in one."

"I keep thinking I might end up here one of these days myself."

"Me, too," she said in a bleak tone.

Before he could reply, a man in an electric cart came racing toward them. Kasey and Tanner both jumped aside just as the old gentlemen grazed a wall.

"Hey, Sam, you're driving a little fast, aren't you?" Tanner said, trying to hold on to his laughter.

"Damn cart," Sam muttered. "I guess I'm going to have to trade it in for a new model."

"Looks that way," Tanner responded, his lips twitching. "Meanwhile, though, you'd best be careful you don't put more dents in it. It'll lower your trade-in value."

"Thanks, Mr. Hart, I'll keep that in mind." He took off again, all the while muttering, "Galdarn vehicle."

Once he was gone, Kasey shifted her gaze back on Tanner. They both grinned.

"How many times have you been here?" she asked as they continued down the hall.

"Too many to count."

"You never cease to amaze me."

"Why?"

"Never mind," she said, shaking her head.

"Come on, there's someone else I want you to meet." He darted into the next room and she followed. A tiny, apple doll of a woman, with features to match, looked up. Instantly her face brightened. "Is that you, sonny?"

"You bet." Tanner leaned over and kissed her on the cheek. "So how's my girl today?"

"Oh, fair to middlin'."

"Good. I have a friend with me. Opal Puckett meet Kasey Ellis."

"Come closer, dearie. These old peepers aren't what they used to be."

Smiling, Kasey did as she was told and grasped the old lady's frail hand in hers. "Hello, Mrs. Puckett."

"Opal, dearie."

"Opal it is."

"So how's Janie?" Tanner asked, motioning for Kasey to sit down in the chair across from Opal. He then took the one next to her.

Opal lifted the doll that was in her lap and held it out to Tanner. "She's not having a good day, either."

Kasey looked on, fighting a lump in her throat, as Tanner took the tattered doll and placed it in the crook of his arm, then began to rock. If she hadn't seen this display of affection with her own eyes, she wouldn't have believed it.

Blinking back tears, Kasey smiled at Opal who took the doll from Tanner. "Thanks for getting her to sleep, sonny."

"Any time, Opal." Tanner stood. "We're going now, but I'll see you soon."

"You promise?"

"Cross my heart," Tanner said with feeling.

"You come back with him, dearie."

Kasey spoke around her tears. "I will."

Fifteen minutes later they stood at the door of her apartment. Darkness had fallen, but the lights from the complex allowed her to admire Tanner's face.

His eyes burned down into hers. "Thanks for going with me."

"You're welcome," she whispered in a shaky voice.

He reached out with the back of his hand and stroked her face. Her heart melted as their eyes continued to hold.

"I want to kiss you so badly I can't stand it."

Her lips parted. "What's stopping you?"

With a groan, he reached for her.

Thirty-Five

Once inside the apartment, Kasey barely managed to lock the door before Tanner grabbed her again, his hot, moist lips seeking hers.

Moaning, she wrapped her arms around his neck and met his tongue thrust for thrust. She was on fire for him and couldn't exist another moment without him inside her.

As if reading her thoughts, he began removing her clothes, then his. His mouth was adhered to hers as he backed her up against the wall.

"Oh, Tanner," she gasped when his fingers nudged her legs apart and entered her while his mouth moved to a nipple and sucked it.

Once her head rolled back as she reached a shuddering climax, he lifted her by the buttocks and entered her. With lips locked on hers, he thrust high and hard. Moments later, they sagged breathlessly against each other.

"I'm sorry," he said roughly against her damp neck.

Her heart faltered. She should be the one sorry, not him. "You are?"

"Yeah, for my lack of patience."

"Do you hear me complaining?"

He laughed as he nuzzled her neck. "It's a good thing, since the wall seems to be a place of choice."

"Whatever works," she muttered against his chest.

"When I get my hands on you, I seem to go crazy." He lifted her and carried her into the bedroom. They lay facing each other on the bed as Tanner reached out and stroked her face.

Kasey couldn't say anything. She felt herself drowning in those deep brown eyes.

"I can't believe this is happening," he finally said in a raspy voice.

"Me, either." Though she had tried to keep her distance physically, she had failed. *Just one more time and that would be it.* Unfortunately she hadn't kept those promises she'd made to herself. She was content, if not eager, to take the detour around them.

"It's fate. I have to think that."

"Tanner—"

"Hey, don't start crawfishing on me now."

Crawfishing? God, if he only knew.

He draped a leg over hers and inched her closer, so close that she knew he was hard again. It would take only one tiny move on her part, and he'd be inside her and everything else but bodily pleasure would be forgotten.

"Hear me out, okay?" he asked in a strained voice.

She feared what he was about to say. Even more, she feared her response.

"I've already told you I don't like leaving you."

"You have no choice."

"We all have choices," he admonished her gently.

"Tanner—"

"Shh. You promised."

"I did no such thing."

"Indulge me." He paused, his eyes searching hers. "Please."

She swallowed around a lump the size of a goose egg, knowing she was opening herself up for heartache beyond any she'd ever suffered. A heart was a terrible thing to break. Two was even worse. Yet it seemed unavoidable; by indulging him, they were on a collision course.

"We're good together, right?"

She nodded.

"I knew that two seconds after I saw you again."

"I don't believe that."

"Believe it. I can't explain it, but something happened inside me, an emotion I'd never experienced before."

"But you were married," she pointed out softly. "Are you saying you didn't love your wife?"

"I loved Norma. She was a loving and giving person, but I wasn't in love with her which I often regretted."

"I'm sorry."

"Don't be. We had a good life and I think I made her happy." He paused and cleared his throat. "Let's talk about us, about you coming back into my life."

"I'm not back in your life," Kasey pointed out in a halting voice.

"You can be."

"What are you saying, Tanner?"

"That I love you and want to marry you."

Tanner strode into his kitchen in his skivvies. He'd made himself a cup of instant coffee only to take a sip, then dump it in the sink. It tasted bitter, like tar. Too bad he didn't have time to brew a fresh pot and drink it leisurely. He had three meetings scheduled that morning, the most important one being a television interview that pitted him against Butler. He wasn't apprehensive in the least. The interviewer was a woman he knew and for whom he had a great amount of professional respect. He was positive she would be able to keep the bit in Butler's mouth. If not, he wouldn't let his opponent goad him into saying something he'd later regret.

Besides, he had the advantage. He was ahead once again in the polls, an accomplishment that both humbled him and frightened him. Greer and Butler's ploy to smear him seemed to have backfired.

Carl had been released from hospital with a clean bill of health from the doctor and was back on the job. The construction site had been inspected by his own people as well as the city's, and to date nothing that would incriminate him or his company had been found. Thankfully those incidences had long ceased to be the gossip of the day. Some other poor mullet now had that honor.

Still, Tanner had no intention of becoming too comfortable and letting his guard down. Between now and election day, he would continue on his chosen path which was to stick to the issues that would make Texas a better place to live for young and old alike.

Yet underneath that shield of caution was festering excitement. He could admit that. His adrenaline was charged, and he felt confident he could face a bear with a switch and whip its ass.

Especially since he had Kasey.

Whoa, Hart. You're getting way ahead of yourself. Much too cocky. She hasn't made a commitment. In light of that brutal reminder, his adrenaline almost dried up.

After telling her he loved her and wanted to marry

her, she had pulled back and stared at him, alarm registered in her wide eyes. Her reaction had stoked his anger.

"You knew, surely," he'd said, trying to suppress his feelings.

"I didn't."

"I don't know why. I've been acting like a lovesick teenager around you from the get-go."

Kasey averted her gaze. "I don't know what to say."

That fired his anger. "I think you just did."

"It's not that simple." Her voice was barely audible.

"Either you love me or you don't. In my book, that's pretty simple." Tears gathered in her eyes, and he groaned. "For God's sake, don't cry."

"I'm not," she denied fiercely.

He didn't argue. Instead he flopped onto his back and stared at the ceiling, feeling as though his insides were in a meat grinder. "I was so sure you felt the same way," he finally added in a dull tone.

"Maybe I do."

Tanner swung back to face her and was about to reach for her when she held out her hands, stopping him.

"Please, don't."

He expelled a harsh breath. "Okay. I'm listening."

"I just need time to digest all this."

He tried to see through the veil she had over her eyes, but he couldn't. "So you're not telling me to get lost."

Silence.

"Dammit, Kasey."

"We don't fit," she said in a weak voice.

Her labored breathing affected the rise and fall of her exposed breasts. He focused on them greedily, aching to touch them again, to suck those pink nipples into hard pebbles. He turned his head.

"We fit, all right." His tone was thick. "Perfectly."

"I wasn't talking just about sex."

"Me, either."

"My life is in such a mess right now, Tanner."

"I'm here for you."

"I know. Just give me some space, let me sort through some things."

"Fine."

She turned and was about to get out of bed. He grabbed her arm. "You haven't answered my question," he said in a strangled voice. "Do you love me?"

"I don't know," she cried before fleeing to the bathroom and slamming the door.

Later at the door, he had kissed her; for a second, she had clung to him. Pushing her away had been the hardest thing he'd done. But until she knew her own heart, he had to let her go. He had told her he would be in touch.

Now, after rehashing that conversation in his mind, Tanner wondered if she was playing him for a fool. No. She loved him. His gut instinct told him that. She was scared to make a commitment for reasons he knew and reasons he didn't.

He saw the past as the biggest hurdle to jump.

And if it was time she needed, then time she would get. As long as she loved him, that was all that mattered. Realizing he'd indulged himself long enough, Tanner made his way into the bathroom. His hand was on the shower faucet when he heard the doorbell chime.

"Great," he muttered, turning and striding into the foyer. If it was Irene, he was not going to be happy.

She had a bad habit of dropping by unannounced, a habit he was about to help her break.

By the time he reached the door, the loud chimes had assaulted his ears several more times.

"Dammit, Tanner, open the door."

"All right, already." He jerked on the handle and stepped aside as a red-faced Jack Milstead crossed the threshold.

"Is your TV on?" he demanded without preamble.

"Nope."

He handed Tanner the morning paper from his doorstep. "You obviously haven't seen the news."

"You're right." Tanner forced himself to ignore Jack's sarcasm and remain cool until he knew what had his friend so riled.

"The shit's hit the fan again."

"How so?"

Jack tossed him the paper. "That reporter's done another number on you."

Tanner grimaced.

"It's all there in black and white. But before you read it, I suggest you sit your ass down."

Tanner quirked an eyebrow, then scanned the front page. "I'll be a son of a bitch."

"Is it true?" Jack asked, glaring at him. "Were you and Shirley Parker involved?"

"I don't like the way you say that word, Jack."

Jack's glare hardened. "I don't give a damn whether you like it or not. Is it true?"

"I knew Shirley. I'll admit that. But we weren't involved, not in the way Daisy Greer has insinuated in this article."

"Did you have a relationship?" Jack pressed.

"No, dammit, we didn't."

Jack glowered at him. "Would Parker have said the same thing?"

"I can't speak for her." Tanner's voice was terse.

"Well, it's too bad we can't ask her, isn't it?"

Tanner's lips thinned. "Cut the sarcasm, Jack. It's falling on deaf ears."

"Well, you can bet this article isn't. That woman has dropped another grenade in our lap and it's exploded. Your political career just might be over and done with."

Tanner stalked to the window, his mind in an uproar. If Jack knew what was circling in his mind like vultures over a dead animal, he'd really be livid. *Kasey*. His heart stopped beating for a millisecond, and he broke out in a cold sweat. What would *she* think?

"I can't believe you thought you could keep this hot potato a secret."

"I didn't think about it one way or the other."

Jack cursed again.

"Greer has blown it all out of proportion, Jack."

"Let's just pray the police and the voters see it that way. They're the ones who count. But after reading this article, I'm afraid both are going to think you're a lowlife bastard who might have killed her."

Tanner clenched his jaw so tightly he feared it might snap.

The phone rang.

"Don't answer that," Jack barked. "It's probably Irene, anyway."

"She won't call. She'll show up on the doorstep like you."

"Cancel all your appointments, and we'll gather the troops in the war room and go from there."

"I'm scheduled for a TV interview with Butler this morning."

"Holy shit."

"Maybe I should keep it."

Jack's face turned beet red. "Have you lost your mind?"

"Not hardly." Tanner's tone was as hard and cold as steel. "But I will take your suggestion under advisement."

A heavy silence invaded the premises.

"Tell me, Tanner," Jack finally said, "were you fucking Shirley Parker?"

Thirty-Six

"Have you seen today's paper?"

"Good morning to you, too," Kasey said in response to Ginger's bluntness after answering the phone.

"Go get your paper. Now. Then sit down."

"Not until you give me a hint what this is all about."

"You'd best see for yourself."

"I have a feeling I'm not going to be overjoyed."

Silence.

"Ginger."

"Just go read the paper, Kasey, then we'll talk."

"You're frightening me. It's about Tanner, isn't it?"

"Yes."

"Butler's really done a number on him this time, huh?"

"It's not Butler."

It wasn't so much what Ginger said, but the way she said it that sent chills through Kasey.

"Stop stalling."

"Okay, okay." Frowning, Kasey walked to the table, opened the paper and scanned the front page.

Tanner Hart And Shirley Parker Involved?

"Oh, my God," Kasey cried, grabbing her stomach and sinking into the nearest dining room chair.

"Are you all right?" Ginger demanded into the silence. "Of course, you're not all right. What a dopey question."

"I'm shocked and sick is what I am," Kasey whispered, trying desperately to come to grips with what she'd just read. *Tanner and Shirley?* No way. It made no sense. It was a mistake. It had to be. He would've told her.

"Kasey, I know this has to zing you real bad, especially since you work so closely with him."

Hysteria bubbled close to the surface as last night's event stampeded through her mind. He loved her and she loved him. Oh, God. She grabbed her stomach again and bent over.

"Look, maybe this is just a bunch of garbage. This Greer woman obviously has it out for Tanner, so wait until you hear his side before you make a judgment."

"Thanks for calling me," Kasey managed to say with quivering lips. "I'll talk to you later."

"What are you going to do?" Ginger asked, anxiety upping the range of her voice.

"Nothing at the moment."

"I think that's wise."

Another bout of hysteria almost choked Kasey. *He's my lover and the father of my child,* she wanted to scream. *How could sitting idle be wise?*

"However," Ginger went on, "your work for him is about done, anyway." She paused. "Isn't it?"

"Yes," Kasey said in a numbed voice.

"Then you won't come out any worse for wear if this brouhaha turns into a smoking gun."

"Okay."

"Okay what? Obviously you didn't hear a thing I said."

"I'm sorry, Ginger, it's just that I'm not thinking straight right now." Her mouth was bone dry and her stomach burned like acid.

"I know and I understand. He's a great guy and until somebody proves otherwise, he's still getting my vote." She paused with a sigh. "All that other stuff aside, the idea that he popped Shirley is too ludicrous to be true."

"I agree," Kasey said, trembling all over.

"Promise you'll call me, the minute you know something."

"I promise."

With that, Kasey hung up. For the longest time, she remained at the table, too paralyzed to move. Her mind, however, was on a roll.

Tanner and Shirley.

Tanner and Shirley.

Tanner and Shirley.

Those words, together, kept playing over and over in her mind like a skipping forty-five record.

It was a mistake. It had to be. Like Ginger had said, Daisy Greer was after Tanner in order to make a name for herself. Sensational journalism was what that awful woman was about. A grandstander. She didn't care about facts, or she wouldn't have wasted her time or her readers' by writing untruths.

Yet where there was smoke there was fire. Trite as that may be, it held merit. Tears stung her eyes as she rubbed her head. He had told her he loved her. To think, she had almost told him that love was reciprocated, regardless of how foolish that would've been.

Now, however, if he and Shirley had had a relationship, then...

Kasey's mind simply shut down, refusing to go there. Trembling, she stood, only to then race to the toilet where she lost the contents of her stomach.

Richard Gallain's eyes were on the ceiling. "There is a God."

If it wouldn't have raised eyebrows, he would've pulled a Gene Kelly and danced through the halls of the precinct, kicking his heels together while he was at it.

However, Gallain reined in those heightened emotions, though it was tough containing his excitement. He had finally gotten a break in the Parker case. Although he couldn't take the credit per se—a fact that rankled when he thought about it—he wasn't about to let that stop him from refocusing his investigation.

On Tanner Hart.

Gallain scratched his head and smiled. If he'd been told things would turn on a dime and in such a freakish way, he would've laughed, and not with any humor, either.

He had busted his ass for countless hours on the Parker case only to continue to come up empty-handed. But he hadn't given up, though he felt like he was shitting in one hand and wishing in the other. It was obvious which one was getting full the fastest.

Then Daisy Greer had waltzed into his office with a shit-eating grin on her face and given him a new lease on life. And a real shot at that promotion.

For that reason alone, he had wanted to grab Greer and hug her. He'd refrained, however, fearing she wouldn't think twice about cold-cocking him for such a move.

"How the hell did you uncover this juicy bone?" he had asked after she'd filled him in.

"Like you, I have sources, which will remain unnamed."

"How 'bout proof, Ms. Greer?"

"That, Detective, is your department." She paused. "Though my part is still ongoing."

"There's more?" He felt an added rush.

"Maybe, maybe not."

She was being deliberately coy. Why? Suddenly his good nature took a turn for the worse. "This is not a game, Ms. Greer," he told her coldly. "This is a murder investigation. Need I remind you of that fact?"

She remained unflustered under his sharp attack. "And need I remind you that you and this department have come up with zip so far?"

His anger fired, but he cooled it. "Trust me, I would've eventually nailed her killer."

Daisy's lips curled. "Sure thing."

"Is there anything else, Ms. Greer?" he asked, deliberately letting her insult slide. What the hell? She was one of those women who lived to grow balls. For the moment, he didn't mind helping her do just that. But when he got tired of her and her mouth, he'd put her in her place. Gallain cleared his throat. "You mentioned there might be more. Care to elaborate on that?"

"Not at the moment. When it happens, *if* it happens, you'll be the second to know."

"I'm going to hold you to that, Ms. Greer."

"So what's your feel on Hart?" she asked in a more conciliatory tone. "Do you think he might've killed Parker?"

Gallain played it cool. "In light of what you've un-covered, I'm not ruling that out, though it seems pretty far-fetched, especially without concrete evidence."

"So are you going to bring him in for questioning?"

"I'm not at liberty to answer that question."

She laughed without humor, then said, "Sure you are. You just won't. But that's okay. I understand. You've got to do your thing, make up for lost time, I would imagine."

"That's right," he said.

"So do we have a deal?"

He ran a hand over his jowls. "Deal?"

"Yeah. I've scratched your back. If your investiga-tion of Hart turns up something, then I expect you to scratch mine, so to speak."

"What's with you and Hart, anyway?"

"What do you mean?" Daisy's face was guileless.

Gallain smirked, then indulged her. "It's obvious you don't like the guy. I'm just curious as to why."

"I don't have any feelings for him one way or the other. Tanner Hart is news, pure and simple, with a lot to lose if he screws up. If I smell a story, I attack."

"And if that attack is unwarranted?"

Daisy shrugged, then pinned his gaze. "Like you, I take my lumps and move on."

Gallain merely looked at her.

"So again, do we have a deal?" she asked.

"I'll take it under consideration. Now, if you'll ex-cuse me."

Since that conversation yesterday afternoon he'd thought of little else. But he hadn't made his move on Hart yet, waiting for the headlines to be the first to hit him below the belt. That way Tanner would be good and vulnerable, making it easier for him to move in for the kill.

Wouldn't it be pure gold if that cocky bastard had been the one who put those bullets in Parker? Could he be that lucky?

Man oh man, he'd almost give up one of his nuts to cuff that do-gooder who thought his shit didn't stink because he had more money than he had brains. Gallain peered at his watch. Hart was bound to have seen the papers. Now was as good a time as any to approach him.

Gallain pitched his head back and laughed.

"What's so damn funny?"

He whipped his head around and watched as his boss, Harold Clayton, strode through the door. Gallain instantly rearranged his features back to his old stoic self. "The thought of Hart's tail in a crack."

"Is that reporter on to something or is she just sniffing?"

"I'm about to find that out."

"Where did she get her information?" Clayton asked.

"She wouldn't tell me."

"If this newsflash turns out to have so much as a grain of truth to it, then find out whose hand she greased. We'll need to talk to him or her."

"She may not give up her source."

"Oh, I'm sure you can convince her that cooperating with us is in her best interest."

"She hinted there's more to come."

"Why did you let her off the hook, then?"

"I tried to probe, but she clammed up."

"Don't wait on her. Talk to Hart. ASAP. Go by the book so this one won't get away."

"You got it."

* * *

Don Hornsby ran his tongue over the mole above his lip before he lunged out of the ratty chair at his sister's house. He had just heard the news on TV about Tanner Hart and Shirley.

"Fucking unbelievable," he muttered into the empty room, then walked over and flicked off the tube.

Had Hart been banging Shirley, too? It didn't matter. Innocent or not, it looked like Hart might hang for her murder. Talk about falling in a tub of shit and getting up smelling like a rose, that was him.

He sucked in his stomach, pounded his expanded chest and let out a war whoop. If only Flora didn't make it following her latest tumble from the wheel-chair, he'd be set. Right now, she was in intensive care fighting for her life. He'd made the cursory visits to check on her only because it would earn him brownie points in Kasey's eyes.

Thinking of Kasey made him chuckle. Wonder what she was thinking about their stellar client? If Shirley's murder was pinned on Hart, would that affect the agency? Probably not. Still, it would be a blow to her and she would need support.

And guess who would be there to offer it? *Yours truly.*

Thirty-Seven

"You know, don't you?"

Kasey could barely meet Tanner's hooded eyes much less answer his question as he stood at her front door. He looked like hell. Disheveled. Tired. Exhausted. Tormented. Any and all those adjectives fit. Yet she didn't feel sorry for him. He'd put himself in this deplorable situation.

"I know," she responded in a dull tone, still refusing to meet his gaze.

"Are you going to invite me in?"

She stalled, her simmering rage close to breaking the surface. She was over the shock. Anger had taken its place. "I'm late for work."

"Dammit, Kasey, I...we need to talk."

Only because he sounded like he was teetering on the edge did she comply. She stepped aside and watched as he strode inside, his gait registering his dejection. She steeled herself not to let her love for him cloud her sound judgment or temper her anger. There was no excuse for Tanner to deliberately withhold that information from her.

"Do you want some coffee?" she asked, filling the refrigerated silence.

"How 'bout a gallon?"

His attempt at humor proved a failure. She didn't

smile nor did he. "I'll get you a cup." She turned and went into the kitchen, leaving him standing in the middle of her living room.

But when she had the coffee poured and on the tray, she realized he had followed her. He stood just inside the kitchen door. "Need any help?" he asked, his eyes probing, as though trying to catch hers and hold them.

"No, thanks," she said in a cold voice.

He expelled a harsh sigh.

She handed him his cup.

"Want to sit in here?" he asked.

"Let's go into the breakfast room." The small glass-topped table in the kitchen was too close, too intimate. She needed more space between them. As it was, she could barely breathe with him in the room.

How could you have done this to me?

Holding the silence, Tanner gestured for her to get ahead of him. Once they were seated in the breakfast alcove, Kasey still didn't diffuse the crackling tension. Instead she peered out the window and watched a blue-bird that was perched on the railing bathe itself.

"Kasey, please, don't do this."

She swung her head around, tensing her lips. "What?"

"Shut me out. I need to explain, and I need you to listen." He paused and angled his head. "More than anything, I need you to trust me."

She gave an incredulous stare. "Trust you?"

What little color was in his face drained from it, then it took on a fierce look. "Yes, dammit, trust me."

She flared back, "Under the circumstances, don't you think that's asking a lot?"

"Okay, I should've told you."

"Yes, you should have." She paused and took several sips of her coffee, using the cup to steady her hands. "So why didn't you?"

"At first, I didn't see the need."

"That's a piss-poor excuse."

For a second, a smile relaxed his lips. Then it disappeared, and his features contorted once again. "I didn't know I was going to fall in love with you."

Kasey sucked in her breath, her eyes widening. From the outside she heard a car door slam, then a dog bark. Normal things. Mundane things. Not like what was happening in her life right now. She didn't want to be here. She didn't want to be having this conversation with him. She didn't want him to tell her he loved her, for God's sake. Not ever again.

Suddenly her stomach pitched, rejecting the coffee. She set the cup down and tore her eyes off him.

"I realized how I felt, but then I just couldn't find the words."

Hurt, anger and betrayal were all lumped together. She didn't know which one was the stronger. "No matter how hard I try, I can't put you and Shirley together."

"We weren't together," Tanner countered in a savage tone, lunging out of the chair, his coffee untouched. "Not in the way you mean, that is."

"Were you sleeping with her?" The words were so softly spoken Kasey wasn't sure he heard her.

He swung around, his eyes narrowed to slits, his breathing heavy. "No, dammit."

"Then what does involved mean?"

"You'll have to ask Daisy Greer that."

"I'm asking you."

"We were business acquaintances and friends."

She wanted to believe him, but there was more. He

wasn't telling all. Her instinct told her that. God, why was she putting herself through this torture, anyway? She loved him, but since they had no future, it didn't matter whether he and Shirley had something going or not.

"You believe me, don't you?"

"I don't know what I believe anymore," she whispered, finally meeting his eyes. "But I'm not the one who matters."

"To me, you are."

"What about your constituents?"

"Screw them. They'll either believe me or they won't."

"Which means you could lose the election."

"Then I lose the election."

"You don't mean that, Tanner."

"Yes, I do. It's you I don't want to lose."

Kasey's heart twisted under his husky confession, but she remained strong and didn't give in to her urge to jump up, launch herself into his arms and tell him she forgave him. Unfortunately it wasn't that easy. While they couldn't ignore the fire that still burned between them, their relationship had undergone a major blow. "If you and Shirley were just friends, then you should be all right," she finally told him in a halting voice.

He swallowed hard, making his Adam's apple work overtime. "I have nothing to hide. That's why I'm going to tell you this."

She cringed inwardly. She'd been right. There was more, only she didn't want to hear it. She feared her heart couldn't hold up under the load.

"Tanner—"

"I was with Shirley the day she was murdered."

Kasey gasped, then sank her teeth into her lower lip to stop it from trembling. "I'm not surprised."

"You knew?"

"Of course, I didn't know," she snapped. "It's just that I sensed you were hiding something."

"I wasn't hiding anything," he stressed vehemently.

She shrugged, which seemed to fuel his anger. She didn't care. Right now, she just wanted him to just go away and let her nurse her misery in solitude.

"We had an argument."

He paused, and she knew he wanted her to ask him what it was about, but she had no intention of doing so. Anyway, she felt sure he would tell her even if he sensed her reluctance to hear it.

"She wanted more from me than I was prepared to give."

"She wanted to sleep with you," Kasey said, cutting to the brutal truth.

"Yes, though I never gave her any reason to think I was interested in her that way. Finally I told her that wasn't ever going to happen, and she might as well move on."

"Never in a million years would I have put you two together."

"We *weren't* together," he stressed again.

"You must've given her some reason to think there could be more between you." Her tone was venomous along with her thoughts. Both unfair, which tapped into her own guilt, resulting from the secrets she was keeping from him.

Tanner trapped her gaze. Instantly the air crackled with tangible sparks. "I swear I never led her on. I took her to dinner several times, that's all. She was interested in politics and wanted to help with my campaign. Or so she led me to believe.'' He crammed his hands in his pockets.

"Did anyone hear you argue?"

"Not to my knowledge."

"What if that Greer woman uncovers that?"

"Then, I'll deal with it. Meanwhile, I'll fear the worst and hope for the best."

Kasey ran a finger around the top of her cup, her mind scattering in a million different directions.

"When I left Shirley, she wasn't happy with me, I'll admit. But she was upright and breathing."

"I just wish I'd known her better. If I had, maybe I'd have a clue who would want to murder her." Kasey shivered.

"Then you know it wasn't me," he said in a grim tone. "That I could never do such a thing."

"Oh, Tanner, I just wish you'd told me you knew Shirley, that you two had a relationship."

"Dammit, stop saying that."

"What about Gallain? Don't you think he'll be knocking on your door?"

"Let him knock. I'll do whatever it takes to clear my name."

She attempted another sip of coffee. When she put the cup down, Tanner was staring at her again. "I want to know how you feel, Kasey. How you really feel."

He didn't try to hide his pain which didn't make her reply any easier. "I can't say because I honestly don't know. The fact that you were *friends* with Shirley and never told me is hard for me to accept."

His jaw knotted with tension. "Maybe that's because you don't want to."

"Maybe you're right," she lashed back.

Kasey jumped as his cell phone rang.

Tanner cursed, then barked, "Yes," into the tiny receiver. After listening a few seconds, he snapped the case shut. "Jack and Irene are waiting for me. I have to go."

Her chest rose and fell. "That's a good idea."

They looked into each other's eyes until the silence turned stifling.

"Promise we'll talk later."

Her gaze didn't flinch. "I won't...can't make that promise, Tanner."

Kasey glared down at the paper one more time. And winced one more time.

Senatorial Candidate To Be Questioned In Parker Murder

Kasey crumpled the headlines into a tiny wad and tossed it in the trash. Otherwise, she would continue to read it over and over as if to punish herself for falling in love with a man who was forbidden to her.

And whom she no longer trusted.

It had been three days since she'd had that painful conversation with Tanner. He hadn't tried to call her nor she him, although she needed to run some new brochure ideas by him. But that could wait, she reminded herself, knowing he had more important things on his mind.

Proving his innocence, for starters.

Pushing a strand of hair out of her eyes, Kasey poured cereal into a bowl and sat down at the table. But she couldn't eat. Her appetite was nonexistent. Her gaze strayed to the trash. The balled article seemed to taunt her. She jerked her eyes away.

She had been afraid the reporter would uncover the fact that Tanner and Shirley had argued the day of her murder. What she hadn't counted on was that someone had heard them and seen Tanner leave the scene.

Feeling herself unraveling on the inside, Kasey grabbed her stomach and leaned forward.

Moments later, the doorbell peeled. *Tanner?* With her heart pounding overtime, she went to the door. With relief, she opened it.

"Don't you just love it when I show up on your step unannounced?"

Kasey hugged Ginger. "I'm really glad to see you."

"I bet you are. So you've seen the headlines?"

"More times than I care to share."

"I'm on my way to work, so I can't stay."

"Sure you can, at least for one cup of coffee."

Ginger half smiled. "You twisted my arm."

Moments later they were in the living room, silence filling the space between them. Ginger was the first to break it. "You've been crying, haven't you?"

Kasey's first thought was to deny it, then knew it wouldn't do any good. Ginger would know she was fibbing. "That I have."

"I'm afraid he'll never beat Butler now. Today's headlines probably nixed his political career for good."

"I agree."

"And after all your hard work." Ginger paused, added in a rushed tone, "Thing's have gotten serious between you two, right?"

Shock froze Kasey's hand.

"I've suspected it wasn't just a casual affair for sometime now, but I haven't said anything. I respected your privacy. More than that, I wanted you to confide in me."

Kasey blew out an uneven breath. "I don't know what to say."

"The truth would do."

"Okay, I've been seeing him much more than I should."

"Which means you're still sleeping with him."

Kasey felt heat sting her face.

Ginger grinned and raised a thumb. "All I'm going to say is bully for you."

"It's not what you think," Kasey said in a rush.

Ginger looked taken aback. "And just what am I thinking?"

"That we're...we're—" Kasey broke off, batting the air with her hand. "An item, but that couldn't be further from the truth."

"Hey, you don't have to convince me. I'm just glad you found someone to see."

"It's really much more complicated than that."

Ginger raised her eyebrows then said, "I'm sure, in light of what's just happened."

Kasey wanted to tell her that Tanner's liaison with Shirley was only one of many reasons she couldn't be a part of his life.

"I can't believe that little twit of a reporter insinuated that Tanner could be Shirley's killer."

"That's a low, dirty blow."

"Why, it's ludicrous. Why would a man like Tanner Hart throw it all away on a woman like Shirley Parker?"

"You'll have to ask him that."

"Did you know about any of this?"

"He told me about his argument with Shirley," Kasey said, "but not that he'd been seen. That's because he didn't know it."

"I imagine Gallain smells blood and is nipping at his heels about right now."

"It makes me sick just thinking about it," Kasey said.

Ginger took several gulps of her coffee, then stood. "Gotta go. Let me know if anything else develops. Meanwhile, keep your chin up. Tanner Hart's a survivor. I'm betting on him."

Once Ginger was gone, the apartment was too quiet. Suddenly Kasey didn't want to be alone with her thoughts. She shuddered to think what Tanner must be going through with the media circus, the new polls popping up, and the police interrogation.

She wanted to believe every word he told her if for no other reason than that he was the father of her child. But there were other reasons that she couldn't ignore. She'd slept with him. She loved him.

But did she know him? Really know him?

Thirty-Eight

"**Y**ou should've taken counsel with you."

"I didn't need a lawyer, Jack." Tanner tried to keep the testiness out of his voice but wasn't successful. "I went to see Gallain voluntarily."

"I still don't think that was a smart idea," Jack argued. "But then, you were always one to do things your way." A deep cough forced him to pause. After clearing his throat, he went on, "The police would love to arrest someone for that woman's murder. And the thought that someone could be you must have them dancing in the precinct halls, especially Gallain."

Tanner tightened his lips as he flung a glance at Jack. A strategy meeting between Irene, Jack, Woody and several others on his front-line team had just ended. The main topic of discussion, of course, was how to repair the damage that had been done by the morning's headlines.

When the powwow had ended, the others had gone their various ways each armed with his assignments. The only critical one missing from the get-together had been Kasey. Tanner had wanted her input since they planned to counteract some of the damage with a new advertising blitz.

But he had refrained from including her, knowing that wouldn't have been wise since they had parted on less than amicable terms. She had been teetering on the brink of mistrust then. After this latest fiasco, he didn't want to think about what was going through her mind. His heart wrenched out of fear and need.

"So what went down with Gallain?" Jack asked.

"I've already told you."

"Not really. You just touched on the high points in front of the others. I want to know in detail what the little prick said to you. And what he thinks."

"Little prick, huh?"

Jack battered his hand. "Whatever."

Tanner's smile never quite matured. "He just kept drilling me about my relationship with Shirley, especially why we argued."

"I'd like to know that, too. I should've learned about the argument from you, not from the media."

"I apologize for that, Jack. It was poor judgment on my part, but that's water under the bridge now."

"So back to why you argued," Jack said in an exasperated tone.

"She wanted us to be more than friends, and I said no."

"That's it?"

Tanner grimaced. "Pretty much, although it wasn't that simple to Shirley. She didn't want to take no for an answer."

"Did you ever give her any reason to think you had a thing for her?"

"Nada. Zip. She was a friend and a staunch supporter, and that's all. Oh, I took her out to dinner several times during which we discussed my chances of beating Butler."

"Only she wanted more."

"That's the bottom line."

"And the fact that you told her no made a fool out of her."

"That certainly wasn't my intention."

Jack merely shook his head at the same time he fingered his mustache. "Go on."

"Shirley started screaming at me, accusing me of leading her on, and as you pointed out, making a fool out of her."

"A woman scorned," Jack muttered.

"The more I tried to reason with her, the more upset she got."

"So what did you do?"

"I told her I was sorry and headed for the door. She followed me outside where she stung me with a few more zingers. Apparently that's when someone heard her."

"How did you respond?"

"I told her she should get a life."

Jack cursed. "Not so great a comeback. I bet that sent her back into orbit."

"Probably. But that's when I got in my car and drove off. I never saw her again."

"And that evening she got popped." Jack shook his head.

Tanner pinned Jack with narrowed eyes. "You don't think I had anything to do with her murder, do you?"

"Shit, you know better than to ask that. But my opinion doesn't count, not with anyone who matters, that is."

"It damn sure matters to me," Tanner countered fiercely. Just like it mattered with Kasey. It was imperative that people closest to him believe in him.

"You have to know I'm going to do everything in my power to save your ass along with your political career,'' Jack said. ''So is Woody. He's not even thinking about jumping ship. In fact, he's going to kick in more money to make sure you win.

''That aside for now, how do you think Gallain's going to play this?''

''He's looking at me as a suspect.''

Jack rattled off several expletives. ''All the more reason why you should've had your attorney with you.''

''Then I would've looked guilty. And I have nothing to hide.''

''I'm assuming you held your own.''

''He didn't get to me, if that's what you're wondering.''

''Thank God. But if he considers you a suspect, then he won't give up. He'll dog you to death.''

''Let him. It won't do him any good.''

''No, but that nipping could sure as hell shitcan your political career.''

Tanner kept his emotions intact, though his stomach was churning. ''I'm going to do my level best not to let that happen.''

''Do you think Parker told anyone about her feelings for you?''

''Gallain asked the same thing. I told him I didn't have a clue. Apparently, though, he hasn't found anyone, or he would've beat me over the head with it.''

''Trust me, he'll find something else to beat you with. Since the cops have been batting zero on this one, they're going to sink their teeth into you and not let go.''

''Let Gallain and whoever else take their best shot. I never laid a hand on Shirley. I'll go to my grave swearing that.''

"You may have to." Jack rubbed his forehead. "I just wish Kasey Ellis would remember something."

The mention of Kasey's name sent a jolt through him. "Well, she doesn't."

The rough edge to his voice wasn't lost on him or Jack who gave him a strange look. "How can you be so sure?"

"What does that mean?" Tanner asked, stalling. He didn't want to discuss Kasey with him. Where she was concerned, he was too vulnerable.

"Maybe she's hiding something." Jack shrugged. "Hell, after all, she was the woman's partner, and the business was in trouble." He broke off with another shrug. "Get my drift?"

"I get it, all right," Tanner responded in an icy voice. "But you don't want to go there."

"Why the hell not?"

"Because Kasey Ellis is not involved. Period."

Jack's bushy brows shot up. "You sound awfully sure about that."

"I am."

"Well, I still say it's a damn shame she doesn't know anything. It would certainly get you off the hook."

"I don't want her involved in this."

"Only she is involved."

"You know what I mean."

"Dammit, Tanner, you need all the help you can get. If this woman can—"

"She can't," Tanner bit out. "Gallain already had several runs at her, and she doesn't know anything. She's been through enough."

Even if that hadn't been the case, Tanner wasn't about to use Kasey to further his own agenda. That thought was so repugnant that it hadn't even crossed his mind. He was just sorry it had crossed Jack's.

He wasn't ready to share his feelings for Kasey with anyone. In light of the political race, anything and everything he did was news. If the media so much as got a whiff that he was seriously involved with a woman, especially Kasey, they would turn it into a feeding frenzy.

No way would he set Kasey up to take that kind of abuse. He would protect her against further hurt at all costs.

"You sure are going out of your way to defend that Ellis woman."

"She saw her partner murdered, for heaven's sake."

Jack seemed to weigh those words before adding, "Is that the only reason you're protecting her?"

"Yes," Tanner said with stern emphasis, "it is."

Jack's eyes never wavered. "Why do I get the feeling I'm missing something here?"

Tanner ground his jaws together, though he couldn't control the flood of color that invaded his face.

"Holy shit," Jack muttered in an awed tone.

Tanner continued to hold his silence, though he felt like he could chomp a nail in two.

"Ah, so I get it. You and Kasey—" Jack broke off and rubbed his jaw, activating his ruddy color. "Well, well now."

"Drop it, Jack."

"I hope to hell you know what you're doing, son."

Tanner held his silence.

Jack looked like he wanted to explore that subject further but Tanner's tone apparently discouraged that, so he moved on. "What say we talk about your upcoming press conference, what you're going to say and how you're going to say it?''

"Good idea. But let me get Irene back here first. She'll have a conniption fit if I don't.''

Tanner reached for the phone, then a few minutes later rolled up his shirtsleeves and picked up his pen, feeling more helpless than he'd ever felt in his life.

"I hope I'm not intruding.''

You're lying, Kasey thought, staring at Detective Gallain. *You don't care if you're intruding or not.* In fact, she would bet his poor timing was planned just like everything else he did. However, she had no intention of letting him see that she was hesitant or leery that he had come unannounced into her office.

"What can I do for you, Detective?'' she asked, wondering how many times she'd asked that same question.

"My agenda never changes, Mrs. Ellis.''

"Nor does my story.''

"Story? Ah, now that's an odd choice of words.''

"You know what I mean,'' she said tersely, her temper flaring.

"So you're sticking to your statement?''

"Yes. If it ever changes, you'll be the first to know, Detective.''

"Mind if I sit down?''

"Not at all.''

After he'd taken a seat, he took his time saying anything, which stretched her nerves. However, she wasn't about to give him the satisfaction of knowing that.

"I'm sure you've seen the papers,'' he said at last.

So that was why he was here. Tanner. Her heart took a nosedive. "Yes, I have.''

"I'd like your opinion on that."

"I don't have one."

"Sure you do," Gallain countered with seemingly easy confidence.

"Why would you think that?"

"You work for him, quite closely, I would imagine."

"What are you saying, Detective?"

"I'm saying, or rather hoping, that he might've said something about his involvement with Ms. Parker."

She got up, turned her back and walked to the window. Through the double-paned glass, she could feel the heat outside. Texas in July was a bitch. Suddenly her thoughts, still centered on Tanner, pictured him on the campaign trail, his face and body glistening with sweat under the sweltering heat.

"Did he, Mrs. Ellis?" Gallain pressed.

She swung around, keeping her features bland. "No, he didn't."

"Ah, so you didn't know he'd had a relationship with the deceased?"

"It wasn't a relationship," she said before she thought.

"He did talk to you, then?" Gallain voice was on high alert.

"He admitted he and Shirley were acquainted," she said with reluctance, "but he never mentioned they argued."

"Sure about that?"

"I'm sure," she snapped, taking umbrage to his assumption that she was lying. She didn't owe Tanner her allegiance, yet she was giving it to him. She had chosen to take his side against this persistent man's. Probably not a wise choice, either.

''We now consider Hart a suspect, Mrs. Ellis.''

Kasey gave him a stunned look. ''You actually think he killed Shirley Parker?''

''I think it's a good possibility.''

''That's ludicrous.''

''Is it? Think about this. What if he's using you?''

''I don't know what you mean.''

''Then I'll explain. What if he hired your agency in order to keep an eye on you?''

''I'm not following you, Detective.''

''Okay, I'll make it real simple.''

Under his patronizing tone, Kasey's temper almost got the best of her. But her only response was to glare at him.

''You're the only person who witnessed the murder. Right?''

''Right,'' she said in a bored tone.

''Now, supposing Hart is the killer.''

She shook her head in disbelief.

''Hear me out, Mrs. Ellis. Then you'll get your chance to rebuff me. What if hiring you to work for him would enable him to keep an eye on you, to make sure you don't remember anything?''

''That's crazy.''

''No, it's smart.''

''His only motive for hiring my agency was to help him win the election.''

''You're positive about that?'' His eyes bored into hers.

She didn't flinch, but then her insides were wound so tight, she couldn't move. ''If I did remember something, are you saying he would kill me?''

''What do you think?''

''I think you're wrong,'' she spat. ''Dead wrong.

Tanner Hart might be many things, Detective, but a killer he isn't.''

Yet Gallain's words had shaken her to the core, planted seeds of doubt inside her head. From the start, she had questioned Tanner and his reasons for hiring her, knowing she probably wasn't the best person for the job. But he had insisted with words of praise, praise that had fed her defunct self-esteem back to life. God, had she… No. Absolutely not. Tanner was not capable of murder.

"Then prove it."

"Excuse me?"

"I said prove it."

"You know I can't do that," she lashed back.

"There's a way, if you're willing."

She ached to slap that smug, condescending look off Gallain's face. Instead she demanded, "How?"

"You can agree to undergo hypnosis." Gallain paused, a challenge in his eyes and a smirk on his lips. "If you're so convinced Hart's innocent, that is."

Hypnosis? That meant a stranger probing inside her head, encouraging her to reveal her innermost secrets. Her blood suddenly turned to ice. What if she revealed the truth about her son? What if she identified Tanner as Brock's father?

Her breathing almost stopped. In order to vindicate him, there was a possibility she would implicate herself and Brock.

Brock.

She couldn't do it. She couldn't sacrifice her son or herself on a gamble. But how could she *not?* If there was a chance she could clear Tanner, remove him from the suspect list, wouldn't that be the right thing to do?

If not, could she live with herself, especially if he was found guilty of a murder he didn't commit?

"Mrs. Ellis?"

"You're on, Detective," Kasey said with unblinking force. "Tell me when and where, and I'll be there."

Thirty-Nine

The staff, along with Tanner, had just finished a planning session. "One last thing before you all go. I want you to know I've agreed to undergo hypnosis to see if it'll help find Shirley's killer."

For a long moment, silence filled the room. She dared not look at Tanner, who was sitting across the table from her, though she heard his muttered curse.

Following yesterday's media fiasco she hadn't spoken to Tanner personally. It was as if they both needed time and space to come to grips with what had happened. However, she had received a frantic call from Irene asking her to come up with some damage control ads ASAP.

Without hesitation, Kasey had agreed, glad to have her mind occupied so as not to think about the sudden turn of events. They had just gotten started batting ideas around the table when she looked up and watched as Tanner strode through the door.

"May I join you?" he'd asked, his gaze finding hers and holding it.

For a moment she found it difficult to speak. Then swallowing hard, she'd said, "Take a seat."

That had been two hours ago. Now as she concentrated her gaze on Red, Don and Lance, who were staring at her, slack-jawed, she put a choke-hold on her emotions.

Red was the first to speak. "I don't have to guess whose idea that was."

"That detective needs to mind his own business," Don said in a strained voice.

"I couldn't agree more," Lance added quietly. "The thought of someone messing with my mind makes me squirrelly as hell."

Red narrowed his eyes while pulling on the fiery-red goatee he'd recently grown. "Is that something you want to do, Kasey? Or are you being coerced because Gallain hasn't nabbed Shirley's killer?"

She continued to keep her gaze off Tanner, though her peripheral vision told her Tanner's face was growing grimmer by the second.

"No, Red. I'm doing this of my own free will."

"I just wanted to make sure," he continued. "If not, I'm prepared to bust his chops."

"And get hauled to jail," Lance said drolly, cutting his eyes to Red. "Smart."

Kasey held up her hand. "Hey, guys, this isn't up for discussion. I just wanted to keep you posted on the latest with the investigation."

"Do you think it'll work?" Don asked, his features scrunched in a frown.

Kasey gnawed at her lower lip. "I have no idea. But I guess we'll soon find out."

"Why now?" Red pressed. "Why didn't Gallain suggest that right off?"

"He did," Kasey admitted reluctantly, "only I wouldn't do it."

"When are you going under?" Lance asked.

"Maybe tomorrow. That's up to Gallain."

Don got to his feet. "If you're not one hundred per-cent sold on the idea, then don't do it. Ever. Tell Gal-lain to shove it. From day one, I've thought that cop needed an attitude adjustment."

Kasey rose with a sigh, then said lightly, "He's just doing his job which is what I suggest we do." She nodded in Tanner's direction, though she still didn't look at him. "Keep in mind, we're on a tight leash to get Tanner's new ads off and running. So get to work."

Once the room had emptied with the exception of Tanner, a heavy silence ensued while his eyes locked on her.

"Why?" he asked, sounding like he needed to clear his throat.

"Why what?"

"Why did you agree to do something you don't want to do?"

She heaved a sigh. "I just explained that."

"You never gave a reason."

"I should've already done it, then maybe Shirley's killer would be behind bars."

"You don't really believe that, do you?"

"No," she admitted in a small voice.

"Then stick to your guns and tell him no."

"I can't," she cried.

"Look at me, Kasey," Tanner pleaded, his mouth drawn in a tense line. "I know you're doing this for me."

She picked up on the torment in his voice and it wrenched her heart. "What choice do I have, Tanner? Gallain thinks you—" Her voice broke.

He finished the sentence. "Killed Shirley. I know."

"Enough said," she murmured.

"I never laid a hand on Shirley, Kasey. I swear to God, I didn't."

Her eyes shifted off him and her voice wobbled. "Maybe we should talk about this some other time and place?"

"No."

His sudden and curt tone took her aback. She felt her gaze widen on him.

"Sorry," he said, his frustration apparent, "I didn't mean to snap your head off."

"Apology accepted."

Tanner stared at her another moment before he got up and walked to the window. Kasey couldn't help it, but she found herself watching how the toned muscles in his shoulders and arms flexed when he raised his hand and rubbed the back of his neck.

She liked looking at him. And for several labored breaths she did just that, thinking she was physically addicted to him. It was all she could do not to get up and wrap her arms around him from behind and try and comfort him. Only she couldn't do that. Not now, not when so much was at stake.

"I have to know," he said, swinging back around, his features rigid. "That you believe me. That you know I could never take a human life."

"I believe you," she said with feeling.

Suddenly he closed the distance between them, but stopped short of touching her, clenching his hands at his sides. "I'd give anything if you weren't involved in my nightmare."

"What if the hypnosis doesn't work?" she asked, biting her lower lip. "What if it turns out that I really didn't see the killer?"

"Gallain will be back to square one."

"He's not going to be happy."

"That's not your problem."

"Do you think he'll focus the investigation on you?"

Tanner shrugged. "Probably."

"It would be awful if that happened."

His eyes turned warm, and he trailed a finger down one cheek. "I don't want you to worry. It'll be all right. I'm innocent, and I'll prove that. Eventually."

"But even if you prove you're innocent but get arrested in the meantime, your political career will be over."

"Then it'll just be over. But at least my life won't be."

But mine just might, she wanted to cry. If she let herself dwell on what she might reveal under hypnosis, she would shatter into a million pieces.

"What's wrong?"

"Nothing."

He caught her gaze and held it. "I love you so much it hurts, Kasey Ellis. It's all I can do to keep my hands to myself."

"And I love you," she finally admitted.

"Can I see you tonight?"

"Tanner—"

"Please."

What could it hurt? She needed him and he needed her. Maybe when all this was over, she could walk away and not look back. But not now. She needed him to hold her, to make love to her, to make her forget the real world for a while.

"I'll be waiting."

At that moment, the door opened. They both stiffened, then turned around.

"Hiya, Mom."

* * *

Don Hornsby paced the threadbare carpet in his sister's dump. Though he was higher than the wind on a blustery March day, he hadn't lost complete touch with reality.

No amount of coke had been able to mellow him out. Rather, he felt dizzy and nauseous. The urge to vomit was gaining momentum by the second.

How had his luck taken such a nasty turn?

For once in his life, things had finally gone his way. Then wham, down the crapper. What a pisser. It was all that dick cop's fault, too. Unfortunately he couldn't vent his fury and frustration on him. Kasey, however, was another matter.

He had to keep her out of the hands of that shrink.

"But how?" he asked out loud, his voice breaking on a croak.

Time was running out. *It had run out,* he reminded himself, clenching and unclenching his fists. He had to make a move of some kind before this day ended. He paused, his gaze resting on the bag of powder in the corner of the room. Maybe another snort was what he needed to activate his mind into the proper channel.

Yet he didn't move. He couldn't afford to pass out which was likely to happened if he further indulged. Sweat poured off him. But God, how he wanted to put himself out of his misery.

But he was too chicken-shit. He'd rather inflict that on Kasey. She shouldn't have gone along with Gallain. She should've told him to suck a rotten egg, but she obviously didn't have the nerve.

Which left him no choice but to take matters into his own hands. Thinking of hands made him smile.

He had a plan. Don grinned. The perfect plan.

* * *

Kasey tiptoed in his room and found Brock sound asleep. She simply smiled as she stared at her son's body draped across the bed, one arm hanging off the side. He looked so young, so innocent, so precious.

At times like this, she still couldn't believe that she'd been given such a gift. But attached to that gift was an awesome responsibility. She must protect that gift at all costs. Her heart wrenched. She couldn't ever let Brock down. She had to continue to do what was best for him, no matter how it may collide with her wants and needs.

As for the upcoming hypnosis session, she realized she was making the ultimate sacrifice for the man she loved. And if she were to divulge her secret, then it would be safe with the shrink. That was her stronghold and allowed her to go forward.

She didn't want to think about anything unpleasant this evening. Her mind and heart belonged exclusively to her son. Deciding to leave Brock in that uncomfortable position, Kasey turned off the glaring overhead light and tiptoed back out, though the tiptoeing wasn't necessary. He could sleep through a tornado or worse. When he was tired, like he was this evening, he was dead to the world.

He didn't get those good sleep habits from her. Maybe from his dad... Kasey paused midstride in the hallway, fear knotting her lower stomach. She had to stop thinking of Tanner as his dad. Even though he was gone, Mark would always hold that honor. She couldn't afford to think otherwise, for her own sanity and peace of mind.

But when Brock and Tanner were together, she

nearly had heart failure. Little things—mannerisms, movements, gestures, even smiles—were so much alike. She would notice those, like she had that afternoon in her office, and fear would paralyze her.

What if Tanner noticed? What if Tanner saw himself in Brock?

Those questions had circled her mind like vultures. So far, however, her mind continued to be her own worst enemy. If Tanner had picked up on anything, he hadn't said a word or acted any differently. If he had, he wouldn't have kept quiet.

The thought of that ever happening almost triggered a heart attack. But it wasn't going to happen, Kasey assured herself. Again, her overactive imagination was her worst enemy. As soon as the election was over, she wouldn't see Tanner again no matter how much she may love him. It was too risky and the strain was too much. She had to whisk herself and Brock out of harm's way.

Meanwhile, she would have to get through this nightmare and continue walking that thin line, even though it was something she abhorred.

That thought was front and center in her mind when she walked into the kitchen to prepare dinner. She loved cooking for Brock. On the way home from the agency, they had stopped by the grocery as she didn't keep much in the way of food in the apartment.

After they had finished eating, she hoped they could spend a quiet evening together, a far cry from what she'd had in mind before Brock's arrival. Suddenly Kasey felt heat sting her face. If he hadn't shown up, she and Tanner would have spent the evening and night making love.

As it was, she wouldn't see him, although Brock had invited him to dinner.

"I appreciate the offer," Tanner said. "But you and your mom need time together."

"Aw, she doesn't care," Brock countered. "Do you?"

Before she could answer, Tanner cut in. "I do, though."

"But I have to talk to you about the Web site. That's one reason why I came home. I've hit a snag."

Tanner had smiled. "We'll unsnag you tomorrow. Count on it."

As if realizing he'd run into a brick wall, Brock didn't pursue the issue. Shortly thereafter, they had parted company with Tanner.

Now, Kasey couldn't wait for Brock to awaken so they could have some quality time together, something that hadn't happened in a long time. The only important tidbit that had come out of their conversation on the way home was that he and Nancy had broken up.

"You're joking?" Kasey had asked while stopped at a long red light.

"Mom, I wouldn't kid about that."

"What happened, or am I allowed to ask?"

He gave her a sheepish grin. "Okay, so I acted like a jerk."

"I never said that."

"Right, you didn't. But I was a jerk and I know it."

She was so proud of him in his budding maturity; she wanted to pull off the road and hug him. "So who did what to whom?"

His mouth curved down. "I dumped her."

"That's not a very nice way of putting it."

"It's the truth. She kept pushing me to get married and I freaked."

"But I thought that's what you wanted, too." Kasey kept her tone light and nonjudgmental, but secretly she was overjoyed that her son had come to his senses before it was too late.

"I did, only not now."

"Now?" Kasey was appalled. "She wanted you to marry now?"

"Yep. Wanted us to elope."

"Oh, my God." Only her firm grip on the wheel kept the car from swerving in the other lane.

"That's not exactly what I said," Brock muttered.

"Don't tell me your response. I can figure that out on my own."

Brock laughed. "It wasn't that bad, Mom. I was nice."

"I'm sure you were. So are you okay with it?"

He shrugged, then turned his head toward the window. "I guess. I miss her."

"I can't say that I'm sorry. You know that. Having said that, I don't want you to be hurt, either."

"Aw, I'm all right. I have football and my job with Tanner. But she doesn't seem to have other interests which makes it harder for her."

"I'm sorry," Kasey said lamely, though she wasn't. Oh, she was sorry the girl was hurt, but if she had forced Brock into marriage... Kasey shuddered, unable to even let her mind go there.

After that, they had discussed football and his work for Tanner, the latter having Brock as enthusiastic as his time on the gridiron. And while his association with Tanner kept her anxious, she continued to hold her tongue and bide her time.

The smell of boiled over rice jolted her back to the moment at hand.

''Great,'' she muttered, reaching for a cloth and moping up the mess. That done, she decided to take a shower before waking Brock. Suddenly she heard the floor creak behind her. She frowned while the hairs stood up on the back of her neck. Before she could turn around strong hands circled her throat and squeezed.

Oh, God help me, Kasey cried silently, fighting against the blackness that threatened to suck her under.

Forty

*D*on't give up! Fight!

Those words screamed inside her head as Kasey struggled mentally to overcome her attacker. Finally her mind and body connected. Using a foot, she beat against his legs at the same time she jabbed his stomach with her elbows.

"Be still, bitch."

One of the elbows apparently hit a vulnerable spot because he relaxed his grip momentarily giving her the chance to let out a bloodcurdling scream.

"Shut the fuck up!"

The front doorbell chimed.

For another second, the attacker's hands stilled around her throat. Taking advantage of that second lapse, Kasey let out another cry, then began delivering blows to any part of the torso within reach.

"Kasey!"

Tanner. Thank God, he had come after all.

"Mom, what's going on?" Brock hollered from his room. "Are you okay?"

Brock! Ohmygod. Ohmygod. Ohmygod. Stay away, son! Don't come in here!

It was then she heard the loud splintering of wood like someone had either knocked down the front door or crashed through it.

"You son of a bitch, get your hands off her."

Tanner was inside her house. He would help her.

Still in the clutches of her attacker, Kasey felt herself being dragged backward all the while fighting to hold on to consciousness. But she was fast losing that battle as her knees were buckling and she was breathing in gaspy spurts.

"Let her go!"

Suddenly her throat was no longer bound by hands. She bent over like a question mark, then fell to her knees, gasping and coughing. When she could pull enough air through her lungs to regain touch with reality, she looked up. Just in time to see Tanner ram his fist into her attacker's belly sending him groaning to the floor. After several muffled groans, the man slumped over onto the tile.

"Mom, Tanner, what the hell?"

"Brock, call 911," Tanner demanded, then dropped to his knees beside her. Ashen-faced, he grabbed her and cradled her against his warm body. "My God, Kasey, are you hurt?"

She clung to him and sobbed.

"Shh, it's okay. I've got you."

When her gut-wrenching sobs were finally under control, Kasey peered up at him and said in a hoarse voice, "He tried to kill me."

About that time Brock fell to his knees, panic darkening his eyes. She removed herself from Tanner and hugged her son. "I'm going to be all right."

"Who would do this to you, Mom?" His voice shook.

Tanner got to his feet. "That's what we're about to find out."

Kasey let Brock help her up, and leaning against

him, watched as Tanner leaned over and yanked the stocking off the unconscious man sprawled in the middle of the floor.

Kasey let out another cry, then covered her mouth with her hands.

"He works for you, right?"

"Yes," she whispered in shock. "That's Don Hornsby."

Forty-One

"Jeez, no one can accuse you of not leading an exciting life."

Kasey cut Ginger a meaningful look. "If you call nearly getting strangled by one of your trusted employees exciting, then you're right."

Ginger had stopped by the agency on her way to work. Kasey had poured them flavored coffee, and they were sitting at the table in the small kitchen.

"God, I can't believe that actually happened. But since I'm looking at your bruised neck, it's obvious it did and that you went through hell."

Even now, a week following the incident, Kasey's nerves remained frayed, though she knew she was no longer in danger. Once Don had been cuffed, hauled to jail and grilled until he admitted he had shot Shirley, the cloud that had been hanging over her lifted.

Yet much of the fallout remained, especially here in the office. It would be a long time before the agency returned to normal operating procedure. The fact that a bona fide killer had worked in their midst, with no one the wiser, had had a profound and chilling effect.

"You're still spooked by Hornsby, aren't you?"

"Not Don himself." Kasey paused and sipped on her coffee. "It just boggles my mind that he had all of us fooled, especially me."

"Like they say, you never know what goes on behind closed doors."

"I'll have to hand it to Gallain," Kasey said. "He did a great job of exacting the truth from Don—starting with his addiction to coke and ending with him killing Shirley."

"All for love and money." Ginger shook her head in disbelief. "Who would've thought it?"

"I don't know so much about the love," Kasey replied, "but the money was the motivator on Don's part. That list I came across was exactly the amount Shirley had given him to feed his habit. As for her, her obsession might have been love or sex."

Ginger made a face. "Apparently he made her happy in bed, and she made him happy by doling out the money to keep him in drugs."

"A match made in heaven," Kasey quipped with no amusement.

"Until she found out the truth, then she dumped him."

"Leaving a scorned drug addict running amok."

Kasey released a sigh. "I should've picked up on that."

"Not necessarily. Apparently, he was a pro at covering his tracks. But you were responsible for nailing him. The fact that you were open with staff about your plans to undergo hypnosis turned the case. You should be proud of that."

Kasey shuddered visibly. "I'm just glad he's behind bars and that I didn't have to put myself at the mercy of a shrink."

Tanner will never know. No one will ever know. My secret is safe forever.

"What I'm damn glad about is that Tanner decided to come over. Otherwise—"

Kasey took a deep breath. "I don't even want to think of the otherwise. He saved my life. And Brock's."

"You know what they say about that," Ginger said with a twinkle in her eyes.

Kasey gave her a stern look.

Ginger chuckled, then her face sobered. "I just hate that Brock had to witness it."

"I still can't think about that part of it. If Don had hurt him—" Kasey broke off with another shudder.

"Well, he didn't, thanks to Tanner who turned out to be a hero." Ginger smoothed a wrinkle out of her linen skirt. "I noticed this morning he's back up in the polls. I have no doubt now that he'll boot Butler's butt right out of office."

"I agree. We've certainly been working hard to make that happen."

"Speaking of working." Ginger rose, then took two more gulps of coffee. "I should've been at the office twenty minutes ago." She set her cup down and peered closely at Kasey. "You need to fill me in on what's happening with you and Tanner."

Anxiety filled Kasey. "Nothing's happening. He's busy and so am I."

"Poppycock. I know when I'm getting the runaround, but that's okay." Ginger grinned. "I'll get it out of you sooner or later. I'm not worried."

"How about you and Matt?" Kasey asked, switching the subject. "Your final divorce hearing should be coming up soon."

"It is, praise the Lord."

"I still want to go with you, okay?"

"I'll take you up on that. Now I really have to go."

Following a quick hug, Ginger was gone. Kasey sat back down, feeling like a whirlwind had blown through. Yet she always felt better after having been in Ginger's company. She had a knack for looking at life through uncomplicated eyes.

Sighing, Kasey got up and refilled her cup, then sat back down. Like Ginger, she should be at her desk working, but she still hadn't gotten her sea legs back, so to speak.

The trauma of that awful night continued to play havoc with her peace of mind. She knew it would take time to heal her body and her soul. If only she could stop replaying those events in her head, she could move on.

She couldn't get past the feel of Don's hands around her neck, squeezing the breath out of her. Every time she swallowed, she was reminded of the nightmare.

Like Ginger had said, thank God for Tanner. If he hadn't had second thoughts about dinner and working with Brock, they both would be dead. And if he hadn't been there for her since it happened, she wouldn't be as far along as she was.

Following the sirens and the cops' arrival, Tanner had taken her to the hospital. Once the E.R. doctor had checked her over, he had released her. Tanner had insisted she and Brock spend the night at his place.

She hadn't argued. The following morning, once Brock judged for himself that she was indeed all right, he had returned to Waco, which was fine with her. She wanted him as far away from that mess as possible.

Tanner was a different matter. He had refused to leave her alone, knowing how the ordeal had affected her.

"It's not your fault, Kasey," he had told her the following day after Brock's departure. "Don't think for a minute you did anything wrong."

"I know you're right, but I should've picked up on something in Don's behavior that should have alerted me."

"Often times people who are walking time bombs appear the most normal."

"He came to work some days looking like hell, but I thought that was because of his sister's plight and him having to take care of her. He played us all for suckers."

"He could've blown a fuse at any time. Your decision to undergo hypnosis was the catalyst that lit it. He feared you'd remember something after all, and he'd be screwed. He couldn't take a chance on that."

"So he took matters into his own hands." She gritted her teeth. "If it hadn't been for your timely intervention—"

"I just couldn't stay away from you."

"I'm glad," she whispered. "Have I ever thanked you?"

"Yes, several times."

"You could've been hurt yourself."

Tanner's eyes turned cold. "That bastard's lucky I didn't rip his head off. I was tempted to bypass the justice system altogether and save the taxpayers a lot of money."

"Then you would have gone to jail."

"Sometimes I think it would've been worth it. Hearing your cry was bad enough, but when I saw his hands on you, I went insane. He's lucky there was enough of him left to haul off to jail."

Kasey swiped at the tears that pooled in her eyes.

"Hey," he said in a gentle tone, placing his hand over hers. "It's over. He can never hurt you again. He'll be behind bars for the rest of his life."

"And Gallain will get his promotion," she said with a wobbly smile. "And you will get the senate seat."

"Screw the senate seat," he countered in a gruff tone. "I'd gladly have given that up if it would've spared you that ordeal."

Her heart melted under those tender words and the look radiating from his eyes. Then she looked away, unwilling to acknowledge verbally the incredible tension that had hovered over them since he'd crashed into her apartment. He felt it, too, she knew. Yet he hadn't so much as made a passionate move toward her. Instead, he had held her throughout the subsequent nights while she cried in his arms, consoling her with soothing words and strong arms.

However, she knew the day of reckoning was near. Tanner was simply biding his time before pushing her for a commitment. She loved him so much and she knew he loved her. But how could they build a life together that was based on a lie?

"Kasey—" His voice had dropped to a husky pitch.

She got off the sofa and crossed her arms over her breasts. He stood also, and for a long moment they devoured each other with their eyes.

"We should go," she said in an uneven voice. "We need to finalize your new TV ads."

"That wasn't exactly what I had in mind."

"I don't know what you want me to say."

"Sure you do, only you're not saying it. But that's okay. If more time is what you need, I'm willing to give it. Meanwhile, just know that I love you and want you in my life forever."

Each time she thought back on that conversation, it upset her. Today was no exception. The need to feel his lips and hands on her body was a constant, aching need. Don't, she told herself. She had to stop beating up on herself for something that could never be. He could never know about Brock, and she could never marry him without telling him the truth.

"Kasey," Monica said, thankfully interrupting her thoughts, "you have an urgent call on line one."

Wordlessly, Kasey reached for her phone. Seconds later, she cried, "I'm on my way." The receiver fell out of her hand as she lurched out of her chair.

Brock. Injured on the football field. Another nightmare. Oh, please, God, not my son. Don't take him from me.

In all the years he'd played football, she had prayed this day would never come. Now that it had, she was ill-equipped to handle it, especially in her fragile emotional state. But Brock needed her, and she wouldn't let him down.

Rubber-legged, she grabbed her purse and dashed out the door. "Monica, I'm going to Waco. Brock's been injured and is in the E.R."

Tanner gave her a fierce look.

"No doubt about it, you've gone from villain to saint. You're a freaking hero."

"Can it, Irene. I don't want to hear that shit."

Her chin jutted. "Why not? As of this morning, you're back in the driver's seat. If the election were held today, you'd win by a landslide."

"But at whose expense?"

Her face turned beet red. "It's not your fault

Hornsby attacked Kasey, for God's sake. You saved her life.''

"That's not the point.''

"That's exactly the point. You saved her life *and* your political career.''

"You're exaggerating, Irene. I would never have been charged in Shirley's death.''

"Well, we'll never know that for a fact, will we?''

"Cut the sarcasm,'' he said in a clipped tone.

"Do you want to win this election, Tanner?''

"What kind of question is that?''

"A valid one, I can assure you. Even Jack's noticed how distracted you've been since Hornsby's arrest.''

"I've had a lot on my mind.''

"Kasey Ellis, right?'' she muttered loud enough for him to hear.

"That's none of your business.''

"It damn sure is,'' she hissed, "especially since I'm working my ass off on your campaign. Right now, you're your own worst enemy. I suggest you get your head on straight before it gets chopped off.''

Following those words, she marched to the door where she slammed it so hard behind her that he winced.

The cords in his neck strained to the breaking point before he finally calmed down enough to think rationally. Irene was right. He was about to blow everything wide-open. His obsession with Kasey was to blame. The thought of how close she'd come to dying had shaken him to the core. It had made him aware of what was really important in life—loving someone more than life itself.

He hadn't found that, of course, with his deceased

wife. He had loved her, but he hadn't been in love with her.

Hence, he'd conjured up in his mind some grand illusion about the type of woman he'd fall head over heels in love with—young, gorgeous, and sophisticated who enjoyed the limelight—the perfect woman and mate for him.

First though, he'd known he would have to prove himself worthy of such a woman since his upbringing had left him feeling unequal and inadequate.

Then Kasey had come back into his life with her sweet personality and unsophisticated ways, knocking him for a loop. And she didn't give a damn whether he had a pot to piss in or a window to throw it out of.

Still, he hadn't been able to convince her that he was real, that he truly loved her and wanted to marry her. He knew she loved him, too.

Being held at arm's length was ripping him to pieces. What should he do? Force her hand? Was that an option? Hell, yes. He'd been patient long enough.

Fifteen minutes later, Tanner strode into the agency and asked to see Kasey.

"I'm sorry, Mr. Hart," Monica said, "she's on her way to Waco. Brock's been injured."

With a terse, thanks, Tanner shot out the door, punching the numbers on his cell. "Frank, I need a favor."

After having reached the hospital in record time, Kasey raced through the E.R. doors only to pull up short and gasp. A grim-faced Tanner stood just inside the entrance. "How—"

"I went to the agency," Tanner interrupted. "Then a friend of mine flew me here."

Suddenly feeling faint, she reached out a hand. He grasped it and circling her waist pulled her against him. "Let's go see if we can find out something."

Grateful for his support and take charge manner, Kasey didn't argue but rather matched his gait to the E.R. reception.

"I'm Brock Ellis's mother."

"Ah, the doctor's been asking for you. I'll let him know you've arrived."

"How is my son?" Kasey asked around the tightness in her throat. If she let herself she could fall apart.

"You'll have to wait for the doctor," the woman said in a kind voice.

"Mrs. Ellis?"

Kasey and Tanner looked around and faced a middle-aged man with a crop of thick white hair. "I'm Philip Spivey, Brock's trainer. I rode with Brock in the ambulance."

Hands were shaken, then Kasey said with a tremor, "Thank you so much for taking care of him."

"No thanks is necessary. I just pray he's going to be all right."

"What…what happened?" Kasey stammered. "Was he hit in the head?"

"Yes," Spivey admitted.

"Was…is he unconscious?"

"Ah, here's Dr. Keith now," the receptionist said.

Dispensing with the introductions, Kasey asked, "How's Brock?"

"The lick on his head has the potential to be quite serious," the doctor said. "But we won't know to what extent until I get the test results. I'm waiting on them now.''

"Oh, God," Kasey cried in a broken voice.

Tanner pressed her closer to his side and whispered, "Shh, he's in good hands."

"May I see him?"

Dr. Keith's eyes perused them all. "Only immediate family is allowed."

"I'll be in the cafeteria," the trainer said. "I'll check with you later."

Kasey nodded, then disengaged herself from Tanner and followed the doctor. He showed her to the cubicle. "I'm on my way to see if the MRI and X-rays are back."

It was when Kasey paused to compose herself that she realized she wasn't alone. She swung around and faced Tanner who was right on her heels. His features were grim, giving the bones underneath new prominence. Her heart faltered. "What do you think you're doing?" she asked in a weak, shaky voice.

"I'm going to see *our* son."

Forty-Two

Shock froze Kasey. Then her mind reeled against that unexpected and staggering blow. She felt weak and dizzy. This couldn't be happening.

He knows the truth.

But how? And how long had he known?

Though she was rabid to launch an attack, to voice her outrage and pound him with those questions, the well-being of her son took precedence over everything else. After she'd seen her child and assured herself that he was still breathing, she would deal with Tanner and this added nightmare.

"Kasey?"

Ignoring him, she whipped around and made her way inside the tiny room to Brock's bedside. "Oh, no," she whimpered when she saw him lying so still, so pale.

"Brock, honey, it's Mom," Kasey said around her tears. "Can you hear me?"

No response.

"I'm here, son." A sob ripped through her. "I'm not leaving you."

"Kasey, don't."

Tanner draped a hand across her shoulder. She went rigid, then whipped around and hissed, "Don't touch me."

His face blanched as though she'd slapped him. Then his lips tightened and he shrugged. "If that's the way you want it."

"That's definitely the way I want it," she responded in a low, terse tone so as not to disturb Brock. Even though he was unconscious, it was possible he could hear what was being said.

Although Tanner stepped back, he didn't leave the room, she noticed. He leaned against the wall and stared at Brock, his eyes hooded and his features set.

Kasey eased down in the chair next to the bed and took her son's warm, but lifeless hand in hers, placing the palm against her wet cheek. "You're going to be fine," she whispered, trying to convince herself that was true.

She would will him to get well. She couldn't lose him to a stupid football injury. Feeling like she was drowning, Kasey lifted her head and fought for enough air to breathe.

"Mrs. Ellis."

At the sound of the doctor's voice, Kasey rose and faced him, her eyes wide and her heart lodged in her throat.

"Good news," Dr. Keith told her. "His only injuries seem to be a severe concussion and a couple of cracked ribs."

"Thank God," Kasey said in a quivering voice. "I was so afraid, Doctor."

"I understand." His tone was kind. "However, he's not out of the woods just yet. Before we transfer him to intensive care—" He broke off as if reading her mind. "ICU doesn't mean he's critical. He just needs to be monitored more closely than on a floor."

Kasey wilted with relief. "That's good. I want him to have the best of care."

"First though, he's going back to X-ray. I wasn't happy with the clarity of one of the pictures, and I want it repeated."

"May I go with him?" Kasey asked, noticing that Tanner had moved closer to her and the doctor but had refrained from saying anything.

"That's not necessary. I'll direct you to ICU waiting, then I'll call when he gets into his room."

Kasey held out her hand and clasped the doctor's firm one. "Thank you so much."

"That's my job, Mrs. Ellis, but you're welcome. If you and Mr.—" He paused again, his gaze on Tanner.

Kasey introduced them, though it galled her. Tanner had no business being there, her mind screamed.

This is not supposed to be happening. He's not supposed to know Brock is his.

"Right this way," Dr. Keith said, gesturing with his hand.

The silence was thicker than the humidity outside.

Kasey kept her gaze off Tanner who stood slumped against the wall in the waiting room, his arms folded across his massive chest, watching her. They were apparently between visitation times as the area was deserted. She didn't know whether she was happy about that or not. She wanted to confront Tanner, yet she didn't.

"I'm not going anywhere, Kasey."

Rage heated her entire body. She turned and glared at him, finally able to unleash her pent up emotions. "How long have you known?"

"Since a couple of years after you and Mark married."

Once again shock and outrage robbed her of words.

"I suppose your next question is how I knew."

She could only nod, still incapable of speaking. The hits kept on coming, she told herself, feeling her panic mount, assured that a final and lethal blow was imminent.

"Mark told me," Tanner said without emotion. "Go figure."

"Why?" Kasey asked in a hoarse, unnatural tone, no longer stunned by anything Tanner might reveal.

"We happened to meet at a bar one evening. I've forgotten exactly how it came about. Anyhow, we started drinking and catching up on old times. Mark got stinking drunk." Tanner paused and sucked in a breath. "That's when he told me that you had betrayed him with some no good son of a bitch."

Kasey opened her mouth but nothing came out. That was when she began to shake uncontrollably.

Tanner's eyes darkened and for a second, she thought he might close the distance between them and reach for her. She stepped back.

Obviously picking up on that gesture, his face turned stark white before he added, "Mark claimed that SOB took advantage of your virginity, and that if he ever found out who he was, he'd kill him."

Kasey hadn't realized she had stopped breathing until the room began to spin. She groped for the back of the nearest chair and clung to it.

"Kasey."

She heard the frantic concern in Tanner's voice and watched as he took several forward steps. She held up her hand. "I'm all right."

"Dammit," he hissed, "you're not all right. Sit down. Please."

Because her legs refused to hold her upright any longer, she complied.

"Not a pretty story, huh?" Tanner's tone was bitter as his gaze rested on her.

"I never knew," she whispered. "Mark never once let on that he felt betrayed."

"That's because he loved you."

"Nothing is ever that simple." Her bitterness rivaled his.

"Apparently it was for Mark."

"What about you, Tanner?"

"What about me?"

"Don't you dare play that game with me." Kasey's voice lashed him like a whip. "Have you laid in wait all these years for the perfect opportunity to claim Brock?"

Tanner let an expletive fly, then defended himself. "You know better than that."

Bitterness tinged her laugh. "I don't think so." Tanner had used her all right, only not for the reasons Gallain had suspected. "You hired me to get access to *my* son, didn't you?"

"No, dammit, I didn't."

"I don't believe you."

"If I didn't love you so much, I'd walk out of this room right now, and you'd never see me again."

Kasey's next breath caught in her throat, and she stared at him. She didn't know what she expected him to say but it wasn't that. Caught off guard, she fought for a suitable comeback.

He took advantage of her silence and hammered on, "When we made love and Brock, unbeknownst to me, was conceived, I had no means of supporting a wife, much less a child, or—'' He stopped suddenly and took a harsh breath.

''Or what?'' she demanded

''I would've married you in a minute.''

''Because I was pregnant.''

''That, and the fact I think I fell in love with you that night, only I didn't know it until I saw you at Shirley's funeral.''

''That's crazy,'' she whispered.

''It might be crazy, but it's the truth.''

''This is not about us, it's about Brock,'' she countered fiercely. She didn't want to hear him tell her he loved her nor did she want to love him back. On the contrary, she wanted to hate him for the threat he had become.

''So what about Brock?'' he asked in a weary tone. ''Take your best shot, get it off your chest.''

''Are you going to turn him against me?''

''God, Kasey, how could you ask me that?''

''It's easy.'' Her voice broke. ''You have to want to be a part of his life. But he is my life, my greatest treasure.''

''And I wouldn't have it any other way.'' Tanner paused, then crossed to her and dropped to his knees, though he refrained from touching her. ''I have no intention of ever telling Brock the truth. Mark is the one who raised him and deserves the honor of being called Dad.''

Kasey's teeth began to chatter while tears splashed down her face into her lap. Still, he didn't touch her. He just looked at her through pleading eyes. ''I have a confession to make, though, because I don't want any more lies between us.''

Another jolt of fear shook her. What now?

"Don't look at me like that, Kasey," he said thickly. "I've kept up with Brock from afar through the years, seeing to it that he got a scholarship to Baylor. Surely you can't begrudge me that."

His voice cracked, and her heart turned over.

"Say you forgive me for that night so long ago," he begged, "even though I should never have made love to you. I should—"

With tears continuing to trickle down her face, she pressed a finger against his lips. "Shush. You don't have to say anything else. I'm the one who needs to talk, to tell you how much I love you and how thankful I am that you gave me Brock. You're a good man, Tanner Hart, and you've made the ultimate sacrifice for our son. And I can't think of anyone on this earth who I'd rather have as his father than you."

Kasey saw the tears gather in his eyes before he groaned and jerked her out of the chair into his arms, kissing her with a sweet, savage intensity.

When he pulled back, he whispered, "Will you marry me?"

"In a heartbeat," she cried, flinging herself back into his arms.

He remained cocooned in her warmth. All she had to do was move a fraction, and he would get hard again.

Reading her thoughts, Tanner chuckled, "I dare you."

She gave him a saucy look. "You're on, smartie."

Before he realized her intentions, she shoved him onto his back, then rose above him. He felt his dick swell inside her just as she began to ride him. He latched on to her breasts and lifted his hips off the bed, thrusting higher inside her.

She let out a cry that matched his before collapsing on his chest.

A short time later, they sat naked, Indian-style, in the middle of the bed, sipping on wine and munching on cheese. And never taking their eyes off each other.

They had been married for six months, and he was the happiest man alive and knew Kasey was happy, too. Brock had made a full recovery from his injuries. He had long since returned to Baylor to the classroom and gridiron.

The election was over and he had won. Though Buck Butler had put up a good front, Tanner's sources told him his opponent had been a sore loser but was licking his wounds in private.

The news guru Daisy Greer had also eaten crow. But she had fooled her readers. Tanner suspected he was the only one who picked up on the arsenic covering her candy-coated words.

But he had the last laugh, having been sworn into the Texas senate, an honor he'd shared with his wife and son.

And while Kasey had adapted to life as a politician's wife, she had maintained her own identity by making the ad agency into a solid and thriving business, though not until she'd gone to court and won the lawsuit against Shirley's cousin.

Life was good. No, better than good, Tanner reminded himself. Paul was running his construction business and doing a great job. Irene had opted to move on after learning about him and Kasey.

Most of all, he had married the woman he loved and

was finally getting to know the young man who was his son. He dared not ask for anything more.

"Well, Mrs. Hart?" he asked when he realized she was staring at him, a puzzled look on her face.

"Well, what, Senator Hart?"

He grinned, then said huskily, "For starters, I love you."

She leaned over and kissed him. "What a way to wake up and face the day."

He tongued a breast. Her deep moan was music to his ears.

"Tanner, don't you ever get enough?"

"Never, my darling."

She pulled his head off her nipple then cradled his bristled chin. "It's almost daylight, my love. We need to finish our midnight picnic and get up."

"Aw, do we have to?"

"You can't be late for work your first day on the Senate floor."

"Oh, yes I can, if it means leaving my precious wife. You're just too damn sexy for your own good." Then on a serious note, he added, "When's Brock leaving?"

"He's due back in Waco by noon." Kasey fell quiet for a moment, looking at him through clouded eyes. "We've been married for six months, right?"

"Six of the happiest months of my life."

"Mine, too," she said sweetly, "even though I didn't know it would be so difficult being married to a politician."

"Ah, no sweat. You're a natural at it."

She smiled. "Thanks for the compliment, but that wasn't what I was fishing for."

"I'm listening."

She wet her bottom lip. "I want to tell Brock."

His gut tightened. "About me?"

"Yes."

"Why, Kasey?"

"Because he should know," she said, touching his face. "He deserves to know."

"I meant it when I told you I had no intention of him ever learning the truth."

"I realize that, but this is something I want. Brock is being cheated, too."

Tanner's eyes probed hers. "Are you sure about this?"

"As sure as I've ever been about anything."

Tanner swallowed hard. "Just the fact that you want to tell him is enough for me."

"We'll tell him together."

"When?" he asked in a raspy voice.

"Today."

The thought of approaching his son with that bombshell struck terror inside him. "How do you think Brock will react?"

Kasey didn't so much as hesitate. "Knowing my son and how he feels about you, I think he'll feel he's the luckiest person alive to have another great dad."

Tanner's heart jumped with joy as he smiled, then reached for her. "I love you."

"And I love you more."

They clung to each other in blessed silence.